ECHOES

THE TRILOGY

Book 1

Adrian Raynor-Krill

First Revelations

*From the blood of the Colosseum to present-day
rural England; a love that spans
2,000 years and beyond...*

 New Generation Publishing

A story for women by a man who adores women

AUTHOR'S NOTE

'Echoes' takes place over two millennia – from the late 1st century A.D. to present day although, strictly speaking, the story has no definable beginning as, indeed, it has no end.

'Echoes' takes the form of three books:
    Book 1 – First Revelations
    Book 2 – The Night of the Eighth Day
    Book 3 – Gallicus! The Spirit and the Sword

'Echoes' is a story encompassing powerful spiritual links and many human traits and emotions; love and friendship, passion, murder, self-sacrifice, violent death, the will to survive another day and, in the latter stages, sexual gratification and butchery before the immense crowds who fill the amphitheatre. It is set primarily in the modern world, specifically, the gentle hills of rural England but is also deeply rooted in a time where the democracy of republican Rome is a distant memory and the conquest of empire sees men of all nationalities conscripted to fight in the arena. However, not all gladiators are slaves in the same way not all gladiators are male and each is motivated by an array of driving ambitions; fame, wealth, public adoration, revenge and a consummate desire to walk proud among the greatest who ever lived regardless of the price in blood spilled or, ultimately, self-destruction.

    'Echoes' principally involves four main characters with varied and colourful backgrounds where their distant pasts have been forged in blood and tragedy. Each has their own story before an untimely transition to the afterlife sees their paths inevitably converge in a more forgiving world where class-differences are of no concern and a woman does not have to form an unholy alliance with the sword to prove she is as good as any man.

    The tale predictably alternates between past and present where relationships bloom and prosper in one world and are rent asunder by hatred, jealousy and murder in another. Perhaps one of the most enduring friendships is that of the two main female characters whose unearthly spiritual bond proves to be as vibrant and potent as ever, assuming new levels of intimacy, heated passions and discovery.

As much as possible, I have tried to weave the fiction of 'Echoes' into the known facts of ancient Rome whilst utilising the processes of past-life regression to access and develop the foundations and ongoing theme of the story. One point perhaps worthy of mention is that in the ancient Roman lexicon there were no words for 'lesbian', 'homosexual' or 'consent' as these were looked upon and accepted as perfectly normal practices and carried no social stigma.

ACKNOWLEDGEMENTS

The fact this first part of Echoes ever reached completion at all is largely down to others who gave unselfishly of their time and expertise and without whose assistance the book would have remained just an idea.

First and foremost I would like to thank Michael Challen, Dip. Hyp. M.C.T.T., who answered all of my many questions on the subject of past-life regression and provided me with an essential grounding into the workings of this type of therapy. Whilst I have indulged in an element of inventiveness in my description of Tyra's regression back to ancient Roman times – especially the duration of the session and extraordinary content, I hope readers will permit me a degree of latitude in order to realise the sense of authenticity I strove to achieve for this part of the story.

When I approached Andrew Stableford, Bsc. M.N.I.M.H. at the Lincoln Herbal Treatment Centre it was with caution and reservation for I was unsure as to how he would view my inquiry into naturally-occurring agents which could ultimately be utilised as a means of suicide. However, we had a most interesting conversation and he gave freely of his time and vast knowledge, enlightening me considerably on the subject of herbs and poisons which would have been found in the Mediterranean 2,000 years ago and how they might have been prepared for their most lethal application. Michael would take no payment for his time spent with me and I can only thank him again for his invaluable assistance when the writing had assumed an incredibly sad and tragic level.

The short poem at the start of Chapter 44 is an extract from 'Echo and Narcissus' by Ovid.

For Karla

Any writer of fiction is constantly searching for inspiration and I found mine in the form of Karla, my lovely wife of thirty-one years who contributed so much more than she will ever know. When I first visualised Tyra and Sophie – or Drusilla and Quintina, depending upon the reader's historical preference, it was Karla who made the characters come alive and put flesh on the bare bones of possibility. Despite the obvious physical dissimilarities I feel all three women possess certain common endearing qualities and I love each and every one of you in different ways at the same time.

No other person ever truly believed in me and accepted, unreservedly, my few strengths and many weaknesses. I am deeply humbled when you say you are proud of me and in my sixty years upon this earth I can honestly own up to the fact you are the only person I ever genuinely wanted to please.

When I first put pen to paper six years ago it was with the impetuosity of an over-eager and ill-informed novice who believed he had something of value to impart to the world. Since then I have come to realise pride can be an expensive commodity and the story of 'Echoes' has been rewritten and edited many times and only now am I coming to view it as a credible piece of fiction.

You have always been the calming influence in times of trouble, the port of sanctuary in the storm, the candle in the night and the reason why I do anything at all. I remain eternally indebted for your assistance in many aspects of the story, particularly those pertaining to female attire and jewellery and, in books two and three, the German language and geographical area around Frankfurt.

It is with immense pleasure I dedicate this trilogy to you with all the love shared by the characters depicted in the story.

FOREWORD

Upon his arrival in Rome in the late summer of A.D.70, the newly-acclaimed emperor, Vespasian, faced the daunting task of restoring a city and government ravaged by recent civil wars. He encouraged building on vacant lots, restored the Capitol (burned in A.D.69) and also began work on several new buildings. A temple to the deified Claudius on the Caelian Hill – a project designed to identify Vespasian as a legitimate heir to the Julio-Claudians while distancing himself from Nero, a Temple of Peace near the forum and a magnificent edifice known as the Amphitheatrum Flavium located on the site of the lake of Nero's Golden House.

In A.D.79, after contracting a brief illness, Vespasian died and completion of the Amphitheatrum Flavium (after Vespasian's family name) passed to his son and heir, Titus, and was duly completed in A.D.80.

We know it today as the Colosseum.

"....I have vowed to give the public something different – something they have never seen before and for this reason alone they will remember me. I have sworn the oath of allegiance and it is what I have trained for...."

Crixus to Senator Caius Attius Caecilius,
Ludus Gallicus Gladiator School,
Rome A.D.82

"....You must die erect and invincible! It is not important if we gain more days or even years in our life but it does matter very much how we die. We were born into a merciless world...."

Seneca: Epistulae 37, 2

1

England – Present Day

It was hot, the hottest July anyone could remember for years. Even this early in the morning, just after nine, the sun was a demon in the clear, blue sky as it beat down upon the land but Adam revelled in it as he moved the oil-stone across the steel, his manner thoughtful and reflective. There had been nothing for almost three months now, Adam pondered with an odd mixture of relief and disappointment, but experience had taught him not to dismiss lightly nor even attempt to interpret the mystical and often capricious ways of the spirit world.

Today was the 20th – Saturday the 20th July and the city would be coming together once more in anticipation of Ludi Victoriae Caesaris – the games of the Victorious Caesar, spread over ten days and featuring all manner of lavish public entertainment with no expense spared. It had been something of an iconic moment and a turning-point in the civil war where Caesar had defeated Gnaeus Pompeius Magnus at the battle of Pharsalus in 48 B.C.

How had he known that?

Detailed events pertaining to ancient Roman history had not formed part of the curriculum at school and he certainly had not researched such in-depth specifics when studying for his architectural degree.

But, for now, he concentrated on those issues that brought him into the elegant formal gardens of the great house. There was precious little grass to cut throughout the heat of summer but around the edges of the extensive lawn and up against the bases of the many statues and busts on their plinths, the terra-cotta urns and Corinthian fluted columns, the growth was prolific in the wake of recent thunderstorms.

Adam, as always, worked stripped to the waist and as he moved, so the large and clearly-defined muscles of his upper torso – already slicked with sweat, rippled as he applied the stone to the shears. The blades shone, reflecting the early sunlight and for a few minutes longer he lovingly worked the steel. They were a good tool, he mused, sharp and precise, made for close work and in an age where most people preferred the convenience of electrical trimmers, they were fast becoming outdated.

"Shame how so many of the old ways have died out," he told the shears as though they were a living entity and setting the oilstone aside and hefting the pleasantly-familiar weight in his right hand he moved lithely across the grass to the first of the columns and knelt before it. It was pure white, dazzling him as it reflected the sun's rays but as he touched it he found the surface was surprisingly cool.

That was one of the properties of marble; it was cold as well as beautiful and durable, lending itself to any number of applications....

The touch became a lingering caress and for the briefest instant he felt the old but enjoyable sense of familiarity he had come to know over the years welling up inside him again. The column seemed to tower above him and now there were others too, forming a majestic colonnade and as he looked skyward he could see their apexes were topped off with sumptuous capitals – each bearing a meticulously-carved scroll at its four corners and a double row of acanthus leaves beneath. He was kneeling in the centre of a flight of wide steps at the top of a lofty podium and through the great open doors of the temple he could make out the inner sanctum where fragrant smoke from incense braziers spiralled up into the gloom of the high fresco-adorned ceiling.

He savoured the experience for just a few moments before, almost reluctantly, shaking off the sensation of having been here on other occasions too. He was at odds to comprehend the scenario which was disturbingly real in its content and even more mystifying in the way it remained random and fleeting in its nature, always presenting him with a tantalising glimpse of this other place before vanishing like a will-o'-the-wisp on fleet wings.

This wasn't marble, it was concrete! Mass-produced stuff designed to look like the real thing only on a much smaller scale. They turned them out by the hundred. Poured into moulds, it only took minutes but the real columns – now that was something completely different. A team of stone masons would be engaged for days carving and perfecting just one of the decorative supporting structures while others laboured over the exquisite capitals adorning their apexes. Just imagine the sweat and exertion that killed men and maimed others breaking the stone out of the quarries at....

Where was it? Ah, yes. There had been others too but the vision of this one seemed permanently imprinted for some reason.

Marathi Paros in the Cyclades off south-eastern Greece.

His mind was wandering again. He went at the grass with a concerted effort, moving between the plinths, columns and urns until the job was done and he stood up and admired his work. His shoulders and upper arms ached from the effort but the memory of this other world lingered and for the briefest instant he cupped the feeling to him once more, like a candle flame in the night.

How long before she beckoned to him again and what secrets would she impart?

"Who needs the gym after a workout like that?" he told the shears, finally shrugging off the sensation and smiling contentedly but his good spirits were not attributed entirely to the physical effort. After cleaning and oiling the blades he returned them to the tool shed, locked the door and made his way back to the house.

Tyra glanced up from the morning paper as Adam halted briefly in the doorway carrying his khaki safari shirt, ready in an instant to cover up if she had visitors. He was silhouetted by the early sun and she felt her body react as she gazed upon the muscular, sweat-moistened form of her husband who appeared to tower over her. Instantly, she felt her nipples swell and harden and became aware of that all-too-familiar delicious melting sensation in the pit of her stomach.

"Coffee's ready and there are hot croissants," she greeted him and then moistened her lips with the tip of her tongue. Her subtle, educated tones conveyed an undertone of invitation and he detected that slightly husky element in her voice. She was in her terry towelling robe which had only been casually fastened at the waist while the upper part hung open to reveal a deep cleavage and much of her large breasts. The urge to reach inside and touch her nipples was almost overpowering and he felt himself hardening and swelling involuntarily.

What if she read his mind and pulled the material aside, flaunting and offering herself as she had done on numerous other occasions?

Her wet, black hair – slick as an otter's pelt, was wrapped in a turban-style configuration, something that had always intrigued him and, he reckoned, a mystery known only to women. Without knowing the reason why, he paused to study the lovely face. At fifty she was still as appealing as she had been twenty-five years earlier but in some respects he was certain he had known her a lot longer. There were no frown wrinkles and her skin retained its lustre as if the ageing process had been suddenly halted whilst she was at her most desirable. The only indications of her true age were the tiny, barely-discernible chiselled marks at the corners of her eyes and mouth – one of life's little legacies which, in a way, made her even more attractive and mysterious.

Probably her most captivating feature was her eyes. They were so dark as to be almost black but shot through with tiny flecks of light. The first time she had smiled at him he had gone dizzy on his feet and felt his world turn upside down but when he looked into her eyes lately he could swear there was something else – something he couldn't quite put his finger on that wasn't there before. It was intriguing and disturbing at the same time but he knew he had not imagined it. Something had definitely changed and was now mirrored in her seductive, penetrating gaze which appeared to be challenging him, mocking him, daring him to....

"I said coffee's ready," and she was staring at him oddly, with a slightly bemused expression. "Penny for your thoughts," she teased with her head canted at an inquiring angle and her voice had now assumed a different note in light of his lingering scrutiny. She fixed him with a heart-stopping candid invitation and in that same instant he became aware of her perfume. It was a perfect balance between slightly-sweet aromatic fragrance and the understated bitterness of Madagascan sandalwood. It must have been made for Tyra for it seemed to mingle with and accentuate her natural feminine scent and always left his thoughts in disarray whenever she wore it. She had been unusually moved and surprised by his choice of gift all those years ago for Adam was not known to spend time pondering the finer aspects of feminine trappings. At the sterling equivalent of 2,150 dollars an ounce, the tiny but elegant coloured-glass phial of Clive Christian No. 1 had been an impulse purchase and he had presented it to her one night over dinner.

The intoxicating musk filled his head and made his senses reel but his brain was already full of confusing messages – some as a result of his experience in the garden just now and others as a direct consequence of the sexual overtones she was clearly making.

'Please, God, not now,' he thought.

"Coffee would be good," he managed at last as he focused his thoughts through the barrage of conflicting emotions, "and then I need a shower."

It was a lame attempt to defuse what had in seconds become an overt, sexually-charged situation for his arousal had been swift and unbelievably demanding. He downed the coffee, black and heavily-sweetened and munched one of the delicious croissants but when he looked across at Tyra again she seemed to have become totally absorbed with the newspaper and made no further comment. He kissed her briefly on her forehead and then walked to the bathroom and closed the door – away from that dangerous intimacy.

2

Sophie Harrington's mood was pensive as she walked through the rooms of her elegant Georgian country house methodically closing the heavy drapes and lighting the many candles. It was barely nine-thirty and would be light for at least another half hour but Sophie was impatient to be rid of the daylight and longed for the hours of darkness for, essentially, she was a creature of the night.

The imminent twilight lifted her spirits as the shadows gradually lengthened with agonising slowness but the approaching dusk seemed to dwell in perfect harmony with the mystique and intrigue which always accompanied the close of another day. For as long as she could remember this had been her favourite time. One of her fondest recollections was of a child walking home from school in late autumn, inhaling the wonderful smell of fallen leaves and watching spellbound as the blood-red sun finally dipped out of sight over the far horizon leaving in its wake that peculiar orange glow – unique to the time of year, in a washed-out pale blue sky that heralded the arrival of another cold and frosty night.

Whilst most of Sophie's friends and acquaintances regarded it as strange she should nurture such an affinity with dark nights and cold winter days she thought it was they who were odd in their longing for endless summer months and foreign beaches packed with seething masses of humanity, risking it all for that elusive tan and most likely falling victim to premature ageing and malignant melanomas.

The house was a parting gift from her father who, ten years previously, had found himself in a loveless marriage and realised he was going nowhere. The ensuing divorce was amicable but costly and as Sophie's mother had always hated the place and it had not formed part of the financial settlement, it followed Nick should leave it to his daughter. Katharine had moved on at the earliest opportunity, finding someone new to begin the cycle over again but had since distanced herself from Sophie. Nick, however – always the one to look to the future in pursuit of life's golden opportunities had, by supreme effort alone, taken his construction company to new heights and now boasted offices in the Middle East and South Africa. The house was set in three hundred acres of picturesque English woodland and grazing pasture and was accessed via a winding half-mile lane flanked by mature copper beech trees. It enjoyed relative seclusion in a shallow depression between the low hills surrounding it and the nearest properties were over a mile away beyond visual range.

Two weathered, life-size statues announced the otherwise inconspicuous entrance leading from the main road and to the ignorant and uninformed who passed by, the significance of these would be meaningless; to others more intimately acquainted with Sophie's vocation, just another indication symbolic of the woman who lived here and indulged in her quirky lifestyle.

To the left of the gate and standing on a lofty plinth which towered above the entrance the jolly figure of Bacchus, Roman god of wine and partying – synonymous of all things representing pleasure, excess and drunken revelry. On the other side, his Nemesis, the goddess, Minerva – patron of wisdom, learning, the arts and industry and, sitting on her shoulder her symbol, the wise owl. These stone figures were archetypal of what Sophie's clients could expect when they arrived at her front door and merely hinted to those who remained unversed in such matters as to the sense of balance she strove to achieve in all things; male and female, light and dark, work and pleasure, harmony and conflict.

As Sophie moved through the rooms of the large house, lighting the candles and embracing this new ambience where the dancing flames became living entities, she felt herself come truly alive. Her senses became more acute and the petty strivings of the outside world were consigned to insignificance. In this ethereal setting Sophie was truly happy as she saw how the candle flames and ever-moving shadows endowed the paintings and sculptures with life of their own. Some of the more sinister gargoyle-like busts and figures of gods from the Pantheon had been placed in niches and alcoves and their features contorted and twisted as the shadows played upon their faces.

There were sculpted cherubs on the high walls and a frieze depicting a heavenly choir while below, good battled with evil and defeated it in a bloody confrontation between the soldiers of Christ and the dark forces of Satan's army. On the ornate seventeenth-century mantelpiece, the Greek god, Pan, played his pipes and again the tricks of light and shadow emphasised the facial features of this impish character.

There were paintings too; beautiful cloudscapes and sunrises, peaceful shorelines with lapping waves and white doves in flight and, at the opposite end of the spectrum portraying the darker side of man, depictions of hell and the underworld in vivid reds and oranges with souls in despair, doomed to eternity in the fires of damnation.

Sophie looked upon all this as a balancing effect. Good versus evil, light against dark; hope and despair, yin and yang; in nature, all things in equilibrium.

Yes, this was Sophie's favourite room by far. This was where she brought her clients in order that she might soothe their troubled minds and provide answers to their many questions. In here was one of her most prized possessions for the couch on which her clients lay was hewn from a solid oak trunk. The tree had blown down in those catastrophic storms of 1987, narrowly missing the house and Sophie – interpreting this as a good omen had contracted a local craftsman to do the work. It had cost a small fortune but once it was in place she knew it was exactly what she had been looking for. She covered it with large cushions purchased from a bazaar in the nearby town and over these she spread oriental blankets and sumptuous tasselled pillows. The end result exceeded all expectations. Her intuition told her she would soon be welcoming a special visitor; not a casual acquaintance or long-standing client in search of their monthly top-up of positive energy and anger management, but her best friend.

She knew there was something going on in the lives of Adam and Tyra but she would not pry. They had always been close enough to speak openly with each other on all manner of subjects but she suspected within the bounds of their unusually-close relationship all was not quite as it should be. Where Adam was concerned she had detected a disturbance in his aura when he last visited her and it could not be explained away by day-to-day, run-of-the-mill events and occurrences. There was something going on in his life over which he had no control and she had yet to discover what precipitated it although she was reasonably certain it was directly connected to his line of work. There was a seemingly-random element to his experiences which was also becoming increasingly noticeable whenever he came into contact with certain physical features or materials.

Already there was a theory forming in her mind as to what was going on here and whilst she was eager to explain it to Tyra so she could be forewarned in the event of Adam exhibiting any strange or unaccountable behaviour, she would not intervene – just yet.

There was also the other possibility, that what she suspected was happening to Adam would also, inevitably, affect Tyra but the idea was so preposterous and unbelievable she dare not voice her opinions too soon or too loudly lest they think her introvert lifestyle had unbalanced her and she had taken to the bottle!

3

Tyra Grant was becoming increasingly agitated by Adam's unusual behaviour of late and since that disturbing incident in the kitchen on Saturday morning when he had finished cutting the grass, she was convinced things were far from normal.

Now, when she looked back, there were other times in the recent past when Adam had been his usual self one minute and, quite literally – within the blink of an eye, he had changed as if something came over him and completely diverted his attention away from the present.

It wasn't that his personality altered or he became threatening or menacing in any way – *Please, God, don't ever let that happen!* Their relationship was too unique, too special to allow anything to come between them.

In their twenty-seven years together he had not once raised his voice to her and she had been aware from those first electrifying days which followed their initial meeting at Russ and Julia's, this was a union of man and woman based not just on love but trust and respect, each having a deep understanding of the other's strengths and weaknesses and using these to further reinforce the bond between them.

It was almost as if they had been.... and she mentally chastised herself for she was not given to romantic twaddle found in fairy tales; it was almost as if they had been destined to be together from a time much earlier than when they had met, as if it was all part of a bigger picture pre-ordained by powers immensely superior to anything found in this mortal world. There had always been that extra special *something* since the beginning, something they were both acutely aware of but could never find adequate words to describe or explain.

A love like theirs, especially these days, was a gift to be cherished and nurtured in a world where they regularly witnessed acts of extreme disrespect, both of the physical and verbal kind and even violence between terribly mismatched couples. Adam had coined a phrase for this kind of behaviour whenever they came across it – *'Ugly by sight, ugly by nature!'* and to Tyra this just about summed it up perfectly. Why did people do this to one another? Why remain with a partner and make both lives a misery when clearly all chemistry and passion had long-since vanished?

Tyra felt she was indeed blessed by the influences of providence to have a man like Adam as her partner, lover, soul-mate and confidante. Not only was it glaringly obvious she was deeply loved by him, she knew deep down she was still *in love* after all this time. So why was she concerned? Was she losing Adam? No, that was definitely not the case; she knew they were still crazy about one another. So, was their relationship changing? She didn't have the answer to that one but something had changed lately. When Adam had come back into the house on Saturday morning and looked at her with that piercing gaze while she studied his muscular form still fresh from his labours in the garden, even though she had only just showered she wanted him fiercely and had been aware of his own response.

And then, without warning – quicker than it had begun, it was over and he was making feeble excuses to leave her presence. One thing she did know – recently, when he looked into her eyes he seemed to be studying her in a way which was unfamiliar to her. It was not an uncomfortable sensation for she loved this degree of scrutiny but at the same time she felt he had either seen or was searching for something but of what she remained unsure.

What was she supposed to be looking for? She prided herself she had always been able to see into his mind, but not this time. Should she tackle him about it and if so, what should she say? She was going round in circles, getting nowhere. Adam had never been prone to mood swings. He was the most placid and even-tempered person she had ever known so what was it that could trigger a reaction in a man like him to seek solitude in the bathroom when on the verge of passionate sex?

There must be a clue somewhere. She had to think harder, beyond the physical attraction they had for each other. She was sure she was missing something. Whatever it was seemed to have manifested itself only recently; either that or Adam had done a convincing job of covering it up. Could it be connected to his line of work? Could it be something from his past – an issue he had never broached and was only now after all this time troubling him so deeply? Again she considered this an implausible explanation; they knew each other too intimately for that. Could the company be in financial trouble and it was playing on his mind? Adam was tremendously proud of his work and ability to maintain such a high standard of living for them while Tyra remained blissfully content in her role as homemaker. With the exception of

Sophie, perhaps, most of their friends were acquaintances of Tyra and although Adam always went out of his way to be convivial and the perfect host, he was not particularly outgoing.

Adam had told her a long time ago that once in a while he *felt things*, only fleetingly before they were gone. Performing certain tasks or seeing something on the rare occasions they watched television together sometimes made him feel good about himself, almost as if these were familiar to him. He seemed reluctant to say more. Maybe he thought she would laugh and tell him he was working too hard and needed a break, that sort of thing. He had always been a very private person, channelling all his time and energy into work and ensuring Tyra was happy and wanted for nothing.

She herself had never felt any of the things he described nor had she seen anything which triggered emotions that were familiar but unaccountable at the same time. This did not affect the feeling they were destined to be together and it was frustrating because she was trying to think logically but common sense kept rearing its stupid head.

"So ask yourself a direct question," she spoke aloud as she attempted to lend credibility to a situation whose solution was proving to be increasingly evasive the more she thought about it. "You've always held a strong belief you and Adam were destined for each other and kept an open mind on the subject. The question is could you and Adam have been intended to meet from a great deal earlier in time than either of you realise? Think about some of what Sophie told you."

'We've all had previous lives, darling, whether we choose to acknowledge it or not. Some of you lucky ones have actually met in previous lives and not realised it.'

"Could Adam be having flashes from an earlier time and becoming curious about what it all means, but at the same time being scared to death by the implications? Why has he been looking at me differently just lately? Is he seeing something or some*one* vaguely reminiscent he is not entirely sure of, something that strikes a familiar chord? If that's the case and we are as close as I believe us to be, then why am I not having similar experiences also? What does it all mean? I need Adam spiritually as well as physically and I need him to touch me and show he needs me also and wants me as much as I want him. What happens if this situation begins to take over our lives and we end up drifting apart...?"

She was truly frightened now and a tear welled up in the corner of her eye and rolled down her cheek.

"Should I ask Adam if there's anything troubling him he wants to talk about or will I simply make matters worse? I need him to talk to me. Is Adam's lifestyle today serving as a reminder in some indirect way of what he did a long time ago? Is that it?"

There was something else too.

"Could the reason for my not sharing Adam's feelings and visions be attributed to the fact in an earlier time we were not actually together, as a man and wife or maybe just a couple?"

That sounded like a credible explanation and she made up her mind to broach the subject with Adam as soon as the ideal opportunity presented itself but in the meantime she desperately needed some answers to questions she was not entirely sure about. It was time to talk to Sophie again and she would call her in the morning when Adam had gone to work.

Adam's black BMW pulled up outside their house a little after six and Tyra watched as he walked across the gravel drive and up the steps to the entrance, admiring the way he looked in the smart grey suit and white shirt. She loved the way he carried himself – head held high with shoulders back and despite the deceptive air of relaxation he also imparted the agility of an athlete where he could launch himself into action with no prior warning, *'Like one of the big African cats,'* she thought with immense pride and barely stifled the giggle.

"Where the hell did that come from?" she surprised herself and went into the hallway to greet him. "Hello, Adam. How was your day? I've really missed you," was all she could manage and before either of them knew it was happening they were kissing with the urgency of lovers who have been parted for too long and tearing at one another's clothes. There would be time later for all the nuances and refinements of love but for now their immediate needs were too cruel and demanding to be denied.

When they awoke hours later from that exhausted, death-like sleep which invariably follows passionate love-making, it was already dark. They showered together and then, in their terry towelling robes, sat at the kitchen table over a steaming pasta bake and a bottle of the finest Chianti. When the meal was finished and the dishes washed, she judged the moment to be right and poured herself another glass of wine.

"Adam, is there anything bothering you lately? Are you truly happy with me and all we have here? I know you work extremely hard and the pressures on you are mounting as you become more successful but is there anything at all unsettling you?"

He considered the question for a few moments and his expression became serious. The brief incident of Saturday morning was completely out of character and he knew she must also have picked up on some of the other fleeting occurrences he had encountered over recent months and were inexplicably increasing in both frequency and intensity.

"Yes, I am happy," he replied at last. "Who wouldn't be? I am the most fortunate man in the world to have found a woman like you. When we are out together with you on my arm I see the envy in other men's eyes. I knew before we met you would be the one. I knew a long, long time ago there would be no other but the endless waiting would prove to be worth it."

She had been caught unawares by his words for it was not at all what she had expected.

"How could you know that?" she demanded and instantly regretted the hard edge to her voice. "How could you possibly know you must wait for someone you were not even aware existed?" she continued in a noticeably softer tone, her thoughts in complete disarray.

"I knew," he stated flatly. "I just knew. Do you remember when I told you I occasionally felt things that were familiar but had never encountered in this life? It didn't happen very often and at first I paid scant attention. Sometimes years would pass before I felt or saw anything again but when I did the sensation and the memory was all-the-more intense.

"After a while I began to understand there seemed to be a pattern to what I believed was totally random. Certain things seemed to trigger these events. They only lasted for seconds but became imprinted on my mind as though they were yesterday. It's a really strange sensation, Tyra, and something I have no control over. I feel someone....somewhere, is trying to call me and part of me wants to find the answers.

"The feelings are not unpleasant – quite the reverse. It's like a fond memory which rekindles intense pleasure but there are only snippets and flashes and the picture is disjointed and fragmented. I can't tell you what the eventual outcome will be or if the picture's ever going to be complete but there's one thing I know for certain and it is that you are a part of it."

She was both shocked and beautifully surprised by his words for only this morning she had been mulling over in her head ridiculous theories and possibilities about all this and thought she might just be going a little potty. Now, as plain as day, here it was out in the open, *but what now?*

"Tyra, there's something else too – something in your eyes that wasn't there before. If you've noticed anything different about the way I've been looking at you recently, that's the reason. I can't place it with any degree of sureness but there's definitely a change. Sophie would

23

probably latch onto it straight away but I'm at a loss to interpret the meaning."

She most certainly had seen a change! It wasn't a mesmeric stare or something she regarded as intimidating or disturbing; in fact it was quite a satisfying but curious feeling knowing the man you love is gazing into your soul and seeing – *what? Something you were not even aware of yourself?*

"Tyra, you fit squarely into this situation but I don't know where. All I know is whatever I did or whoever I was in the distant past, you played a major part. I cannot tell you whether or not we were related or were lovers, friends or sworn enemies. I may not actually have been aware of your existence but you were there and you were influential in my life to a greater or lesser extent. I have seen these things and your eyes confirm they are neither trickery nor delusion. There is a burning need to find out who I was and what made me the person I am today but I have no idea what to do. Tyra, I'm deeply sorry for what happened on Saturday. When I touched one of those columns in the garden something happened and for the briefest moment it felt as though I was knelt before the real thing at the top of a flight of wide steps – somewhere.

"There's also the matter of the garden shears and sharpening them by hand - the look and feel of holding the blades. What the hell is all that about? At the time it felt good and the sensation ended all-too-soon but when I came in here and saw you, saw into your eyes I....I just couldn't face you. If anything, the experience in the garden should have heightened the occasion because I wanted you with a passion when I looked at you with your hair tied up and I knew beneath the towelling robe you were naked. My emotions were so mixed up and I just felt drained and confused. I'm sorry for that and I'm sorry it spoiled your weekend."

Tyra was thinking hard. The implications of this were simply enormous. Some of the pieces had already fallen into place and were starting to make sense.

In the darkness of their bedroom where a single candle flame cast eerie shadows, they made tender love before falling into a dream-filled sleep.

She desperately needed to make that call to Sophie.

4

"Hello, Sophia Harrington speaking. How may I help you?"

"Sophie. It's Tyra. How the devil are you?"

"Tyra!" she squealed with glee. "How lovely to hear from you again. How long has it been - seems absolutely ages, darling."

"Two weeks, three days and this morning. Listen, Sophie, I need to talk to you. It could be important."

"Friend or therapist?" and Sophie smiled to herself.

"Both," Tyra replied. "How are you fixed for lunch – I'm buying?"

"I have a free day," Sophie answered, warmed by Tyra's unexpected invitation and the feeling this was, perhaps, the call she'd been anticipating.

"I'll pick you up at twelve, Sophie. 'Bye for now."

Tyra replaced the phone in its unit and went upstairs to change. It was just after eleven and the trip to Sophie's would take a good half-hour so it was with mixed feelings of urgency and excitement she dressed and put on make-up. One way or another, this meeting could change many things. It should certainly provide answers to some of her many questions as Sophie was one smart woman. She could see beyond all the fog and clutter that complicated people's lives and come up with some pretty startling revelations. They had both known Sophie for years and been visiting her regularly for their much-loved spiritual therapy sessions.

She had also been a damned good friend! Tyra reflected. She listened and gave advice when asked but never judged. Sophie and her 'room' were a powerful combination where total relaxation and brutal honesty were the order of the day and the only stipulations she attached to any therapy. Sophie knew more about you than you knew about yourself and Tyra smiled as she imagined her slightly eccentric but all-seeing friend.

Distanced by her mother whilst her father ran a successful business abroad, she had few visitors save for her clients. She lived a bit like a recluse, scorned the daylight hours, deplored any kind of artificial lighting and kept her curtains closed most of the time. Sophie had a weakness for candles and if you'd ever been to one of her sessions you'd come away loving them too!

At five feet ten inches, Sophie was considered tall. She was voluptuous with an amazing figure and had flaming auburn hair, generally piled up on top of her head and held in place by several beautifully-ornate Etruscan clasps. The long strands which hung down the sides of her face were apparently a constant source of irritation and she was forever brushing them aside with her hand.

She had an oddball dress style, sporting mainly long, black dresses displaying her ample cleavage and stiletto heels which further accentuated her height. Sophie had never married nor sought any permanent relationship with another person. Most of the time she spoke perfect English with an accent that gave hint to her education at Cheltenham School for Ladies but if the need arose she could swear like a sergeant-major bawling out the latest intake of rookie troopers on the parade ground. She could drink Adam and Tyra under the table without blinking and awaken three hours later refreshed and ready to face anything the world was capable of throwing in her direction. They both loved her like a sister and were agreed she was the focal point around which their lives revolved.

With Sophie belted safely into the passenger seat of the white Mercedes Tyra sped along the country lanes with a flair and panache many a racing driver would envy. Sophie eyed the lavish interior of Tyra's most recent acquisition with critical appraisal and ran an admiring glance over her beige Chanel skirt and expensive open-toed high heels.

"Blessed are the rich!" she intoned and they both laughed delightedly. They parked behind the restaurant in one of the 'patrons only' bays and the two of them walked, arms linked, round to the entrance where the owner greeted them like family.

"Ladeez, you do me a great honour," he piped in his halting English. "Will it be your usual table in the corner? You have much to discuss, no?" and he eyed his shapely customers lasciviously.

"You are very gracious, Carlos," replied Tyra. "Thank you."

Once seated in their secluded corner the waiter brought menus and only after Tyra signalled did he return to take their orders.

"We'll both have the sea-bass, thank you." She ordered a carafe of house red for Sophie and a spring-water for herself. She needed a clear head for what was coming.

As the waiter turned smartly and headed for the kitchen Sophie came straight to the point with her usual flair for assessing the situation.

"This is about you and Adam isn't it?"

"How could you have known that?" Tyra was astounded.

"Not just plain old feminine intuition, that's for sure. It's Sophie Harrington you're dealing with now, you know."

"I'm beginning to realise."

"So tell me and let's see where this goes."

"Adam's been experiencing feelings and images from what he thinks may be a time before he was born. They're only brief, mind you, but are unsettling him and, I fear, may damage us as a couple unless we can get to the root of the problem. He says he's had them on and off for years but now they're back with a renewed intensity. Apparently they're not unpleasant but they leave him confused with his emotions in turmoil. It's as if there's something calling to him and he wants to go out there and meet it."

She looked around her and even though she was speaking in hushed tones she was afraid of being overheard and attracting unwanted attention. Leaning over the table toward Sophie, she continued.

"He talks about a picture with many of the parts missing – a fragmented and hazy image with gaps and spaces and he's curious to find out what it all means. What's going on, Sophie? He says he's wondering if it's partly due to his lifestyle – you know, always sharpening the garden tools and his fascination with Roman architecture. Something happened the other day when he touched one of those columns on the lawn. When he came indoors he looked at me in a way I've not seen before and we were on the point of ravaging each other when he walked away."

They were interrupted by the arrival of the waiter bringing their meal and after he had left Tyra continued.

"Also, Sophie, have you seen his work just lately – some of his designs? They're building enormous structures with huge columns, podiums, fountains and statues, shopping malls and piazzas with marble floors. They're fantastic but he's sold his ideas to the clients and it's what they want. Everyone else is building with the boring old traditional materials like bricks and concrete and he gives them granite and Italian marble."

Sophie nodded as she ate, sensing instinctively where all this was leading for she had been expecting it. She drained her third glass of wine and gestured for the waiter to bring more. "Please continue, darling. I find what you are saying most interesting."

"The company's got more work on the books than it can handle and I think this latest project of theirs is going to prove the crowning achievement of their lives. Have you been keeping pace with it, Sophie? It's the biggest thing to hit Warchester in memory."

"I have to admit to being largely in the dark apart from accounts in the local papers but do tell me. I can see the beginnings of a pattern emerging here."

"It's a near replica of the old Roman forum in Italy with a completely covered-in part at one end. They've modelled it on the Pantheon with its huge domed roof and even the oculus to admit daylight. Oh, there's something else too...," and she had to stop again as Sophie's second carafe of wine arrived at their table.

As the waiter left them alone again Sophie's attention lingered on the form of his retreating backside in the tight black trousers before returning once more to her friend. "Sorry, darling. You were saying...?"

"I don't know what to make of this but Adam told me I'm part of this convoluted scenario and played a direct part in whatever ultimately happened to him. He can't say if we were lovers, enemies or friends or were even known to each other, just that I'm a part of some other bigger unfinished picture and he won't rest until he has the answers. What does it mean, Sophie? What's happening to Adam and where are we going as a couple?"

Sophie placed her empty glass on the table and adjusted her seating position before fixing Tyra with her penetrating green eyes.

"Darling, I'm surprised you took this long to broach the subject of Adam's apparent connection to his past. He once told me, and I really don't recall when, about some strange sensations he'd felt under certain but very specific conditions and what amounted to be flashes from a past existence he could neither explain nor understand. On the surface he appeared more curious than troubled and as we talked about it and I explained how these things sometimes manifested themselves, he seemed to accept it.

"If you are particularly receptive it is quite possible to be presented with images from a previous life when the conditions and circumstances are favourable. We've all been there, darling. It's just that most people either refuse to believe such notions or are simply unaware. Ignorance is bliss, as they say. How many times have you heard people describe life in the womb and some can go back an awful lot further than that, even without hypnosis and regression?"

"Why are Adam's visions, sensations – call them what you will, why are they becoming more intense and increasing in number?"

"Tyra, listen to me carefully before committing to any judgement about Adam. Since we've come to know each other we've built up a bond of trust and friendship to the extent where we no longer question the wisdom, counsel or advice of our coveted little circle."

Keeping her voice to little more than that of a raised whisper and looking around to satisfy herself they were not being overheard, she leaned a little closer to Tyra and began.

"Darling, you know I love you and would never say anything to cause pain or discomfort so I'll try and put this as simply as I can. It is my belief, and I have evidence supporting the claim, in his past life Adam was deeply hurt. I can't give you precise details but there is reason to suspect immediately prior to his death he was faced with a terrible decision. I can also confirm you were known to each other but at precisely what level is unclear. Your father was an important figure within the body of government – a politician seeking enhancement of his career to much higher office. There was some kind of scandal, not public at first where it remained known to only a few."

Sophie's expression became grave and her mysterious green eyes misted over. Tyra knew better than to interrupt. It was just as well for her face was suddenly a mask of tragedy and she began to weep, making no attempt to wipe away the tears that rolled down her cheeks.

"Tyra, you and Adam went to your deaths within twenty-four hours of each other and your father died by his own hand soon after. Something tells me all three of you were linked by a combination of fate and circumstances but the full details have yet to emerge. Adam said you were a part of this picture but I don't think either of you realised how big that part was until now."

"Adam doesn't know," Tyra replied. "How long before he works it out for himself or is made aware at some point in the future? He's already started looking into my eyes for something or someone – what's he searching for?"

"Perhaps he already knows and is merely seeking confirmation."

"Sophie, why don't I have these same flashbacks and visions if, as you say, I was part of what happened, whatever that may have been?"

"Perhaps the moment to be reminded of your own past experiences is not yet at hand, Tyra. Nothing in the spirit world happens by chance but you may rest assured in the days ahead your time will come and you will know beyond all doubt how your fates have been intertwined and predestined for millennia. As for Adam, there is little doubt his recent insights and sensations are attributable to his former self calling to him, willing him to remember a far-off time when the world was a dangerous, brutal and unforgiving place and the two of you were about to meet as strangers. For what it's worth, I can reaffirm you are his first woman in this life. Adam has waited an incredibly long time for you."

Tyra's world dissolved into a state of turmoil and she covered her face lest Sophie should see her emotional distress. After several moments she lowered her hands to reveal cheeks wet with tears and dark stains around her eyes where her mascara had run and smudged, imparting an even greater sense of tragedy to the story unfolding.

"He told me that himself less than twenty-four hours ago," she sniffed and reached into her bag for a tissue. "He said I was the only one for him, always had been and always would be. He said we were destined to be together and had waited for me since before this life began." At last, satisfied she had her emotions under control, she continued. "Sophie, we keep talking about then and now and a long time ago. Just when, exactly, was *then?*"

Sophie's eyes sparkled with her own tears and she looked at Tyra mischievously.

"Think about it, darling. It doesn't take an educated scholar to fit the pieces together - marble columns, statues on their plinths, fountains and beautiful structures atop lofty podiums. Your daddy was making a name for himself in the senate and now Adam seems to have some fixation with metal blades when he's in the garden. Darling, your man was a warrior and by that I don't mean a soldier. I've been doing quite a bit of after-hours research over the months when you probably thought I was tucked up safely in bed and it turns out Adam – or the man who became Adam, was a popular figure in his day, loved by the masses and feared by those sent against him."

Tyra had adopted an expression of wide-eyed disbelief and her food remained untouched as she listened to the outrageous conjecture unfolding before her, but she would not interrupt Sophie. Regardless of how far-fetched the explanation appeared on the surface, she was not given to sensationalising or over-dramatising events purely for effect.

"Don't you see it, darling? Your man was a star of the arena!"

"Are you telling me Adam killed people for sport?" and she had found her voice again with some difficulty.

"That's exactly what I'm saying. I can offer no hypothesis as to why he embarked upon such an odyssey but he does appear to have entered into the profession of his own accord as opposed to being purchased as a slave and forced into it. He seems to have chalked up an impressive list of victories in a relatively short time and the crowds loved him. I can tell you for a couple of years he was Rome's best and set the benchmark for future entertainments in the arena spectacles."

"But Adam isn't a violent man. He's never hurt anyone or even made threats to another person. He's the kindest, most considerate man I've ever...."

"Stop right there!" Sophie interjected. "You're missing the point here. We're not talking about Adam as you know him today. We're discussing the man who became Adam in another life. Everyone knows about the violence and blood-letting of those days. The cruelty and barbarity were an accepted and integral part of Roman life just as boxing, football and all manner of contact sports are for us today. In order to stay alive it was necessary to win favour with the crowds and keep them on your side. He consistently gave them what they wanted and they adored him."

"Okay, I'll buy that for now, but who was this celebrity and the man I subsequently married? He must have had a name. What did they call him?"

"Yes, darling, he had a name and it was daubed on walls all around the city at first. It was a name spoken with pride by the populace for he was one of them. Unfortunately, after a couple of years things changed and it was only after his death the senate passed a decree of Damnatio Memoriae where his name was dashed from all writings and forbidden mention in public which must have incensed the crowds who had witnessed his contests in the arena. His name was Crixus and we can only attribute this draconian action by the senate to the fact you and he were involved in some kind of affair right from the start. When it became public knowledge there would have been hell to pay."

"Oh God, Sophie!" Tyra tried to digest the enormity of those things she had just heard. "This goes so much deeper than I ever could have imagined. Adam said I was involved somewhere along the line but was unable to be more specific. It now seems he and I shared some kind of relationship after all but everything points to the fact it didn't endure for whatever reasons. Sophie, are you able to be a little more specific about when all this took place?"

"To within a year or so, yes," she nodded. "The Colosseum was not completed until A.D.80 but soon after, Crixus began training and making a name for himself in some of the smaller arenas in and around the city. He never fought in the inaugural games but made numerous appearances thereafter. Try and appreciate this little sentiment, darling, and you might begin to understand. In those days Rome was a predator society. A display of mortal combat and its contempt for death perfectly represented what it meant to be a Roman."

Her head was reeling; she could not take it all in but retained absolute faith in Sophie's extraordinary psychic abilities and visionary windows into the past and trusted her pronouncements implicitly.

"Tyra, there are many clues here about Adam's life before, although I cannot give you any details about his death. That particular information is still shrouded in a veil of mystery but may well emerge at some future point. Tell me, darling, when you've seen Adam in the bedroom, the shower or maybe even in the garden, is there anything different you've noticed about his upper body when compared to other men? Take your time, darling, and think carefully. Anything at all. Any irregularities for instance – any marks and I don't mean tattoos?"

"Well – now you mention it, yes, there is. High up on the left side of his chest and just below the collar bone there is a faint horizontal scar about three inches long. I've never inquired and he's offered no explanation as to how it came to be there but it looks like a very old scar."

"It is," Sophie replied with an air of the seasoned anthropologist in her voice. "Approximately one thousand nine-hundred years old."

Tyra looked at her with mouth agape and was about to say something but Sophie hadn't finished.

"Is Adam right or left-handed?"

"He's right-handed, Sophie. Why do you ask?"

"Let's go back to distinguishing marks or differences if you like. Think of balance and uniformity. If you had a life-size photograph of Adam and folded it in half, would the left side fit exactly over the right?"

Tyra considered the matter carefully. Adam's physique would have commanded attention from any quarter but there was one unique and rather prominent feature that stood out above all other athletic males she had seen over the years.

"Of course...! Yes, I see what you mean now. It's been there all the time but I've never really paid too much attention to it. Yes, there is a difference. The muscles on Adam's right side are much larger and more clearly-defined than those on the left. It's quite pronounced. Is this another of your clues, Sophie?"

"Absolutely. Skilled fighters who used the type of heavy weaponry employed in the schools had massively-overdeveloped musculature of their sword-arms. It all fits, Tyra. You've just given me another part of the puzzle. You know how we've spoken about equilibrium and balance in nature being important, well try to appreciate this view," and Tyra edged a little closer as Sophie expounded her theory.

"In his past life the man we know as Adam killed and destroyed because that was what he had trained for and he became rather adept at it. But, on the other side of the coin, look at what that man has become today – quite the reverse and the complete antithesis of his former self. He creates and builds beautiful and lasting monuments. We've all seen his work and he is considered one of the best in his field. Two thousand years further on, the man we know as Adam is still giving the public something they want, something different and on a scale of impressiveness that will see his name elevated to virtual legend for his achievements. Once again they will come to love him but for a completely different reason. It's almost as if, subconsciously, he is making reparations for his past life and this latest chain of events will see his destiny come full circle.

"Don't forget, darling, this is no longer just about Adam. We know for certain part of your own distant past is locked away somewhere in here too but I'm at a loss to see any of the details at the moment. Perhaps in a few weeks or months...."

Tyra was still considering Sophie's words carefully, trying to assimilate her thoughts into some semblance of logic. She was treading on unfamiliar territory here but her next question served only to confirm she remained abreast of the situation and her instincts were correct, if only in the short term.

"Do you think that's why he designs and builds on such a grand scale, employing all manner of expensive materials because only the best will do? Are his ideas rooted in his time here before when he would have been surrounded by structures identical to the one's he's replicating today?"

"Undoubtedly so," Sophie was quick to add substance to the apparently nebulous thread linking their present world with the far-distant past. "He publicly displayed his skills and abilities for the world to see when he embarked on the life of a gladiator. He's doing exactly the same thing now."

"Could he be conscious of the connection between the two, do you think?"

"He may not be aware at a conscious level of any connection at the moment but I'm almost certain he will before too long. Look at the materials he's working with. He spends hours every day poring over drawings he's created and then goes out to the construction sites and rubs shoulders with the physical results of his ideas. He told you himself under certain circumstances contact with those materials can trigger what you and I know as his flashbacks and sensations which, by all accounts, are becoming more intense and numerous.

"Yes, Tyra, I'm sure every time this happens Adam is going to gain a little more of this picture he tells you about. I don't think he will be particularly devastated to learn about his previous macho image and high-standing among the people of Rome. The screaming crowds in the auditorium, rich women wanting to bed you on the eve of the contest, some of the most powerful and influential figures in Rome chanting your name. The sweat, the muscles, the blood, the adrenalin and the glory – it's a guy thing! What concerns me more is how he reacts when he finds out how it all came to an end and who was responsible...."

There was little to be gleaned from further speculation and it was almost reluctantly Tyra caught the attention of the waiter and mouthed silently, "Bill, please." When he finally approached their table and enquired as to whether they had found the meal to their liking, Tyra handed him several crisp notes and smiled, "Excellent, as always, thank you, and please keep the change."

"Signora is too kind," he beamed and Sophie made lascivious eyes as he kissed each of their hands in turn and held the door open as they exited.

"He's nice," she commented dreamily as she looked back over her shoulder. "I wonder if all Italians are so utterly charming."

"Behave yourself, you wicked woman," Tyra admonished her fondly. "All that wine's gone to your head!"

They both giggled again and loped off arm-in-arm to find the car.

The journey back to Sophie's country home was uneventful and after their animated banter in the restaurant the conversation was strangely subdued as they pondered the implications of their lengthy discussion and those issues requiring answers.

"Thanks for lunch. It was lovely to see you again, darling. Don't forget, if there's anything I can do, call me but I know you will anyway."

She leaned across and bussed each of Tyra's cheeks theatrically and then, having found her key, stepped out of the car and opened the front door to the house.

Tyra drove away down the narrow country lanes and out onto the main road. She always felt a twinge of melancholy after she'd dropped Sophie off and it was just her again; she loved their meetings.

As always she looked forward to Adam coming home at the end of the day but tonight, however, there was another feeling too. There was a slight fluttering in her stomach and, lower down, that pleasant melting sensation. Was it fear? Was it excitement or anticipation, or could it have been all three?

She would not have to wait long to find out.

5

Adam Grant was filled with a deep sense of pride and satisfaction as he stood and admired the great edifice taking shape all around him. It was a huge undertaking and had not been without its most basic and exasperating problems. Part of the 1,280-acre site had historically been an old sand and gravel workings but was now slowly but inevitably yielding to the processes of nature once more as weather eroded the steep banks and wild grasses mellowed the scarred earth. Wildfowl continued to proliferate in the reed-beds and sheltered waters of the deep excavation and the occasional intrepid wind-surfer was not unknown in the summer months.

The town of Warchester, close to where Adam and Tyra lived, desperately needed large-scale investment in order to create new opportunities within a potentially large workforce, many of whom had not been able to find regular local employment for years. Where other towns and cities boasted cathedrals, state-of-the-art sports pavilions and stadiums, marinas or perhaps dramatic geological features which brought tourists into the area, Warchester had nothing.

Nestling in a gap between the hills it had been ideally situated to ship out its coal on the deep, wide canal intersecting the complex of waterways in the midlands industrial region and eventually, after the advent of the railways, by train.

Coal which until the 1980s had been its lifeblood and provided work for considerably more people than lived there now. Following the strikes of the 80s and the Thatcher government's search for alternative fuels, came the inevitable pit closures and Warchester's economy collapsed overnight. Seeing no future by remaining in a run-down area without hope of recovery on the horizon, many of its residents moved away, never to return.

Over the years various half-hearted rejuvenation schemes had been started in an attempt to put the town back on the map. The canal had been cleaned up and was now a popular stopping-off point for narrow-boaters during the finer weather.

There was an attractive riverside pub with terraced gardens and the houses on the quaint, cobbled streets had all been freshly painted. Most people adorned their frontages with window boxes and hanging baskets and during the springtime and warmer months that followed the area was a riot of colour.

But it was not enough and in the wake of much soul-searching and a burning desire to put this town back on the map Adam decided it was time to do something about it. Warchester was only ten minutes from the motorway and there were several other A and B-class roads close by, all capable of bringing in the masses – *and their money!* In the past, Warchester had been a strategic Roman garrison town but, like so many other locations up and down the country, little remained at surface level and only archaeological digs continued to resurrect vital artefacts as a reminder of its once-great beginnings. What more appropriate way of restoring Warchester's illustrious past could there be than by recreating the very pulsating heart of Roman life itself – the hub of social and political activity echoed in every settlement throughout the provinces as Rome continued her policy of imperial expansion?

When Adam had shown his preliminary designs to his partner, Russ Templeman, there had been wide-eyed surprise and only a couple of minor reservations even though he regarded the basic concept as sound if a little adventurous. First and foremost there had to be interest in a project of this size and it was going to be necessary to sell their idea and procure financial backing if it was ever going to get off the ground at all. Warchester, as a centre for tourism, or anything else for that matter, was completely off the map and below the economic horizon. They needed someone who would be willing to take a chance, an astronomically-large chance. If it paid off the rewards for the investor would be enormous. For the company of Templeman Grant Architectural Consultants the increase in prestige, reputation and standing would be incalculable.

Their big break had come just a few short weeks after Adam had delivered his ideas and Russ had been hard at work arranging meetings, entertaining clients and calling in favours in a bid to stimulate interest in their proposed scheme. He had influence, right at the top which was probably why the order books were always full and he could be sure they only ever dealt with the most powerful and respected names in the business.

Because of the sheer scale of the project Adam was proposing and the enormous amounts of capital required throughout its construction,

Russ had sought to channel and amass great sums of money and pledges of backing via a kind of unofficial consortium where each investor would ultimately receive a stake in the finished complex as well as having their own status elevated considerably. Adam had given his assurances they were onto a winner in every respect and his signature on the initial contract of approval was written in blood.

When Russ assembled his group of backers in the company's spacious and luxurious boardroom and shown them Adam's designs, they were clearly impressed but at the same time a little sceptical such an enormous edifice could be built on time and within budget.

"Think of it this way," Russ had encouraged them. "Two thousand years ago the Romans were building stuff like this all the time. They pioneered concrete as we know it today and developed waterproof mortar for use in their aqueducts. They didn't have tower cranes or bulldozers or any of that heavy earthmoving equipment so commonplace nowadays on sites the world over. But look at what they accomplished. Their buildings and monuments have withstood the tests of time and are still with us today. They knew how to drain lakes and build on marshes without the foundations sinking. They could tunnel through solid rock and build straight roads because they knew how to survey the land and make the best use of natural contours.

"Gentlemen, this project is called simply, The Roman Forum, after the popular open-air shopping malls of ancient Rome and which also served as the social and political hub of the city. In its concept Adam Grant has tried to reflect some of the glory and opulence of those days and it is, predominantly, a complex of shops on a huge scale with bars, restaurants and open expanses ringed by porticoes. The chief difference you will see is the great edifice at the northern end of the site which is domed and incorporates a large oculus to admit natural daylight. Around its circular interior will be another complex of shops, hopefully on a theme to reflect their illustrious surroundings and, in the centre of the floor and directly beneath the oculus, a huge fountain modelled on a combination of those found in Rome today. It is calculated in direct sunlight through the top of the dome, wherever a person stands around the fountain there will be a rainbow visible.

"When the original of this building was completed back in the second century A.D. it was called the Pantheon which is derived from the Greek, 'all the gods.' Taken in isolation it was not only one of the most splendid and lavish structures in existence it also boasted the largest dome anywhere in the known world. The walls of the Pantheon were originally thirty feet thick in order to support the weight of the dome on top. We propose to mirror this detail but by employing a matrix of internal load-bearing arches within the main body of the walls we will not only be able to cut down on materials but also facilitate the circular arrangement of shops and stalls."

He was almost irresistible and affected every one of them with his enthusiasm.

"Gentlemen, are we all in agreement this project should go ahead, subject to the usual red tape and bureaucracy of local government planning restrictions of course?"

The laughter echoing around the boardroom was in many ways a release of nervous tension, breaking the spell of Russ' words which had so captivated his small audience. In unison they voiced their approval and he breathed a sigh of relief. He pressed a concealed button and within seconds an aide appeared through a side door carrying a tray with bottles of champagne and a number of elegant lead-crystal flutes. After the popping of corks and charging of glasses Russ Templeman called for silence and addressed all those assembled.

"Gentlemen, a toast! To something new reflecting the wonders of the past. Something magnificent that will not only stand as a monument of national pride and endure in the same way as its predecessor, but a symbol of excellence and prosperity for the town of Warchester and its people. The Roman Forum! May all who gaze upon its splendour be touched by a little of the passion which inspired the man who designed it, Adam Grant."

"The Roman Forum!" they echoed in unison as their raised glasses clinked.

The largest civil construction project of the modern age had just been born.

6

Now, as Adam contemplated the scene before him with a new critical evaluation he could truly appreciate what a monumental task it must have been for the Roman engineers who - in the absence of specialised mechanical equipment as we know it, had raised huge and majestic structures which would endure for thousands of years.

Just draining the lake and levelling the site had been a massive undertaking. It constituted less than a third of the total area but the ground, which had become saturated over the years, had to be made stable and reinforced using steel pilings and countless thousands of cubic metres of hardcore and concrete. It was simply mind-blowing for the average man on the street to try and comprehend the amount of material below ground level, hidden away from view but every bit as vital as the finished structure which would eventually dominate the skyline for miles around.

A major part of the project was situated on a nearby steep-sided hill. Oddly, despite its precarious location and obvious difficulties encountered when preparing the ground, this particular phase had gone well and was already ahead of schedule. The multi-level shopping area comprised three long rows of buildings in terrace formation stepped one above the other against the sloping profile of the hill and were interconnected by escalators and covered walkways whilst the roofs were finished in characteristic red tiles.

The side of the hill was south-facing, thereby enjoying one of the sunniest aspects of the whole site. Even though Adam was standing at a fairly low elevation he could discern clearly the beautiful Mediterranean palms imported in their thousands, their fronds nodding and swaying in the early afternoon breeze.

Other parts of the site were less complete and this was born-out by the volumes and diversity of materials stacked wherever he looked. If construction of the complex had proved challenging enough then maintaining the supply of materials required was a herculean and unenviable task.

The whole site was a hive of activity but progress was impressive. Mixer trucks seemed to be arriving every few minutes, discharging their loads of carefully-blended concrete into the steel reinforcing basket-like meshwork of the floors – thousands of cubic metres, day after day.

At night, arc lamps and sodium lights cast their garish orange light over the scene as work continued. In one corner of the site where one of the immense, sprawling car parks would eventually sit, was the accommodation for the workforce. Hundreds of portable cabins and even personal caravans were arranged in neat rows and, stacked one above the other just a short distance away, more terraces of huts and cabins housing the site offices with their large tables and filing cabinets bulging with blueprints, drawings and plans.

This little village and its army of workers had already made a dramatic impact on the local economy and many had struck up relationships with girls and women who welcomed this sudden influx of male company into their midst.

Adam walked a little further until he came across some of the thirty-foot white travertine columns that would eventually hold up much of the exterior facades of the great buildings. There would be hundreds of these around the site – their numbers varying according to the type of structure they were designed for. Some would be situated in freestanding rows whilst others would form enormous porticoes and colonnades connected by sumptuous capitals and entablature. Moving on still further Adam discovered another recently-arrived batch of marble floor slabs from the Italian supplier. These would ultimately occupy an equally-prominent position to that of the columns only they would line the inner floors of the covered structures and provide an opulent finish to the stepped entrances and high podiums.

Here too, clearly-labelled and in the now-familiar plastic wrapping, were some of the many pre-assembled mosaics which, two millennia earlier, would have adorned the walls and floors in the homes of the rich and powerful among Rome's elite. Their themes incorporated a multiplicity of subjects from intricately-worked Greek designs to scenes of a military nature; soldiers and weaponry, specialist gladiators fighting not just their heavily-armoured counterparts but also exotic wild animals and expressing Rome's self-portrayed dominance over nature in addition to the rest of the known world. Depictions of the sea and its diversity of life would also have featured prominently as well as the more common erotic and mildly-pornographic illustrations.

Adam walked on, lost in thought and although immensely conscious of his surroundings where he was dwarfed and rendered insignificant by the towering structures taking shape all around him, he was suddenly startled to find himself plunged into shadow for up until now he had been walking in virtually uninterrupted sunshine. His steps had brought him unerringly to the northern extremity of the site and he had passed through two huge, majestic marble columns guarding the entrance like sentinels to find himself on the opposite side of the lavish portico.

He could never quite take in the scale of this structure even though it was he who had replicated much of the original design after careful research. The lower part resembled a huge, upright cylinder with its curved walls of immense proportions already being given their final outer covering of dressed travertine blocks and red brick. As he reached the interior a sight greeted him like no other and took his breath away. In the high, domed roof the last of the steel was going into place and men worked at dizzying altitude on scaffolding that appeared frail and incapable of supporting their combined weight.

Clearly identifiable was the circular framework for the oculus that would admit much of the daylight into the building when completed but unlike its counterpart in Rome which boasted a completely open and unprotected apex, the oculus in this design would comprise a single piece of concave armoured glass, purely to keep out the unpredictable English weather.

There would be mosaics and frescoes in here too, Adam mentally referred to the specifications; shops all around the inner circumference of the great hall and a vast open space beneath the dome. Stallholders who kept their businesses on a Roman or Mediterranean theme would be given preference when space was duly allocated and would receive discounts on their rentals. In the centre of the circular floor, a huge fountain circumscribed by some of the more popular deities from the Pantheon would gush and spray water over opulent marble terraces before plunging into a deep pool where Poseidon stood guard over a harem of nymphs and sirens.

In the labyrinth of tunnels and cavernous spaces beneath the structure, an arsenal of pumps would supply the many millions of litres of water needed to keep the hundreds of fountains going throughout the complex of piazzas, gardens and malls. Dwarfed by the scale of his creation Adam felt humbled and looked around him with all the reverence of a man knelt before the high altar in a great cathedral. He was on the point of leaving this particular phase of operations when he hesitated and looked upward once more. As he tilted his head skyward

41

a shaft of sunlight broke through a patch of fine-weather cumulus, illuminating him with the intensity of a theatrical spotlight. It was like being touched by the gods and he closed his eyes briefly, savouring the wonder of the moment before turning and walking out of the vast interior.

He took a quieter route back to his car in order to escape the ear-numbing cacophony of heavy industrial machinery that was seemingly everywhere and also to compose his thoughts into some semblance of order. He could not help but wonder if, even at this comparatively early stage, his career was already at its peak and it was simply a matter of maintaining this level of excellence and achievement in order to secure the financial future of the company. When this latest project was unveiled to the world it would be the proverbial icing on the cake, he reflected. The fees and commissions alone had effectively doubled his salary and there would be bonuses too, especially for the construction teams if the job came in on time and within budget.

He thought of Tyra and how their relationship was faring at the moment. *Had it suffered lately?* He was spending so much time at work these last months; even weekends. He promised himself when this was over he would devote more time to her, just doing the things couples did together. All this work, it was for both of them but it would be worth it in the end. They would go away on a well-deserved holiday; he would let her choose where they went.

She was a rare beauty, was Tyra. Tall, elegant and stylish with that long graceful neck emphasised by the way she wore her hair piled up and secured at the back of her head with one of those flamboyant clasps Sophie appeared to have an eye for. That dark hair, black as anthracite and always smelling of – *something;* something other than her chosen fragrance and was quite simply, her.

He thought of her eyes, as black as her hair and bottomless; you felt you could read your own destiny when you looked into them and at other times they were veiled and revealed nothing. He thought of her body. She wasn't at all small and dainty – quite the reverse in fact. She was fairly large-boned but did not carry any surplus flesh. She had an incredible figure and was curvaceous beyond belief. Seeing her in a summer dress or a tight skirt had the effect of making his pulse race, and then he thought of her legs; Tyra's legs in high heels and his erection was swift and aching. He wanted her now, right now, this very instant. God, how he wanted her, it was almost painful.

Financially speaking they were assured for life. Materially they wanted for nothing and eventually Adam would be able to fall back on his more-than-adequate pension to secure them through their autumn years.

Yes, the fates were indeed plying him with largesse but it hadn't always been so, Adam reflected on a more serious note. From his earliest memories as a child Adam was uncomfortably-aware he didn't fit in. Other kids had mates and went around in groups, did things after school, met girls – that sort of thing. Adam was a loner through no choice of his own and at times it seemed he must remain this way indefinitely; all through school, primary, secondary-modern and college, he attracted little attention from the opposite sex and was generally excluded from their social groups. He was particularly aware of this on the playing field when, as teams formed up and the captains selected their favourites, Adam was never picked to be on anyone's team. Most of the time he was placed here or there to make up an uneven number but on many occasions he was left a sad, lonely boy on the touchline.

Consequently, he failed at sports and his end-of-term reports often contained such barbed and confidence-sapping statements as, *'Does not apply himself to this subject,'* or, *'could do better.'* But it was the deeply-poignant and hurtful remark, *'Not a popular boy,'* which cut like a knife. Adam needed to be wanted, but it was not to be.

In desperation he applied himself with a vengeance to his studies, especially mathematics, history and science. He adored the English language when spoken articulately and he cringed when he heard it abused. He had a feeling for certain aspects of history, especially the rise of the Roman Empire and its subsequent influence on the world thousands of years after its demise as a superpower. He couldn't say for certain just why this period fascinated him so much but he told himself one day he would know – he was certain of it.

At college he further applied himself to his chosen subjects and worked as intensely at night as during the day. Here he broadened his sphere of interest into architecture and it was again Roman influence was to play its part. Outside class hours he pored over every book and archive detail he could lay his hands on and became totally absorbed. He loved the style of construction, the elegance, the majesty, the opulence and sheer boldness that seemed embodied in every structure the Roman engineers put their name to and, even at this early age, he knew one day he would design and build something equally as grand which would make the world sit up and take notice. Adam Grant might be insignificant and scarcely noteworthy at the moment but it would not always be so and he inwardly swore a sacred oath.

There was something else too. Whenever he immersed himself in his studies of the great city he experienced an inordinate sense of well-being he could not interpret. It was almost as if she was breathing the passion of rediscovery into his soul, imparting her most elusive and intimate secrets and willing him to remember; and yet during some of his more private moments as he sat alone in his room with only a single lighted candle for company, he felt she was subconsciously nudging him gently with the solution to a problem he had no recollection of voicing.

His eventual grades reflected his unceasing efforts and enthusiasm and he was duly allocated a place at university where again, hell-bent on achieving his dream, he worked all-out, single-mindedly going for the goal he knew he must attain. He sought no relationships with other students and after a few weeks they ignored him completely.

However, his endeavours did not go unnoticed and he eventually came to the attention of his mentors for his unswerving approach to his studies. During class lectures he openly challenged his tutors with sharp, no-nonsense, straight-to-the-point questions which appeared to be lost on the other students. They looked vacantly at one another while the lecturers loved his pointed remarks and sharp mind.

He mastered his course subjects of architecture, mathematics, civil engineering and engineering science and ultimately, his fifty-thousand word thesis entitled 'Ancient Roman Construction Projects and Methods of Calculating Stress' won him the applause of his seniors and much grudging admiration from his fellow students.

He was now in a position to write his own ticket and knew immediately what he wanted to do – design buildings and replicate others from a bygone age; huge, lasting structures and monuments built from some of the most durable and beautiful materials known to man. Not for Adam, the ugly skyscrapers of concrete and glass that adorned every city around the world; the horrific brick and pre-cast concrete tenement buildings advertising the slum areas where poverty and crime were out of control.

No. His materials were going to be marble, granite and travertine in all their resplendent colours – the foundation blocks on which empires were built.

He was twenty-six years old, single and unemployed. He had everything going for him and for the first time in years he admitted to himself he was lonely. When he looked back he pondered life's vagaries and fortunes and how the winding path of destiny had ultimately brought him to his present position. He had studied unbelievably hard for years, locking himself away for endless nights while the rest of the world was out there enjoying itself, forming relationships, living life and having fun.

None of that for him; his future was too important. He had a strange awareness that all through his further education and attainment of the handsome credentials he now possessed, he had never once visited the city responsible for his fascination and decision to embark upon this chosen career. Rome had inspired him deeply and he had never been there.

Or had he?

During his more intent periods of study when he had been poring over photographs of the historic centre, especially those of the Colosseum and the area immediately adjacent, he had the vaguest notion something here was familiar and it annoyed him because he was unable to identify it. This was crazy. It was like looking at an old map of a favourite town where you hadn't been for decades and things had changed slightly in your absence. He had the strangest feeling he actually knew this area – knew its streets and where they led. He had not studied any actual maps of the centre because it had never seemed a vital part of his research. He had only read detailed accounts of construction and surveys undertaken in the last hundred years or so, concerning himself specifically with calculations the ancient Roman builders and engineers must have known about in order to bring their designs to fruition.

But the feeling of familiarity was never far away and returned like an old friend whenever he thought of her and contemplated her glorious history.

Try as he might, Adam could no longer disassociate himself from her beguiling voice and although he was accepting of the fact this whole scenario was a little daunting and slightly eerie, he allowed her into his mind and soul whenever she spoke to him, calling him, beckoning him like a temptress and seducing him as Rome seduces all men with her beauty.

After six months doing nothing he was finally approached by a company specialising in top executive placements. Their client had seen Adam's impressive list of credentials and would be interested in offering him the position of partner should he be willing to consider it. At the salary they were offering and the chance to show off his work he took no persuading.

Russell Templeman and Associates became Templeman Grant Architectural Consultants and literally, overnight, Adam's dream was realised and Russell Templeman had a new business partner. It was to be the making of them both.

And then, Adam met Tyra.

7

He had been with the company just over a year but in that time had managed to impress Russ Templeman with not just his full-blown enthusiasm for the work but his apparently boundless energy, natural flair and bold imagination. Realising he had a rising star and budding genius in his midst Russ gave Adam full rein in order that he might exploit his full potential.

Adam's demeanour was quietly self-assured and his easy manner and obvious love of his work instilled confidence in their clients. In the ensuing months the workload increased dramatically and Russ was somewhat self-congratulatory as he realised his hunch about Adam had been right all along and was now paying big dividends.

Word on the street and Russell's connections through the *'Old Boy'* network appeared to confirm this and the only concern seemed to be Adam might not go the distance in the true sense of the word and burn up before the first hurdle.

But Adam had only just begun and he certainly would be seen to go the distance. The plan was already forming in his head.

He would give them something they had never seen before. It would take years of diligent planning and scrupulous attention to detail but some strange, deep-seated feeling told him before he was much older his dream was about to be realised. A haunting and, as yet, undiscovered part of his distant past was soon to assume the dominant role in his life and see his name acclaimed the world over and accorded all the respect snatched from him at the eleventh hour by a cruel twist of fate.

Trying to get Adam out of the workplace was a major undertaking for Russ but after numerous suggestions and unsubtle hints he needed to unwind and relax in more conducive surroundings, he eventually prevailed and Adam duly arrived at Russ and Julia's small, informal get-together at their lavish country home. Julia had prepared dinner and the rooms were full of the tantalising aromas of roasting meat, open log fires and a hundred other equally-pleasant smells that enveloped Adam in a shroud of well-being and caused him to momentarily reflect how such a lifestyle was not entirely beyond his own means.

As he and Russ were enjoying some light banter and pre-dinner drinks, Julia walked into the dining room linked arm-in-arm in a manner suggesting great closeness and friendship, with the most stunningly-beautiful woman Adam had ever seen in his life. Literally, she took his breath away.

"Adam, I'd like you to meet my very good friend, Tyra. Tyra, this is Adam, Russ's new business partner."

She looked directly into his eyes and smiled and in that instant Adam's world fell apart and he knew, as if it was written in stone, she was the one he had waited for all these years.

"I'm really pleased to meet you at last, Adam. Russell and Julia have told me much about you."

She cast an appraising glance over Adam's dark suit and crisply-ironed white shirt and, looking further, she could see he appeared to be in fine physical condition. He was a fraction under six feet tall, a couple of inches more than her and wore his sandy-coloured hair fashionably longer than most young men these days. It was clear he carried no excess flesh on his body for his muscle-tone was further accentuated by the tailored clothing and she gained the impression he was hard and fit.

By contrast, Adam, who was usually so calm and collected and never found any challenge too daunting, simply stared and cursed his inability to come up with some original and flattering remark suitable for the occasion. This woman was simply gorgeous and his thoughts were thrown into complete disarray. There were undertones here reaching back further than he could remember and he felt as if a fire within his soul had suddenly been rekindled and blown into a raging flame. Could it really be as he had first dared to wonder – she had come back after all this time?

In some ways she appeared vaguely familiar but in others she remained a delicious, sexual conundrum, enigmatic, deeply mysterious and inviting the attention of his eyes. Her skin was flawless and that long, graceful neck was somehow further emphasised by way she wore her hair, piled up and secured with an ornate jewelled clasp. There were curly tendrils of it hanging down the sides of her face – just a few, but he found himself totally captivated by the effect, *and those eyes!* They were nearly black and he could see himself reflected in them.

After a few moments it suddenly dawned on him he had not spoken a word yet for he was unable to think clearly. Most women would have killed to look like that, he reflected. She had a relatively narrow waist but her hips flared out beneath the stylish black evening dress and she wore fashionable open-toed high heels. He decided hers were undoubtedly the shapeliest legs he had ever seen on any woman anywhere. The neckline on her dress was cut sufficiently low to reveal a hint of her ample cleavage and again his senses swayed as he imagined what lay beneath.

Around her neck she wore an interesting cameo pendant on a gold chain and he was intrigued to see it depicted a faithful reproduction of Anubis, the Egyptian god of the underworld. In its real-gold surround the head of the half-man, half-jackal added a further subtle hint of mystery to this beautiful creature standing just inches away and he wondered if she possessed even the slightest notion of how she had affected him.

She was desirable beyond words and he felt his body react to her presence with a violence that startled him.

"The pleasure is all mine, Tyra," he replied lamely but he smiled one of his rare and irresistible smiles and saw how she had still not taken her eyes off him and seemed to be studying him intently.

Russ and Julia had been carefully watching the two of them during their introduction and both were acutely aware something intense and meaningful had just taken place. The chemistry was instant and buzzed between them like static electricity. It was an almost tangible sensation and Julia audibly breathed a sigh of relief when she saw how Adam and Tyra reacted. These two were made for each other.

"I think you're going to be just fine," she announced happily. "Shall we go through? Dinner's almost ready."

Julia had arranged the seating so each person sat opposite their partner. Candles flickered in the subdued lighting and soft background music accentuated the mood of intimacy and relaxation. The conversation flowed back and forth as easily as the refills of full-bodied Chianti and it was clear the evening was turning out to be the unqualified success Julia could only have dreamed of. Every so often she would give Russ a knowing look for her intuition had been correct all along.

This was a match made in heaven!

She observed with great warmth and happiness how Adam and Tyra were so easy with each other and apart from the apparently-innocent exchanges of dialogue flowing between them there were other, unspoken messages and sentiments where eyes flashed and the body language was suggesting of more intimate contact.

It ended all too quickly and as Adam reached for his mobile to call his taxi, Julia took hold of Russ's arm and steered him into the lounge, her eyes saying, *'Can't you see what's happening here? It's wonderful. Give them some time alone together.'*

Adam made his call and then pocketed the phone.

"Fifteen minutes," he commented flatly and Tyra detected a note of sadness and resignation in his voice – a barely-disguised reluctance to leave this place where life would never be the same again and the fates had conspired to bestow upon him riches and untold happiness the envy of any man who ever walked God's earth.

"Tonight was just simply, perfectly wonderful and I can't believe it's over. I can honestly say I've never felt like this in all my life."

She was standing directly in front of him, those mesmerising, black eyes staring into his own and he could smell her perfume. Again his senses swayed with the effect of her presence and he knew it was not the wine.

"Tyra, I...," but he got no further. She placed a single slim, manicured finger upon his lips, silencing him.

"Don't talk," she whispered huskily and before either of them knew it was happening they were locked in embrace, brushing their lips against each other's with delicate, featherlike touches. Her lips were sweet and she smelled of crushed orange blossom and the feel of her body in his arms was like nothing he could ever remember.

For her it was as if a star had exploded in her head and as her nostrils flared at the clean, virile smell of him combined with that heady brand of body spray, she could feel as she had previously surmised, he was hard and fit.

Their kisses became firmer, more searching, more demanding and she thrust her breasts against him, slowly and deliberately gyrating her pelvis against his own volatile reaction. He transferred his kisses to her lovely neck and instantly the goose-flesh came up on her arms and she clung to him with a need verging on desperation.

Completely oblivious to the fact Russ and Julia were only yards away in the lounge they were overcome with each other and Adam's arousal was almost too painful to contain.

"We can't, not here," he exclaimed a little breathlessly. "My God, what's happening to us? I never thought it was possible to feel like that. I was completely out of it for a few minutes there, almost like being in another place and impervious to the rest of the world."

She smiled dreamily at him and was conscious too of her own reaction. Even through the material of her dress her nipples pushed out, hard and swollen with her wanting and proud testimony to the intensity of the feelings stimulated by the man now ensconced in her warm embrace.

"When will I see you again?" he asked a little breathlessly.

"When do you want to see me again," she teased and her black eyes imparted an unimaginable promise.

"Now I've met you, I don't think I ever want to take my eyes off you again," he told her and had become deadly serious. "I want to see you tomorrow and the day after that and every day for the rest of my life. When I wake up in the morning I want to see your face before I open my eyes and I want you to be there at night when I turn out the light. I felt something tonight – something deep down and so intense but I'm at a loss to describe it."

She was looking at him and lingering on his every word before replying.

"When Julia introduced us tonight I knew it would be good and we were meant for each other. I have never seen another man look at me the way you did – such passion, such wanting and I think even you realised our paths had crossed once more despite the improbability of the situation. I too felt that sensation deep down and it was as wonderful and special for me as it was for you. I am hungry for you, Adam, and there is a wanting deep inside me aching to be satisfied like a fire that that will be not be put out. Adam, I need you to make love to me but not here – not just now, but soon when we can be alone together, when there will be no disturbances and the mood is right again."

As Adam's taxi pulled up outside the house and honked the horn, Julia and Russ came through from the lounge.

"Taxi's here," announced Julia, taking in the scene of Adam and Tyra holding hands and realising from the looks on their faces there was much, much more going on here than just two people holding hands. She was just so happy for them. Tyra had been without a man for as long as Julia could remember, saying she was waiting for the right one to come along. It would appear he just had.

"Thank you for a lovely evening," he addressed Russ and Julia. "I enjoyed being here." And to Tyra, "Can I offer you a lift?" but she declined graciously.

"Thanks, but I'm staying over tonight and going home tomorrow. You've got my number. Call me when you can."

She touched his lips briefly with her own and gave him another of her special smiles while her hooded, downcast eyes attempted to conceal her more basic emotions.

"Goodnight, Adam."

"Goodnight, Tyra," he wished her and was then gone into the darkness.

8

Caught up in the maelstrom of site-visits, board meetings and the negotiation of new contacts that were now becoming routine for Templeman Grant Architectural Consultants, Adam was not able to call Tyra for several days and in a way it was an exquisitely-delicious form of self-denial. Also he did not wish to appear too eager but, like Tyra, he was aware their time together would soon be at hand. No matter how he tried he could not put their meeting out of his mind for it was a constant, beautiful distraction and he savoured the whole episode over and over.

"Adam is that you – is it really you? God, it's been ages. I thought you were never going to call."

"Sorry, there's so much work at the moment, I've hardly had a minute."

"I'm proud of you, Adam. I've known Russ and Julia for a good many years and they've always been there for me. Since you've become a part of Russell's organisation things have gotten so much better for them. The wealth and prestige are only a part...."

"And now I want to become a part of you," he told her and felt his eyes swim as he said it.

"Adam," she continued and her voice had become a husky whisper, "I've simply got to see you again soon. Since that night when you and I....you know, I've not been able to think of anything else. It's driving me crazy. I've got so much I want to say to you. Can we be together before I go out of my mind?"

His insides were tied up in knots and the sound of her voice reminded him of the spellbinding effect she still wielded over him. The need to hold her in his arms, to inhale that intoxicating fragrance and feel those firm breasts pressing against him was a constant fire in the pit of his belly and he knew he was just as desperate for them to be together again.

"How are you fixed for dinner tonight? Sorry it's rather short notice but under the circumstances...."

"I thought you'd never get around to asking," she teased and felt her spirits soar.

"I know how to find your place. Is seven o'clock okay?"

"I'll be ready and waiting. You can count on that."

"I have to go. See you later."

Despite his many appointments and the constant need to check and recheck drawings and calculations the remainder of the day seemed to drag interminably. Russ was out, entertaining a prospective client and as Adam had caught up on the backlog by four he tidied his desk and left soon after.

He managed to avoid most of the peak-time traffic and made his own house in a little over twenty minutes. Adam's lifestyle had improved dramatically since teaming up with Russ Templeman and the building he had subsequently purchased was not only a gauge of his meteoric rise to success, it was also way beyond his immediate requirements – *for now!*

With a fine entrance of tall, wrought iron gates and a long sweeping approach flanked by copper beech and silver birch trees the majestic grey stone edifice with its many chimneys, fine courtyard and adjacent stable block made a suitable impact and statement of opulence to any visitor.

The word *house* did the structure no justice at all. *Hall* would have been a far more suitable description. At a mere £400,000 Adam regarded it is a bargain and although he knew all-too-well it was far beyond the needs of just one person, perhaps one day there would be someone to share it all with. Some of the original grounds had been sold off over the centuries to pay death-duties and also ensure the short-term integrity of the main building but the remaining grounds were still impressive enough where the designs of William Kent and Charles Bridgeman had revolutionised English garden landscaping.

The house could boast several affluent owners over the decades including Richard Boyle, the 3rd Earl of Burlington and the 4th Earl of Cork - the Lord High Treasurer of Ireland.

Adam employed a grounds-man on a regular basis in order that the immense flower beds, manicured lawns and vegetable plots always looked their best for gardening had never been his strong point and nowadays there was simply not the time.

On the west-facing gable of the main structure a Virginia creeper clung to the stonework and at the onset of autumn each year this blaze of colour was always a welcoming sight and a sombre reminder winter was just around the corner.

As Adam breezed through the entrance hall and up the stairs to shower and change, he could hear sounds coming from the kitchen and knew Francesca would be hard at work preparing tonight's menu. When Adam had called her earlier with instructions to set an extra place for dinner she had nearly wept with joy.

"About time too, young mister Grant," she exclaimed in her heavily-accented English. "You shouldn't be living alone at your age. All that energy – Mamma Mia! Is she beautiful, Adam – are you going to marry her?"

"You're getting carried away again, Francesca," he had to interrupt her. "We've only just met. It's a dinner date, that's all," but he was deluding himself for he knew it was everything but a mere dinner date; it was to be confirmation of the fact Tyra had walked into his life and turned his world upside down where things would never be the same again.

Adam remained under the pummelling, high-pressure jets of the shower for a full ten minutes, feeling invigorated once more as the trials of the day were effectively removed by the hot water. As he dressed he felt his spirits begin to lift once more where the vision of Tyra pushed all else from his mind. She was coming here, to his home, and the feeling multiplied tenfold.

He went back downstairs to see how Francesca was progressing in the kitchen and already the aromas were mouth-watering. She loved people to be pleasantly surprised by her creations so he wouldn't ask what she'd be serving and spoil it for her. Looking around him he could see she had everything ready, even the two bottles of Chianti he had selected to go with the meal tonight. He hoped Tyra would approve; he knew she adored red wine as much as he did.

Leaving Francesca to her work he stole out of the kitchen and made his way along the hallway to the immense dining room. He told himself it was only a perfunctory inspection for he trusted Francesca's judgement in these matters implicitly but as he looked around him he could see everything was perfect. The lavish 17th century Jacobean oak table had already been set with two places utilising the dinner service she had personally selected on one of their days out looking for tasteful additions to the house. It was one of Davenport's few chinoiserie patterns featuring polychromatic enamels with a stork, chrysanthemum and peony in an oriental garden portrayed in stunning shades of cobalt blue, orange, pink, brown and gold.

Pride of place in the centre of the table was a splendid piece of crafted imagination finished in dull pewter – his Celtic candle holder. With space for three broad church candles instead of the traditional tapered and much slimmer variety, this creation depicted a Celtic warrior in full regalia complete with fearsome expression, helmet and sheathed sword. In his right hand he held aloft what might have once been a flaming torch but was, in reality, the broad stem of the candle holder.

Francesca had used a beautiful white linen cloth with autumn leaves around its edges to cover the bare polished wood of the table and, in its centre and breaking up the large expanse of plain cloth, an overlay of all the colours depicted in the border but in the shapes of every leaf it was possible to imagine. The effect was more than he could have hoped for and as he took in the scene one last time he nodded in satisfaction, closing the door quietly behind him and walking to his car at the bottom of the entrance steps.

It was time to go and meet his guest.

The smells of the early summer evening seemed to enhance his mood of well-being as he drove along the country lanes. It was warm but not oppressive and the air was filled with the evocative redolence of wood-smoke and mown hay making him appreciative he lived away from the noise and bustle of city life.

He saw hardly any other traffic and pulled up outside Tyra's modest dwelling at two minutes to seven. She must have heard him arrive for she left the house within a moment and, checking the front door with a tug, turned and walked toward Adam in the car. She stepped gracefully in and closed the door behind her.

"Hello, Adam," she greeted him in her husky tones. "I thought this moment would never come. I've missed you so much. It's been three days and it feels like three months." She placed a hand upon his lower arm as she regarded him with the candid appraisal of those near-black eyes and he felt his heart miss a beat.

"It was only the thought of seeing you again that's kept me on an even keel. I left a large part of me with you the other night when we said goodbye."

She leaned across to kiss him warmly and he met her half way.

"You are more beautiful than I remember," he told her quietly and felt his pulse race at the touch of her lips and the scent of her fragrance.

"And you, sir, will have my violation upon your conscience if you continue to kiss me like that," she teased and studied him again. "Now, are you going to take me to dinner or shall we sit here and just talk?"

They chatted like old friends for the twenty-five minute journey back to Adam's place and as they swung in through the tall gates and made their way along the elegant tree-lined approach Tyra exclaimed, "You live *here, in this, all by yourself?*"

"Actually, I have a confession to make. There *is* another woman but she's much older and I don't see her all that often," he joked.

"And I thought you only had eyes for me," she feigned hurt.

Adam parked at the bottom of the steps that led into the house, switched off and then turned to her again.

"Francesca is a real den-mother. She speaks English and Italian with an accent that can break your heart, cries into her apron whenever she hears good news and is probably the finest cook anywhere. I think you'll like her." She took in the sweeping grandeur of the courtyard and stables, the rugged majesty of the ancient English oak trees and the extensive but lovingly-tended flower gardens.

"You only told me you lived in the country," she chided him. "That would appear to be something of an understatement if ever there was one."

"That's right, I did," he replied smiling mischievously. "I don't do the show-off scene - it's just not me. This is comfortable if a little ostentatious. It's big but I can afford it, certainly at the moment with things the way they are at work."

"It's much too big for one person, Adam. How on earth do you manage? This is the sort of place earls and dukes live in."

"Francesca cooks and cleans part time and there is a nice old chap who tends the gardens most of the year. I need space, Tyra, and I get that here. The thought of living in a terrace or a flat is enough to scare the life out of me. I could never be a city dweller."

"It's still too big for one person," she continued with an imperceptible shake of her head, pondering the secrets, scandals and colourful history of the great building before her.

"I suppose it may be seen as a little pretentious and extravagant for a bachelor," and he took her right hand and fixed her with his steady gaze, "but it would be perfect for a couple...."

His words appeared not to register and then, after a few seconds, it suddenly dawned on her what he had meant with that barely-cryptic remark and her eyes flew open.

"Adam Grant, are you asking me what I think you're asking me?"

"Tyra...," and his voice had suddenly dropped to little more than a whisper as he took her hand and pressed it to the side of his face. "Tyra, there is no precedent for this especially as we have only just met but I know we share common feelings and there is still much we have to discover about one another. I have been lonely for too long – longer than I care to remember. When I met you it was as if a curtain had suddenly been drawn back allowing the light into my world for the first time ever."

She sensed unerringly he was about to say something that would turn her life around completely and drew even closer to him.

"All of a sudden there was something beautiful standing there before me and a new purpose to my very existence. I dread to think of losing you now and going back to the way it was before. You are right. This place is far too big for one person. What it needs are laughter and love to bring it alive. It needs warmth, feelings and emotions within its great walls so it will become a home in the true sense of the word and no longer be just a house. It needs the daily routine of two people who are in love and look forward to spending as much time in each other's company as they can. It needs....you. I can't think of any other way to say it. Tyra, will you come and live with me here? Will you come and share your life with me? You need give up nothing and would not have to work. I just have an incredible feeling this was all meant to happen."

It was too much and as she listened so the tears welled up in those dark, mysterious eyes.

"Oh, Adam – Adam," she exclaimed. "We have both waited so long for this moment. What are the forces in play that bring two lost souls together in such a way? I didn't know when you would come, Adam, or even what you would look like but the fact we would eventually meet was an absolute certainty."

He reached into his inner pocket and found a clean handkerchief with which he gently dabbed the wetness from her cheeks and softly kissed her forehead.

"Thank you," she smiled. "I think I'll be alright now. We don't want Francesca thinking we've been fighting on our first date, do we?"

"The very thought of us exchanging angry words tears me up inside. I'd much rather fall *into* something with you."

"When Julia introduced us I knew within seconds my waiting was finally over and you were the one. There was never any doubt about it, and now this. You bring me to this wonderful place and ask me to share it all with you. My answer is yes, Adam - the most confident and assured yes I have ever uttered in my life. Let us not speak of marriage tonight for that is another matter for another time but for now, for the next few hours, let us be together as a man and a woman should be together."

He leaned closer toward her and kissed away the last of the tears which had rolled down her cheeks and felt his heart would break with the strength of his love.

"Shall we go inside and see what Francesca has rustled up for dinner?" and he gripped her hand reassuringly.

"That would be lovely," she replied softly.

Hand-in-hand they ascended the front steps and he held the door while she entered the great house. Immediately she took in the scene of the splendid edifice and was filled with admiration for Adam's tastes for she could see nothing here that might be described as over-elaborate or vulgar. On the contrary, everything seemed to complement its surroundings from the rich walnut panelling to the expensive Aubusson carpets. The heavy drapes at the windows must have cost a small fortune and the high ceilings still retained their characteristic solid oak beams, blackened with age and the smoke from the enormous brick fireplace. It was a truly wonderful house made all the more special by the fact the man who was fast becoming her obsession had just asked her to share it all with him and she wondered to herself, *'Is the bubble about to burst and I find this is only a cruel dream?'*

But she need not have concerned herself. At the sound of movement and voices Francesca had left her kitchen and come to welcome Adam and his guest.

"Mister Grant, I see you are back safely with the lady who...," and the words dried abruptly when Tyra, who had been admiring one of the many paintings, now turned and smiled in greeting. Instantly Francesca's hand went to her mouth and her eyes opened wide as she saw Tyra for the first time. "Mamma mia! Che bello! But you are beautiful. I cannot believe it is possible for someone to look so.... Adam described you but his words - they did you no justice at all."

"Francesca, this is Tyra who literally stepped into my life just a few days ago," and Francesca detected the note of pride in his voice even as she was dabbing at her own tears, clearly overcome by the moment. In turn, Tyra embraced her with genuine affection and wrinkled her nose mischievously.

"Adam's told me quite a lot about you and reckons there's none can compare with your culinary skills. Oh, by the way, I simply adore your name. It really is wonderful to meet you."

"Sorry. Look at me getting all emotional," she apologised in her heavily-accented English. "I must be getting back to the kitchen. Dinner will be ready soon and then I'll be off so the two of you can enjoy each other's company." She retreated through the mahogany doors leaving Adam alone with Tyra once more.

"You certainly know how to make an impression. Shall we go through to the dining room?" and he led the way down the impressive hall while she followed close behind.

"This is simply divine," she exclaimed as Adam threw open the double doors to reveal the lavish interior. "I'd be hard-pushed to describe a more romantic setting than this," and he could see the moisture forming in her eyes once more as the ambience in the room began to affect her. He could so easily have taken her out to any of the restaurants in town where even the most secluded corner would never have afforded them the privacy and intimacy of this opulent setting. Also, it was made all the more special by the fact there were no memories of another woman. She was coming here to make a life with Adam where they would create a beautiful and lasting partnership and not replacing someone who had made a brief appearance and moved on.

The table setting was a masterpiece of inventiveness and she studied every detail, from the sparkling silver cutlery and expensive 19th century Davenport china plates to the embroidered napkins and heavy lead-crystal wine goblets. There were flowers, not in a vase but a spray of red carnations whose heady scent further accentuated the mood of well being. Not for Adam the clumsy and ill-prepared arrangement of roses because other men naturally assume all women will love roses and she was astounded by his foresight.

"How delightful – carnations. I simply adore carnations. How could you possibly have known? I bet you asked Julia," she teased, but she knew he had not.

In the background a tape of Ben Webster and Coleman Hawkins saxophone melodies played soft, seductive sounds and as she again took in the setting of the lavish table where the ethereal glow of flickering candle flames was reflected in the silver cutlery she was deeply touched by Adam's sense of wanting everything to be perfect for their first date. As their fingers interlocked and he drew her closer to him he stared into those dark, fathomless depths and wondered at the dancing flames and many shades of honey and amber. He loved the way she wore her hair, just like that first time only tonight there was a decorative slide of red feathers to match exactly the stunning dress. The awareness of her perfume made his blood quicken uncontrollably and as she smiled that achingly-tantalising smile he felt his senses becoming light and his heart melted like wax in the candle flame of her beauty.

"Kiss me," she implored and as they embraced, touching so lightly the sensation made them catch their breaths, she snuggled deeper into his embrace trying to draw out all the *man-smell,* amazed at the strength he commanded and the softness of his mouth. They remained this way for perhaps a minute and then the sound of the kitchen door heralded the imminent arrival of dinner and they must draw apart. As they took their seats Francesca made her appearance through the double doors, pushing the heated trolley containing tonight's gourmet meal.

"I hope so very much you are liking this," she beseeched her guests, removing the lids from the serving dishes.

"It smells absolutely heavenly," Adam encouraged her. "I really should start paying you more for service like this. Would you do us the honour...?"

"I'd be delighted, Mister Adam. I've so enjoyed doing this today and I know the evening is going to be just wonderful for both of you."

She was giving them pork fillets cooked in calvados with delicate apple slices and creamy lyonnaise potatoes and even Tyra who was no stranger to the pleasures of hearty cuisine complimented her in suitably extravagant terms.

"This is simply wonderful, Francesca. Thank you so much for doing all this and making me feel so welcome."

"I am having all the pleasure," Francesca trilled in her halting English. "Please, when you have finished, there is a little something special in the way of dessert. I will be going now and will return tomorrow to clean the dishes. Please be having a most happy evening. You are two special people meant to be together, like ships that meet in the night I think. I will let myself out," and with that she was gone.

"She's lovely," Tyra observed thoughtfully as Adam poured the rich, red Chianti into their glasses. "Wherever did you find her?"

"Believe it or not, she came with house. When the previous occupants moved out and put the place on the market they had no further use for a cook and housekeeper. She comes highly recommended with a string of references and we seemed to hit it off from day one. She dictates her own hours and the house is always immaculate so I can't really complain."

"That accent is going to break hearts before she gets much older."

"Speaking of hearts," Adam recognised the appropriate moment, "I think this is a suitable time for me to say something," and he gave her his full attention with a glass raised in salute and greeting. "Tyra, in an incredibly short period of time you have brought great warmth and beauty into my life and I drink to our friendship which, I know, will swiftly grow into a deep, meaningful and lasting love. All I have to give is yours if you will share it and allow me to love you in the manner you deserve. If I'm perfectly honest I'm at odds to adequately describe the sensations which seem to have taken over since meeting you. There's all the excitement, exhilaration and uncertainty of the first date and yet I feel I already know many things about you, things you've never disclosed but which at the same time make our situation all the more delicious and mysterious."

Solemnly and with that great presence she exuded so naturally, she raised her own glass and declared, "Until a few days ago my life was relatively dull and lacked true purpose – and then I met you. I have never gone without, Adam, but in some respects I feel I have missed everything a woman needs in her life. For as long as I can remember I have declined male company. Don't ask me why but something kept telling me not to give myself to another person until the moment was at hand. How would I possibly know, I asked myself on numerous occasions and the answer was always the same. When the time is right he will come again and your heart will tell you. In the wake of that life-changing evening when we met, you bring me to this wonderful house and ask me to become a part of it with you as the man in my life. I accept, Adam, and I drink to our future together. May it be filled with love and all the magic that makes being together so utterly special."

They sipped at the rich, dark wine they both adored and as each gazed at their partner with eyes that declared their love in a manner beyond the words of any poet or philosopher, each was acutely aware of this precious turning point in their lives. Once again the chemistry that was so right crackled between them like a high-voltage discharge as they began to see this was no chance or accidental meeting but a preconceived and deliberate move on the part of the forces governing their lives. In the coming months and years they would both have irrefutable proof as to how this reunion had been preordained for millennia but for the next few hours where time and far-distant events were lost to them their only thoughts were of the night ahead and such mutual sentiments as '*I love you,*' were completely unnecessary.

The meal exceeded all their expectations and once again they chatted in the easy, relaxed manner of old friends. Tyra was curator at the Warchester Museum and Archives Office, a position which allowed her a reasonably extravagant lifestyle after the mortgage repayments on her two-bedroom detached cottage. Whilst the work was interesting to a degree she felt locked away and stifled, not realising her true potential. Warchester had, in the distant past, been the site of a Roman fortification owing to its strategic position and the museum contained a great many artefacts from that era. Most of these were pottery and items of jewellery but recent archaeological digs had uncovered ancient weaponry, gold coins from the reign of Claudius and even a partially-preserved sandal. There were oil lamps, a couple of beautifully restored cart wheels, several ladies' hair clasps and even a letter from a Roman legionary written on a wax tablet requesting socks and underpants for additional warmth in this dismal frontier outpost.

But it was not enough and inwardly she knew she was destined for greater things and she had yet to embark upon the spiritual voyage of discovery she was certain awaited her at some point in life's not-too-distant future. Adam's unbelievably generous offer had just opened another door in her life and she could now afford to walk away from the dark vaults and dusty books.

'Come and live with me here, Tyra. Come and share your life with me.'

His wonderful words still echoed inside her head and she knew she needed the job no longer. She would draft her letter of notice in the morning and put her house on the market the same day. She would be coming here to live with Adam, where she truly belonged.

He recharged their glasses and then sought out the 'little extra' Francesca had left them in the chilled compartment of the food trolley.

"Is there no end to her talents?" Tyra asked as exquisite things happened to her taste buds when she sampled the mouth-watering peach and passion fruit mousse served with raspberry coulis.

"It just gets better and better," Adam agreed.

When dinner was over he cleared the dishes from the table, stacking them tidily where they could be removed to the kitchen when Francesca returned in the morning.

"Would you like coffee?" he asked.

"I'm okay with the wine, thanks. It's lovely," and after a short pause, "Adam, you seem an awfully long way off. Could we get comfortable together somewhere?"

"I know just the place. Follow me," and taking their glasses with them Adam led her into the spacious lounge with its subdued lighting and soft pastel colours where she sat gracefully down on the elegant high-backed sofa and patted the cushion next to her.

"Come and sit next to me," she invited. "I need you to be close to me." She placed her head upon his shoulder and he took one of her slim hands with its finely manicured nails and held it in his own. "For the first time in my life, Adam, I am truly happy – not just because of these beautiful surroundings and untold riches you have invited me to share with you, it goes much deeper than that. I feel if I never had anything else I could not possibly want for more. You have honoured me tonight, not just with your generosity and the fact I've been treated to the most romantic dinner of my life, but because you've declared in all but the spoken word you love me, Adam."

"Yes," he admitted quietly, nodding his head imperceptibly. "In everything but the spoken word for that is the strength of my feelings. I could have told you that first night at Russ and Julia's and there have many instances this evening when I knew it was true but I could not take the risk of causing embarrassment or driving you away so soon. When the time is right you will have my word as well as my heart."

"Kiss me again, Adam, before I say the words I feel in my own heart for soon I know we will utter the same words together."

With no limit to the hours they became lost in their searches for one another. The warmth of her body and the intoxicating fragrance of crushed orange blossom filled his world once more as he angled his head to one side and kissed that slender, almost regal neck which had captured his attention in the first instant of their meeting. Immediately the goose flesh came up on her bare arms and as she began to gyrate her pelvis in slow, sensuous movements it was as if a living entity had taken hold of her body. Her stomach cramped and the contact of clothing against her breasts was almost unbearable as she felt her nipples harden and thrust out. She reached forward and began to unbutton the front of Adam's crisply-ironed white shirt, burying her face in the large pectoral muscles and flaring her nostrils at the clean virile smell.

As the last of the buttons finally yielded to her demanding fingers she pulled the material from his shoulders and he shrugged the item to the floor. The rain of kisses falling upon her neck and lips now became a deluge and she felt the delicious thrill of her deep-red evening dress being unzipped and teased down to her waist, exposing her large shapely breasts and stomach. She wore no bra and his attentions moved lower, kissing each of her nipples in turn until they thrust out even harder, teasing with the tip of his tongue before returning to her neck and lips once more. As the first orgasm swept over her, causing her to arch her back involuntarily and part her thighs in sensuous invitation, it felt as though a fire had been rekindled in her lower belly and was now burning out of control.

He feasted his eyes upon her and could not believe it was possible for a woman to be so utterly desirable, so physically perfect and as she at last gave herself up completely to those feelings which were rapidly consuming her with desire, Adam began to explore her wondrous body. Those open-toed high heels only served to accentuate the curvature of her calves and he kissed every inch of her feet that remained uncovered, moving deliberately along the back of her legs with agonising slowness and pausing once more to kiss and tease the little dimples at the backs of her knees. As he continued on his journey of sensual discovery she sensed his intentions and her breathing became more laboured, her actions more urgent.

"Yes, Adam, touch me. Touch me as I have wanted you to touch me since that first night."

Inch by tantalising inch his tongue teased a path along her inner thighs until he came to the place where the heat and the scent of her feminine musk drove him to new heights. She was smooth and as luscious and ripe as a soft fruit, her full, slightly-parted lips inviting him to taste her secret flesh. With skilful fingers and delicate touches, assisted by the wetness of his tongue and her own copious lubrication, he opened her like the petals of some exotic orchid, smothering his face in her warmth and drawing her unique womanly scent into his lungs. As she unfolded before him he could see her inner surfaces were like mother-of-pearl, a glossy satin sheen, slippery to the touch and sinking away into mysterious, lustrous depths.

Moving imperceptibly higher he came to the tiny bud of firmer flesh and the centre of her arousal which, at the slightest pressure with the tip of his tongue, caused her to call out with the delicious rippling sensations of another climax as the world was suddenly filled with dazzling, vibrant colour and the darkness behind her eyes exploded with the blinding intensity of a thousand suns.

"Oh God, Adam, it's been so long. It was never like this."

She was wild with abandon, her head rolling from side to side as the first tears squeezed out from beneath her eyelids, disbelieving of her love for this man who was touching her body, her mind and her soul. He probed deeper and deeper, seeking the very centre of her being, the way a humming-bird might delve for the precious nectar and as her actions assumed a new level of soaring, unbridled passion where her breathing was reduced to short, sharp pants he touched the little bud again and she thought she might faint amid this kaleidoscope of pulsating light and myriad bursting stars.

While she came back down to earth again he moved his head away and studied her body in the muted light of the opulent lounge. Her stomach was not quite flat but he found himself completely entranced by this singular detail for there were undertones of Rubens and many celebrated Baroque painters who also possessed an appraising eye for the female form. He kissed her skin and inhaled her warm smell, leaving little damp marks from his caresses. He could just about discern the outline of her ribs and saw again in this new light the relative narrowing of her waist which flared out into her hips like a beautifully-crafted drinking vessel from which he had just sipped the very essence of his woman. Her breasts were the crowning glory of her body; firm and perfectly proportioned, they were large but not requiring any artificial support and he remembered that night at Russ and Julia's when he had yearned to press his face into the deep cleft of her cleavage. In her current state of arousal her nipples were the size and consistency of ripe olives, dark and swollen with her wanting and he closed his mouth over each of them in turn, teasing and licking with the tip of his tongue and pausing every so often to nibble gently while he listened to her sighs and soft moans announcing her readiness to continue.

"You are beautiful beyond description," and the words caught in his throat. "Will there ever be a more appropriate moment to tell you I love you." Sensing too her own time had come she reached out for him and was startled by his size, feeling slightly giddy she could exert this degree of reaction in him.

"Love me, Adam," she pleaded. "Love me as I love you. Give yourself to me completely. I want all of you." His own mounting passions could be denied no longer and he wondered how he had managed to exercise such restraint when the urge to lose himself inside her slippery, welcoming depths had been virtually overpowering all evening. As her fingers found him and guided him into her, they at last became one, united in mind and body. The delights seemed without end. Like waves on a benevolent sea there were gentle troughs of tranquillity and calm, gradually building up into towering waves and great peaks of intense pleasure that burst inside their heads. After many hours the sea grew calm as the waves subsided and they fell, still entwined, into a drug-like, dreamless sleep. At some point they drifted upstairs to the bedroom and through the night hours when one of them awoke to adjust their position or visit the bathroom so the other would come awake also and with teasing fingers and kisses their lovemaking would resume until, eventually, the mists of sleep enshrouded them once more in a warm, protective veil.

In the morning with the sun long-since risen and peeking through the heavy drapes they awoke, still frozen in the act of love and when he saw Tyra owl-eyed with hair fallen out of place his response was aching and demanding.

Much later and only after their immediate needs were sated, they rose and showered together. It was midday when they made the breakfast table in the dining room and already Francesca had been and gone. Last night's dishes had been removed and there were cereals, fruit juice and a pot of freshly-percolated coffee awaiting them on the clean linen tablecloth. Dressed in terry bath robes with Tyra sporting a turban-style towel around her wet hair, they occupied the same chairs from the previous evening.

"I keep feeling the bubble is going to burst and any moment I'm going to wake up in the vaults of that dusty museum," she observed dreamily. "By the way, did I tell you I love you? I forget."

"It's something of a dream-world for both of us," he replied seriously, barely able to accept how fate had smiled upon him once more and he had spent the whole of last night with this woman in his arms, loving her – making love to Tyra. Could it ever get better than this? He had waited so long; waited for what seemed like an eternity for her to come back to him. But it had been worth it, he mused; every minute of it. He left his seat and went to kneel beside her, taking one of her slim hands in his own and kissing it as a man might kneel and kiss the hand of his emperor as he pledges loyalty unto death.

"Tyra, with all my heart I love you and hope one day when you feel the moment is right you will further honour me by consenting to become Mrs Tyra Grant. I make this oath to you now on the foundation of what we have already found together, I will always respect and love you for the person you are and will never attempt to change you. God forbid, if we should ever drift apart there will never be another. I have waited too long for this and in a strange way I know to be the truth but cannot explain, I feel the waiting has gone on for longer than I can remember, a seemingly endless succession of months and years blurring into the mind-numbing expanse of eternity.

"In my loneliest, darkest hours when I was studying for my exams I used to feel someone or something was watching over me like a guardian angel, telling me although I was a virtual outcast and unknown to the world it would not always be so. Night after night in the isolation of that small room, poring over photographs of the buildings I wanted to replicate, there was – something – a voice – a feeling, something telling me, *'She continues to search for you, Adam, and one day soon when the time is right, you will meet again as it was written in the fates.'*

"I just have this incredible, eerie and yet beautiful feeling all of this – all of us, is somehow inexorably linked. We've only just met and look at us! This is more than chemistry and compatibility. We're both certain we were waiting for one another and have denied ourselves the pleasure of others in anticipation of that very meeting. Why would we do that if there was no truth in it? Tyra, do you think the two us, here like this could all have been decided a long time ago – that it was meant to happen? Are we destined to live this life again now because we were denied it in the past?"

He suddenly realised the glaring implausibility of his suggestion and he was complicating the wondrous situation of a man who has just shared his bed and declared his undying for a woman he met – *how long ago?*

"I'm sorry. I didn't mean to be so serious. I suppose I'm just overcome with the deeper meaning of all this and I refuse to believe it's all down to chance or something completely random."

"Adam," she addressed him in her husky tones that again heralded her sexual arousal, "you lovely, romantic, wonderful person. What more could a woman possibly want than the man who has spent the entire night making love to her, put his head in her lap and declare he believes all their love, indeed, their very meeting, to be predestined? I wasn't just waiting for someone different, Adam – someone who ticked all the right boxes, pressed the right buttons and swept me off my feet. I was waiting for you!

"Okay, I didn't know what you'd look like or even what your name would be but one thing was certain from the very beginning. When you turned up, I'd know about it and boy, did I know about it! That night at Russ and Julia's when we met – the chemistry, the distant recognition, the spark igniting the fire in both of us. I saw it in your eyes too. It was still there and I wanted you as much as you wanted me. It was instantaneous. I wanted you to take me right there in the dining room. I was aching for you so much it almost hurt and I could sense your own need. Don't question it, Adam, let it happen. We're meant to find each other at last."

Her words wove spells of longing and desire about him and now he was burning up inside again. Raising his head up from her lap he tugged open her towelling robe and closed his mouth over one of her engorged nipples. The sensation made her cry out and she pulled his head toward her so he might feast upon her breast. He transferred his kisses to her mouth and she ripped his own robe from his body and moving her hands down she found him hard and thrusting and desperate to be inside her once again.

"Oh God, you're so hard," she panted. "Take me now, here, in this very room. Oh God, it's been so long," she cried real tears. "Love me again, Adam, as you did once before," and so in this beautiful room with its rare treasures where they had shared their first meal as a couple, they were once again united in a frenzied, impassioned coupling of their flesh as if they had been parted for many lifetimes.

And, of course, they had!

Tyra duly wrote and posted her notice of resignation from the museum and archives office and later that same day Adam drove her into Warchester where she advertised her house for sale. All that remained was to clear out her possessions and it was done. As predicted, the house sold quickly and the day came when Tyra must say goodbye. With the removal van disappearing down the narrow lane carrying the remainder of the house contents, she closed the door for the last time and he held her while she cried and kissed the tears from her eyes.

"One door closes, another one opens," she sobbed and it broke his heart to see her this way. However, after only a few minutes she was cheerful and bright again as she recognised the first part of her ultimate destiny had already been fulfilled and it was now time to begin living the rest of her life with the man she had waited for.

9

Sophie Harrington was exuberant as she stood over the two bulky wooden packing cases the couriers had obligingly deposited next to the opulent couch in her treatment room. Without a doubt it was her single most expensive purchase since taking possession of the house and she was somewhat self-congratulatory as she saw how the next piece of the puzzle had been placed on the board and the picture was, at last, beginning to take shape. All that was needed was for the players themselves to assume their rightful parts in the little drama soon to unfold and then their immediate questions would be answered, if only in the short term.

The more she thought about it, the more the mystery seemed to unfold itself anew and so it was with great excitement she began stripping away the wooden boards from the two seven-foot-high crates standing end-on where she decided they must rest. As the outer layers came away, exposing the straw and bubble-wrap of the interior she felt the goose bumps come up on her bare arms, knowing what she would find beneath. Reverently, as an archaeologist might gently brush away the remaining soil from a priceless discovery she pulled away the last of the protective packaging. As the likenesses were revealed and the little hairs stood up on the back of her neck she gasped in wonder and knew they were going to be just perfect for the task she had in mind.

For the next half hour Sophie busied herself cleaning and tidying and removing the wooden planks from the packing cases. She bundled the straw and plastic wrapping into the dustbin and then vacuumed the room from end to end. She trimmed the candle wicks and replaced those burned out with fresh ones from her vast supply. At last, satisfied the work was complete, she sat on one end of the couch and treated herself to a client's-eye view of her wondrous purchase.

Barely two metres away and strategically placed one either side were two life-size statues carved from white marble. The likenesses were frighteningly-real and Sophie mentally applauded the sculptors for what they had recreated based on the information and photographs supplied. They had been unbelievably expensive but were going to be worth every penny.

Her gaze was drawn to the portrayal of a wealthy young Roman woman of aristocratic birth dressed in an exquisite stola and sandals. Her hair was purposely styled into braids and pulled up on top of her head, held in place by a decorative clasp which matched exactly the one Sophie wore now. Down the sides of her face hung delicate curly wisps of hair which served to emphasise the softness and alluring beauty of her features. Her arms remained bare and she wore large decorative fibula and brooches securing the fastenings of her clothing and a pendant on a slim chain depicting Anubis, the half-man half-jackal god who ruled over the Egyptian underworld. She was approximately five feet ten inches tall and the long, slender neck heightened her grace and stunning looks. Beneath her stola which was cut sufficiently low at the front to reveal much of her cleavage, her hips flared out from a narrower waist and there was a subtle hint of roundness to her belly. The effect was startling and Sophie could see they had captured every detail of Tyra's great beauty – a lasting monument to an extraordinary woman who nurtured an even more special bond with the man whose image Sophie now studied.

It was the most wondrous replication of a Roman murmillo gladiator she had ever seen and was, perhaps, something of a rarity since most surviving images of gladiators were to be found in either fresco or mosaic form. At a full six feet in height the statue portrayed all the characteristics of this heavyweight fighter, from the linked-mail protection for the sword arm with its double leather securing straps buckled across his otherwise naked chest, to the heavy and robust sandals extending to mid-calf. On his lower left arm he wore a thick, bronze-studded wrist protector and his mid-section was covered by the traditional subligaculum and heavy leather balteus. The most intricate and perhaps disturbing aspect of this sculpture was the head, completely covered by the large bronze helmet which flared out around its lower edges to afford a modicum of protection for the neck. The face was totally obscured by the decorative mesh-like screening of the visor which effectively removed all vestiges of humanity. No opponent could ever see what lay beyond; fear, anticipation, anger, blood-lust, triumph, pain, uncertainty and maybe even pity. It was all hidden from view.

His left hand grasped a circular shield with ornate depictions of sun, moon and stars around a centrally-located wolf's head whilst his right held onto the gladius – a broad-bladed sword about two feet in length with a viciously-tapered point. Gladius was also the colloquial for 'penis' where the gladiator was often looked upon as a much-revered sex-object, a god of the arena whose services could be purchased on the eve of the contest.

'*He was equally adept with his 'gladius' in the bedroom as the arena!*'

"Goodness, what a testimonial!" and Sophie smiled to herself as she recalled the candid description of these sex-god sports personalities of the day. The most pleasing replication was the man's physique. The great muscles of the sword-arm were clearly in evidence whilst his pectorals bulged without the restraint of chest armour. Across his back, the broad definition of shoulders was in stark contrast to the narrowness of his waist and his sinewy calves and thighs writhed like mating pythons. Altogether he was a fine specimen of the fighting man she felt deserved a presence inside this room beside his woman.

'*What a pity,*' she thought, '*the identity of the man remains a mysterious and delicious secret,*' but all would be revealed soon she knew. In just a short while the last pieces of this intricate little puzzle would fall into place and all that was needed was the telephone call from Tyra to set events in motion.

Once again, her visionary windows into the future and powers of perception told her the call would not be long in coming.

10

Adam glanced at his watch. It was just after three and his last appointment was at four. Best be getting back. The site inspection had gone well and he was impressed by the rate of progress. All aspects and phases were on track for completion within their projected dates and others were ahead of schedule and nearing completion. As he approached his starting point again he took in the splendid view of the terraces on the outer mall as they hugged the profile of the steep slope. At this hour of the day the sun had passed its zenith but was still high enough in the sky to pain the eyes if not shaded. It reflected off the thousands of red roof tiles and many pure white vertical columns already in place – some supporting the frontages of the larger structures while others were arranged in free-standing pilasters. With the brilliant blue sky forming a backdrop and the palm fronds nodding gently in the afternoon breeze, it stopped Adam in his tracks and he stared in wonder at this enigmatic Mediterranean scene. Part of the marble flooring was already in place and the effect of virtual completion was eclipsed by the rippling heat haze which caused the buildings to dance and shimmer to the point where they appeared to lift up and become detached from the ground.

As he continued to ponder the scene laid out before him he suddenly regarded it as strange that an area so close to being finished should have such an inordinate number of people bustling about when there were other sections in need of manpower. He strained his eyes, frowning with the glare of the fierce afternoon sun and could not believe what he was seeing. Was this a trick of the light? He closed his eyes tightly but when he opened them again nothing had changed. The crowds of people were not site-workers they were citizens, hundreds of them, all milling about in the various attitudes of daily life. Most were simple folk clad in inexpensive, drab clothing, the hallmark of the majority while the nobility, patricians and upper classes wore fine white linen togas and chitons, some outlined in purple with decorative leather belts and ornamental daggers.

And there were smells! Cattle and poultry from the pens, fruit and vegetables laid out on open barrows and carts in all their attractive colours. There were traders and merchants selling bolts of fine cloth in a myriad shades, herb and spice sellers, jugglers, acrobats, clowns, magicians, fire-eaters, snake-charmers – *and soldiers!* Some stood around in groups, chatting idly and whistling lustfully at the women while others walked suspiciously among the crowds, maintaining order, looking for trouble – hoping for trouble. There were no beggars or whores in the forum, only reasonably well-dressed men and women whilst the perimeter was lined with hundreds of shops and stalls advertising their wares; mosaic makers, jewellers, potters, carpet makers and rug weavers, coffin makers, stone masons, silver and goldsmiths, wine merchants, barbers and carpenters – the list was seemingly endless.

A short distance to the right lay the most recent of Rome's majestic creations, the Flavian Amphitheatre in all its glory and operational for little more than two years. The sunscreen had already been drawn across the top to keep the worst of the heat off the crowds; the midday executions would be completed by now and the long-awaited entertainment of the day would just be getting under way. However, the results of this afternoon's contests were of little consequence as he was not billed to fight for another three days.

The time would soon pass, he contented himself, *and then they'd see something!*

Adam was confused. The sun had gone and he was now bathed in shadow; the buildings had disappeared too along with the bustling mass of street-traders, the colours, the sounds and the smells. All that remained was a cloudless blue sky and the outlines of men surrounding him; men wearing boots, helmets and reflective jackets. They were talking among themselves and two of them were knelt by his side trying to loosen his tie. He could hear them now.

"Mr Grant, Mr Grant, are you alright, sir?"

Where was he? His position became all-too-clear as he was able to focus on the real world once more; on the ground, laid flat and looking up with curious faces all around him; men, construction workers who'd seen him fall. But how the hell did he get here? He had been standing on this very spot, admiring phase one when all of a sudden there were vast crowds, noises and smells – and an awful lot more! And then the pieces at last fell into place and he knew this was merely the extension of an all-too-familiar pattern of events going on in his life.

He sat up unaided and brushed himself off, feeling a little awkward at this embarrassing scenario.

"Thank you for your concern but I think I'll be okay now. It must have been the heat or skipping lunch."

"If you're sure, Mr Grant...."

"Quite sure. Thanks again."

The group dispersed to their respective locations while Adam retrieved his hard hat and donned it for the remainder of the walk back to his car. Some of that earlier good feeling had evaporated and he was slightly dazed and more than a little confused. Everything was back to normal when he looked around him; no crowds, no markets, stallholders or performers. They had all gone and even the towering bulk of the great Flavian Amphitheatre had been replaced by caravans and site offices. He called his secretary and apologetically cancelled the last appointment of the day.

Scattered at regular intervals around the vast sprawling site were portable cabins housing toilets, showers and general wash facilities and Adam headed to one just a few yards away before returning to his car. Strangely, the little building was deserted and he was at least thankful for not having to share the cabin or make awkward conversation when all he needed at the moment was to be alone with his thoughts. Climbing the three steps he removed his helmet and hung it on one of the numerous coat hooks provided and then stood in front of the basin, running the cold tap until it was full. His head was still muzzy after the incident but the water would help refresh and revive him and hopefully clear his thoughts a little.

He loosened his tie and unfastened the top two buttons of his shirt before lowering his head to the basin and scooping up double handfuls of the icy water and splashing it over his face until he at last felt revitalised. With his eyes still closed he reached for the paper towel dispenser on the wall next to him and dabbed the excess moisture from his face. As he came back to check his appearance in the mirror he froze in the act and blinked, disbelieving of what he saw. His experience of only a few minutes ago had caused him to doubt his soundness of mind – but this! As he gazed totally fascinated into the mirror it was not his own reflection staring back at him; rather, it was the image of an incredibly beautiful young woman and she appeared to be moving toward him, either walking or running in slow motion but without actually drawing any closer. Her arms were open and outstretched in front of her as if in a gesture of supplication and that alluring face was sadly marred by a countenance of profound grief or pain.

This was crazy. Was he going mad? He shook his head and squeezed his eyes tightly shut but when he opened them once more she was still there and he recognised her. It was Tyra. It just couldn't be anyone else. The hair, the voluptuous body, the swell and promise of those breasts he knew so well but most of all, it was the face of his woman; a face which belonged on a gleaming marble statue atop a lofty pedestal as it gazed serenely down on a world at her feet. It was Tyra but the dress was all wrong. It didn't resemble anything Tyra owned or ever had done as far as he knew. The clothing she wore was simply exquisite and left him a little breathless. It was exactly the style of dress adopted by wealthy Roman women, especially those of the nobility and she wore it with such grace and elegance he felt his heart rate increase alarmingly. Her arms remained bare and had been gilded by the sun and the folds of her stola were secured at each shoulder by expensive golden fibula. Her feet were hidden in swirling mist and there were no background details to identify her surroundings. It was Tyra but why was she dressed like this and why the aura of tragedy about her? She appeared to be calling to someone but he was unable to read her lips – and those outstretched arms. Was she looking for someone or had she seen the object of her searches and was now rushing to embrace whoever that may have been?

Slowly, the image began to fade and after a few moments had disappeared completely, leaving his own reflection in the mirror – a face whose expression bore an element of concern and a frown posing yet more questions relating to this bewitching scenario. There could be no doubt this was tied up with his earlier experience and was yet another insight into his past – but why two events in the space of half an hour? Was this a foretaste of what he could expect in the future until the issue was finally resolved? He knew she was a part of it and whilst this latest incident served only as confirmation it failed to shed any more light on what part she had played in his life.

He retrieved his helmet and walked back to the car, still slightly shaken by this latest revelation regarding his past but completely unable to purge the image of Tyra from his mind. She had looked absolutely stunning and the memory burned like a flame in the pit of his stomach.

The journey home was uneventful and, a little earlier than usual he pulled up against the steps of the house, wondering how he was going to explain all this to Tyra. For some reason which only became apparent later, she was not there to meet him in the entrance hall and it was only after peering through the doors of several downstairs rooms he eventually found her in the elegant lounge, semi-reclining on the large sofa. Instantly, the afternoon's events were relegated to insignificance as he observed the manner of her dress – or rather the lack of it. He had never grown accustomed to the power she seemingly wielded over him and was always surprised by the intensity of his own response. His mind was in a state of turmoil again. He knew she had been meeting Sophie for lunch today so had their appointment been the catalyst for what was unfolding now? What exchanges had taken place and how much more enlightened had Tyra become as a result? It must have been significant for she was clearly desperate for them to share intimacy once more and had taken matters into her own hands.

She was clad in a black under-slip with a neckline so plunging it was barely able to contain her breasts. The topmost part of her nipples was already exposed above the thin material and he could see they were swollen and angry red as the tips thrust forward. The only other item she wore was a pair of black open-toed high heels which always had the effect of adding that final touch of eroticism to a beautiful, semi-naked woman. Her thighs were parted and she was flaunting herself before him, her smooth opening slick with lubrication that had already coated the inside of her thighs and moistened the cushion beneath her.

"Wouldn't you like to get those clothes off and sit down with me?" she asked huskily and as he stood next to her and removed his suit and underwear he watched as she pulled the thin straps from her shoulders and began to tease her own nipples. As the first orgasm overtook her and she briefly shuddered with the intensity of it, he placed himself next to her and she reached out for him with a slim hand. She kneaded and stroked and teased with her nails and then, leaning forward, closed her hot mouth about his length. He ran his fingers through her lustrous black hair as the heat and wetness of her mouth intensified, and then, just as it seemed he must lose control and submit to the exquisite torture, spending himself in the way surf crashes upon the shore, her expert touches and skilful manipulating ensured the wave receded and was able to gather itself once more.

Again and again she brought him to the edge of his endurance where he must surely surrender to her attentions and teasing fingers and at last, as she sensed he had reached the point of no return, her movements quickened and it was as if his entire being – his mind and his spirit, were being drawn from his body in that single volatile action. She continued to tease and stroke lightly until he came back to earth once more and then she reclined against the cushions, displaying herself for him again. He placed his head between her parted thighs and her scent drove him wild. At the slightest pressure from his tongue on the firm little bud her back arched and she climaxed involuntarily; again and again she cried out as the spasms and contractions of orgasm wracked

76

her body while perspiration beaded her brow and her head rolled from side to side. Her eyes remained tightly closed and she was moaning softly as a fever patient might call out in the nightmare of delirium.

It was hot, so unbearably hot and the tiny room was lit by only a single candle. The small window remained slightly open and the heavy fragrance of bougainvillaea and orange blossom drifted through on the warm evening breeze. How she craved these stolen moments together. Merely thinking about tonight's encounter had precipitated that pleasant melting sensation in her belly and the delicious secret stirring of her flesh. He was poised over her at this very moment, filling her entire being with his presence and for a man of his size he was a particularly skilled, sensitive and inventive lover, taking her over the edge time and time again with scant regard for his own release – and his gentleness belied the strength and cruelty lurking beneath the surface. This afternoon in the arena, she had seen him kill his hundredth man in a contest where the odds were stacked seemingly impossible against him. They were sent in as a group to face him and at one point he was surrounded with no avenue of escape, save for death. But he had defeated them all and tonight, while the crowds celebrated and daubed his name on the public buildings of the city he was here with her in their secret place, towering over her, loving her, driving her out of her mind with lust and abandonment – skilled, magnificent and deadly!

"Crixus, Crixus," she called out in her mind but the words that reached her lips were, "Adam, Adam, what are you doing to me?" But Adam was still caressing her depths with the tip of his tongue and, at last, she submitted and gave herself up to the stars and colours that flashed and streaked across the darkness behind her closed eyelids, trembling with the strength of it.

As he pondered the scene of Tyra in this state of raw, unfettered wantonness, he knew his own moment was at hand and could be denied no longer. The musk of her sex lingered in his nostrils and as he came over her, so the breath whooshed from her lungs and another great wave which had been gathering momentum far out to sea finally rushed in and with a violent explosion of surf spent itself against the land. Hours later and still in the attitude of love they woke from a dream-filled, deathlike sleep. As they moved apart and took their respective turns in the shower, Adam noticed she appeared a little pensive and unusually at a loss for words. He gave her a few minutes and when he saw her expression still bore an uncharacteristic frown he knew something was wrong and sought to draw her out on the matter.

"You look so serious. Was it something I did...?" and in reply she kissed him and squeezed his hand.

77

"Adam, we are close, are we not? Close enough we don't hold back or keep secrets? Something – something happened just a while ago when we were making love. In all the time we've been together I've never known the feelings to be so intense. For a few moments there I was somewhere else. That's the only way I can describe it. I was aware of all those incredible feelings and was responding to everything you were doing but...," and the words failed her for in her eyes it was tantamount to betrayal. In the end she decided honesty was in their best interest for now and she would deal with the long-term implications later.

"Adam, I don't know the best way to say this but I was with another man in another time, another place. It was a stolen, illicit moment and I knew the man who was making love to me. It was something which could have had far-reaching consequences for both of us but I didn't care. All I wanted was to feel him touching me and driving me crazy with lust. Adam, I'm frightened by what this means for it goes so much deeper than I ever realised. First it was you and now it's me. Where is it all leading? I called out his name, over and over. I can't believe you didn't hear me. I knew what we had was more than just a romantic notion – with us it was so much more than that...."

"Adam, I know what's been happening to you these past years. The visions, the sensations, the feeling someone or something is there talking to you, calling you and willing you to remember. It's all starting to make sense now. In the beginning I didn't know what to think and if I'm perfectly honest I felt a little left out because I wasn't experiencing the same things too. I've been seeing quite a bit of Sophie lately and she knows exactly what's going on in your life. You know Sophie – can't keep anything secret for long with her! She knows all about your past - what you did and at what point in history although many of the finer details are still a little sketchy.

"That episode in the garden with the column a few days ago – something comes over you when you're working with shears or sharpening the blades. Your work too! Look at your work and what you're creating – or recreating. Your fascination with Roman architecture. You're almost obsessed with marble and granite structures, fountains, arches and statues and now you're replicating the entire political and social heart of Rome itself – a task which took centuries to complete and you're doing it in four years! I can still remember that morning after our first night together when you told me about studying for your exams, being locked away in that lonely room night after night where your only company was the voice inside your head telling you, 'She's still there – searching and waiting,' that's what you said."

"In the beginning I interpreted that as meaning the city itself and her secrets. Rome is the mistress and sooner or later all men bow to her. If you keep searching you will find the answers to her deepest mysteries and she will find you. She's still there – just don't give up when you're so close to achieving your ultimate goal. I was thinking about her buildings and kept wondering why I felt I knew them so intimately whenever I saw photographs, even though I had no memory of ever being there before. I knew all the streets and where they led. It was a comfortable feeling, like going home when you've been away for ages."

"Adam, listen to me. Those streets – the ones you feel you know so well. You know them because you were part of them a long time ago. Let's just say for argument's sake your initial perception of the things you heard in your room was, for the most part, correct and the city's history was in fact calling and preparing you for the great project you would undertake when you eventually qualified. But what if there was also another aspect to the scenario where something else or someone else was involved? Sophie told me you and I shared some kind of intense relationship for a little over two years before it ended violently and we both went to our deaths within a period of twenty-four hours. She doesn't know the precise circumstances but left me in no doubt since our first parting each of us has been searching and waiting for the other whether we choose to admit it or not. You yourself told Sophie you felt you'd been waiting for me since before this life began and you'd never had a woman before me."

"That's right, I told her that at a time when there were not so many pieces of the puzzle assembled as there are now. I was only having odd visions and glimpses without any discernible pattern to what was happening. It was just a gut feeling but also something I was utterly sure about."

"Adam, recently you told me I was definitely a part of this picture but couldn't say where I fitted in, just that I was there."

"Go on," he replied with an eerie suspicion of where this might be leading.

"When we were making love just a while ago and things really started to happen to me, I told you I felt I was somewhere else, in another time. The man driving me crazy with pleasure and lust was a star of the arena, a celebrity gladiator and earlier that same afternoon I'd seen him kill his hundredth man in a contest with four others. He was the people's champion and while he and I were alone together the crowds were scrawling his name on buildings all over the city because he was their hero and they adored him.

"Adam, that man was you and his name was Crixus. It was you, Adam. It all fits. You even look the same. Sophie knows an awful lot about Crixus. It was her who told me the name. I could never have known that. He died sometime during A.D.84 but like I said, the precise circumstances remain a mystery. Do you see where I'm going with all this? Those comforting voices you heard in your room as a young man were not purely the great city imparting her secrets. One of them was me or rather the woman I had once been, urging you to persevere with your architectural quest for it would ultimately provide the means for our paths crossing once more."

He nodded in acceptance of her words for recent events now appeared to make a lot more sense and he was no longer stumbling around in the darkness of uncertainty and speculation.

"Tyra, there's one more thing and after all you've just told me it's probably the confirmation you need even though it may sound a little far-fetched. This afternoon I was over at the forum inspecting the site, checking progress, seeing what materials had arrived, nothing out of the ordinary. I was on my way back to the car and stopped to take a look at phase one, the elevated terraces on the hillside. It was a wonderful sight, the blue sky, the red-tiled roofs and palm fronds nodding in the breeze. Some of the marble flooring was in place along with many of the columns and several rows of freestanding pilasters. The sun was in front of me and I had to shade my eyes but apart from that everything seemed normal.

"My attention was repeatedly drawn to what seemed like a large group of site-workers only this particular area was nearing completion and the activity was focused on other parts of the site. As I continued to watch it suddenly dawned on me what I was really seeing and the whole scene changed before my eyes. I was looking at the forum all right, but not the one we were building. This place now took on the appearance of how it would have looked two millennia ago. There were people – hundreds of them, stood around in groups socialising. Wealthy citizens in fine clothes, politicians with robes outlined in purple, commoners going about their own business, market traders, stall holders, fruit and vegetable carts, animals, everything – even the smells.

"There were soldiers keeping an eye open for trouble and close to where I was standing I could see the Colosseum only it wasn't called that. I can remember a huge inscribed plaque on its walls designating it as the Amphitheatrum Flavium because that was the place where I made a living only I wasn't scheduled to fight for another three days. I can tell you exactly what was going on inside its walls and how I was eagerly anticipating my own turn before the great crowds again. Next thing I know, I've passed out and I'm on the ground surrounded by a group of construction workers. They were genuinely concerned but I knew I'd be okay after a couple of minutes and a freshen-up in one of the ablution blocks."

After much careful deliberation he had decided to defer mention of Tyra's mysterious appearance in the mirror until a more suitable moment. In light of this afternoon's events which left them both in little doubt as to the extent of their former relationship and the revelation they had in fact been known to one another on such a level of intimacy, there was a limit to how much their minds could cope with. The question posed by all this was, *what now?*

She was deeply concerned after his disclosure of the fainting episode and placed a comforting arm about his shoulder.

"Are you alright, Adam? God, I feel awful now, inveigling you into a situation like that as soon as you walked through the door when it was probably the last thing on your mind. Strange as it may seem it was Sophie's explanation of past events that was responsible for me being so in the mood when you came home. I just couldn't wait for you to walk in and find me like that. I knew exactly what I wanted but I could have had no idea where it would ultimately lead or how intense the feelings would be. By the way, sorry about the shirt," and she indicated the pitiful remains discarded and devoid of buttons on the lounge carpet.

"You're just the tonic I need after a lousy day," and then he became serious again. "If I'm honest I think what troubles me most is the manner in which I appeared to have entertained people. It's one hell of a way to make a living compared to what I do now and yet when I was looking at the centre of the city this afternoon just before I passed out, I was impatient to be standing before the crowds again, to be about the business of giving them what they wanted to see."

"We shouldn't be so surprised, Adam. It was considered as normal a part of daily life as most contact sports are today and Sophie was quite emphatic you signed up for the activity of your own volition. Why would a free man embark upon such a drastic course of action unless he had reached absolute rock-bottom and had nothing left to live for? Sophie told me you – or *he*, were good and for years no one could ever come close to defeating you. It seemed to matter little how great they were or how many they numbered. You were unstoppable."

"Something put an end to it though, didn't it? Something or someone...."

"I just can't help seeing that image, Adam, over and over. Tens of thousands of people all chanting your name, the amphitheatre vibrating to the pulsating chant of the masses all screaming and punching the air with raised fists. You and he are so much alike, especially in looks and physique – do you know that? He may have been slightly more developed but under the circumstances it's hardly surprising. The overdeveloped musculature of your right side - have you never seen it before or wondered why it should be so? I couldn't believe I'd missed it until Sophie pointed it out and she was right."

Her words could not be denied and it was all the proof he needed. He was astounded she and Sophie had come up with the answers so readily but after seeing the way she had been during their frantic lovemaking and listening to her *with him* in that other far-off place which now appeared to be taking on a more disturbing air of reality with each day that passed, all doubts were dispelled. There was also the issue of their ultimate demise still shrouded in mystery and then, out of the blue, a nagging, unpleasant possibility suddenly reared its ugly suspicious head. *What if...?* He felt like a traitor for even thinking it but what if she had been responsible for their downfall whether it was accidental or by her own hand? Was there treachery involved – betrayal? He hated himself for the thought and instantly dismissed it as the ravings of a tortured mind. Tyra was not capable of such monstrous cruelty, then or now.

'But she wouldn't have been Tyra when I knew her before, would she? So who was she and what was her place in society? Did she have lovers?' Best not dwell on that possibility. It twisted his guts to imagine her sharing what they had now with someone else. *'I'll find the answers if it kills me,'* he mentally promised himself, not realising it had already done so in the far-distant past.

"Adam, I think we've both reached the point where we need to address the situation before we become obsessed with it. This latest episode for you is just one of hundreds but look how revealing the content was. I can't bear to think what might have happened if you'd been somewhere else – up in the roof or on scaffolding...," and she closed her eyes and shivered involuntarily. "Now things are happening to me too and I seem to have learned more about our pasts within the space of a few minutes than you have in years. Are you happy for me to talk to Sophie again and take this matter as far as we possibly can? This is about both of us, isn't it – you and me?"

"Call her tomorrow," he agreed. "I can't see any other way."

11

"Sophia Harrington speaking. How may I help you?"

"Sophie, it's Tyra."

"Darling, this is simply delightful. When are you coming to see me again?"

"Sooner than you think. Sophie, listen and I'll come straight to the point. When we met for lunch you told me an awful lot of things about Adam I didn't know myself."

"I did, indeed, and it was all true – every delicious fact. Tell me, darling, are things starting to happen to you as well as Adam?"

"They certainly are, hours after we spoke in fact. It was incredible. There was no warning at all and within the space of a few moments I saw all those things you spoke of."

"I won't inquire as to the nature of the catalyst which sparked this great illumination of yours. I'm far too polite but I've an educated notion you and he were engaged in...."

"Sophie!" Tyra cut in. "Not over the phone if you don't mind. This is somewhat delicate, *and private!*"

"Quite so," she teased. "I was only joking but the manner of your reply suggests I'm not a million miles from the truth. When do you want to come?"

"Are you free tomorrow some time?"

"Let's have a look," and she made a show of consulting her diary. "I have one client at ten and another at three. I could see you in between. Shall we say twelve-thirty?"

"Sounds good to me, Sophie. It'll be fun to see you again. I've missed you."

"You too, darling. Give my regards to Adam. I'll see you tomorrow."

12

At twenty-five minutes past twelve Tyra rang the chimes, nodding imperceptibly as she heard the muted sound echoed from somewhere further along the lengthy hallway beyond. Within seconds she was rewarded by the heavy door being swung open and Sophie's dulcet, upper-class tones filling her ears.

"Darling! You look simply ravishing. Your sex life must be doing absolute wonders. That little sparkle in your eyes.... Can't keep any secrets from Sophie, can we?"

"Apparently not," Tyra replied as she stepped into the hallway and immediately became aware of the great aura of peace and well-being that went hand-in-hand with Sophie.

"Come on through, darling. There's someone I'd like you to meet," Sophie invited.

"I thought it was going to be just the two of us," Tyra was immediately suspicious. As Sophie opened the door leading into her treatment room and beckoned for Tyra to follow, it was like stepping over an invisible threshold into a different world altogether, a place where fears were dispelled, secrets divulged and just about every kind of emotional torment rationalised and confronted.

"Well, what do you think, Tyra, darling? Good likenesses, hey...?"

Tyra's mouth seemed to fall open with surprise as she gazed upon this latest addition to the room where all three of them had spent hours in recent times searching for answers and venturing into the realms of the unknown with only Sophie's visionary giftedness acting as their guiding light.

"Christ, Sophie! You can be really spooky sometimes. How the hell did you manage this? These must have cost an absolute fortune. Where did you get them?"

"Custom made, darling, based on a few photographs, drawings and detailed written accounts of precisely what I was looking for. They turned up only a couple of days ago from Italy. Impressive, aren't they?

As for the cost – well, it's immaterial in the bigger picture of things. What else is money for if not spending? I can't take it with me when I die and I've no family other than you and Adam. If I have to spend a little to help a couple of friends answer some mystifying questions and get their lives back on track, where's the harm in that?"

Tyra studied the image of herself, moving around and appraising it critically from different angles while Sophie looked on before dropping another bombshell.

"Adam's already seen you dressed like this, but not for the best part of two millennia. He has no idea about these statues either. It took simply ages to decide on the finer details but I think we've got it about right," and Tyra could only shake her head in wonder. Clearly there was more to Sophie than met the eye.

"I never realised I was so voluptuous," she commented at last, returning to the front and contemplating the thrust of her breasts beneath the material of the elegant stola. "It must be down to always seeing them from a different perspective."

"You should ask Adam about that sometime," replied Sophie with a raised eyebrow.

"I suppose my only criticism is that it's all in white. It's so stark."

"My dear, some of the most beautiful and celebrated statues in the world today are of women, naked women, reproduced in this very material. It's all about effect and the way beauty is perceived by the discerning eye, don't you see? If we're going to start daubing you in paint and all those frightful theatrical accoutrements of the modern world you're going to end up looking like some grotesque mannequin posing in any high-street shop window. You can be such a philistine sometimes, darling. I thought you were a little more cultured than that. At least you've still got your clothes on. I'd be more than happy if someone wanted to sketch my outline in charcoal with the lights off, let alone carve me in Italian marble," she added unsubtly"

"Sorry, Sophie. It was purely an observation. I didn't wish to appear ungrateful. I just never thought I'd ever see myself portrayed in such a manner. I really love it, even though its origins are still rooted in uncertainty."

"I should bloody well hope so," Sophie sniffed her indignation. "Most women would kill to look like you on any day of the week, let alone when you're dressed like a goddess straight out of Roman mythology."

After several more minutes where she compared herself to the gleaming marble figure before her, Tyra's attention wandered to the second sculpture and many of the finer details which had remained hazy and indistinct during her more intimate recollections of recent days, now became sharp and frighteningly real.

"This is incredible, Sophie. Imagine being out there in the arena facing this. It's a killing machine."

As she stared at the helmet and her eyes attempted to bore through the mesh-like screening of the visor, the hair came up on the back of her neck, realising with delicious terror whose representation this must surely be.

"It's him," she stated flatly. "This is precisely the way he looked when I saw him in the arena but obviously he was devoid of all that mail and leather armour when he came to me later and made me call out in my....my...."

"Abandonment...?" Sophie prompted her. "Let me guess, Tyra, and correct me if I'm wrong. Something happened to Adam earlier that afternoon, another of his insights into the past, yes? He comes home early and you're all fired up because of what I've told you over lunch and you're ready for him as soon as he walks through the door. One thing leads to another and bingo! But this time it's different, isn't it? Whatever Adam saw out there at the site had a profound effect upon him, further confirmation of what he already knew or suspected."

"He said he fainted and woke up on the ground surrounded by workers who'd seen him fall. It was hot and he was looking into the sun and then all of a sudden everything was laid out in front of him, just as it would have been all that time ago. He could even describe the smells and different types of produce laid out on the barrows and carts and...."

"And then he comes home, slightly confused and maybe smarting a little from the truth of this latest revelation and you're there, ready for him. It's almost as if he's seeking solace in your body for what more effective way could there be to discard the event than to give in to the basic male urge of making love to a beautiful woman, especially when it's handed to him on a plate. This is the most intense it's ever been for both of you, yes? But it's different this time, isn't it? Something happens and takes you by surprise. Adam keeps getting pieces of the puzzle and you hit the jackpot with your first dollar, am I right?"

"It was so real - the single lamp flame in the small room, the heavy scent of flowers coming through the open window on the early evening breeze and the sounds of wild celebrating out on the streets. And there was him – poised over me, driving me wild and I was revelling in the wickedness of it all, a stolen, illicit moment because I knew what we were doing was against the rules of society and the knowledge of our mutual connivance served only to spur us on to greater heights. I was even calling his name, over and over but thank God it didn't come out like that. What would Adam have thought?"

Her gaze lingered on the image and she ran her slim fingers over the great muscles of the sword-arm which were barely masked by the linked-mail armour held in place by two broad straps across his back and chest.

"It truly is an amazing likeness but what mysteries lie beneath that helmet? It's quite an eerie sensation to stand here and look at the man again, knowing what this figure represents and my own part in his past. Yes, there is an element of terror when I appreciate his lifestyle and how many men he sent to their deaths but on the other side of the coin there's a wicked excitement because I know we were lovers, not just for a moment but something longer than that, flouting all the laws, restraints and conventions of the day in order we remain together. Oh, Sophie. How are we ever going to get to the bottom of all this? I feel we're just going round and round in circles waiting for I don't know what. Even if we carry on just the way we are now and the images and visions keep manifesting themselves in the way they have been, how is that ever going to solve the riddle and give us the full picture. There must be a reason for it somewhere but I'm at a loss to see how...."

Tyra remained oblivious of the fact but for the last few minutes she had been the subject of Sophie's unceasing appraisal, scrutinising, assessing and probing with those deep emerald-green eyes that saw into the mind of a person – and beyond. At length, satisfied with her own conclusions, she nodded imperceptibly as the decision was made.

"Don't fret, darling. You and he will have your time again, along with answers to your questions although it will be largely down to you and your receptiveness – how you respond when confronted with certain issues and phenomena."

"What on earth are you talking about, Sophie? We can't just recreate events out of the blue. What do you propose?"

"Come and sit down, Tyra. There's something I want to ask you." They moved to one of the two-seater leather sofas and sat down next to each other. "How much do you know about past-life regression – anything?"

"Not much I'm afraid although I know it forms a part of what you do in here. I have an idea it is a procedure where, if a willing person is suitable they can, by various methods, be induced into a condition where they are able to go back in time and relive past experiences. Are you suggesting I...?"

"How much do you want this, Tyra? How desperate are you and Adam to finally solve this enigma which is deepening with every day that passes? Have you not wondered why this room looks the way it does – these little additions? I've been expecting this very meeting for longer than you can possibly imagine and your last call was all the confirmation I needed. Tyra, you could do this and I could help you through it. Would you really trust your innermost secrets with a theoretically-disinterested third party when you and I are so close? You'd be perfect. You're receptive, you trust me implicitly and you have the advantage of not being afraid. We're not going in search of any particular traumatic event which has caused you undue discomfort over the years and we're not seeking to cure any phobias by confronting them are we?"

"Of course not," Tyra replied, slightly buoyed by the realisation just how close an apparent solution to their problem was. "Do you really think we can do this between us? I'd love to be able to tell Adam the story of our life before."

"Even if it was something he might not like to hear?"

"Whatever do you mean? I could never have hurt him, could I?"

"I don't know, Tyra. You tell me. Times were different then. Society bore little resemblance to how we know it today. Infringements of the law were dealt with much more harshly. Adultery, for instance could be punished by divorce, flogging, banishment to the provinces or even execution if the circumstances merited. You have to be prepared for discovering truths that, sooner or later, you will have to broach with Adam before he finds out for himself. Whatever they may be, Tyra, trust me, your relationship is strong enough to weather it."

"I understand but I think the risks are small compared to remaining in the dark indefinitely. How long do you think we'd need?"

"If nothing goes wrong and I don't have to intervene and bring you out of it prematurely we could probably do the whole thing in a couple of hours although there are no hard-and-fast rules where these things are concerned. It would be largely down to you at the end of the day. Tyra, you need to be aware that two hours in this room may well equate to many months or even years of your past. There's also the other matter of this little excursion not being solely for the purpose of personal enlightenment. Essentially, you're going in search of two people and we're going to be venturing into relatively uncharted territory. Ordinarily, I would recommend Adam to undergo a completely independent session of his own but due to the circumstances of this case I feel you may well discover the answers to all the questions raised over the past months and years."

"When could we make start?" Tyra attempted to appear nonchalant but her childlike impatience was transparent.

"You're an eager little beaver, aren't you? How about tomorrow evening at seven? It won't be dark but we can draw the curtains and light all the candles so the ambience is perfect. You'll have to talk to Adam, of course, but I don't foresee any problems. He's as keen as you are to see this matter resolved once and for all."

"Seven will be good and don't worry, I'll square it with Adam. Sophie, I have to say this. Your friendship over the years means more than I can ever tell you. There isn't another person in the world who'd do for us what you're doing now. This room and these beautiful statues you've added to complement the setting and add a note of realism. It's just too much. However will we repay you?"

"Don't be silly, darling," she replied through misted eyes. "Why should I want repayment? Seeing your restless souls over the months has troubled me and I am merely the means by which we're going to put things right. My reward will be in the knowledge you have indisputable evidence of your origins in this world being firmly rooted in not just the distant past but another time and possibly even further than that – before always, you might say."

"You lovely, sweet, romantic person," Tyra hugged her and kissed her cheeks. "What would I ever do without you?"

"Be off with you, woman - back to your man," Sophie sniffed and wiped away a rogue tear. "I'll see you tomorrow evening." They parted reluctantly from their embrace and Tyra let herself out. The half-hour journey home was tinged with the mixed feelings of euphoria, expectation and also a degree of uncertainty when she considered what she was soon to embark upon.

Tomorrow would come all-too-soon but first she had to talk to Adam.

13

Templeman Grant Architectural Consultants was rapidly becoming a victim of its own success as completion of the Roman Forum loomed ever closer and the complex inevitably came under the scrutiny of the outside world. New office premises were being sought in two other nearby towns and the company had organised a recruitment programme to fill the many vacancies arising from this unprecedented expansion. Russ and Adam were in constant demand by the media for statements, press-releases and on-site televised interviews for both local and national TV and whilst the barrage of inquiries seemed without end and downright infuriating at times they both realised the importance of maintaining good relations with press and public and gave good-naturedly of their time.

It was a site of truly gargantuan proportions and was now beginning to assume a semblance of majesty as the structures rose from their foundations and streets appeared where there had been nothing more than a sea of mud just a few months ago. Adam's designs had taken full advantage of the natural contours of the land and many of the smaller temple-like buildings were perched atop low hills where they looked down upon their equally-grand and substantially-larger counterparts whose frontages were clearly demarcated by the rows of columns supporting vast entrances and porticoes. Elsewhere, fountains spewed forth gushing torrents into basins and pools adorned with depictions of Poseidon while Hercules supported the world and gazed with envious eyes upon semi-naked nymphs and sirens reclining flirtatiously in the shallows while the sun danced and sparkled on the shimmering water.

Estimated completion time was a little under six months away and the complex was being hailed by the media and critics alike as the most innovative construction project of our time.

Having completed yet another session with the cameras Adam shook hands with the female interviewer, glanced at his watch and decided it was time to be moving if he was going to beat the traffic. No point in going back to the office today. As he drove out of the site he felt the feather of excitement at the prospect of being with Tyra again. It was a feeling that never waned nor varied and was one of the great constants in his life. He wondered what she would be like tonight after that last welcoming of hers when he had walked into the lounge and found her – *like that!* Just thinking about her in a towel, a summer dress or one of those revealing under-slips and a pair of high heels was enough to make him catch his breath and he felt the first stirrings in his lower body.

The traffic lights were kind and he parked the black BMW outside the entrance a little after quarter to five. Tyra's white Mercedes was in its usual slot to one side and he remembered she'd been seeing Sophie again today. He wondered what this latest meeting had revealed. As he walked into the hallway those earlier stirrings were suddenly rekindled as he smelled her perfume. He checked the lounge and dining room but to no avail. The kitchen, maybe, but this proved fruitless too. He climbed the stairs and her fragrance immediately became more intense. Quietly he inched forward on the thick carpets and peered through the small gap in the partially-open bedroom door. She was here, asleep, with one arm thrown up above her head on the pillow and wearing a thin cotton jacket with matching beige skirt. She had not even removed her shoes and he wanted her with a violence that startled him.

His heart was pounding and he could hear the blood thumping in his ears. He could not resist her and as he lowered his head to her feet, feeling the intense ache of his own arousal, he kissed and teased each of her toes. He had always been fascinated by this particular style of shoe she wore with its elongated heel and open-toe configuration. As he inched higher on his journey along those incredible calves he paused to lick at the backs of her knees for she was laid partially on one side and the sight of those little dimples seemed only to inflame his desires. As the intensity of his caresses increased and her upper thighs now became the object of his affections her eyes fluttered open and she came dreamily awake.

"Hello, Adam," she purred contentedly. "You're home early tonight," and stretching out like a cat she rolled over and gave herself up to his attentions.

When they awoke much later, still entwined from their lovemaking, she kissed him warmly and ran a slim finger over the muscles of his chest, tracing the outline around and around and marvelling over his appearance in the subdued lighting of the slowly darkening room.

"Who was a hungry boy then?" she asked now they had both come back down to earth once more. "I sensed your need by the things you were doing. Had a bad day...?"

"On the contrary, I've had a great day and it just got a whole lot better when I came up here and found you like this. I couldn't get you out of my head on the way home and wondered what you might be doing. I can't believe the strength of the feelings just lately. It seems to get more and more intense every time. Driving home I was imagining you in a skirt or a dress and those high heels and I was kissing your legs. It's a good job I didn't drive off the road or something like that. When I saw you asleep on the bed it was all too much and I knew I had to touch your body. The urge was almost painful."

"I'm so glad, Adam. I don't ever want us to drift apart, physically or spiritually."

"Regarding the spiritual how was your meeting with Sophie today?"

"Amazing, Adam - truly amazing. She seems to know what I'm going to say before I say it. You just can't surprise her. She knows things are starting to happen much more frequently for you. She's been expecting it and when I told her about that unbelievable vision I had when you and I were....you know, she'd been waiting for it to manifest itself as if it were all a perfectly natural progression of events and merely served to confirm her initial instincts.

"Adam, she's purchased two life-size statues for her room and placed them next to the couch where everyone can see them. One of them is a depiction of me only the clothes are not of the modern world. She must have spent an awful lot of time researching the finer details because I've come out of it looking like a wealthy woman of the ancient Roman aristocracy," and Adam's attention was immediately diverted to that eerie scenario in the washrooms at the site when Tyra had appeared in the mirror dressed exactly as she had just described. He resisted the urge to own up but all of a sudden it was starting to look as if Sophie was involved in all this too – and not solely as the friend and therapist providing answers!

"You said there were two statues, Tyra," he prompted her, hoping his inner unease was not etched overtly in his expression.

"Yes," she replied, "and the second one is clearly an image of the corresponding half of this mystery and, ironically, the very same man who was the subject of that frighteningly-real situation I found myself in the other day. Obviously, the facial details remain a mystery, hidden behind the visor of the helmet but in every other respect it's a carbon copy of the man I saw that afternoon in the arena. You and he share some pretty disturbing similarities, Adam, and I can't help but wonder how Sophie came to be in possession of so much hard fact pertaining to your physique. There are depths here I haven't even begun to explore but I have a strange feeling Sophie's implicated in this bewitching conundrum much more than she's prepared to admit."

Funny how she arrived at the same conclusion!

"So, how did you leave things with her – can she help?"

"I think so, Adam. She hinted I'd be a perfect candidate for regression."

"You mean regression as in hypnosis – going back in time to a previous existence?"

"Exactly that. It's all done in a strictly-controlled environment and should anything untoward happen she can bring me out of it in seconds. How do you feel about me doing this, Adam? The way I see it, our options are somewhat limited if we're going to get to the root of what's actually happening to the two of us. I've arranged to be at Sophie's for seven o'clock tomorrow evening but if you're not happy I'll call it off."

"Just as long as there are no appreciable risks. I couldn't bear to see you traumatised in any way or left emotionally scarred for the rest of your life. I know you won't actually be going anywhere, at least not with your body and I trust Sophie as much as you so I guess as long as she doesn't do anything crass you'd better keep that appointment."

"There's one other thing, Adam, and whilst it probably won't have any bearing on the overall outcome of the evening, I can fully understand Sophie's concern at what we might uncover. Under normal circumstances a person undergoing regression therapy goes in search of events relevant and significant to their own life, reliving past experiences which have played an important part. The chief difference in this case is I'll be going back in your life as well or at least to those parts of it where I appear to have been influential to a greater or lesser degree. Sophie's never presided over anything quite so ground-breaking and it'll be an experience for her too. She can't say for certain how long the session will last but I know she won't intervene and call a premature halt if everything looks okay. Are you still happy to proceed?"

"How can I possibly object when you put forward such a convincing argument? I'll make sure we're there by seven."

14

It was an unfamiliar and slightly disconcerting feeling to admit for the first time in his working career the job was devoid of any sense of reward. The hours merged into a mind-numbing oblivion of client-meetings, site inspections and planning details. It was endless and he even removed his watch to check the movement at one point because he thought it had stopped.

For Tyra it was the same as she roamed the great house cleaning, tidying and generally taking inordinate pride in this wonderful place where the colourful history of its previous owners was always present as a reminder of bygone days. The hours dragged by and as the day wore on with agonising slowness she detected that slight fluttering sensation in her stomach which became increasingly pronounced the more she thought about tonight.

Was it fear? She attempted to rationalise the feeling. Surely not; Sophie had put her mind at ease with a simple explanation of the session and she wouldn't actually be going anywhere or encountering supernatural manifestations. Sophie had given her word nothing would happen and she would always be in full control, even while Tyra remained under the veil of gentle and non-intrusive hypnosis. The secret would be complete and utter relaxation, to allow her body to relax sufficiently for Sophie to assume control and take Tyra back in time to where, hopefully, the final parts of this story would be pieced together.

But she felt far from relaxed at the moment and considered finishing off that second bottle of Chianti they had made a start on last night. She needed a lift but it was vital she maintained a clear head and accordingly the idea was dismissed. Depending upon the outcome of tonight's venture into the unknown, the wine might later serve to assist consolation or celebration. It certainly was a rather poignant fact the waiting seemed to be the most nerve-wracking aspect of any forthcoming encounter, especially as she had no real idea of what she was walking into. She was also curious as to how the evening would unfold and, more to the point, how she would fit in to the sequence of events as they unfolded. Would she actually be experiencing events for herself as they happened and responding to the stimuli of grief, bereavement, passion, anger and pain, or would she be observing the proceedings as a spectator or just a casual bystander? The latter sounded a little far-fetched as it would be akin to watching a mirror image of herself, devoid of control and influence. Questions, so many questions; at this rate she would be tearing her hair out before too long and so it was with considerable relief she heard Adam's car pull up outside the main entrance a little before five and rushed out to meet him.

"Missed you," she told him, hoping her earlier trepidation was not mirrored in her voice. "Are you ready to eat?"

"That would be good," he replied. "Lunch didn't happen, I'm afraid. Just couldn't manage to get away from my desk. I can't believe how the time's dragged. It just went on and on."

"I think we've both got the same thing going on inside our heads, haven't we? Can't seem to concentrate on anything."

"You still want to do this – no reservations?"

"I'm a little apprehensive, Adam. Anyone would be but we both trust Sophie like no other and if she gives her word on any singular issue or predicts some future event will come to pass, then that's good enough for me. We've never had cause to doubt her yet, have we?"

"No, you're right. She's the only person in the world I'd trust you to be doing this with. Anyone else and I'd have done my damndest to talk you out of it."

15

With the evening meal behind them they set off just before six thirty for the half-hour drive to Sophie's. It was still light and they chatted about nothing of any great concern but as the miles sped past so the knot in Tyra's stomach tightened like the noose around the neck of a condemned man and the sensation was still there when they parked up at a couple of minutes to seven. Hearing them arrive, Sophie rushed out to greet them on the doorstep in a theatrical barrage of kisses and bussed cheeks.

"Welcome to my humble abode," she trilled. "It's so good you both came."

"Why do I always feel like a different person whenever I see you?" Tyra smiled as she held Sophie at arm's length and stared into her eyes.

"Because I am your guiding light in a dangerous and unforgiving world full of mysteries and darkness, darling," Sophie wrinkled her nose mischievously.

"You look stunning," Adam admired her shapely form with his steady gaze.

"Adam, you lovely man," she teased. "Always the charmer. I see the Pantheon has an empty pedestal tonight."

"Yes," he agreed, "and if you and I were alone together I'd be doing some decidedly ungodly things with you," and she giggled wickedly at the suggestiveness of his remark. She led the way in and Adam closed the heavy front door behind them. Once in Sophie's room his attention was immediately drawn to the two marble figures strategically placed one either side at the foot of the sumptuous couch.

"My God, these are incredible! The likeness of you, Tyra. It's unbelievable – the face, the hair, that graceful neck and the clothing," and his observations lingered on the sensuous depiction of her breasts. "All of it, it's just perfect. I don't know how you did this, Sophie, but it's mind-blowing. The level of skill and accuracy...." He then turned to face the second statue and he could only shake his head in wonder as he studied the intimidating figure. "Is this him?" he asked after a short pause. "Is this the man who appeared to you that afternoon when we were...?"

"Yes, Adam, it is," Tyra replied with an air of the seasoned anthropologist. "This is the man I saw in the arena and who, by the law of averages, should never have survived a contest where the odds were stacked so impossibly against him. This is the man Sophie has known about for years but was reluctant to speak about until I approached her first. This is Crixus. This is the man I waited for all these years without ever realising it. It's you, Adam."

Sophie came to stand next to him and laid a gentle hand upon his arm.

"She speaks the truth for many years ago it was written she would come to him again and their questions would be answered. You are he and Tyra is your woman. There was never any doubt and tonight you will discover your origins in this world and why the crossing of your paths was predestined in the same manner of the sun rising at each new dawn and setting at its conclusion."

"The helmet and visor, it takes away every aspect of personality and humanity. It's quite frightening. Imagine being thrown into the arena and told you had to fight – this!"

"These will be our two witnesses for tonight's proceedings, Adam. They were only chosen after much soul-searching on my part because I knew this meeting was going to happen years ago and I wanted the setting to be as near perfect as I could hope for."

The room was, indeed, perfect and Sophie had done her work well. In the virtual darkness the only light was provided by flickering candles which made the shadows dance while they cast eerie reflections. It seemed the characters depicted in the wall murals and on the high ceiling were looking down at them; the cherubs, gods, angels, gargoyles and heavenly choir formed the expectant audience. Tyra was the subject and Sophie was the master of ceremonies presiding over tonight's performance. The atmosphere was one of utter peace and Tyra was suddenly aware the knots in her stomach had dissipated and she was now ready to face the journey she would soon embark upon.

"Would you like to make yourself comfortable, darling?" Sophie invited and Tyra swung herself up onto the great carved-oak couch and smoothed out her clothes. She wrinkled her nose at some faint aroma, unable to place it.

"Why is that smell so familiar? We don't have anything at home like that and I've not been aware of it here before. It reminds me of something I recently...."

"Your perception is quite correct, darling," Sophie agreed. "If you cast your mind back a day you'll remember how you encountered it when you were enjoying your little interlude with Crixus and the window was open allowing the fragrances of bougainvillaea and orange blossom into the room on a warm summer evening...."

"Of course. I should have known. You're absolutely right, Sophie. You think of everything."

"Just another of those little touches which might have the effect of jogging your memory. Adam, I know I'm being a bossy-boots but I have to ask you to remain absolutely quiet until the session is over and Tyra is safely back here with all her faculties fully restored. She will not in any way be traumatised and will be conscious of my voice at all times so please do not be alarmed by anything you see or hear. I give you my word nothing untoward will happen and I will retain full control throughout the entire period of regression. As I explained to Tyra yesterday, this is something of a ground-breaking event for me too as I will be presiding over one person's regression into two different lives and it promises to be interesting."

"We both have absolute faith in you, Sophie," Adam nodded in agreement, "and I understand perfectly not to interrupt or cause distractions."

"You're a darling. Okay, shall we make a start?" Sophie asked confidently.

"Ready when you are," Tyra replied, hoping the slight tremor in her voice was not glaringly-obvious. "I'm quite comfortable now. This couch is amazing."

"Oh, good. That should certainly assist the relaxation process. Okay then, I want you to close your eyes, Tyra, and keep them closed. I won't let you sleep but they will start to become heavy." Obediently, she closed her eyes and adopted the attitude of calm and total relaxation. On the surface she appeared serene and perfectly at ease with no fluttering of eyelids but Sophie pondered how this deceptive pose would, in all likelihood, change dramatically as the secrets began to come out.

"Concentrate on your eyes becoming heavier all the time until you start to feel drowsy. It's a wonderful feeling because you don't have to open them or do anything at all except listen to the sound of my voice. Allow the sense of well-being and relaxation to soak into your entire body, Tyra, flooding your veins from head to toe and driving out all the tension, the fears, the worries and any concerns you may still harbour as to the nature of your journey this evening.

"Just give in to the feeling of softness beneath you and relax. For a moment, think about that first large glass of wine at the end of a long and tiring day and how the sensation of warmth travels through your body, purging life's trials and tribulations and rendering them inconsequential. It's a wonderful feeling, Tyra – every bit as good the way you feel now, slipping further and further into the next level of calm and tranquillity.

"Relax and listen to the sound of my voice as the weight falls away from every part of your body – your arms, hands and shoulders first and then your torso, legs and feet. With all that weight gone you feel as if you want to float up from the couch and leave the physical world behind for your body is now devoid of substance where you can no longer feel it. There are no intrusions into this peaceful place you are beginning to enter and the only sound you will hear is my voice, guiding you along the path to your ultimate destination."

Already, the tone of her breathing had noticeably changed and become deeper and sonorous, as if on the point of sleep but slipping no further while her chest rose and fell in a slow and regular pattern.

"You're perfectly safe, Tyra, and in the company of people who love you more than you will ever know. Soon you will relinquish those final threads which bind you to the present world but first I need to be sure you're comfortable and happy to proceed with the next phase of your journey. You do not have to speak, Tyra, but gently nod your head if you wish to continue."

The movement was so imperceptible Adam nearly missed it but Sophie's trained eye picked up the tiny change in position confirming Tyra's acceptance. She turned to Adam and mouthed silently, 'She's okay!' and he merely smiled his acknowledgement. Sophie continued and it was clear Tyra was at a point where her journey back through the years was about to commence.

"Tyra, I want you to imagine you're standing at the top of a flight of steps. There are only ten steps and there's absolutely no hurry to descend. As I count down from ten I want you to take a step each time until you arrive at the bottom. Okay? Nice and slowly then – nine – eight – seven – six, take your time and enjoy the new lightness in your step now all the weight has gone from your body. Let's continue – five – four – three - two – one, and you're there. Good girl, Tyra. We're doing really well. Are you still with me...?" and she moved her head in reply.

"Alright, Tyra, as you look directly ahead you will see a long corridor stretching away into the distance. There are no lights to dazzle you but your vision is good and you can see normally in the shadows.

On either side of the passage are doors. There are many doors, Tyra, and each one has a large number on it, like a date. Can you see them and you may speak to me?"

"I see many, many doors, all the same and merging with the distance and swirling mist. There are so many doors...," and she seemed a little perplexed even though it was clear she was 'under.'

"Let me help you, Tyra," Sophie encouraged. "The numbers on the doors are actually dates and begin with the present. We don't want that, do we? What are we looking for, Tyra?"

"The truth," she replied and Sophie smiled.

"Yes, and what else, Tyra? What else are we looking for?"

"The past," she came back after a short pause.

"Correct and how far back in the past is the truth you are seeking – a long time ago?" Sophie prompted.

"Yes, a long time ago. A long, long time ago," and there was a note of weariness in her voice.

"Tyra, I want you to simply walk along the passage looking to your left and to your right. See how the numbers change as you advance along its length. You may have to walk a considerable time but the journey will not be arduous for there is lightness in your step. Tyra, are you making progress down the years – away from the present time in search of your past?"

"Yes, and I am nearing a date familiar to me. I am hardly aware of my journey but I know I have come a great distance."

"When you arrive at the door where the desire to enter is strongest I want you to stop and wait." There was a gap of many seconds and at last Tyra spoke again. There was neither excitement in her voice nor trepidation but rather an element of agonised pleading and Sophie knew she had located the portal into her former world unerringly.

"I am here. This is the place. I feel I am being drawn irresistibly to its interior. This is where the truth lies – where I must begin my search. Please, let me go now...."

"Tyra, before you go through there is one more thing I want you to do."

"I understand."

"Tyra, read me the number on the door and then you may enter."

"Eighty-two," came the reply. "Eighty-two," and with a sense of urgency she opened the door and was gone.

16

Rome – A.D. 80

There had been no rain for ninety-three consecutive days and Rome sweltered in the unrelenting summer heat. The prolonged dry-spell had inevitably resulted in accidents and arsonists were known to have started several fires, promptly extinguished by the city's *Vigiles*. Consequently, the senate had seen fit to convene and debate the ongoing volatile conditions and passed emergency legislation warning citizens as to the results of carelessness with cooking utensils and open fires. Damage to state property arising from such negligence would be punished harshly and this edict was publicised widely in the form of verbal announcements and posters affixed to buildings at regular intervals.

Following the great fire of A.D. 79 which burned for three days and nights, large sections of the city had been reduced to rubble and ashes and the ensuing reconstruction programme was still under way. Whilst several temples and public buildings were damaged in the conflagration, the real losses and hardship had been suffered by the people themselves. Huge swathes of residential properties had been totally destroyed and many lives lost due to the dry timber construction and sheer density of the dwellings. There was little in the way of an organised fire department and any minor blaze would soon engulf an entire tenement. Escape was impossible.

However, the rebuilding had gone well and with the ever-increasing use of concrete and mortar the city was taking shape once more. The fire-ravaged areas had been completely cleared and redesigned with safer structures, running water, improved access and egress and wider streets. Tenements were now constructed of brick which was not only fireproof but much stronger and less likely to collapse in the event of a catastrophe.

Julius Quintus was overseer for the public works programme in the *Subura,* the area outside the protective limits of the New Forum of Augustus with its thirty-foot-high *tufa* wall. Situated in the low-lying region between the southern end of the Viminal and western extremity of the Esquiline hills, the *Subura* was a busy, crowded and noisy area also housing trades and manufacturing. Unfortunately, crime and prostitution were rife too but in some ways the great fire had done its work most effectively. Hopefully, the regeneration now under way would improve life for the majority and create new opportunities.

Julius' record of efficiency without cost-cutting at the expense of safety was legendary and the primary reason for his being awarded this prestigious task. At any other time he would have been assigned to the construction and maintenance of larger public buildings but urgency dictated his skills were required here. Concrete – particularly evident in the construction of the great amphitheatre, was revolutionising building on a huge a scale. Walls and floors could be fabricated in hours and after the initial setting time had expired, the wooden shuttering could be removed and the new walls faced with red brick, or, in the case of larger public buildings, travertine and marble.

Yes, this was the construction material of the future – the foundations upon which empires were built, Julius mused as he observed one of the younger men prepare yet another batch for a section of flooring in the block they had started on yesterday. He was particularly conscientious was this one, never complaining, turned up for work every day and did whatever was asked without questions – *and those muscles!* He was built like an athlete – *or a god!* His shoulders were wide, tapering to a narrow waist and his thighs and calves would be the envy of many gladiators Julius had seen over the years. He watched with interest as the young man methodically blended the crushed aggregate with hydrated lime and pozzolana before adding water in just the prescribed quantity to produce a mix of optimum strength and workability; too little water and the concrete would be stiff and unmanageable, too much and it would be considerably weakened - its consistency excessively fluid where the drying-out process was noticeably extended. The finished product would be light but immensely strong; just one of the advantages of utilising volcanic rock of which there was an inexhaustible supply. The ash, or pozzolana, formed the binding agent along with hydrated lime and there were various types of naturally-occurring stone to be employed as filler or the main body of the concrete. Pumice saturated with gas bubbles was light enough to float on water and ideally suited to roofing applications where strength was paramount but weight came at a penalty. For heavier situations granite and basalt could be used - much denser materials where the additional weight was of no concern.

This young god had displayed an unusually-avid interest in the basics of construction since Julius agreed to a three-month trial period just over a year ago. He wanted to see plans and drawings of everything, from the tenements they were building now to the great temples and majestic structures of the forum, the focus and heart of social and political life in Rome. He was full of questions which Julius answered readily for he was unaccustomed to this degree of keenness in his subordinates.

How was the marble and travertine quarried and where did it come from? Why did columns differ from one building to another? Why were some of them fabricated from sections whilst others were enormous monoliths? Why was it a certain temple might have six columns across the frontage while another had eight and what was the purpose of free-standing pilasters and colonnades when they didn't seem to be holding anything up? Would Julius please show him how to carve stone into those wonderful shapes and designs adorning the capitals that sat atop those elegant columns?

Yes, he was indeed a rare find in every sense of the word. As far as Julius knew there were no women in his life and unlike many freeborn young men today he showed no interest in joining the legions where a man could achieve wealth and property, not to mention untold glory whilst expanding the empire or suppressing tribal revolts in the provinces. The young man had proved his worth many times and Julius could only ponder the results if his workforce boasted a few dozen more like him. He had never seen such a tragic and completely devastated figure as poor Crixus here upon learning of his father's untimely demise in Germania. Having also lost his mother at the tender age of seven, Julius had taken the young man under his wing and whilst uncomfortably aware he could never replace the father, became instead friend, mentor and confidante to a lost young soul who would make him as proud as any son.

"The work goes well, young Crixus," Julius observed with a nod of satisfaction.

"Yes, sir, it does. I estimate two more days for completion of this section and then we can start on the next."

It was no less than Julius expected. Give this one a task and he attacked it single-mindedly until it was done. Another man would have taken longer and attempted to justify the delay but Crixus seemed to regard everything as a personal challenge, constantly pushing himself in pursuit of his own goals.

"I have a proposition for you, young Crixus. How would you like to leave all this and train for something else – something more in keeping with your potential and that passion I see every day, simmering away beneath the surface?"

"Something else...?" Crixus replied hesitantly. "I don't know anything else, sir. This is what I like doing," and there was a mischievous glint in Julius' eyes as he surveyed the crestfallen expression of the young man.

"I have been watching you closely this past year and answered your many questions. You are unlike the others on this project who are engaged in similar work and I feel you possess a certain natural flair, a talent and a willingness to achieve great things. Such a gift should not be squandered when the fire that drives you burns so brightly in so few. How would you like to work in the quarries for two years and learn how to cut marble and travertine from the ground? There will be craftsmen to teach you the ways of dressing the stone so one day you will be able to reproduce what you see in the city with your own hand.

"I warn you now, the work is challenging and dangerous but should you succeed in your task the rewards for your efforts and perseverance will be great. When you return after two years I will show you the ways of building the true and lasting structures proclaiming Rome's dominance to the world. What do you say, young Crixus? Are you willing to do this? Do we have a bargain?"

He was overcome by the overseer's generous offer for it was akin to a door opening in his life and all he had to do was prove himself worthy. He had never really pondered the concept of destiny or dwelt on the possibility of life being preordained. The gods and fates were too mercurial and capricious at the best of times, giving with one hand and taking away with the other but now it seemed his dream was about to be fulfilled – on his own merits! The passion for architecture was mingled with the blood in his veins and he simply had to know more, to be able to design and give this great city something of his own.

And, one day – one day, he knew he would.

"You do me a great honour, sir," Crixus replied with a lump in his throat and humility in his heart. "I accept the offer and will come back at the end of two years."

And so it was that a twenty-one-year-old Crixus embarked on the first part of his vocational enlightenment and a journey which took him to Euboeia, an area separated from western mainland Greece by the narrow Euripus Strait. Much of Rome's Cippolino marble was quarried here and Crixus was put to work alongside slaves and other young men driven by similar ideals, extracting great blocks of solid rock from the exposed faces and vertical walls while yet others laboured in the long underground tunnels. As he worked with the teams so his expertise and, indeed, his muscles grew under the daily exertion of wielding the heavy hammers that drove chisels into the enormous slabs of rock. As they worked the faces in appalling heat, the blinding sun reflected back at them and the mortality rate through exposure and dehydration was high. Accidents were commonplace and tempers flared regularly as a badly-judged hammer blow dislodged a splinter of rock that took an eye out or laid open a flap of skin on cheek or forehead to the bone. Inevitably, angry words and fists were exchanged but these instances nearly always resulted in handshakes. It was a good way to clear the air and the overseers generally ignored the less-serious affrays.

After six months Crixus moved on to the Marathi Paros quarry in the Cyclades area off south-eastern Greece − an island group of the Aegean archipelago infamously renowned for the cataclysmic eruption of Santorini volcano in historical times. This was the work he truly loved as he watched a block of stone, devoid of life and character up to this point, suddenly become a thing of great beauty under the skilled hands of the masons. Using a variety of chisels and mallets they lovingly sculpted the four scrolls at the corners of a Corinthian capital, followed by successive rows of acanthus leaves. Even the deep vertical flutes on the columns themselves were mathematically precise to within a millimetre so perfect symmetry was always achieved.

His tutors were patient and whilst they too recognised his latent talent and burning ambition they initially made him practice his carving on old, spoiled blocks of stone that had no future use as building material. When at last he was permitted to begin work on a full-size column, one of many assigned to a new temple of Jupiter on the Capitoline Hill in Rome, he approached the task with great reverence, muttering prayers to Minerva, goddess of wisdom, learning, arts and industry to guide his hands.

The final part of his journey took him back to the outskirts of Rome itself, to a travertine limestone quarry in the hills of Tivoli where the basic skills were repeated for a softer and more-workable stone generally utilised in lining the facades of great buildings but which also lent itself to numerous other applications. The end of the second year came all-too-quickly for Crixus and on the final day the overseer, Severus, came to him with a letter.

"Give this to Julius Quintus when you return to the city for his trust and confidence in your abilities has been vindicated. You are a strange man, young Crixus − never seeking the company of others and yet you are a source of inspiration to us all. I have never witnessed such dedication and willingness to learn and I know you will achieve great things one day. May the gods always walk with you and guide your hand."

They embraced and patted one another's shoulders for the last time.

"I will never forget the things you have shown me here and I thank you for your patience. One day I will give Rome something she has never seen before – something to make you proud...," and with that he turned and strode away, eagerly anticipating his reunion with Julius, a man who had shown him more kindness than he had ever known.

17

Rome - A.D. 82

The restoration work was virtually complete by the time Crixus returned to the city and his searches for Julius among the isolated pockets of ongoing activity yielded nothing.

"Where's Julius Quintus?" he asked as his steps took him around the rebuilt and completely modified area of the *Subura*. But the answer was always the same.

"Julius didn't show up for work this morning or yesterday. He was here the day before but that's the last time anyone saw him."

Crixus wandered back to the heart of the city, a feeling of unease descending upon him like a pall of gloom. Something must have happened. Julius always turned up for work no matter what. He was pivotal to the whole operation and could usually be found at some location or other solving a particular problem. In the end, out of frustration he went straight to the public-works building and asked if anyone knew the whereabouts of Julius. At length, satisfied his concern was genuine, a secretary showed Crixus through a heavy curtain into a side office where he was confronted by a seated figure attired in a splendid white-and-purple *toga praetexta*.

He was one of several *curule aediles* responsible for the upkeep and maintenance of the city's buildings and public works programmes. They were powerful people, eager to please the populace and win their approval, especially at election times when their policies might secure or lose them crucial votes in a bid to ascend the political ladder.

"My name is Caius Attius Caecilius. How may I be of service?" He was typically-unremarkable of the breed Crixus had seen entering and leaving the senate over the years – grey and balding with hair only at the sides and back of his round head whilst the lack of height seemed only to draw unwanted attention to his rotund and portly physique. The eyes were cold, the features unsmiling and despite Crixus' immediate aversion to the seated figure he decided against deliberately antagonising the man further for he detected his presence here was an intrusion.

"Sir, I am seeking the works' overseer, Julius Quintus, whom I have not seen for two years. At his invitation I have been away from the city, learning my trade in the marble quarries of Greece. Now that I am returned to resume my instruction bearing letters of commendation he seems to have vanished and my searches have yielded nothing. He has been a father to me and a dear friend."

Caius Attius' lugubrious expression became even more downcast and the colour seemed to drain away from his florid cheeks at Crixus' mention of the name.

"Julius Quintus, you say. I know him well. A popular man with an enviable reputation for achieving results without, shall I say, ruffling the feathers of either his seniors or subordinates." His eyes bore into Crixus own and as he took a deep breath and exhaled with a sigh, Crixus sensed a terrible presentiment and portent of looming disaster. "Come and sit down a moment. You will need to for it is clear you have not already heard."

He spoke clearly and concisely for his position dictated he regularly addressed the senate and assemblies and his education in rhetoric was evident.

"Heard what?" Crixus demanded a little more harshly than intended. "What has happened?"

"I am deeply sorry to be the bearer of sad tidings but Julius was the victim of a drunken and totally unprovoked knife attack two nights ago and he was gravely injured. My personal physician has been attending him at his private residence but I do not care for his chances. The assailant was apprehended soon after the attack, still the worse for drink and, of course, denied any involvement but the knife was later found concealed on his person and there were traces of blood on his hands. After two witnesses came forward there could be no doubt. He is being held in custody awaiting trial but I think the outcome is indisputable."

"Death. Plain and simple for taking a good life with no regard for the consequences."

"Death, yes. Execution in the arena. He will suffer the fate Rome reserves for murderers. That is the way."

Crixus leant forward with his head in his hands, scarcely able to believe what he had just heard. It was indeed a cruel paradox for once again the gods had given with one hand and taken away with the other.

"Sir, you said he was at home. I must see him. There are things I need to say before he...," and he could not finish the sentence for the thought of Julius being torn away from him like this ripped at his insides and threatened his powers of reason.

"I understand perfectly," and Caius Attius' voice had softened noticeably. "If you walk along the Via Valeria for half a mile his house is directly opposite the statue of Mercury and has a large fig tree close to the door."

"There is one more question I have before I leave. Who did this? By what name is he known?"

"The man is a common thief and now it would appear he has broadened his sphere of notoriety into murder too. He is completely without scruples or morals and is at home in the gutter with the rest of his kind. His name is Ferox. I am truly sorry for your grief but you must let justice prevail now. Ferox will have his day in court and then Rome will make an example of him."

"I am indebted to you for your assistance and kind words but I have to go before it is too late. May the gods watch over you, Caius Attius Caecilius, and bestow upon you greater favour than they have seen fit to award me."

18

The home of Julius Quintus was small compared to other more-ostentatious local properties where development was on the increase due to its picturesque, semi-rural location. Tall, slender cypresses lined the road while palms, figs and cicadas abounded in the gardens of wealthy Patricians who regarded the presence of interlopers with suspicious, envious eyes. The south-west-facing side of the hill which sloped away to meet the Tiber in its wide valley was a sun-trap and natural haven for the propagation of juicy red grapes that reached as far as the eye could see in their ordered, regimental ranks.

The door was opened to Crixus after his first polite knock by a tearful and sombre-faced woman about sixty years old whom he judged to be the housekeeper.

"You must be Crixus," she decided. "I knew you'd come. I don't think it will be long now. He is very weak."

Julius was laid on a low cot in the coolest and most comfortable part of the house and although his eyes appeared locked in a vacant stare he recognised Crixus' presence immediately. He knelt beside the old man and took one of his hands – scarred and calloused from a lifetime's labours, and held it to his face. Julius' voice was hoarse and broken as he looked upon the young man for what, he knew, would be the last time.

"Crixus – Crixus, I fear you must continue life's odyssey alone despite my promise we would journey together. I knew you would come back and make me a proud man – to reaffirm my initial feelings were no delusion."

Crixus made as if to give Julius the letters of commendation from the quarry overseers but Julius understood and waved away the gesture with tired hand.

"There is no need. I know what is written, otherwise why would you have come?" His complexion was grey and brittle as old parchment and his eyes seemed to have sunk into his skull. There was a new *oldness* about him, a resignation to the fate rapidly overtaking him and Crixus merely gazed upon the tragic figure in the manner of a helpless spectator.

"I can't believe this is happening. How could the gods remain so indifferent...?" and he was momentarily aware of grief being overtaken by something infinitely more powerful – something alien, unfamiliar and deeply disturbing that threatened to undermine his composure and shake the foundations of his world to the very core. Julius' voice was a whisper and Crixus sensed the end was near, leaning a little closer lest he miss the final words.

"Rome is not all she appears to be, Crixus. There will always be pools and dark shadows affording sanctuary to lurking predators. It is the way things are. Before you returned I was filled with the fear of death but now I have seen your face again I can rest safely in the knowledge you will continue my work – if not tomorrow then at another time when you are ready. Crixus, I am tired and cold and my bones are weary. Now make an old man happy and embrace me as the son I never had."

He leaned forward and with huge muscular arms cradled the frail, broken form of the man who had come to symbolise the way forward – a bright light at the end of a long, dark tunnel.

"I will always remember you, Julius Quintus, and I will honour you in everything I do from this day forward. Someone will pay for this – I do so swear upon it. I give you my pledge, the one who bears the mark of culpability will curse the day his bitch of a mother brought him into this world and I, Crixus, will be the instrument of that retribution."

There was the hint of a smile on the pain-wracked face as the old man drew his final breath and relaxed in the attitude of death, closing his eyes for the last time. Crixus gently lowered the frail body back down onto the cot once more and covered his face with the single linen sheet. Grief and sorrow merged into one soul-destroying force, now fuelled by terrible, overwhelming and destructive anger. It welled up inside him, deep, corrosive and monumental – threatening to consume him and destroy any last vestiges of reason or coherent thought.

Roman justice was about to deny him the means of purging his soul of the demons who now dwelt there, teasing, mocking, scorning and pointing their fingers accusingly. In the semi-gloom of the cubiculum, a tiny ray of hope pierced the darkness that filled his mind and he cupped it to him, nurturing it like a candle flame in the night as he voiced a silent prayer to Nemesis – goddess of chance, fortune and revenge.

111

19

When it was taken into account the circumstantial evidence and testimony of the two witnesses there could be no real doubt as to the outcome of Ferox' trial. A street thug and known criminal nurturing an inbred contempt for authority and all things decent, he represented just the kind of vile canker Roman society was doing its utmost to be rid of.

Julius Quintus had been a much-revered figure in the public-works sector and befriended many people over the years. His senseless killing by the leering character now standing before the court in chains had provoked a sense of outrage and as the guilty verdict was announced they gave vent to their feelings. With raised arms and clenched fists they punched the air and demanded angrily, "Death, death, death...."

The magistrates conferred among themselves a few moments longer and then, reaching a unanimous decision, nodded and the senior judge held up his hands gesturing for silence. Reluctantly the court fell quiet and he delivered his pronouncement.

"You see before you a miserable wretch who displays no remorse for his violent, cowardly act against one of our brothers. Like a vile leech sucking the lifeblood from its host, this – criminal – is content to prey on the weak and vulnerable, robbing, stealing and murdering to fuel his filthy and unearthly habits.

"We have conferred among ourselves and agree death is the only sentence we can pass here. However, even we senior judges recognise mere death – execution in the arena by whatever means will not in itself serve any great purpose other than a few minutes of entertainment for the crowds and we are therefore on this occasion willing to give the condemned before you a chance to repay something of his debt to society before he leaves this world for ever."

Focusing his steely gaze upon Ferox again the senior magistrate now spoke for the last time as punishment was duly awarded.

"As a show of clemency you are hereby sentenced to be taken to the gladiatorial school of Capua where you will work and train with the scum and rabble abounding within its walls. You will find the harsh regime a contrast to what you have become familiar with on the streets of Rome and we are further agreed you will never leave that place unless under transportation to fight in the great arena should you ever aspire to such prominence. Take him away - sentence to be carried out immediately."

The court dispersed amid shouted protests and murmurings of both disapproval and incredulity. Ferox might live for years, become a champion and a hero of the people or, in the worst possible scenario, be awarded his freedom at the hand of some ill-informed and fawning emperor. But, for one man, the verdict was something in the way of a reprieve and a bizarre indication perhaps the gods had not completely deserted him after all. Since holding Julius Quintus while he drew his last breath there was hope at last to avenge personally the old man who would now never pass on the knowledge of the great buildings.

Crixus knew exactly what he must do. In the wake of Julius' mindless slaying this was to be his new chosen path and he relished the outcome as inwardly he vowed to give his utmost in mind and body in pursuance of that objective. It would be five years out of his life and the first three months would either make or break him but he saw it as his only escape from the demons that now haunted his soul. He would not enlist at Capua – that would be too easy for he would surely kill Ferox the first time they met. No, this would be a far more appropriate way and eventually he would have his revenge for all to see. He was filled with renewed anticipation of the work he faced and in light of this change of fortune he felt the blood quicken in his veins, heightening his senses as he set out on the walk to Ludus Gallicus, his new home for only the gods knew how long.

20

Ludus Gallicus Gladiator School

From the outside it might have been the gateway to the afterlife with only a small decorative portal set into the high stone walls surrounding the main complex of buildings. Although the regime was less harsh compared with other schools – especially since the Spartacus rebellion of 73 B.C. there were still many guards in evidence and Crixus pondered what awaited him on the other side.

In exchange for a handful of gold he had sold his freedom and Roman citizenship for five years as part of the contract he now entered into with the owner of the school. The *lanista* was a celebrated ex-gladiator, awarded the *rudis* or wooden sword by the emperor, Nero, back in A.D. 50. A free man and Roman citizen, Lentulus Fulvius had gained a reputation for fairness and persistence without the associated brutality and was consequently turning out some of the most dynamic and skilled fighters Rome had ever seen.

Standing in line with the rest of his current intake, Crixus had sworn the gladiators' oath of allegiance to the lanista, submitting himself unreservedly to the demanding training regime and agreeing to punishment by fire, sword and death if he should disobey or attempt to escape. There were other free men here too and dressed in fine clothes, either having fallen on hard times and seeking to redeem themselves or simply in it for the thrill – to be a gladiator!

"Many of you will not make the grade!" Lentulus Fulvius told them flatly with hands upon hips and fists clenched. "Those freeborn among you who fail the training will have your contracts cancelled upon return of the gold paid out. For the rest, if you train hard and make your mark the rewards will be great. You will be well-fed and receive the best medical care available. As you progress and begin to make your first public appearances, there will be women and they will pay much to be with you on the eve of any contest when you will feast well. But that is all in the future and first there is much work to do. I have a reputation to uphold and by all that is sacred I swear to continue in the same unblemished manner. This school is second only to the great Ludus Magnus but within a year that position will be reversed if the gods are willing."

He allowed them a few moments of contemplation before continuing, "Rest well tonight and bathe yourselves for tomorrow the training begins in earnest. Some of you have gone to fat – a measure of your over-indulgent lifestyles. Too much rich food, too much wine with scant regard to work and discipline. You will find the training hard. Others...," and he indicated Crixus with a slap to the shoulder, "others like this man here are clearly no stranger to hard work and for you the training will be easier. Until tomorrow....you are dismissed to your quarters."

They were marched away by their escorts to the barracks that would be their homes for the next few years but as Crixus turned to follow the others, the lanista, who had been watching him keenly, pointed an outstretched arm in his direction.

"You there! Wait a while." He approached Crixus who appeared troubled at being singled out while lesser men had been allowed to walk away apparently unnoticed. "My eyes tell me you are different to your fellow novices. You are cultured and respectful and I'd like to wager you didn't get those muscles pouring wine in any street tavern. Clearly you have not been forced upon me by any magistrate so what brings you to a place like this? Fame in the arena? The prospect of riches, perhaps? Women? Come, you make speak freely."

Crixus pondered the question for a moment before answering. In the end the truth was always best.

"Have you heard about the recent trial and sentence of the man, Ferox?"

"An unsavoury character to say the least," Lentulus Fulvius made his position all too clear. "His crime was an act of mindless brutality against a person not able to defend himself. I heard as a reprieve he was sent to train at Capua if you can call that a reprieve. But what is that to you? He was a common murderer, a street thug from the gutter, a man with neither principles nor honour. The sentence should have been one of drawn-out execution there and then."

"His execution will indeed be a long and drawn-out affair if the two of us should ever meet," and the lanista began to pick up the thread of where this was leading. "His victim was a man called Julius Quintus, a public works official and the best friend I ever had. He was like a father to me. We worked on many projects together and I had just returned from a two-year spell in Greece learning how to cut marble. When I eventually found him he had lost much blood and was weak from the wound. His last request was that I embrace him as a son and he died in my arms."

"Go on," Lentulus prompted, nodding imperceptibly as the motives became clearer.

"If the sentence of the court has been simple execution I would never have seen Julius' death truly avenged."

"You do not place great store in Roman justice," the lanista regarded Crixus seriously.

"I have the greatest respect for Roman justice. It's just now, all of a sudden this has become extremely personal and I should be the one responsible for Ferox' eventual demise. Executions are carried out every day in the arena and they're becoming so numerous people are leaving their seats through boredom and visiting the taverns. I don't want Ferox' death to be insignificant and fleeting or part of an entertainment interval. When he dies it will be my own hand that rips the heart from his body, in the same way he has pierced mine with a dagger of hatred and burning vengeance. I couldn't do that if the sentence had gone the other way but if I can meet him in the arena – on equal terms, then it becomes a different matter."

"A noble sentiment indeed, young Crixus. I knew you were different to the rest. That you would give up your freedom and Roman citizenship to avenge the death of a friend tells me many things about you. You are built like a gladiator but can you fight and think like one? It's a big stage out there and the crowds are unforgiving if you get it wrong. Tomorrow we shall assess your fitness and only after you have been deemed suitable will we put a sword in your hand – a wooden sword. We do not single men out for special treatment here. If you do not measure up you will be gone within a month. If you show promise and originality we will develop that and you will be the recipient of privileges.

"The crowds are hungry for new blood and they become easily bored with the same routines day after day. A quick kill no longer provides them with the thrills they seek but a man who can go out there and win their hearts with flair, talent and natural acumen will become a champion. They will adore him and cheer for him – tens of thousands of them! Are you that man, Crixus? Have you got something to give the crowds they will love you for? I will make you an offer. If you can prove you possess some quality or attribute other than being able to wield a gladius and kill your opponents in the same old predictable manner, if you can demonstrate an inner fire to be the best – better than anyone who has gone before you, I will arrange for your pairing with Ferox and you may have your revenge. Are we agreed?"

Crixus could well empathise with the lanista's predicament for it was a brutal reality that the capricious and volatile crowds often booed and jeered fighters in the arena – not through boredom alone but as a result of heavy drinking during the midday interval where tension built throughout the heat of the afternoon and restlessness surged through the packed terraces like opposing ripples on a pond. An otherwise forgiving and good natured gathering could turn instantly into an ugly, riotous mob, high on cheap wine and demanding the death of a gladiator purely for the hell of it.

"Until yesterday I had never considered myself a fighter. Now, in light of the court's verdict, everything has changed. I understand the training will be difficult and the risk of death always present but I give you my word I will bring credit to your school. Already in my mind I know what is required if I am to win the crowd and keep them on my side and I accept your offer with gratitude."

"Splendid! It is done then. We have a bargain. Now, be off to your quarters for tomorrow we will see what you are made of," and with his escort of two guards Crixus marched away to join the others in the barracks. Watching him, Lentulus Fulvius allowed himself the luxury of a smile as an inner feeling told him one door had just closed and another was about to open.

Could this be the one – after all these years? Was Crixus that man – at last?

21

The first days of training were already showing up the weaker members of the group and several had been singled out as not worth pursuing. In the first few critical weeks attention was devoted to body strength with a variety of activities coupled to a high-fat, high-protein diet designed to promote body mass. Squatting exercises with enormous weights placed upon the shoulders improved calf and thigh muscles whilst traversing high beams by hand with a second person clinging onto the waist and dangling below developed grip, hand strength and powerful arm and chest muscles.

The pace was gruelling and there were times when even Crixus, who was fittest of the group by far, doubted his ability to continue the punishing routine. Every few days another would drop out through fatigue and exhaustion and miserably await transfer to some lesser establishment as he cursed his inadequacy in not meeting the strict requirements. Just as it seemed their bodies must surely break under the pressure the lanista addressed the group one morning – a group now significantly reduced in number.

"Those of you who remain have already overcome the most physical demands of the training and now it is time to master the ways of the sword. You will learn how to strike, how to guard, how to deceive your opponent and to survive in a situation where it seems all is lost and you are on the point of being defeated. And you will learn how to kill cleanly a defeated opponent who has lost favour with the crowd. At the end of it all you must learn how to confront death yourselves. As gladiators you must embrace it with courage, unflinchingly, with dignity and not begging for your lives. Death comes to us all sooner or later and the best a man can do is smile back and spit in her face. If you fight like men and die like men the crowds will love you and your names will live on long after you have vacated this earth.

"Those of you who possess swift reactions and reflexes will live longest. If you are slow and half-witted you will not survive long and the time and money invested in you will have been wasted. Until I deem you ready for the steel you will fight only with the rudis."

The next real test was to gauge any natural tactical ability they may possess when faced with an opponent. In turn they mounted the rostrum to face a skilled fighter with a blunt wooden sword. The first managed only a single blocking manoeuvre before he was overcome by a rain of blows and sent tumbling onto the straw bales below. The second fared little better and within seconds he too was falling backward through the air onto the dust and straw beneath. It didn't look good and as Crixus was finally handed the rudis by his defeated predecessor the head trainer turned to Lentulus Fulvius apologetically.

"I fear they still have much to learn and I have seen nothing to inspire confidence. One-armed men with blindfolds have been known to give more convincing performances."

"I am keen to see how this one acquits himself. He is different to the others."

Seeing how his comrades had been knocked off their feet in seconds gave Crixus an idea. None of them seemed to know where the blow was coming from until it landed. Too late! Any element of surprise was lost in self-defence. No time to attack. He concentrated, studying the man before him. *Remember the training! Do not meet force with force. Turn the opponent's attack to your advantage!*

Crixus watched the other man, waiting for that first tell-tale sign of movement and when it came he was ready – a direct thrust that would have gutted him like a fish had it connected. He did not step back but rather angled his body so the wooden sword cut the air where he had been standing. The man's impetus carried him forward and with lightning speed Crixus delivered a powerful reversal with his right hand, a cracking blow that smacked into the lower back of his adversary. The impact raised a huge welt that drew blood and began to swell immediately. He came back with another flurry of well-aimed blows which Crixus seemed to regard with amusement. He either sidestepped or, with feet planted firmly on the heavy timber of the raised platform, simply moved his body out of harm's way.

As the duration of the contest increased, Crixus sensed his opponent was tiring and then did what no other fighter under training had ever done before. He dropped the wooden sword and smiled at the other man, goading him. As the opponent delivered another thrust there was something in Crixus' expression that told him it was to be a wasted effort. When it came he grabbed the wooden blade of the rudis and wrenched it free of the man's hand, jerking him off his feet and toppling him over the side of the platform onto the straw below.

Unemotionally, Crixus picked up his own rudis, walked down the steps and handed it to the next man.

"Reflexes, strength, agility and most of all, surprise!" the lanista smacked a fist into the palm of his hand four times to stress these key elements. "Take the fight to the other man. Don't just stand there and react to whatever he does. The crowds always like to be surprised and kept on the edges of their seats. That was good, young Crixus. Slightly clumsy at the end but you show great promise and inventiveness. I've never seen anything like that before. We need to refine your sword work a little but I am pleased with what I have seen today.

"The rest of you need to work much harder if you're going to stay off your arses. Your moves are uncoordinated and lack style. The training will continue until sunset and tomorrow you will be paired off to learn the rudiments of attack and defence. Oh, Crixus – just one more thing. If you want to keep that left hand of yours attached to your body I wouldn't recommend disarming an opponent in such a manner. On a steel gladius you'll lose more than your fingers. If it goes wrong the crowds will regard it as a desperate, suicidal move and never let you forget it."

The lanista was still smiling when he left the training area and his remark to Crixus had been good-natured rather than a criticism. He knew the man was clever enough to work that one out for himself.

"Do you think we have the makings of a champion in our midst?" he asked the senior trainer as they walked away.

"Even at this early stage he bears the hallmarks of greatness. He has lightning reflexes, the speed of which I have never seen before. He is agile for a large man and possesses the strength of Hercules which is always an advantage if other crucial qualities are also present. His eyes are those of a hawk and he appears to gain the measure of his man in seconds. There is still much to teach him about the sword but he is willing and eager to please. He has an inner fire and the steel in him is bright and strong. With a little sharpening he will make a fine gladiator within two months and I'll wager a purse of gold on my instincts."

"He is burning to meet Ferox, the criminal who killed his friend. He has been sentenced to an indeterminate period of incarceration at Capua and I have sworn to bring them together at some point where Crixus may exact his revenge."

"If Crixus is half the man I think he is then Ferox may already be dead. It will not be a quick contest but even before they meet I suspect our man will find favour with the crowds when they look upon him."

22

During the next two months Crixus and the remaining novices who had survived the initial training and mock combats, were introduced to metal weapons and the wooden swords were consigned to basics. The chief difference they all noticed was the weight of the gladius and although several times heavier than the rudis it was still light enough to be wielded effortlessly. Less than two feet long it was a relatively short, broad-bladed stabbing sword with a viciously-tapered point, a weapon that would revolutionise combat techniques in the Roman army and become an iconic piece of military equipment.

Flesh and steel are an unlikely alliance but Crixus knew this was the ultimate fighting weapon as soon as his fingers closed around the grip that terminated in the definitive ball-shape. He used it as an extension of his own body spending hours on the training ground before the others were up and about going through the motions of combat with his eyes closed when the sun was still below the horizon and the air fresh and cool. At his own insistence, he mastered the art of fighting with two swords where he assumed the role of the dimachaerus, wearing neither helmet for protection nor carrying shield for defence. For a big man he was surprisingly nimble on his feet and could dance away effortlessly from a strike that would have gutted a lesser fighter – like one of the big predatory African cats, sleek and menacing.

The strength and determination of his attacks was overwhelming and he struck with the speed and venom of a mamba. His fellow gladiators both respected and venerated him for there was not a man among them who had not heard the story of Julius Quintus. In the wake of Ferox's incarceration at Capua, Crixus had stepped forward like an avenging angel, a man whose place was among the great buildings of the city, a man who knew nothing of gladiatorial combat, of vengeance, death or public spectacle. Would Ferox even survive the training at Capua? Would he be branded a failure and sold on to another school or would he be killed before he and Crixus ever faced each other across the sands of a packed amphitheatre?

It all seemed to be hanging by a thread and only the gods would be instrumental in bringing it all together one day – *and then...?*

At the end of the third month Lentulus Fulvius came to him in the training yard, taking him by one arm and steering him to a private corner where they might not be overheard.

"I have watched you closely these last months, closer than I have watched any man who has found himself under my charge for one reason or another and I am indeed pleased with those things I have seen. If all men who came through those gates were half as good as you I would be an exceedingly rich man by now."

It was a truism in every sense of the word for emblazoned in the stonework above the elegant gates depicting, Ludus Gallicus Gladiatores, was another motivating source of inspiration – Amat Curam Victoria, victory favours those who take pains.

"Before we let you loose on the unsuspecting Roman public I wish to see you fight here in our own small arena. It will be a contest to 'first blood' only and your opponent will not be from this school. Before you ask, let me put your mind at ease by quelling any preconceived ideas you may have already formed about Ferox being the other man. Do not concern yourself at this time. Your day will come all-too-soon and I give my word you will have your revenge before a packed amphitheatre."

"Who is the man I will face in my first contest?" Crixus asked. "Is he a champion with many kills to his credit or a novice like me?"

"I have arranged for you to be paired with a man called Septimus. He is a retiarius and is renowned for his skill with net and trident. I would urge caution on your part as this man has been victorious in three contests. You will fight this afternoon and if you defeat him, as I believe is a distinct possibility, then we will prepare you for much greater events."

"I feel I am ready as I ever will be. The training has been hard but others have found it more taxing. In a way it will be good to face a real opponent rather than a straw man with a wooden sword. I just hope I'm as good as you believe."

"I know you will not bring shame upon me, Crixus. Septimus is good but you are better. Watch out for the net. If you end up on your back it could all be over in the blink of an eye."

"I will watch out for Septimus and his net and, by the gods, he had better watch out for me!"

23

Four hours later, after completing a warm-up session with three sparring partners, Crixus bathed and then – as his daily personal ritual demanded, he knelt before the statue of Nemesis in his sparsely-furnished cell.

"Great Nemesis, Goddess of chance, fortune and revenge, guide my hand in this first test I must face on the long and difficult road to avenging the death of Julius Quintus. Watch over me, your humble servant, with a trusty sword and if perchance I do not emerge victorious then grant me a swift death and merciful release from the shame of failure."

That should do for now. If the battle with Septimus went as planned he would offer up something more in keeping with the event later.

His escort had been dispensed with at the perimeter of the small semi-circular arena. The place was packed and there was little room to move on the tiers of steps overlooking the area where the first contests were taking place. Apart from a discerning cross-section of the general public lucky enough to have gained access there was evidence of the more wealthy too, their presence advertised by fine white and purple togas and not here out of curiosity alone. Truly skilled fighters were something of a rare commodity in Rome these days and citizens of the nobility and Patrician classes were constantly scouring the training schools in search of promising new material to feature in the spectacles they would host as part of their election campaigns.

Lentulus Fulvius had shrewdly delayed Crixus' appearance to the end of the bouts and, as a precautionary measure, had not pre-empted the situation by giving away any secrets concerning his best fighter's tactical acumen and brute strength. They would see for themselves. The boisterous crowd numbered about three thousand, the absolute limit of the public enclosure and had clearly entered into the spirit of the occasion as they cheered, booed and yelled at the two combatants giving it their all out on the sand a few yards away. The fighters appeared well-matched and anything from a few denarii to a small fortune would have been wagered on the outcome. As the duration of the contest lengthened it seemed neither man could find and exploit any weakness. Inevitably - as energy levels dwindled and combat fatigue took its toll, so the referee stepped in and ended it. The result was a draw, greeted by a mixture of applause, curses and oaths from the crowd but also reflected on the training and fitness of the two gladiators who walked away unscathed.

Crixus was attired in full armour and as an attendant handed him sword and shield a cheer went up on the far side of the enclosure when Septimus made his entrance and acknowledged the applause of the crowd. As the cheering died away in expectancy of Septimus' opponent and Lentulus Fulvius introduced his own man, the gate was flung open and Crixus strode in to a smattering of applause. Septimus assumed the readiness stance – dangerous, confident and threatening with the circular wide-meshed throwing net dangling from his left hand whilst the trident was held out horizontally in his right. Crixus, on the other hand, chose to ignore the crowd and strode aggressively up to the other man, coming to a halt less than six inches away and brushing the trident to one side contemptuously with the shield. He stood a good head taller than Septimus who appeared intimidated by the huge figure and retreated half a step. Behind the concealment of the helmet, Crixus glowered and there could be no mistaking the belligerent thrust of that jaw.

It might not be Ferox confronting him but it would be a good place for the crowds to gain their measure of the new man.

Start as you mean to go on. Give no quarter and expect none in return. Every opponent you defeat from this day forward brings you one step closer to Ferox. This is where it all begins...!

The referee approached them carrying his wooden baton which conveyed as much authority as any senatorial mace or legionary standard and addressed both combatants in the small arena now fallen into silence.

"This contest is to first blood only. If you are injured and unable to continue, kneel and raise a finger. At this point your opponent will be declared the winner."

Crixus maintained his stance, forcing Septimus to back off and place distance between them.

"Begin," the barked order signalled the start of the contest and Septimus immediately thrust at Crixus' abdomen with the long-handled trident, swinging the net in a wide arc as he attempted to confuse and divert Crixus' attention. He was light on his feet and moved with

124

deceptive speed as he searched for gaps and weaknesses in his defence. The razor-sharp prongs of the trident danced and weaved just inches from Crixus' helmet and he could see how Septimus' expression betrayed his anger at being unable to force a retreat. Crixus gave no ground and merely swayed like a willow in a gale to avoid being hit. Whether the crowd's whoops and cheers were attributed to Septimus' skill with the trident or his own spirited defence, he could not gauge but decided it was time to make a decisive move.

As the trident struck out again, rather than meet the blow head on he angled his body to the left, allowing his shield to guide the weapon out of harm's way. But there was still the net and just as it was about to imprison him like some grotesque spider's web Crixus allowed the momentum of his left turn to carry him in a full circle, raising his sword arm as he came back to face Septimus and catching him a powerful forehand to the side of his head. Fortunately for Septimus the gladius landed flat-side on or he would have lost the top of his skull. Either way the retiarius was stunned by the force of the blow and for a moment his grip on the trident faltered. Crixus' sword arm was still raised and, reversing the action, he caught the net on the point of the gladius and flicked it over Septimus' head to the accompaniment of another great outburst of applause and cheering from those who looked on. Ensnared by his own net, Septimus could do little but thrust ineffectively with the trident but the game was over. And then, Crixus did the unthinkable – he dropped sword and shield into the sand at his feet and wrenched the trident out of Septimus' hands and snapped the heavy wooden shaft cleanly in two, breaking it over his knee. At last Septimus disentangled himself from the net, hurling it from him and reached for the dagger – his last means of defence – *or attack!*

This would be the ultimate test of his courage and fortitude, he reasoned. He had discarded his own weapons and now faced a wickedly-sharp knife in the hands of an angry opponent. But he would not be cowed at this stage of the proceedings where he had already given good account of himself as an unblooded novice. As the blade hissed and cut the air just inches from his chest and the noisy spectators lapsed into uneasy silence once more, he judged the moment and blocked the attack with his left forearm, delivering a crashing blow to the side of Septimus' jaw with a balled right fist and his opponent fell to the ground like a sack of corn.

The crowds were on their feet with rapturous applause, stamping and whistling for this new sensation yet to make his first appearance in the great amphitheatre. What manner of man threw down his weapons and overcame an adversary bare-handed? But Crixus was not quite finished yet and rather than leave the small arena he removed his helmet and laid it next to the sword and shield while his audience ceased their riotous accolades.

"Citizens – citizens of Rome, you insult me! I came here today expecting to fight for my life. I have trained hard, unbelievably hard for three months and you send me this – this piece of shit!" and he spat on the recumbent form of Septimus. "When you have a worthy opponent for me I shall return," and he walked away without another word as the resurgence of thunderous acclaim rent the air asunder all about him. Watching his man storm out of the arena glowering with rage, Lentulus Fulvius could not hide the huge grin that creased his sun-bronzed face and exposed the square white teeth for whilst he retained every confidence in Crixus to defeat his opponent, he had not quite envisaged this display of self-disregard and utter contempt for death.

24

Curule aedile, Caius Attius Caecilius was in an ebullient mood as he assessed once again his chances of ascending the political and social ladder another step. There could be no doubt life had been satisfying and rewarding these last years since his election as one of the twenty quaestors automatically granting him eligibility for membership into that noble body of government – the senate. In this relatively junior position he had administered the finances of the state treasury and, as was the case with all military men of officer status, served in various capacities throughout some of the nearer provinces. Essentially he was a sun-lover but even Spain with its unrelenting, eye-searing heat and vast expanses of sun-parched wilderness and barren landscape had proved too much.

Two years ago he had been elected to the rank of curule aedile, one of four who supervised public places and oversaw games and spectacles. He had also presided over many of the public works contracts including the rebuilding of those areas devastated during the great fire.

Again he pondered those other celebrated and illustrious men who had gone before him and heralded from similar aristocratic backgrounds. Without exception they had all risen to the lofty heights of general and commanded whole armies as Rome expanded her borders and filled the treasury coffers with untold spoils from conquered lands. There was Lucius Licinius Lucullus who had eventually quelled the Spartacus rebellion after nine of his contemporaries were defeated by the slave army. Gaius Marius had been uncle to the legendary Gaius Julius Caesar and, his Nemesis and bitter political rival, Lucius Cornelius Sulla, famously notorious for his proscriptions among those he saw as a threat to his continued hold on power. There was Gnaeus Pompey, another great statesman who had reluctantly taken up arms at the senate's insistence when Caesar returned from Spain and crossed the Rubicon. Pompey the Great had been subsequently murdered in Egypt by the Ptolemy dynasty as the civil war took the fight to even more-distant shores and Caesar had been appalled by the pointless slaughter of his former friend.

In Caius Attius Caecilius' mind, if a man could not rise to the top by virtue of his own merits and the senate remained blind to such potential, then there were other ways a man could still see his dream realised and Caesar himself had been a master, employing violence, public disorder and threats to political rivals. Least of all, what remained inviolate could ultimately be bought.

They all lived a reasonably extravagant existence in the splendid villa on the Via Sacra, he mused. It was a huge pretentious dwelling set among tall umbrella pines that helped shade the house from the fierce summer sun. Just beyond the atrium and its surrounding portico where figs grew up through the tessellated paving, a large private swimming pool caught the best of the sun from mid morning to late afternoon. The roofs had all been recently stripped and renovated with bright red tiles and the surrounding walls were lavishly decorated with mosaics and frescoes.

Yes, this latest position had served him well and he had been able to procure the house's purchase for a fraction of its real worth.

And yet there was something missing in his life. Despite the relative security of his position within the senate and the luxuries surrounding him there was an ominous brooding lack of fulfilment and happiness within his marriage. Agrippina was a rare beauty when he had married her thirty years ago and he thought life could not possibly give him any more. Drusilla was born three years later and the image of her mother, tall and naturally elegant, that long graceful neck and proud bearing endowing her with the grace and allure of a deity and he reflected how he had watched her grow from gawky, long-limbed child into full luscious ripe womanhood, the envy of his colleagues and the source of limitless trouble from potential suitors who saw Drusilla as a means of gaining access to the family wealth.

But his passionate affair with Agrippina had been short-lived when, for no apparent reason, she had become sick and never recovered. One moment she could be calm and lucid and then, without warning, she would adopt a strange and disturbing countenance, falling to the ground writhing and foaming, biting her tongue and lips. There was little he could do but recoil in horror as the woman he loved convulsed on the floor in front of him, her body twisting into impossible shapes while her eyes rolled back into her skull. Over the years love had been replaced by revulsion and he could no longer stand to be in the same house, especially as her condition appeared to have worsened dramatically.

Happy and somewhat relieved for Drusilla to look after her mother he made excuses to be away from the house whenever possible, voicing the heavy responsibilities of office as his reason.

They both sensed and resented his discomfort and constant need to be away from the family home but the situation was ideal for Caius in a bizarre and perverse way for while the mother was ill Drusilla was kept tethered by the firm rein of her conscience and sense of duty looking after her. He provided for them, kept a roof over their heads and nothing more. He would have liked their gratitude and recognition for his continued achievements in the political arena but it was not forthcoming. As he lingered on the vision of his daughter he realised he had not once asked her if she was happy, and who could blame her if she was not? She had lost contact with her circle of friends because most of her waking hours were spent caring and looking out for Agrippina. She never spoke of meeting men, going out and having fun or doing any of those normal things that might fill the world of a young, wealthy and extremely desirable woman of the aristocracy.

These last weeks Caius had even more reason for spending extended periods away from the house. There were elections on the horizon again for the influential and esteemed appointment of praetor and all the enhanced benefits of power, wealth and status it would bring. There were eight praetors and they served primarily as magistrates in the law courts but could also convene the senate and assemblies on matters of urgency or times of crisis. They assumed the administrative duties of consuls in their absence and when their term of office was up they might govern one of Rome's many provinces as a propraetor.

In his mind's eye he saw himself governing one of the more exotic corners of the empire, not one of those miserable postings he had endured during the early part of his aedileship. He had money and could surround himself with those luxuries and pleasures he ought to be enjoying at home but the more he thought about *her,* the greater was his aversion to being a part of it and inwardly he shuddered. He was still in reasonably good shape, had most of his own teeth and apart from a little middle-age spread had not yet developed those sagging old-man's tits many of his colleagues sported. He had seen them in the public baths with their great bloated, hairy bodies and skinny legs and even at banquets and social functions they still had women and girls fussing over them.

He missed the touch of a woman as he briefly recalled how it had once been between him and Agrippina but she was gone from him now and he would never know her that way again. The prospect of a future posting to a more distant territory could change all that and his lower body began to ache as he thought about some of the women he had seen on his travels and wondered what it would be like to have one of them. Persian women were reputed to be extraordinarily skilful lovers and those large-breasted African matrons could drive a man out of his mind with their Nefertiti beauty, pleasing fingers and sensuous dark flesh.

With a considerable effort he shut the images out of his mind and concentrated on the forthcoming elections and what would be required to secure the votes of the electorate. Improved conditions and regular employment would ease the situation for many where taxation was a constant burden prone to increase overnight but there were limits to his powers and he was in no position to alter or overturn government legislation. People seemed to like gifts, especially money, and that would mean delving into his own personal coffers with no guaranteed results of a successful outcome on the day. However, there remained one means of reaching tens of thousands with a single throw of the dice and had been utilised by political rivals and their predecessors for more than two centuries; entertainment, public spectacle, games – *gladiators!*

The mob was hungry for entertainment, lavish spectacle – *and blood!* Rome boasted a population of one million souls, the largest single collection of human beings anywhere on the planet. It also nurtured a correspondingly large number of unemployed. What more effective way could there be of reaching eighty-thousand people bored out of their skulls by the daily repetition of nothing going on in their lives? Give them what they wanted – an above-average pageant and extravaganza of martial prowess and superior fighting skills and the rewards could be incalculable.

Another question then floated across the horizon of his mind as he attempted to gauge the possibility of providing and financing such a show or series of shows in the arena. In the pursuance of popularity among the voting public, the only effective means of procuring the desired result was by securing the services of a proven champion, a man capable of outclassing all those sent against him. Such a man would immediately win the hearts of the tens of thousands who flocked to see the best spectacles in the empire and the same would apply to the local politician financing them.

This would be his chosen route then but it was not without its basic problems. The greatest obstacle as Caius saw it, was finding the right man for the job. There had been no serious champion material emerging from the schools in years and no exceptional fighters still under training, waiting to make their first public appearances. He had visited the arena contests many times in recent months and there was nothing promising in evidence. Perhaps he should search the major training schools for an update on any up-and-coming stars while the outside world remained blissfully unaware. There were four principal schools in Rome – three of which trained and developed the various categories of gladiator while the fourth specialised in the bestiarii and venatorii who stalked wild animals. There was a huge school at Capua where Spartacus had begun his slave rebellion but they trained mainly slaves, renegades and scum from the gutters. Any one of them would slit your throat as soon as look at you.

He would confine his searches to the city for the time being and then move outwards if his diligence proved unrewarding. He would take Drusilla with him for men always seemed to perform with greater style and panache when the eyes of a beautiful woman were upon them. Drusilla had been speaking recently of an apothecary, one of her closest friends who appeared particularly gifted in the manufacture of preparations, potions and mixtures which, allegedly, relieved the symptoms of certain afflictions and ailments and cured others completely. If it pleased her to embark upon this fool's errand in search of a fictional panacea for her mother's illness then so be it. No harm could result and if it gave them something else to talk about instead of bemoaning his own shortcomings, then that was all right by him.

But not until he had found the object of his searching. In the morning they would visit Ludus Magnus first, reputedly the finest school in all Rome. It shouldn't take long; he need only speak with the lanista and inspect the goods personally to verify whether or not there was anything worthy of investment. He simply had to have the right man and it needed to be soon. If he settled for anything less than absolute best he would not only be risking potentially huge sums of money, he could end up the subject of ridicule when it all came crashing down and he stood dejected amid the remnants of his dream.

He couldn't bear the thought of sniggering and joviality directed at him from all quarters so he imagined being the recipient of congratulations and public acclaim, pleasant and deserving rewards just beyond reach of his grasp but not altogether a million miles away. One successful throw of the dice was all he needed. It all hinged on finding the right man for the job and it was virtually assured from then on. He had seen it happen so many times before. Promises were no longer enough these days. The populace had come to distrust politicians over the years and not without good reason. They were impressed by deeds that lent credibility to those performing them and failure was no longer an option. If Ludus Magnus was unable to come up with the goods, then, as second choice, he would move on to Gallicus where, hopefully, the pickings might be a little richer. He had heard somewhere this school was a little more selective in who it admitted and the lanista was particularly jealous of his reputation regarding the standard of fighter it turned out. It was rumoured he would never send an undertrained or poor-quality fighter into the arena purely to satisfy demand and would rather sell them on to another school rather than waste their lives and bring shame upon his establishment.

Both Caius and Drusilla could have no possible idea how in the next twenty-four hours, their lives were to be changed for ever. At the Ludus Gallicus, plans were already being set in motion which, shortly, would dramatically revolutionize the concept of gladiatorial combat in the arena.

25

Drusilla was seated at her mother's bedside, thankful now sleep had come to the tortured figure who lay exhausted before her. Accustomed as she was to seeing Agrippina in the throes of violent convulsions after collapsing to the floor, she had been truly frightened by this latest and most devastating attack so far. She could not be restrained from the flailing arms and serpentine writhing motions of her torso and it was as if her body had been possessed by evil spirits intent on destroying their host.

Her strength was superhuman and all Drusilla could do was watch in horror and let the fit run its course – fearful for her own safety if she should attempt to intervene. When it was over she lifted Agrippina onto her bed with the assistance of the domestic servants and held her hand, crooning softly as, finally, sleep overcame the dreadful spasms and the body relaxed.

"This is the last straw!" she made the decision, both to Agrippina and any of the gods who might be bold enough to be listening. "This simply cannot be allowed to continue. The physicians are worse than useless with their leeches and mumbled inanities. I will go and speak with Quintina in the morning. She is wise and will know how best to treat such an affliction. I should never have allowed your condition to deteriorate to this level without consulting her. Forgive me, mother. I could have spared you much suffering these last months but I seldom venture out and have ceased contact with those I once looked upon as friends."

She gently dabbed the perspiration from Agrippina's brow and carefully wiped away the last vestiges of froth and spittle from her mouth.

"Why can't father be here at times like this when he is most needed?" and her voice had risen again as she gave vent to her anger and frustration. "He only thinks of his precious reputation and social standing among others of his kind. I would gladly give up all we have here to see you well again, mother."

Recognising the need for sleep and rest, Drusilla left Agrippina alone and closed the partitioning curtain behind her. The atmosphere in the house felt heavy and oppressive and she walked through the atrium with its palms and figs and sat down next to the cool waters of the pool, watching the sunlight play upon the ripples stirred by the warm breeze. It was indeed a cruel scenario as she pondered how her life had changed these last years, what with Agrippina's ever-worsening condition compounded by her father's reluctance to spend any time with her. Yes, they lived well and wanted for nothing but it grieved her to see how a love once so transparent had degenerated into revulsion, especially for him. Drusilla was existing in every sense of the word, from one day to another. This was no life at all when she considered what she could be doing. She used to have friends, meeting regularly, going out and having fun. Most of them were doing exciting things now, she reflected sadly. They had good marriages and prominent social status – and she was here confined like a prisoner within these walls.

They would meet in one another's homes or visit taverns and sit together in their clique over an amphora of wine, discussing the type of men they would like to meet and describing in the most finite detail the circumstances of such assignations. It seemed all but herself had fulfilled their dreams, lived the fairy tale and she had been left behind – a cruel and bizarre form of collateral damage and the price to be paid for nurturing any form of conscience.

"Selfish bitch!" she berated herself, snapping out of her melancholy in an instant as she recognised just how well-off she really was compared to her mother. But the feeling of life passing her by was not so easily shrugged off and she yearned to live the fairy tale herself and be swept off her feet by....and she could not think who this fantasy character might be nor even put face or name to him. But for now she contented herself with her own powers of recognition and an unquestioning awareness that destiny worked in the most unpredictable ways.

I will know him when I see him. If he is the right one I will know him beyond all doubt. My heart will tell me. Cast aside any preconceived ideas you may be harbouring about this man. He will love you above all others and pledge his blood in defence of that love!

Inwardly she thrilled at the prospect of such an encounter and forgot, briefly, the anguish and sorrow she had felt just a short while ago.

It would be good to see Quintina again. It had been months since they last made love and she immersed herself in the delights of her friend's warm, sensuous flesh – enjoying multiple climaxes as they explored one another's bodies with moist tongues and teasing fingers. They shared all manner of secrets and spoke openly but, she remembered, as all good and true friends do, even after a protracted period of separation they would pick up on each other's lives as if it had been only last week. She would slip away early in the morning to visit Quintina and leave word with the house slaves to guard her mother vigilantly until she returned a short time later. She smiled as her thoughts lingered on her friend, lifting her spirits and rolling back all those unpleasant issues which seemed to gradually encroach on a world no longer carefree and untroubled, smothering and crowding her with gloom and the heavy weight of oppressiveness.

She could be so many things; funny, scary, extremely vulgar when it came to bodily functions and unbelievably descriptive about her fleeting sexual encounters with the young gods who were apparently never in short supply, although her intimate relationship with Drusilla was sacrosanct in her own mind where their mutual soaring abandon always left them spent and depleted. Drusilla could well appreciate why men found her so attractive. She was quite tall – around five feet ten and her deportment was suggesting of aristocratic or noble breeding giving rise to an aura of aloofness depending on her mood. She had the most piercing green eyes and wore her flaming auburn hair tied up for the most part while strands and wisps hung down the sides of her face. She paid scant attention to the restraints and conventions of society where dress-codes were concerned and did pretty much as she pleased, adopting stolas and rough-woven garments that showed off much of her shapely legs and voluptuous cleavage.

She loved rare and expensive jewellery and admitted to a weakness for huge ostentatious brooches and fibula which secured the folds and fastenings of her more elegant garments. They were of a similar age and had known each other since early childhood although their social differences had never been allowed to come between them. Her laugh was infectious and when she had been drinking she could be loud and raucous. In addition, depending upon which prominent politician or emperor might be the subject of topical debate at the time, she was known to offer theories purporting to the man's birth and number of fathers implicated in conception.

Quintina lived only a couple of miles from Drusilla where the Via Sacra left the main built-up areas and headed out into the open spaces beyond. The house was larger than she needed, with rendered and whitewashed walls and traditional red-tiled roof. The rooms were spread over one level and contained mostly shelves stacked with the accoutrements of her trade. There were herbs and spices of every description – some native to Italy whilst others had their origins in the distant reaches of the empire where Rome's commerce routes were still expanding and her merchant fleet ventured ever further in search of new lands and opportunities.

There were oils distilled from trees and plants; roots, mosses, seeds and dried leaves, creams and lotions. There were preparations and embrocations for just about every kind of human ailment, from piles to nose-bleeds and any spaces not already occupied by this vast array of jars and amphorae were taken up by yet more stacks of books and journals she had accumulated over the years. The house was set back from the road on a small rise and a spring on the side of the slope gushed cool, sweet water in abundance and cascaded into a deep rock pool before flowing on again to join the Tiber some three miles away. The large gardens front and rear were full of beautiful scented blooms that proliferated in the rich soil while others spread their flower-laden branches over rustic arbours and clung to the rough render of the house walls.

There were bees here too for honey formed an essential base constituent in many of her treatments and was always in abundance. Elsewhere there was lavender of every variety and colour, adding its heady aroma to the warm summer air. There was rosemary and thyme, feverfew for the treatment of headaches, sage and hyssop and, adding further vibrant colour and beauty were dense bushes laden with orange flowers. From the leaves came petitgrain and from the rich petals, neroli and bergamot used for relaxation and the treatment of sleep disorders. The garden to the rear was circumscribed by a high wall offering privacy and seclusion – not solely for Quintina but any of her visitors who might wish to spend time alone reflecting upon a particular issue in their lives; an incurable disease, the imminent death of a loved one or a recent bereavement – *and there was always romance!* How to attract that elusive, distant and seemingly-unattainable member of the opposite sex with all its problems of desirability, self-confidence, tongue-tiedness as Quintina liked to think of it and basic good old-fashioned physical attraction. In her mind nothing could surpass that age-old earthly element – chemistry. It was a key ingredient and any relationship was doomed to failure before too long without it. What better portent for the future could there be than the fire which suddenly ignited inside the breast of man and woman alike when they recognised the person destiny had brought their way?

There were interconnecting paths here where a person or persons might stroll at leisure and take in the delights of the warm sunshine and heavy scents of herbs and flowers. Insects of every kind were drawn to this peaceful haven and in the summer months especially, damsel and huge multi-coloured emperor dragon flies abounded in the reed beds of the slowly meandering stream. The only onlookers here were the many busts and statues gazing out upon the world with their unseeing eyes while strands of variegated ivy encroached upon their tall plinths. In this tranquil setting where the only sounds to be heard were the hum of insects' wings, birdsong and the stirring of the benevolent breeze through the palm fronds and cicada leaves, Quintina lived her introvert lifestyle and sought to alleviate a small part of humanity's suffering.

"Drusilla, are you there?"

That dreadfully-familiar voice conveyed just a hint of irritation and startled her out of her reverie. She had been sitting by the pool much longer than intended and now, unbelievably, her father was here, shattering the mood of peace and quiet and instantly replacing it with tension and animosity. With a sigh she stood up and walked back through the atrium, meeting Caius in the living area. Despite his obvious annoyance at her delay in presenting herself immediately, she detected an aura of smugness and self-congratulation in his demeanour – and he had been drinking again for she could smell the wine on his breath.

"You might show a little respect when you enter this place and keep your voice down," she went straight onto the offensive, her dark eyes flashing angrily while inwardly she seethed. "Mother remains gravely ill and as I recall you have forfeited all rights to enter our home. Your very presence sickens her and I have come to despise the person you are. What possible reason could you have for being here?"

Instantly, any good feelings he may have been nurturing were swept away by Drusilla's unpredictable outburst and he responded violently.

"You insolent bitch!" he snarled, the rosettes of anger blooming high on cheeks already flushed with alcohol. "How dare you address your father in such a manner? You are my daughter and will conduct yourself in a suitably-appropriate manner at all times."

"It's a pity the acknowledgement of your responsibilities does not extend as far as your wife," she came back, now fuelled and armed for a direct confrontation. "I may exhibit all the frills and trimmings of a lady and simpering virgin in public but don't you ever dare test my patience or you'll see a side of me you don't care for. I ceased to be afraid of you the day you walked out of that door. You can bully and threaten and intimidate but you will only succeed in making me loathe you even more than I do now. Why don't you get straight to the point of your business here? It must be something monumental or life-changing since you hardly show your face these days."

He sensed further conflict at this point would only serve to exasperate matters and he needed her cooperation, if only in the short term. He had never witnessed her so angry and belligerent, standing with hands on hips with her jaw thrust out in a challenging manner. She had certainly undergone some changes since he vacated the family home and he could only attribute it to the constant demands of nursing her mother and the fact her so-called friends no longer called or sent invitations to join them.

"I will be visiting two of the training schools in the morning in search of promising gladiators to sponsor in the forthcoming games and it is imperative we find the right material if I am to emerge victorious in the praetorial elections."

"We...?" she was immediately suspicious of his motives but he chose to ignore the distraction.

"The crowds are volatile and unpredictable and only the best in entertainment will pacify them, thus securing valuable votes at the ballot. Your presence will add an element of spice and refinement to those squalid places where only death and misery prevail. Men in their positions somehow give even more of themselves when in the company of a beautiful woman and I like to see the hungry looks on their faces."

It was no less than she had expected and his superior attitude inflamed her once more.

"You should be wary not to topple from those lofty heights where you piss on the rest of the world."

"Guard your tongue, woman," he seethed and she could see her words had found their mark. "You will obey me in this matter."

"I have my own business to attend before I accompany you on any such trivial foraging."

"And what of your mother?" he demanded. "Who will tend your mother so early in the day when you are out on the streets?"

Her anger boiled over and she screamed back at him with such venom he drew back a pace and seemed to cringe beneath the verbal onslaught.

"My mother! My mother! Always my mother! Never your wife! She is still the woman you married and the mother of your daughter. Why don't you be a man for the first time in your life and face up to your responsibilities? You deserted us both and I hate you for what you've become. You're so puffed up with your own self-importance you have no time even for your own family. All that matters is you, you, you and your precious ego! You're insufferable!" and she stabbed an accusing finger repeatedly in his face.

"You keep me a virtual prisoner inside this house day after day, month after month, looking after mother. I have no friends, I have lost contact with everyone and what do you do? You contribute absolutely nothing to her care. You swagger in here when it suits you, stinking of wine and issuing your demands and expectations. Where were you this afternoon when she needed you? Today was the worst it's ever been and where were you? Drunk with one of your whores...!"

Despite the unfamiliar visage of his daughter with her features twisted into a mask of hatred he recovered somewhat from her scathing indictments and slapped her back and forth across her face, two stinging blows that left livid angry marks. It was the first time he had struck her and instantly he experienced a pang of remorse for this brutal action but it was too late. The damage was done.

"You ungrateful bitch!" he snarled. "How dare you speak to me that way? Have I not raised and provided for you all these years, given you a good home, wealth and status and you repay me with your insults? How dare you?"

"You have given everything but yourself!" she came back at him and he could see the two slaps had done nothing to knock the fire out of her. If anything she was more determined than ever. "How can you call me ungrateful when I am the one who nurses your wife while you are out drinking and whoring and living the high-life with your friends? You should be the one with the troubled conscience – not I."

He made as if to strike her again and she stood her ground, her head angled to one side, daring him to hit her once more and he lowered his hand. She sensed this small capitulation on his part and continued, her tone and body language underlining the uncomfortable awareness she was, as she had previously stated, no longer afraid of him.

"It is already agreed the house slaves will watch over mother for the short duration of my absence and I thought even you might have arranged for her care during the day if I am to be at your side like some faithful lap-dog. If she was to suffer an accident or take a fall during one of her seizures it would suit your purpose rather conveniently wouldn't it? Oh, and don't you fret about me being out on the streets so early in the morning. That little errand I'll be going on is to the apothecary – the only true and lasting friend I have in this world. She may just be able to alleviate some of mother's suffering while others, apparently, are doing nothing and remain indifferent to her needs as a human being."

"Make sure you're back here by the time I arrive. I have arranged for transport to convey us to the Ludus Magnus in the first instance and if that particular inquiry proves fruitless we will go on to Ludus Gallicus. Two schools in one day should be sufficient and, who knows, if I find what I am looking for and my election is secured in the coming weeks you may be rid of me for ever."

"And just what do you mean by that?" she was scarcely able to believe they might be left in peace at last.

"Divorce, my dear, founded on irreconcilable differences and the fact your mother is no longer able to provide the services of a wife. It's all the fashion these days. If I win this next election I can walk away for good and you can afford to let me go. As a parting gift I will leave you this house and all that goes with it. As you so rightly point out, your mother needs full-time help and I am in no position to be even a small part of that. Anything there may once have been between us is now gone and I feel only loathing – not even pity."

"I hate you!" she spat back and her fists were balled. "I hate you more than I thought it was possible to hate another person. I'll be glad when you're gone. In fact I hope one of your gladiators slits your traitorous throat."

"Just be ready in the morning when I come for you!" and he was scarlet with rage. He turned to leave and was about to walk away when Drusilla's deceptively calm but menacing words filled him with icy fingers of doubt and an eerie confirmation of his own mortality.

"Before you go there is one more thing you need to know. If you ever lay a hand on me again, I swear I'll kill you. Now get out!"

Her own words appalled her for she was not given to thoughts of violence but Caius had overstepped the mark and gone far beyond the limits of anything she was prepared to tolerate. His expression mirrored shock and something that disturbed him deeply as he saw how her black eyes glared into his very soul and flashed cold fire.

26

His hands were awash with blood and it was daubed on the rough woven fabric of his simple tunic. He was not in the arena but walking through the streets of the city with the old man's limp and broken form cradled in those powerful arms while his life ebbed away and splashed onto the cobbles beneath. Curious onlookers opened a path for him, their expressions echoing the grief and lancing pain that surged mercilessly through his own breast without respite.

"You are my son," the words were seemingly nothing more than a hoarse whisper before the eyes rolled back in death and Crixus felt his heart might break.

"Where is Ferox?" he demanded angrily of the crowd.

"Gone where you will never find him," they taunted. "No peace for poor old Julius. His spirit will wander this earth for eternity and never know the glory of Elysium." Their distorted and magnified faces closed in all about him, leering and accusing, their very numbers squeezing the breath from his lungs. "Julius is dead, Ferox is gone. You failed Julius, a man you called a friend. Who will avenge him now? Failed – failed – failed...." Their fingers pointed at him like daggers and he felt like a condemned man at his trial.

As he struggled upward from the depths of the now-familiar but gut-wrenching dream into full awareness, Crixus was thankful to be back in the relative sanctuary of his tiny cell. The dream was always the same and left him panting for breath and deeply troubled as their numbers threatened to crush him. He knew it would never leave him until his business with Ferox was settled and he could finally purge the demons of self-doubt and that strange anger he found so difficult to keep in check. He would speak to Lentulus Fulvius in the morning about his chances of visiting an apothecary. These people were reputed to work wonders with their herbs, potions and unearthly bond with nature and the cosmos but could they soothe a troubled mind as well as an ailing body?

In the training area Crixus went through the usual routines with the others and spent even more time perfecting his own unique style of fighting no one seemed able to match. He was the largest by far but could perform feats of agility and fleet-footedness beyond the capability of any opponent despite the weight of armour and weaponry. His chosen style was that of the murmillo, the fish-man, who fell into the league of heavyweight thereby determining although he was well-protected by a combination of leather armour and mail he was disadvantaged by the extra weight. In Crixus' case this appeared to pose no impediment owing to his superior strength and fitness. Murmillo gladiators traditionally fought with a scutum – a large rectangular shield similar to those that equipped the legions but Crixus had dispensed with his own in favour of a smaller circular type emblazoned with sun, moon and stars surrounding a central wolf's head – his fighting emblem that would remain throughout his career.

Even though the lanista's presence was not in evidence this morning Crixus knew nothing on the training ground went unobserved and accordingly he tapped into those hidden reserves of aggression and raw power, seeking to make his mark and come to the attention of Lentulus Fulvius once more for all the right reasons. In just two days he was to make his first appearance in the great amphitheatre where, hopefully, they would pit him against a skilled and worthy opponent or possibly more than one. If he won this contest, as he knew he must if he was ever going to fulfil his pledges to Julius Quintus and the lanista, it would give the mob a taste of what they could expect in the future and also reaffirm Lentulus Fulvius' initial belief Crixus could bring untold credit upon the school.

Secondly, he needed a favour and if the lanista was suitably impressed by Crixus' performance this morning he may then grant permission to leave the school early tomorrow for just an hour or so. Those disturbing dreams were inevitably taking their toll and the continued nights of interrupted sleep were insidiously eating away at his spirit and state of preparedness. He wondered when the right moment might present itself but as chance would have it the lanista strode out of the shadows a short time later when the trainers called a halt to the first session.

"Just as I tell myself you have reached the peak of your performance and excelled in your training yet again, you prove me wrong. My decision to let you fight in Rome's great arena was well-founded and I know the crowds will be more than ready for you."

"There is a matter I would seek your favour upon," Crixus came straight to the point.

"Tell me and let us see if we can resolve the issue between us."

"The face of Julius Quintus continues to haunt me in my sleep. Every night I carry his broken and bleeding body through the streets while the crowds press in ever closer, scorning, mocking and jeering, telling me I have failed the man who was both friend and father. When I waken I am fearful to sleep again lest the images return. I train hard every day with but one goal in mind but as normal sleep and rest eludes me I feel I am less prepared to face the day ahead. The dreams are becoming more frequent and I can ill afford to be unprepared when I must face my next opponents."

"What is the nature of the favour you require from me?"

"There is an apothecary not three miles from here. I have heard she is most proficient in curing all manner of ailments with her potions and preparations. If she can rid me of the sleep demons and restore proper rest then I retain every confidence to defeat those sent against me, no matter who or how many."

"You are asking permission to visit her...?"

"With respect, yes. That is what I am asking."

Lentulus Fulvius made a show of resting his chin in one hand while a thoughtful frown creased his forehead. And then the frown relaxed into a smile and he laughed out loud, slapping Crixus heartily on the shoulder.

"You have served me well these last months and proved your loyalty many times. Normally I would grant leave of absence only with an armed escort but in your case I am prepared to make an exception. When do you wish to do this?"

"Early tomorrow if it pleases you. If I leave before dawn I can be back here in time for the commencement of training."

"Very well, you have my blessing and I will brief the guards on the gate to let you pass. Do you have money to pay the apothecary?"

"A few coins, yes. They will be sufficient."

"A few coins, you say," and his laughter suddenly bellowed across the expanse of the training area. "When we let you loose on Rome you will have more gold than you have ever seen. Later today we will discuss your first appearance in the arena and I think you may find it an interesting proposition."

27

It was well into the night when Crixus struggled breathlessly into wakefulness after yet another vivid and deeply disturbing dream where the whole world seemed full of ugly leering faces and menacing phantoms. It was still dark outside but as he glanced briefly through the small barred window of the cell he could make out the first paling below the eastern horizon as dawn loomed an hour away.

He would not sleep again now for there were other things on his mind and he made his way outside to one of the drinking fountains, splashing cold water on his face until he felt refreshed and revived. Then, as part of his daily ritual, he spent fifteen minutes stretching and warming his muscles in readiness for the walk to the apothecary's home, feeling a light sensation of well-being in anticipation of this small interlude away from the school. A little earlier than planned he made his way to the entrance where a dozing sentry snapped into wakefulness and opened the gate. As he made his way into a world he had not seen for over three months the heavy gate closed once more, leaving him completely alone on the deserted streets. He was only a short distance from the centre and immediately picked up the Via Sacra that would take him the relatively short distance into the hills. At this hour with the sun still a captive of the night the only signs of life were the occasional trader and mule making their way to the stalls and markets of the forum. It felt good to be out in the open again, even for only an hour or so and although he had signed up voluntarily for his stay at the ludus he felt like a prisoner just released from his term of incarceration.

As the vastness of the forum with its temples, basilicas and markets receded further and further into the distance and he passed the houses and villas of the wealthy, so the buildings and manicured gardens at last gave way to open country with gently rolling hills. The sky was lightening rapidly now, throwing the tall cypresses and umbrella pines with their characteristic flat broad canopies into stark silhouette against the paler backdrop. As the rising sun finally teased the world with its presence, so the dawn was streaked with vivid shades of pink and gold on a canvas of pale blue. It was good to experience such basic pleasures again and he briefly forget the harsh regimes of the school but he would not allow himself to be softened or distracted from that singular objective now governing his life. He detected some inner sixth sense telling him the contest with Ferox would soon be at hand and he wondered if the man was even aware of Crixus' existence. Life in the Capua school would almost certainly be more brutal and demanding than Gallicus and he could only hope and pray the gods kept Ferox safe until the day of their meeting and delivered him unscathed into the hands of his executioner.

His long, powerful stride ate up the miles and before too long he approached what he knew must be the house of Quintina even though he had no recollection of having travelled this road before.

How wonderful to live and work in a place like this, perfectly in tune with nature, and for no good reason it suddenly occurred to him she might not even be there and would certainly not be expecting visitors this early in the day. A little guiltily he suddenly reflected his imminent arrival might be interpreted as an unwanted intrusion where she berated him with an off-handed manner and regarded him suspiciously. The narrow path led him through a small gap in the waist-high stone wall and continued around the side of the house where he observed the care and attention to detail lavished on the property. As he turned yet another corner in search of a door he was confronted by a tall, elegant woman carrying an armful of cut herbs and freshly-dug tubers walking in the opposite direction. They both stopped abruptly and she appeared taken aback by the sight of the young god before her. She sported a simple rough-woven tunic that bore little resemblance to the type of garment traditionally worn by females for the hem had been hacked off at mid thigh and the neckline plunged to reveal a large and shapely cleavage.

"Felicitations, Crixus," she greeted him as his mouth began to open in pleasant surprise. "I have a feeling this is going to be a good day. Visitors don't usually present themselves this early. How can I help you?"

He had half expected to be met by some wizened hag covered in warts and reeking of stale piss or some other equally-noxious odour but this woman was the very antithesis of that ill-judged perception. She was tall and wore her rich auburn hair tied up with a band of jewel-encrusted fabric while those piecing green eyes studied him intently. He had seen many females on his travels including some of the wealthier

145

citizens, market traders and whores but none came close to the woman in front of him now who exuded a multiplicity of auras and overtones that left his thoughts in a state of confusion and his body with an aching desire he had not felt in years.

"You know my name and yet we have never met," he found his voice at last. "How can that be so?"

"I know many things about you, Crixus, even though, as you rightly point out, we have not met before today. I have been expecting you for some time and your presence here this morning serves only to confirm my initial instincts."

"And what instincts were those?" he inquired as he regarded her with his own critical appraisal.

"That you would seek the assistance and place your trust in the skills of one such as me when the face of Julius Quintus returned to haunt you night after night. Your training at the school places many demands on your body but the sleep demons ensure you are unable to rest. The body copes well but the mind is less resilient and you grow fearful lest the days ahead see you unable to fulfil your pledge."

"The eyes of Quintina are indeed bright and all-seeing and her words cannot be denied. So tell me, is the future of Crixus shrouded in the mists of uncertainty or have I embarked upon a path of darkness and foolhardiness?"

"Come, walk with me in the rear garden," and she linked an arm through his own. "We can speak freely. Even at this hour of the day you are not my only visitor."

The air resonated to the sound of birdsong and insects delved for pollen and nectar at the heart of exotic plants, their tiny bodies disappearing from view into the elongated trumpet-shaped blooms and petals displaying their startling diversity of colour. She knew much about him and nurtured a healthy respect for his motives and clearly-defined path he had set out upon and whilst she could admire the tanned bulk of Crixus with his overdeveloped musculature and touching politeness, she was not drawn to him in the way another woman might perhaps be attracted. He possessed the rugged countenance and good looks of any god perched atop his lofty plinth in the forum and she found the story of Crixus endearing beyond words but for her there was strangely no sexual magnetism.

'Chemistry rearing its head again', she mused, 'or possibly the pronounced absence of it.'

There was something else too and whilst she would make no reference to it and allow events to take their course, she sensed Crixus' ultimate destiny lay with another and for the short duration of his life upon this earth he would be rewarded with untold happiness.

"I think I know the manner of your distress, Crixus, and I should be able to prepare something to assist natural sleep and banish the demons from your head. These things are often difficult to diagnose but in your case there can be no doubt as to the root cause. I predict you will lose no sleep when Ferox is slain, however, the killing of someone dear to you has proved a traumatic event we need to address right now. It may take a little time as I'll have to prepare the herbs and reduce them into something palatable. Feel free to walk around the gardens or sit and relax as you wish. As I said, there is only one other person here who just also happens to be my closest friend. Her mother, sadly, is gravely ill with demons of her own. A most tragic situation, I'm afraid. I am preparing her medication this very moment but the process is long and arduous. If you will please excuse me I must be about my work. I'll call you when I'm ready."

28

The enclosed gardens possessed a magic and tranquillity of their own and he felt if he died and went to the afterlife right now he would never find anything to parallel this. What sights had these statues and busts seen over the years and what conversations had they overheard? It was a place of extraordinary peace and beauty and for just a moment he could cast aside the unpleasant circumstances of his visit. The soft breeze was a mere whisper as it sighed through the shrubs and smaller trees, caressing his cheek with the tenderness of a lover while the air around him was filled with rare fragrances he had never known. Again his thoughts returned to that initial vision of the apothecary and the way she apparently flouted the conventions of society to suit herself. The memory of those shapely legs with her feet thrust into high-strapped sandals seemed only to confound him for she was clearly no whore or loose woman of questionable morals; indeed, there was something about her that made him suspect she was more than capable of acquitting herself in any situation, could give equally as well as she got and in all probability had a tongue like a viper when required.

If the vision of Quintina had thrown his thoughts into disarray then his entire world was about to be turned on its head for as he reached a point on the narrow path where he could go no further and turned to retrace his steps, he was confronted by a picture of the utmost perfection and beauty. She had approached him from behind on silent feet and now stood gazing at him with eyes that melted his insides and caused his breath to falter.

"I'm sorry if I startled you," and her voice was as melodic as the spring water tumbling over the rocks while her head was canted at an inquiring angle.

"You did not startle me, my lady," he struggled for an opening. "I was lost in thought and unaware of your presence – until now."

"You are no ordinary man," she declared. "You are strong and powerful – a warrior perhaps, and yet I detect many qualities within

148

you, least of all humility and a deep understanding for those less fortunate than yourself."

He was enthralled by the sound of her voice which was clearly a blessing from the gods and he wondered what other secret gifts and splendours she secretly harboured. Those eyes were nearly black and she wore her hair in an almost identical style to the apothecary only tidier with an array of decorative pins and combs. And that neck! It endowed her with an almost regal air and served to emphasise her height. She exuded grace and refinement from every pore and his sensation of breathlessness continued. She was dressed as only a woman of her position and bearing could ever be dressed and his thoughts raced ahead of the situation as he attempted to gauge her position in society. Clearly she treasured her relationship with the apothecary and the mother's life appeared to be hanging by a thread. So who was her father? Who was her husband and why had she not entrusted this simple errand to a house servant? Her stola hung in beautiful folds, a soft creamy ivory perfectly enhancing the colour of her sun-gilded neck and lower arms. She wore a large cameo on a gold chain and he was intrigued to see it depicted Anubis of the underworld – the head of the half-man, half-jackal held in reverence by the Egyptians.

"I make no claim to the glory of Rome's legions, my lady," he replied after a short pause, "but the fates have conspired to put a sword in my hand regardless. I owe my allegiance to Lentulus Fulvius of the Ludus Gallicus, my home for the next five years if the gods are willing I survive that long."

"A contract gladiator!" she exclaimed placing a hand to her mouth. "What brings you to this place for clearly you are no slave?"

"I am a freeborn citizen of Rome, my lady. Until three months ago I was engaged in the restoration of the city's buildings following the great fire. My overseer was a man by the name of Julius Quintus. He was like a father to me and a dear friend. He arranged for me to serve a two-year apprenticeship in the marble quarries of Greece so I might learn how to cut the stone from the earth and fashion it into great monuments. When I returned after two years bearing letters of commendation I could find no trace of him. My searches yielded nothing and when I discovered he had not shown up for work two mornings consecutively I knew something terrible had befallen him."

Her expression became grave as he told her the full story and, still gazing intently into his eyes, she placed a delicate hand upon his lower arm and made no attempt to remove it.

"Please continue," she prompted gently and the sound of her voice, her fathomless black eyes and the warmth of her hand made his senses sway once more. "I detect an unfolding tragedy and an act of great compassion and brotherly love such as I have never witnessed."

"Eventually a man by the name of Caius Attius Caecilius told me of Julius' great misfortune. Apparently he had fallen victim to a crazed thug as he walked home one evening and was fatally stabbed. I was only just in time and he died in my arms. Ferox was never executed in the arena but sentenced to an indeterminate period of incarceration at Capua, training as a gladiator. I have sworn a sacred oath to avenge the slaying of Julius Quintus and one day soon Ferox and I will meet before the great crowds and I will have my revenge. I seek the apothecary's wisdom on a colleague's recommendation because my dreams are haunting me with the vision of a slain man who was in all respects a father. My first appearance in the amphitheatre is two days from now and the business with Ferox will be settled soon after."

The lovely face was a mask of tragedy and her eyes were suddenly filled with tears.

"You gave up five years of your life to avenge the murder of someone dear to you...?"

"That is so, my lady. Otherwise I would have continued along my chosen path – to construct great monuments."

"How are you so called, gladiator? What is your name? What manner of man would do such a thing for a friend and at such appalling risk to himself?"

"I am known as Crixus, my lady," he replied softly as he observed how her cheeks were now streaked with tears.

"My name is Drusilla and Caius Attius Caecilius is my father although at this moment in time I wish he was not."

"I am honoured to make your acquaintance, my lady, although I think it might be improper for us to be alone like this."

She surprised him again when she replied, "And you can drop the 'lady.' Drusilla is my given name and it is I who am honoured to be in the presence of such a man," and she went on to tell him about her father's intention to visit the training schools later this morning, demanding she accompany him. "My father places more importance on his own image with the electorate of Rome than on his own family. The praetorship beckons with the lure and promise of a siren but his ultimate goal is governing one of the provinces."

"I gain the impression you and he are no longer close and there is much enmity and bad blood between you."

"It wasn't always so. We used to be close but not any more. He has vacated the family home and now it falls upon me to look after mother. She is so ill and the fits become worse with the passage of each day. Father and I had a terrible row yesterday. He had been drinking heavily and not once did he ask after his wife. I told him exactly what I thought of his selfish and disgraceful behaviour and he slapped me twice across the face – hard."

"He *struck* you?" Crixus was appalled. "He struck a *woman,* his own daughter?"

"It's an ugly truth, I know. I told him I was no longer afraid of his threats and ultimatums and dared him to hit me again and he almost did. I surprised him with my verbal attack but who else is there to stand up for mother if not me? I swore I'd kill him if he ever laid a hand on me again and he walked away. I probably went too far but the anger was upon me and I simply had to let it go. I know I haven't heard the last of it and the next time will probably be a whole lot worse but I have to fight for what I believe, regardless of the eventual cost."

"For what it's worth I think you are a fine and honourable woman in defending those causes you view as right and just. Your father may be powerful within the political arena but someone has to draw a line in the sand and tell him enough is enough when he oversteps the mark. Tell me about your mother. Are you and she alike? From where I stand you seem to have inherited little of your father's influence."

"In looks we used to be but the fits have aged her prematurely. They have taken a terrible toll these last years. Alas, nature can be so cruel. We used to have such fun together but now she is tired and completely exhausted and spends most of her time sleeping. When she is awake I have to be with her constantly in fear of the next attack. It's just so awful...," and at the mention of her mother's predicament her composure deserted her completely and she covered her face with her hands, weeping bitterly while her shoulders heaved with the pain of it. "Please hold me...," and a little tentatively he encircled the graceful body with his muscular arms as she pressed her face into his chest.

She had not cried for months – at least not like this and in some ways it was a catharsis, a blessed release from the anguish of her mother's plight, the anger of her father's indifference and the compounded frustration, desolation and heartache stored up over the years. He pressed his face into that glossy, stylish black hair, marvelling over the softness and captivating redolence and as he closed his eyes he detected a hundred other evocative fragrances, most of which eluded him. There was lavender and chamomile, apples and wood-smoke, sandalwood, myrrh and frankincense but most of all there was the unique scent of a beautiful woman, the warmth of her body through the material of her clothing and just the indescribable yet comforting *feel* of her in his arms.

His mind quailed at the implications of their discovery under such circumstances. His prowess as a gladiator, no matter how skilled, would not save him from a flogging if this became public knowledge and the repercussions for her were simply unthinkable with the potential for scandal immense. Knowing her father's reputation for bullying and unquestioning obedience, his reaction, predictably, might be measured in blood.

After many moments he became aware her crying had ceased and the front of his rough tunic was soaked with her tears. But still she held onto him and he could feel the pressure of her fingers as they gripped his upper arms, a measure of her reluctance to let him go. This was as close to a real man she had ever come – an unsubtle reminder she had never given herself completely in her steadfast belief the right one was out there – somewhere – waiting, as she had waited these last years. Now, some deep, primeval instinct she trusted implicitly but could not explain told her the waiting was over, at last. Just like her friend, the apothecary, she cared nothing for the rules and conventions of a society that allegedly set her class aside from all others, especially when she was fully aware how her father behaved. The cultured decorum, the articulate speech and rhetoric, the perfect manners and the airs and graces; it was all contrived and a facade, a huge pretentious fraud and one of the reasons she loathed him so.

In a bizarre kind of way that made her skin tingle whenever she pondered the issue, she and Quintina were like opposites that attract. In some respects her privileged, aristocratic position in Roman society sickened her and she longed for the carefree, untroubled lifestyle of someone like Quintina. Quintina, on the other hand, was fully aware of the position bestowed at birth and whilst her chosen occupation might be looked upon as menial and viewed with distaste by the nobility, she frequently adopted the speech and deportment of the Patricians and ruling classes in a convincing display of upper-class breeding and culture as she went about her business in the city. It was this very clash of social differences and the fact they were able to overcome the great cultural divide that made their relationship so enduring and wickedly exciting.

She would never forget the first time she had kissed Quintina, just for the hell of it, wondering what it would be like to embrace another woman and probe her mouth with the tip of her tongue. Rather than shun Drusilla's advances, Quintina had accepted the invitation readily, entering into the spirit of the occasion with more fire than Drusilla could ever have foreseen. As an apothecary, Quintina was well-versed in the finer points of the human anatomy but had been unprepared for the exquisite pleasures available at the hands of another female, especially her best friend. As their clothing was discarded and Drusilla's kisses became more searching, more intimate, her fingers teasing, fondling, caressing and seeking her inner depths, she gave herself up to those sensations rapidly overtaking her body and squeezed her eyes shut. It was just as well for the blinding light, dazzling stars and exploding, vibrant colours threatened to overwhelm her. She had known many men since her adolescent years but none could compare with this woman whose head was now between her parted thighs, licking, delving for the nectar at the centre of her being and making her feel more alive than any man could ever hope to do. She lost count of her orgasms as Drusilla's tongue lapped at her slippery opening, already slicked with lubrication that coated her lips and smeared her inner thighs. As she approached what she knew would be the greatest climax of her life she arched her back, grasping Drusilla's hair and pulling her head forward while the brief darkness behind her eyes was suddenly illuminated by searing white light.

At last, Drusilla raised her head from his chest and blinked away the remaining tears.

"Thank you for holding me like that," she whispered. She looked around her, fearful of discovery but relaxed when she saw they remained completely alone in this wonderful, secluded paradise full of all the special things in nature. "Are we being wicked, Crixus? You and me, flouting the laws of society like this?"

"I believe rules were made for the obedience of fools and the guidance of wise men," he replied in the manner of the seasoned philosopher. "Why should laws prevent two people sharing an embrace and taking pleasure from each other's company if that is what they desire? Who are we hurting?"

She was looking at him that way again and his heart missed a beat. She was a couple of inches shorter than him but there was nothing small or childlike about her. Even while she held onto him in her sorrow he was aware she was a mature young woman, luscious as a ripe fruit and desirable beyond words.

"For me it was more than an embrace," and her voice had altered subtly, becoming slightly husky and imparting overtones of an intimate, more suggestive nature. "For me it was as if something I had been waiting for all my life had just arrived and now it is here I don't think I can ever let it go."

"You are beautiful, Drusilla, and how the mere mention of your name fills me with a strange urge to know more about you. In this haunting odyssey to avenge the death of my friend I had forgotten what it is to hold a woman such as you and inhale her special fragrance. I have signed away five years of my life and I now wonder if I have paid for such hastiness with a heavy coin."

"Will you be there when we visit later this morning?"

"I will be in the training area preparing for my contest. We fight as a group in order for the public and potential sponsors to view us in our natural surroundings."

"What if you are the one who comes to the attention of my father as being superior to all others? How will you feel if he wishes to purchase your services in a bid to secure popularity with the electorate?"

"If that it so I will do as I am asked and when I defeat those who are sent against me it will bring great credit upon the school and its lanista. In time I will be champion. If I cannot bring Rome the great buildings I once promised then she will be appeased by death. The crowds demand blood and I shall give it to them."

"I hope you are the one my father chooses for although I despise the man he has become, his choice will echo the one I have already made."

"I am resigned to a hard and difficult life which will know no respite until my business with Ferox is settled. When Ferox dies, perhaps some of the anger and monumental hatred will die with him and I can concentrate on pleasing the crowds for the next four and a half years – and then, who knows?"

"Crixus, let us not speak of death and revenge any more, nor of the pain and suffering of others. This is such a magical place and so far-removed from such dark and base emotions. Kiss me and hold me close to you. Kiss me as I have never been kissed and let some of your strength flow into me for as the gods are my witnesses, I will surely need it in the days to come."

He cupped the lovely face in his calloused hands and leant forward, touching her lips with his own while the gentle, feather-like touches made them catch their breaths. She placed one hand around his waist and another at his neck, drawing him closer to her and at last she felt her body melt as his arms enfolded about her in delicious, crushing embrace. In the last three months he had made demands of his body that would have broken a lesser man as a great storm might break a ship and discard it carelessly upon the shore. Now, as he kissed this woman in his arms, the most beautiful, desirable and perfect woman he had ever seen, he felt his blood quicken uncontrollably and his heart thump in his ears while a different kind of wave threatened to overwhelm him;

a benevolent wave on a warm, tropical sea and he wanted to drown in it before it broke and dissipated.

For her the feelings surpassed everything she had imagined and dreamed of in her own private moments or discussed animatedly with her friends. She knew from that first instance – before he had uttered a single word that this was he, the one she had waited for. The waiting had been the worst part and there were times when she had doubted her own resolve; month after month, year after year. Would he ever come to her? Would the gods make a mockery of the deep-seated beliefs she held so sacred and deny her the most basic of all human needs? Now, somehow, all those frail insecurities were swept away on a rising current of euphoria and heated emotions as the great strength of his arms made her feel weak and she suddenly experienced that delicious melting sensation in her lower body.

And then, just as the feelings intensified to the extent where he thought his powers of reason and judgement might be compromised he tore cruelly from the heat of their embrace and strode away angrily, leaving her bewildered, hurt and confused. She remained silent and unmoving and after a dozen paces he stopped, still facing away from her with fists clenched and she could see he was wrestling with his inner self; a great struggle with his conscience and sense of honour that what they were doing, even here, was wrong and no good could ever come of it. That he would never forgive himself if ever she was made to suffer on his account. There was a yawning gulf of class distinction between them, the rules of society never allowing them to be together while he remained bound by his oath of allegiance to the lanista of the school. In the outside world he was a freeman, a citizen of Rome with all the honours and privileges it bestowed but within the confines of the ludus he endured the status of a common slave; a rough, frightening outsider, a doomed man beyond hope of reprieve, completely beneath the horizon socially and no better than the conscripts, criminals and prisoners of war who shared the barracks and the dining tables while the nobility and patricians regarded them with disdain.

Fleeing to the farthest corners of the empire where no one recognised them and living the existence of fugitives from the law would be their only future – and it would not be a proper life together, not the kind of life she deserved. It would be merely an existence, much the same as now, trapped by their own love for each other in a world which forbade such transgressions and punished them harshly. And yet he felt that here, now, like this, he would do anything to keep her by his side. He knew he had fallen in love with her – the fates had conspired to bring them together for their bizarre amusement and purely to

155

witness once more how humans are able to tap into those hidden depths of strength, resilience and determination in the face of overwhelming adversity.

He could never tell her of his feelings – at least not yet. Perhaps if they were careful they might see each other again, but where? He could not visit her at her own private residence and she certainly could not be seen alone with him at the school. What was to become of them? All other issues were swept aside for the time being as he thought about her with an urgency that pierced his heart and left him breathless for now he had met her he could not possibly envisage a future where she was not a part of it.

She could see his fists clenching and unclenching as he struggled to make some enormous decision and, at last, after many moments where she remained silent and watched him struggle with the demons of his conscience, he turned and strode briskly back to her with an expression on his face and a determination in his stride that left her in no doubt at all as to what that decision had been.

As he approached her his eyes spoke the words in his heart and he swept her up in those great arms and kissed her with a fire and passion that left her breathless – an embrace born of love and a hundred other emotions they both feared life would deny them; an embrace of desperation fuelled by the uncertainty of the times they lived in and the circumstances that had not only brought them together but threatened to tear them asunder. At length they drew apart, both aware of what had just taken place between them. There seemed to be a tacit understanding concerning the implications of their as yet unspoken intentions and it was as if an invisible barrier had been surmounted.

"Take my hand," she invited. "Let us walk a little and enjoy the delights of Quintina's garden for soon we must part and go our respective ways." He took her slim fingers and they walked along the winding paths savouring the rich, heady aromas and indescribable magic of the moment as they wondered what the fates held in store for them.

"When you come to the school it is vital you remain indifferent if I am singled out for closer inspection by your father. There must be no indication of recognition or favouritism on your part and it would be beneficial to us both if you remained aloof and regarded the proceedings with a degree of boredom."

"It will be difficult," she replied, "but I will try hard. I may be able to lie and feign disinterest with my eyes but my heart will be with you and my body will crave your embrace."

"I will say nothing of our meeting to the lanista – at least not yet. In the days ahead he will be watching me closely and if I live up to his expectations and bring glory to the school and make my mark with the crowds in the arena he may then lend a kind ear to our situation and grant me leave when it is possible. Perhaps you and I will find a way to communicate but only the gods know how we will chance to meet again like this."

The maze of paths eventually brought them back to their starting point and as they approached the rear of the house Quintina emerged carrying two small amphorae containing their respective medications. As her eyes fell upon Drusilla and Crixus with hands still linked she smiled and nodded imperceptibly for events had unfolded as foreseen.

"Behold, Mars and Venus travel the same path through the heavens," she greeted them. "Even the stars grow pale beside such beauty and the great god, Apollo, rants in his jealousy." Then, on a more serious note she spoke directly to Drusilla, proffering one of the two identical containers. "This diluted compound will assist your mother in combating the ailment which has stricken her these last years. It is a concentrated blend of herbs and plants boiled to extract their medicinal properties, mixed with one or two elements you don't really want to know too much about – the stuff of nightmares! As you can feel, the liquid is still hot but do not reheat it before you administer it to your mother. There is sufficient in this container to last four days if you give one small cup morning and evening. After that you must return to me for more.

"I'm convinced what we are dealing with here is born of the mind rather than the body and whilst the concoction is potent and downright lethal if overprescribed, I think it will alleviate only a part of the ailment she suffers. But, with prolonged use, who knows? She may even regain something of her old self. Don't forget – four days!"

"Can't you tell me just a little about what's in this?" Drusilla persisted. "I'd really like to know. You're always so mysterious and secretive in these things."

"Since you ask, it is a blend of four basic herbs – hyssop, vervain, skullcap and lavender, mashed up to a pulp and boiled in fresh spring water. The fibrous elements are then separated leaving the liquid you now hold. That's all I'm saying. The rest of it is a trade secret. Believe me in the wrong hands it could kill a legion. Just before the seal goes on I add a goodly measure of hope and love and a prayer to the gods for the speedy recovery of the recipient. Anything else...?"

She smiled mischievously at Drusilla who was clearly awestruck by this boundless scientific knowledge her friend dispensed with such apparent ease.

"Take this thirty minutes before you are ready to sleep," she addressed Crixus who had remained silent throughout the exchange. "It is a fairly innocuous preparation compared to the one Drusilla's mother must take but the healing qualities are excellent, for mind as well as body. I have to stress that short-term use of this medication can only alleviate visible symptoms. The death of Ferox by your own hand will ultimately bring the peace you seek and quell the fires of hatred that burn inside you. If you are satisfied the medication is working you will also need to return in four days for a repeat dosage."

"Four days...?" Crixus immediately suspected the apothecary's hand was being instrumental in bringing them together once more. "Is that not when you must return also?" and his gaze was fixed upon Drusilla.

"Indeed it is," she replied, her thoughts apparently racing ahead to the possibility of a second encounter.

"I will return just after dawn in four days," and he reached into his tunic for a leather purse. "Will this cover the cost of both amphorae?" he asked Quintina as he emptied the contents into her palm.

"This is a hundred times more than I would have charged anyone, let alone friends. It is too much. I cannot," she protested.

"Take it," he insisted. "When I win the contests there will be more gold than I know what to do with, and besides, it is not possible to put a price on that which I have found here today." And then, turning to Drusilla, "I have to leave now if I am to be back at the school in time. I will never forget our meeting here this morning. You have given my life new purpose and brought great beauty and warmth to where there has only been pain, ugliness and the fires of vengeance. If I am brought before you and your father today I will show no sign of recognition and if I should be deemed guilty of hostility and contempt then I apologise in advance for I mean you no offence."

"I too will look forward to our next meeting here in four days, and now you must go. I will follow a little later." She reached up on tip-toes to kiss him passionately and touched one of her elegant hands to the side of his face. She had promised herself to exercise restraint and employ a little more decorum but she failed miserably, her nipples swelling beneath the thin material of her stola while her stomach cramped and she felt the wetness begin to flow once more.

"Go now, before my resolve weakens and I speak the words I feel in my heart." As he strode away to the road that led back to the city Drusilla reached for Quintina and buried her face in her neck.

"Oh, Quintina, whatever will become of us? We cannot be as other couples – meeting wherever and whenever they choose. Our very differences have made that impossible. As soon as I set eyes upon him in the garden I knew he was the one and my endless waiting was finally over. Have I done a terrible thing – giving my heart to a man who can never truly give himself to me? He is bound by his oath of allegiance to the lanista for another four and a half years and even if he is granted his freedom before the expiry of his contract Rome will never allow us to be together in the true way of a man and a woman."

Their continued embrace provided a mutual comfort and Quintina tenderly kissed the top of Drusilla's head whilst running her fingers through that lustrous black hair.

"Listen to me for it seems you have a distinct advantage over just about every other pair of young lovebirds in Rome today. What is it that eventually kills a relationship no matter how passionate it might have been at the outset? I'll tell you. Familiarity! The boredom and staleness of routine. Look at the potential of what you two could have together. The circumstances of your meeting were the pain and suffering of others but look at the magic that has come of it."

Drusilla's head remained pressed into Quintina's neck, her eyes still moist as she hung onto her every word and being filled with renewed hope where before there was only uncertainty and insurmountable obstacles barring their way.

"You have all the necessary ingredients to make this work for you. Enforced separation for instance. You don't know for certain when or where you're going to meet, at least not after your next little interlude here in four days. You certainly cannot afford to be seen together in public for both your sakes. Any implications of scandal would have far-reaching effects, especially for your father and could be ruinous. You could expect neither sympathy nor mercy from such a man where his retribution would likely be measured in blood. All I'm trying to say is if the love and attraction are strong enough you will find a way to make this happen. Just keep the fires of anticipation burning inside you for the next few days. Why else did you think I arranged for the two of you to present yourselves here at the same time?"

There could be no doubting the wisdom of her words and she began to see how special their relationship could be if it was conducted in secret and how they must both learn to do without one another for possibly many days at a time until it was safe for them to meet.

"The remedies could have been made to last a day or two longer," Quintina conceded, "but I wanted to give you a little ray of hope that being together again was not completely out of the question. Think how

Crixus will long for you also and ache to hold you and kiss your lips. He will undoubtedly train even harder now his life has taken on a new purpose in a bid to maintain good favour with the lanista. You can certainly expect to be sharing your bed with Rome's new champion before much longer but I think you should not lose sight of his original objective. When his business with Ferox is settled he will be yours in every respect."

"How I love you so," Drusilla whispered. "Our moments will be stolen and wicked but we will thrive on the excitement of it all."

"That's my girl," Quintina encouraged her a little breathlessly as Drusilla kissed her neck. "You may use my gardens as often as you wish, assuming young Mars can get permission to be away from the school."

"However will I repay your kindness?"

"If you carry on kissing my neck like that I'll find a way before too long."

"Let's go inside. I really want to feel you close to me." As their lips came together Drusilla felt the rush of blood through her veins and her nipples firm up once more, precipitating that pleasant melting sensation in the pit of her belly and with a note of urgency headed for the open door with Quintina grasping her hand.

29

Ludus Magnus Gladiatores was a well-equipped and imposing school recently constructed by the emperor, Domitian, as part of a radical modernisation programme within the city. The training ground was actually a small arena with its classic elliptical shape circumscribed by rows of seating and an elegant double colonnade of slender white columns surmounted by Corinthian capitals. The viewing terraces held up to three thousand spectators where ordinary people could attend the training sessions whilst remaining confined to the longer sides of the ellipse. On the shorter sides, wealthy citizens, politicians and visiting dignitaries occupied their own boxes and sometimes even the emperor himself was known to make an appearance.

It was from here Caius Attius Caecilius and his daughter, Drusilla, now observed the proceedings with critical eyes. Yesterday's violent and unpalatable confrontation appeared overlooked or disregarded for the time being as Caius studied each pair of fighters sparring with their respective partners. Since the concept of the gladiator as far back as 264 B.C. the sport had undergone some radical changes and many different types of fighter could now be seen in the arena, based on characters from Roman mythology and ideas borrowed from nations conquered in battle. Accordingly, a corresponding variation in weaponry had also been introduced in order to vary the spectrum of entertainment on offer and make the outcome of any contest more difficult to predict.

Although armour for the torso was available in limited forms, most gladiators elected to fight bare-chested or in sleeveless tunics for the heroic nakedness of the upper body made the fights more appealing, especially for the women. The two gladiators closest to Caius and Drusilla were typical of the matched pairs seen in the arena any day of the week. The murmillo was a heavyweight and took his name from the murma, a salt-water fish caught in nets and because he was often entangled in the net of the retiarius it was common practice to pit him against this type of fighter. The murmillo carried a rectangular, legionary-type shield and his main attack weapon was the gladius. He wore a fully-enclosed wide-brimmed helmet topped off with a crest in the shape of a leaping fish and was well-protected by a combination of robust protective leather armour and mail.

Conversely, the retiarius wore no helmet and virtually no protective armour, relying on speed and agility to both defeat his opponent and provide a crucial element of defence. For the most part he wore a loin cloth and sandals and perhaps a galerus – a metal plate at one shoulder to protect the vulnerable side of his neck. In Roman mythology the retiarius was the fisherman and accordingly he sported a circular, wide-meshed throwing net with lead weights around the circumference. His main weapon - the trident, bestowed the advantage of outreaching his opponent's sword and the wickedly-sharp barbs were a constant, menacing threat in skilled hands.

"These two are my finest," the lanista, Marcellus, volunteered in the wake of a protracted, awkward silence. "The others....they are competent but not particularly outstanding. They may survive three or four matches but no more. Since the commissioning of our great Flavian Amphitheatre the demand for gladiators has outstripped supply and it is no longer economically viable to extend the training period. Slaves are not the material from which champions are forged and if a man possesses no natural warrior-like traits or tactical acumen then there is only so much he can learn here. Forgive me but I detect an air of displeasure in your manner. Perhaps you are seeking to find something a little more exclusive – a more choice-cut for want of a better expression. I can assure you this school produces the finest gladiators in Rome. Our reputation is unequalled."

'Your reputation is about to disappear up its own arse into the realms of obscurity,' Drusilla observed just loudly enough for Caius to overhear and smiled to herself as she contemplated seeing Crixus again.

"These two are good, I'll concede against my better judgement," he scowled. "But they're not *that* good! If I am to pay out huge sums sponsoring games for the public I want something better than this. I see nothing here to instil confidence or reassure me I could be onto a winner. I want champion material – something to get the crowds on the edges of their seats and whip them up into a state of hysteria. The mob needs something different and I don't see that here. I am willing to pay handsomely for the right man and this school was my first choice in the mistaken belief you were the best. This is a complete and utter bloody shambles and a waste of time."

"The man you seek does not exist, certainly not in this city. If he did I would already be aware. Perhaps with time..."

"I don't have time!" Caius snapped, his features flushed and twisted with anger as spittle flew from his lips. "It has to be now. Can't you see that? This establishment is allegedly the benchmark for all other schools in the empire. Even *your* contacts and associates should be able to locate such a man and have him brought here."

"Only rarely does a man of the calibre you seek come to the attention of people like me. Slaves come and go in their thousands, along with criminals and prisoners of war for they seek only to survive until the next contest. But a man with a mission – a man who is motivated by different forces and an unearthly desire to prove himself before the people, he is like the gold at the end of the rainbow. I wish you good fortune with your continued search but I fear it will be to no avail, and now, if you will excuse me, I have a school to run," and he turned briefly to acknowledge Drusilla. "My lady...," and he inclined his head politely before walking away to speak with his trainers.

That earlier sense of euphoria had rapidly evaporated, leaving Caius beneath a descending pall of gloom and despondency at this circumvention of his plans so early in the day.

"By the gods! I am not asking for the moon! Greater men than I have won the crowds with far less than I have witnessed here today."

"Perhaps it was their natural appeal that endeared them to the people and the games were merely an added attraction, in which case you're going to be a sad, deluded loser. Whatever will you do, father, if Marcellus is right and such a man does not exist and you have to come back here and grovel for his business? He will probably quadruple the price for being insulted and rightly so."

"Choose your words carefully, young lady!" Caius snarled. "I will not forget your insolence of late. You're becoming just a little too damned sure of yourself. You need to remember your place. Any more of your venomous tongue and I'll...."

"You'll do what?" she threw her head back and laughed at him. "What will you do? Come on, I want to hear it. What will the great Caius Attius Caecilius do? Slap me across the face again? Knock me to the ground and kick me until I'm unconscious?" The adrenalin surged through her veins again as she sensed another volatile confrontation, filling her entire being with an unfamiliar but equally uplifting reckless abandon where her scathing tongue knew no bounds. "Am I to be the subject of a public flogging because I refuse to acknowledge your self-proclaimed god-like status and bow down to your vulgarity, your glaring lack of integrity and cheap, shoddy methods?"

"Keep your voice down!" he hissed like a serpent poised to strike. "There are people watching."

"Good! Let them watch and they might see you for what you are – a fraudster, a womaniser and a devious, unscrupulous cheat. I know all about you and your whores and the way you go about your business in the senate. You're a sanctimonious bastard, do you know that? I wonder what the censors would make of your behaviour. They could have you publicly vilified and removed from office if your activities were made known to them."

"You bitch!" and he was scarlet with rage again but her words had hit the mark. At last she had cut through the carapace and touched raw nerves. "We're leaving here this instant and you will accompany me to the Ludus Gallicus."

"You go," she regarded him with a new distaste. "I'll follow in my own time."

"We will arrive together," he struggled through clenched teeth.

"Don't push your luck, father. You don't own me any more. In a way I really hope you win this next election and then we might be rid of you for good."

"But until then you'll do as I say," and bracing himself with a visible effort he began to walk away.

"You're going to be the loser here, Caius Attius Caecilius," she screamed after him, her voice cracking shrilly with outrage. "I swear it to you. I will see you lose everything!"

He subdued the urge to run and made his way around the perimeter of the arena to the welcoming escape of the gates, holding himself erect while the air around him was rent asunder with the storm of her hatred.

"Go back into the streets where you belong – into the gutter with your whores!"

Once clear of the building he could hurry but found his legs were trembling beneath him, his breath ragged and broken and there was a tight knot of anger turning his guts into a ball of fire.

"The bitch!" he cursed aloud as curious faces turned and stared at the odd spectacle. "The bloody bitch!"

30

Despite his angry threats Caius Attius Caecilius remained alone for the short distance to Ludus Gallicus where, in a deliberate and blatant air of disobedience calculated to annoy him still further, Drusilla arrived a good twenty minutes later, strolling leisurely and nibbling demurely on an apple.

"You test my patience still further with your contempt and lack of respect," he growled and she could see he was still hurting from their last verbal exchange. She chose to ignore him completely and brushed past him on her way through the gates and into the seating area, knowing how it would infuriate him and preserve that dangerous animosity and ever-present conflict between them.

"Your daughter...?" Lentulus Fulvius inquired with a raised eyebrow.

"Unfortunately."

"She has spirit," and he allowed himself the luxury of a smile.

"We're both straight-talking men so let's get down to business and cut the bullshit. You know why I'm here. I have just come from the greatest school in Rome where I was informed the man I am searching for has yet to be born. It would appear this too is to be a waste of time and resources for if such a man does exist, all would be aware by now."

"Perhaps...," the lanista was being deliberately evasive. "Perhaps not. Come, let us talk a while and take a little wine together. Who knows? It may well transpire you have not embarked on a fool's odyssey after all."

Caius' expression remained dubious and suspicious but inwardly he mellowed somewhat at the lanista's invitation of hospitality, quite the reverse of what he had been expecting. Drusilla positioned herself several yards away - both to enhance the sense of rejection toward Caius and also to cover any inadvertent betrayal of emotions when she saw Crixus again. Her eyes remained fixed on some remote point totally unrelated to the day's proceedings although she listened intently for any mention of the name that would send her pulse racing.

"Sometimes it is not always prudent to advertise one's best assets up front even though we are all in the business of making money from what we do and any resulting public adoration may be considered a bonus. That is the prime reason for inviting prominent citizens such as your good self to see first hand the excellence of fighting man we produce here. Regardless of what you may have been told or already seen with your own eyes, this school boasts a higher success rate than all others. The number of slaves and criminals under training continues to dwindle and in their place we now have a steadily increasing percentage of volunteers from all walks of life, willing to give up all the privileges of the outside world. Contract gladiators who sell their freedom and citizenship for five years to pursue fame and glory in the arena. You cannot drill devotion and unquestioning obedience into a slave. You can only threaten him with fear and pain and death if he fails to do as you command."

This was not the type of conversation he had envisaged as they walked into the school. The lanista was clearly endeavouring to make a point but seemed to be relishing the cryptic approach – taking the scenic route rather than getting straight to the heart of the matter.

"Please continue," Caius eyed the lanista, detecting something he had wanted to hear all morning was about to surface.

"The majority of fighters who emerge from this school make a significantly greater number of appearances in the arena than those of any other establishment. Their training is designed to eradicate all fear of death so they will give the optimum performance right up to the end and if it should come to a decision by the editor or perhaps even the emperor himself, they are taught to die well."

Caius fidgeted restlessly in his seat, wishing to hell the lanista would get straight to the point rather than equivocating and keeping him on a knife-edge. The suspense was unbearable. He was facing straight ahead toward the activity on the training ground so his next words came like a clap of thunder from Vulcan himself, delivered almost as an afterthought.

"What if I were to tell you I have in my charge the next potential title-holder of Rome? I have supervised his training personally and no one – I repeat, no one can even come close to him. Three days ago in this very arena he made his first appearance before a crowd where his opponent was a retiarius from another school with three kills to his name. That doesn't often happen. Novice gladiators can expect to be

166

paired with others of similar skills – not professional fighters. Shall I tell you what happened?"

"Already I like what I'm hearing. It may be the situation can be retrieved after all," and that sense of euphoria which had earlier deserted him suddenly made a welcome return.

"Very well, I will tell you and may the gods strike me down if I lie or embellish upon the truth. The contest began, bearing in mind it was to first-blood only and both fighters sized each other up, looking for gaps in defence, weaknesses and signs of hesitation – the usual things. I swear I have never seen a man move with such speed and fluidity. To blink was to miss it. The retiarius had not bargained on facing someone who paid scant attention to his own personal safety and was soon ensnared by his own net. Crixus then stepped in and wrenched the trident from his opponent's hands and snapped it over his knee – a two-inch hardwood shaft and he broke it like a twig. When Septimus went for his dagger Crixus knocked him cold with a blow that would have floored an elephant."

Caius listened to the epic tale with a degree of incredulity as he attempted to visualise the scene played out here just yards away.

"But what of Crixus' own weapons – his sword and shield. How did he acquit himself with those?"

"Never needed them," the lanista added with a note of pride. "As soon as Septimus made his first mistake Crixus' own weapons were discarded, no longer required. He disarmed and defeated his opponent bare-handed. They carried Septimus out of here with a broken jaw. If I'd sent Crixus in to fight without weapons he would have gone unquestioningly and the outcome would have been the same. I did warn him about attempting the same tactic against someone armed with a knife or sword but I think he's smart enough to work that one out for himself."

"You said his name was Crixus. Why do I know that name?"

"Just over three months ago he returned from Greece and you told him about Julius Quintus being gravely injured in a knife attack."

"Him!" and the recognition dawned immediately. "He was so young. I know the story. Ferox was sent to Capua and Crixus sold his freedom in a bid to even the score. His motives are indeed honourable but now you're telling me he possesses the ability to defeat all others?"

"Without a doubt. In two days he fights in the great arena for the first time and has vowed to give the mob something they will not forget in a hurry – whatever that may be. He has pleaded with me to set him up against three opponents and I have acceded to his wishes. If he prevails and kills all three, Rome will have its new champion and Crixus will be worth his weight in gold – literally."

"Three! Three opponents on his debut appearance? By the gods, if he is successful Rome will never have seen such a thing. I must be there to witness it for myself."

"How badly do you want your champion? If you bargain with me now, before Crixus' first appearance, I will offer you a good rate. When he wins the contest – and win it he will, the price will quadruple reflecting his value as an asset to the school. I think he is a man worthy of investment, even at this early stage of his career and if it should become known a certain prominent citizen and patrician had already shown great interest in featuring him in games he was soon to host, then that may just serve as a further incentive to achieve great things and cover us all in glory."

"Name your price, Lentulus Fulvius," and all of a sudden the elusive praetorship Caius desperately sought had moved to where it was tantalisingly just beyond his grasp – but only for now. The next few weeks would tell.

"Five thousand denarii reserves Crixus for your first public games and limits him to two appearances. In two days time, after he has made his name with the people of Rome the price will rise to twenty thousand denarii. If you require him to feature still further as part of your election campaign then you may have him for ten thousand denarii – half of what I will be charging anyone else. After his first appearances you should be able to gauge public reaction to the games and also, to some degree, your own popularity and chances of success at the ballots. In the past I have seen greater men than yourself lose favour with the electorate because they relied too much on their own reputations and ignored the people that really mattered. There are an awful lot of citizens out there – bored and unemployed people living on the brink of poverty and starvation. They need some kind of distraction from the tribulations of every-day life. Give them death on a grand scale and in a manner never seen before and they will be eating out of your hand."

"I agree to your terms, Lentulus Fulvius, and I will not even attempt to barter for something tells me you are a man of your word and I will see a good return on my investment. I will have the money delivered into your hands before sunset – you have my own word on that. And now if it pleases you I should like to see the goods for myself."

"Of course. Forgive me, I will send for him." He rose from his seat and summoned the head trainer who sprinted across the open ground and inquired as to the lanista's bidding. "Bring Crixus and three of the best to go against him."

168

"Three...? Did you say three?"

"That is my wish. Our guests would like to see for themselves the fighting ability of our star pupil. We have spoken at length about the man and now it is time for him to deliver on my expectations."

"I understand. Will this be a contest to the death or first blood only?"

"Neither. This is merely a foretaste of things to come, a hint of true potential. There will be no fatalities."

"I will bring them," and he disappeared across the training ground once more to where the fighting groups were going about their drills in a boiling cloud of dust. Moments later he had returned with Crixus and his three opponents chosen for this contest of skill. In appearances only Caius became animated to see how these four were vastly superior to anything Marcellus was able to offer at Ludus Magnus.

"Crixus, remove your helmet," Lentulus Fulvius commanded. "Your sponsor wishes to gaze upon the greatness I have illustrated." The helmet was duly removed and both Caius and Drusilla were taken aback by his presence and ruggedly handsome countenance. After several hours in the training area he was slicked with sweat and every muscle stood out in startling clarity giving him the impression of a thoroughbred. But Crixus gave no indication of being taxed or his reserves being even mildly depleted and, with the wolf's head shield on his left arm while the gladius sat snugly in the palm of his right hand he presented the visage of the unassailable; the invincible warrior, a towering mountain of muscle and armour with the power to destroy anything put before him. He oozed power and menace from every pore and Lentulus Fulvius could not hide the proud smile that creased his handsome, sun-bronzed features.

"Great Jupiter!" Caius exclaimed. "If this is Crixus he bears little resemblance to the young man I spoke to just a few months ago. Such a change is not possible and yet I am looking upon a man who has been transformed. No wonder you kept him under wraps until now."

"The standards in this school are exacting to say the least but he has pushed himself beyond the limits of physical endurance in the quest for perfection. As you are fully aware, there are other forces and motivations governing him and driving him ever harder in search of his own goals. Those forces have shaped the man you see before you today. Remember though, like you and me he is mortal and as such will be influenced by mortal weaknesses and emotions. He is not a machine totally devoid of feelings. Like you and me also he is aware life is short and is blind to what may lie over the horizon. As with all gladiators he has sworn the oath of allegiance and knows precisely what is expected of him but he will never lose sight of his ultimate mission which burns inside him with the heat of a sword-maker's furnace – to kill Ferox."

Several yards away Drusilla watched with immense pride and her heart was crushed under the weight of conflicting emotions as she listened to Lentulus Fulvius extol the qualities and virtues of the man she had come to love and the limits to which he had pushed himself these last months. With considerable difficulty she resisted the urge to call out in greeting as she saw him in this new, disturbing light and even beneath the confining restrictions of the helmet with its enclosing visor he had donned once more, she remembered the handsome face and soft lips; lips which, just hours ago, had made her weak with desire and left an empty, aching and lonely place when he had gone. Secretly, she too hoped she was one of those motivating forces that would drive him relentlessly onward, sweeping aside all opposition and seeing him triumph where others would capitulate to their own exacting standards and fall by the wayside.

His manner of attire was simply terrifying and she felt a degree of sympathy toward those who would ultimately face him in the arena where sporting chances were rare and a man's first mistake was usually his last. Despite those tender emotions she felt during that all-too-brief glimpse of his face there was now something more bestial, more earthly and basic taking over in its place where his raw power and menace served as a potent narcotic and precipitated the heat and pleasant melting sensation in the pit of her belly.

'Great Mars,' she whispered to herself, *'how I want you and crave the union of our naked flesh. Please, let it be soon before the desire consumes me!'*

"Begin the contest," Lentulus Fulvius ordered good-naturedly, "and let our honoured guests witness how our school produces the finest. Soon the name of Ludus Magnus will no longer be associated with greatness and the barbarians within its walls will be knocking on my door. Watch the movements and don't blink. I think you may find this interesting."

The four combatants took up positions at the centre of the small elliptical arena and all other practice sessions had ceased for the time being. The head trainer would act as referee for this contest and as the lanista nodded his head he cut the air with his simple wooden baton and shouted, "Begin!"

Crixus' three opponents were all in the league of heavyweight and sported different combinations of mail, leather armour and helmet. Their main attack weapon was the gladius and shields varied in size and shape according to preference. Conspicuously absent was the retiarius –

the net man and a popular adversary for a man like Crixus any other day. After much consideration Lentulus Fulvius had decided against including the retiarius in this contest for the swinging net may well have proved more of a hindrance to the others than to Crixus himself. They formed a loose circle about their man, constantly moving, weaving, probing his defences and attempting to divert his attention long enough for one of them to make an attack.

Crixus remained exactly where he was, feet planted firmly in the sand like an anchor securing his upper torso which swayed like tall grass in a summer breeze as he assessed the likely intentions of his opponents, his eyes flicking from side to side, missing nothing like a falcon poised to stoop, seeking the tell-tale movement that would herald the strike. It could be nothing more than a calf muscle flexing or the twitch of a bicep but he sensed they would work as a group coordinating their attack to overcome him by weight of numbers. He formed a clear picture of what they would do for he was a master of tactics and he waited patiently, allowing the others to do the moving and expend their own energy reserves.

"Why does he not move?" Drusilla asked with wide eyes as she sensed Crixus was merely waiting for the others to close in before unleashing a withering assault. "He hasn't made a move yet and stands like the god, Talos, waiting for interlopers foolish enough to approach." It was a perfect comparison for the giant man of bronze stood sentinel over Crete, protecting the island from intruders – a man built by Haphaestus whom Zeus gave a divine fluid identical to that which flows in the veins of the gods.

She could almost sense the energy stored in his great muscles and again wondered at those qualities that gave a man like Crixus the courage to stand unflinchingly before three others and smile in the face of death. It was just as well she had chosen to remain several yards distant from her father and the lanista for as her lower body continued to cramp and spasm while the wetness flowed from her and her nipples ached with exquisite pain, she finally yielded to the demands of her body and touched a gentle finger to the spot that burned with an indescribable fire. She almost gasped audibly with the intensity of her climax and thought she might faint as her heart thumped loudly in her ears and caused her breath to falter. The explosion of light and colours behind her closed eyes was like nothing she had ever experienced with Quintina and she felt her complexion flushing as the blood surged and coursed through her veins.

"Patience," the lanista's voice brought her back to earth. "It will come soon. Wait and see...."

In an explosion of movement that deceived the eye Crixus struck at the man to his left, ignoring the diversionary feint attack from the right, his instincts telling him unerringly the direction of the true threat. The first devastating downward blow from the gladius severed his opponent's sword just above the hilt and before the man could recover from his surprise a crashing blow to either side of the head from Crixus' shield sent him sprawling into the dust disarmed, dazed and clearly out of the contest. The attack had taken less than five seconds and already the odds were reduced by a third. Once again he planted feet firmly in the sand, immovable as a granite boulder, waiting for them to make their move.

It was a ploy. They were all grimly mindful of his speed, skill and unflinching determination for they had trained with him since those first days and there was not a man confident to fight him even with superior numbers in their favour. He was conscious of their reluctance to engage in virtual suicide and for that reason he would not seek to maim or injure men he regarded as brothers in arms. But he would effectively disarm them and destroy their concerted efforts to best him with a convincing display of controlled aggression, swordsmanship and tactical acumen that would leave those who looked on from the seating terraces in no doubt at all as to the outcome of future contests where those sent against him had death as their goal.

Again, the two remaining fighters circled Crixus cautiously, maintaining a respectful distance lest one of his lightning strikes find its mark.

When the odds are against you, always do the unthinkable!

Taking both opponents completely by surprise Crixus launched into his own attack just as the man to his right wearing a brass griffin-crested helmet and black leather cingulum belt with ornate bronze studs made his move. The action was quick while both fighters circled one another, punctuated by fast and savage exchanges of thrust and parry combinations with the violent clashing of shields. As the opponent continued to valiantly launch further attacks while the second man vainly attempted to distract Crixus, he momentarily left himself exposed as the sword-arm was raised and, in a blur of movement, Crixus struck unerringly into the left side, opening his flesh to the bone and the man went down on his knees, clutching his injured side while blood sprayed through his fingers. It had not been Crixus' intention to inflict serious injury but his adversary had left himself vulnerable and open to attack, precisely the weakness to be exploited mercilessly in the arena where hesitation was fatal. If Crixus had spotted his opportunity then so too had the lanista and to have missed it would have invited scathing criticism.

The third man now confronted him with determination reflected in his stance, shield held close to his body with the gladius flat-side up in typical legionary position, ready in an instant to thrust forward into any opening that might appear. Crixus could see he was wearing his own personalised style of body armour he would retain throughout his fighting career; the sword-arm was protected by a black leather arm-guard and hand wraps ornamented by a silver lion's head and he wore a tall crested helmet. The shield bore a menacing visage of Medusa – a sight calculated to chill and instil fear into his most determined opponents. His first thrust aimed at Crixus' mid-section would have gutted him like a fish had it connected but Crixus had gone, pirouetting away on agile feet and the gladius hit nothing but air.

From the terraces alongside the small arena the waves of sound rose and fell, rising up like a storm before falling away into a dramatic hush as they anticipated the next act to be played out in the dance of death. Crixus advanced, forcing the other man to back up and his actions were those of a panther or leopard stalking its prey before ultimately moving in for the kill. The ending was predictable but within a moment Crixus had come to a halt and the tactical advantage appeared to pass to his opponent for the big man now relinquished his hold on the shield and let it fall away.

When the outcome favours you, dispense with your upper hand and they will love you for it!

Again the crowd roared its approval and in the privileged seating area the small group of three sensed they were about to see something unparalleled in combat and which Crixus had promised at the outset. With his left hand positioned on his hip he now held the gladius at chest height, straight out in front of him completely bewildering the other man as to his intentions for what manner of attack was this? And then Crixus began to spin the sword in his hand, rotating it around his wrist in a dazzling display of seamless, perfectly-coordinated movement just inches from his opponent's face. As the speed increased and the metal dissolved in a blur of movement he flicked the gladius to the left and caught it in his opposite hand whereupon the blade continued to hiss and cut the air making any response from the other man completely impossible. And then, without warning, the movement ceased abruptly and those who looked on in stunned disbelief could see the sword of Crixus was pressed into the throat of his opponent. Accordingly, the man dropped his own weapon, knelt on one knee and raised a finger in capitulation.

Again the crowd erupted as one into spontaneous, rapturous applause and wild cheering and even Lentulus Fulvius, Caius Attius and Drusilla were on their feet acclaiming the spectacle. On the sand Crixus lowered the gladius and helped the other man to his feet. After removing the helmet he walked the short distance to where the lanista and his guests were still standing and waiting to greet him.

"That was the best yet, young Crixus. You promised to keep us on the edges of our seats and we were not disappointed. I like a man who delivers on his word. I pity those who are sent against you in the coming months for their lives will end quickly."

His muscles ached but his breathing remained deep and controlled as he eyed Caius Attius while the image of Drusilla hovered tantalisingly close and he tried to shut her out of his mind.

"I understand your last meeting was conducted under somewhat more painful circumstances," the lanista decided no formal introductions were necessary. Both men nodded and seemed to be scrutinising one another with critical appraisal, their gazes steady and unblinking. For Caius Attius it was tantamount to inspecting the largest purse of gold he had ever seen and it was not solely the generous helpings of wine that brought about this new sensation of warmth and well-being. Crixus, on the other hand, was careful not to display the anger and resentment he felt toward Caius, mindful of Drusilla's words just a short time ago where their violent argument had resulted in him striking her twice across the face. Had it not been for the embarrassment to the lanista, the loss of business generated for the school and the wrath that would have descended upon Crixus as a result, he would have had no conscience about beating the man with his balled fists.

"Can I rely on you to perform in the manner I have just witnessed – regardless of who your opponents may be or how great they number?" Caius came straight to the point.

"I am sworn to continue along my chosen path and nothing will sway me from that decision. I am sworn to the lanista, to Julius Quintus and to myself. Send your brave gladiators to me, as many as you choose and we will see who walks away victorious at the end of the day. You may send me Ferox also and the agony of his death will cause mothers and infants to lie awake in their beds for many nights." He was unsmiling but his voice conveyed a silent menace that sent a chill up Caius' spine. The brutal training regime had indeed altered Crixus from the young man he first set eyes on just a few months ago but he also recognised the inner driving force that set him apart from the others, constantly fuelling the fires of burning vengeance that steered him unerringly on his terrible odyssey. At the edge of his vision he was aware of Drusilla's lovely form but he dare not fix his gaze upon her lest it be deemed inappropriate and she should be made to feel uncomfortable. His heart raced and he could feel the blood coursing through his veins with a force that surpassed the exertions of combat a few minutes previously. She was a dangerous, beautiful distraction and he had to force her from his mind.

"Again you have eclipsed my expectations, Crixus, at a time when I told myself you had reached the peak of your performance," Lentulus Fulvius made no secret of his exuberance. "We will speak later, now go and bathe and rest until tomorrow. You are excused further training today."

Carrying his armour he strode smartly away to the armoury and, full of admiration, they watched him leave. For the lanista no further proof was required as to his man's credentials and once more he anticipated with great satisfaction the new elevated status of his school when Crixus was let loose on the unsuspecting world.

For Caius Attius, what had begun as a disastrous morning – both at the Ludus Magnus with its disappointing array of fighters on offer and that violent and unprovoked attack by Drusilla with its barely-veiled threat of exposure, had turned out monumentally better than he could have possibly imagined. He would not forget her insolence and she would pay dearly for her poisonous tongue; but, for now, the gods of fortune seemed to be smiling on him once more. The rank of praetor now loomed closer than ever along with its enhanced social prominence, political leverage and wealth. He hardly dare think of it yet for the very idea made him weak at the knees and his breath faltered for a moment.

What lay beyond the praetorship?

Almost certainly a position as provincial governor if he made his mark and didn't step on the toes of those who pulled the strings of power. After that, in a few short years his accumulated fortune and assets would help him buy his way to popularity again when he sought election as consul, a position second only in power and absolute authority to the emperor himself.

"One thing at a time," he told himself, breathing deeply to clear his head.

As Drusilla attempted to remain indifferent, her own heart continued to pound and her gaze followed Crixus until he was gone from sight. Throughout she had kept her head averted and remained several yards distant lest her father glimpse those more basic desires etched overtly across her face. More than once the tears of her love spilled over as she saw how he moved with the speed, grace and fluidity of a dancer and, when she witnessed how hopelessly outclassed his opponents were, she detected an almost sympathetic air where he afforded them a modicum of advantage and let them leave the arena without losing face or dignity.

He was like no other man she had ever known or even read about in mythology and the annals of Rome's glorious, heroic past. Her need was almost a physical pain and she longed to tell him of her love and aching desire. She hoped it was the same for him also – that outside of training and the haunting demons which filled his restless soul, he thought about her too; thought about meeting in secret where they might explore one another's flesh and yield to the demands of their bodies. The thought of having sex with a man like Crixus caused her cheeks to flush and she felt herself burning inside. She had never known a man intimately although Quintina had been most forthcoming and descriptive about the sensations to be enjoyed at the hands of a skilled and inventive male lover. Quintina knew just about everything there was to know about the human anatomy and Drusilla's initiation into the world of physical pleasure, soaring abandon and limitless, earth-shattering orgasms had been at the hands of her apothecary friend where the two of them had spent many hours in naked embrace, touching, probing, kissing and teasing with moist tongues.

But first there would be Crixus' all-important contest in the great arena and she would be there, shouting his name, cheering him on with the thousands of others, fearing for him and praying to the gods for his successful deliverance. How she wanted him to love her and be damned with their social differences. She wanted to feel his great powerful body next to hers, the excitement, the passion, the wickedness and the tenderness. She wanted to bind herself to him with chains of love so they might never be parted from one another again – not even by death itself!

31

The domestic slaves had been dismissed after Drusilla thanked them for their vigilance and attention to Agrippina during her absence. Normally their day would not have begun at this unearthly hour but with Drusilla's urgent need to obtain her mother's medication and the walk to and from Quintina's home they were required to be up and about just after four o'clock. As a token of her gratitude she handed them each a few coins and their surprise to this kindly response touched her for no such gratuities were ever distributed when Caius was in the house.

Drusilla administered the first measure of the still-warm brackish liquid as soon as she returned from her visit to the apothecary and the house slaves reported Agrippina had slept fitfully and there had been no evidence of the terrible spasms. Now, for the first time in many weeks her mother sat up in bed, clear-eyed and lucid and the two of them chatted like old friends catching up on their lives after a protracted separation while Drusilla brushed Agrippina's wavy black hair until it shone and reflected the afternoon light permeating through the small window.

Even through her illness which kept her confined to her room for days at a time when at its most aggressive, Agrippina had still managed a regular food intake which Drusilla prepared herself, along with a daily amphora of rich red wine from the family's estate. Consequently, she retained her shapely figure and healthy complexion despite the ravages of her condition. A lesser woman without access to the care and attention lavished upon her would have wasted away mentally and physically and degenerated into a pitiful state before the onset of death which was why Drusilla had taken personal responsibility for her mother's care. Caius could no longer be entrusted with any aspect of her well-being these days and his visits to the house were becoming something of a rarity.

"I cannot believe the improvement after just one draught of Quintina's potion. It seems like months since we laughed and talked the way we used to. Quintina said it might alleviate only the very worst of the symptoms but with prolonged use it could have a long-lasting effect and perhaps we might venture into the city again when you feel stronger."

"That would be so nice, Drusilla, my child. I don't know what I would have done without you these last months. All the time you have spent with me and through most of that I just sleep for the fits render me so weak."

"Do not berate yourself, mother. I am more than happy to do these things for you, even if it is only sitting and holding your hand while you rest. The servants have been wonderful and remained with you this morning whilst I visited Quintina. They are always asking after you and I know their concern is genuine."

"Yes, I know. They are loyal and work well. Drusilla, speaking of loyalty, how is that dreadful man, your father, these days?"

It was a grim reality Agrippina finally accepted her marriage to Caius was over and she had become a figure of revulsion in his life. It might have been a little easier to swallow if Caius had simply tired of her and found another love but the circumstances of his rejection and desertion were particularly cruel. Drusilla could well remember how it had once been before the onset of her condition but now the magic had vanished for both of them leaving only bitterness, hatred and resentment; a situation made all the more poignant by her new-found love for Crixus. She recalled fondly some of the banquets the three of them had attended on public holidays and feast days and how grand her parents had looked as they walked arm-in-arm together; her father in a fresh white linen toga praetexta with its rich purple border and classic folds with her mother resplendent in creamy rich silk with her elegant brooches, expensive earrings and opulent Greek fibula at the fastenings of her stola. Apart from being blessed with an unusually beautiful face, near-black eyes and a long, slender neck, Agrippina's greatest asset was perhaps that wonderful black hair, plaited and knotted and twisted into double ropes on top of her head and held in place by a large pink orchid.

They were the perfect expression of affluence and compatibility and it brought a lump to her throat when she now considered how it was all gone.

"Father and I had a most awful row last night. Once I knew you were sleeping I left your room and went to sit by the pool. I was lost in thought and must have been there for ages and the next thing I remember was him shouting to me from inside the house. He was his usual pompous self – full of his own self-importance and did not even bother to inquire after your health. I told him to show a little respect and keep his voice down. It was probably the wine that made him so loud."

"Be careful of him, Drusilla. He has developed a dark and dangerous side and will tolerate no criticism or interference that might impede his political aspirations."

"I couldn't take it any more and told him exactly what I thought of his disgraceful behaviour and underhanded methods. I said some really hurtful things and he slapped me twice across the face but I was so angry I hardly felt it and went back at him again. It was a strange feeling I've never encountered before but I actually enjoyed the confrontation once the anger started to build up and I knew I was afraid of him no longer. It was almost like a release of long-repressed emotions that had built up over the months and I knew something had to give. His arrogance and pontifical attitude were the trigger and it all came out."

"We ceased sharing intimacy on the first day of my illness. How cruel is that? He was so kind in the beginning, before I was struck down with this accursed affliction. When he saw the ugliness of it and how I was reduced to this disgusting, writhing form on the ground in front of him he recoiled in horror and was a changed person from then on. I'll never forget that look upon his face, damn him for eternity!"

"He never speaks of you these days – nothing. It's as if he's trying to erase you from his memory. I'm so sorry for what has become of the two of you."

"I feel only contempt and bitterness now. Even the sound of his voice sickens me. If he died today I would not shed a single tear. You did no wrong speaking to him the way you did, Drusilla, for you voiced the opinions of us both where I have been unable to do so. Perhaps it is the truth that really upsets him and he cannot bear to have his shortcomings illustrated in such a manner."

"He made me accompany him to the gladiator schools this morning, searching for a champion fighter to sponsor in his public games. Nothing else matters except winning this next election and appeasing the mob in his endless search for popularity."

"He has changed, Drusilla. He has become single-minded in his search for wealth and power and will stop at nothing to achieve his aims and I fear he will not hesitate in destroying any person who poses a threat to him and I mean anyone – you or me. He is completely without scruples and bears no resemblance to the man I once knew."

"We had another blazing row at the first school we visited and I know I really hurt him this time. I said I knew about his whores and his

179

dishonourable behaviour and how it would be easy to expose his illegal methods and dishonest, fraudulent handling of government finances. The censors would investigate him and remove him from office. It would be the end of his dream to govern one of the provinces and most likely his political career too. He would be finished."

"You must never do that, my child," and there was a note of panic in Agrippina's voice. "Regardless of what your father has become and however much we despise and abhor his conduct you must never be implicated in the event of his public disgrace or downfall. Given time he will almost certainly dig his own grave. He is vindictive enough to sell this house out from under us and put us both on the streets if there was any scandal or he felt threatened."

"Between us we could destroy him with what we know. It would only take a word in the right ear. He could do nothing. We have enough money to start again somewhere else without him and could manage with a smaller home anyway. We don't need all this. What could he do?"

"No, Drusilla!" and she had become fretful now. "Let him have his promotion within the senate and if the gods are kindly disposed at the end of two years he will be gone to the farthest reaches of the empire, away from us all for good! Come now, my child. No more talk of your father and the darker things in life. I am feeling so much better today thanks to you and your foresight in visiting the apothecary. Let us speak of happier moments, the way we always used to. Tell me, have you met the man of your dreams yet or is it that you have no time these days for such things because you are forever attending your sick mother? Come on," she teased Drusilla, "you can tell me."

It was like a knife being twisted in her ribs. Agrippina's innocent question had caught her off guard and she had no immediate reply. How could she possibly explain after all these years of self-denial she had met, under the most unlikely circumstances, the man she would spend the rest of her life with? There could be no doubt; Quintina had seen it and their union was written in the heavens. Had it been someone her parents could have identified with – a high-ranking official at the very least but nevertheless a patrician or equestrian she would gladly have announced their intention to be together. But Crixus was a gladiator and devoid of any kind of social status. It mattered little that he had sold his freedom and Roman citizenship for five years, that his motives were honourable and his integrity unquestionable. To people like Agrippina and Caius Attius he was every inch a slave forced to fight in the arena for the entertainment of the mob.

"No, mother," Drusilla replied fighting back the tears as she thought of Crixus and felt her heart squeezed. "I have met no one. I hardly venture out these days and those friends I once had no longer call." The denial cut like a blade and she begged his forgiveness but she could never tell Agrippina of her new-found joy and continued reason for living.

"Never mind, my child," her mother continued. "If your apothecary friend knows her business and this condition of mine abates long enough, perhaps you and I can venture out a little. Not too far at first but who knows, with a little time it would be nice to visit the markets in the forum again and look at all the handsome men."

Her illness had indeed taken a toll these last months but Agrippina had lost none of her looks and still harboured that distinctive sexual aura men found so captivating. She was of virtually the same height and build as Drusilla but her increased years had endowed her with an air of sophistication, aloofness and a mood of unavailability – something she was keen to change. She had certainly enjoyed her share of lovers before Caius came onto the scene and she could barely dare to wonder how it might be again one day if she was blessed with good heath once more. While Caius had been away on senatorial business or lusting after young girls there had been many hours to reflect upon her life and now he was no longer a part of it she was formulating plans of her own. Drusilla's kind and unbelievably thoughtful act might just be the key which would unlock the door to her future. Let Caius go and be done with it. He was in the past now. He had never been a particularly gifted and considerate lover when she compared him to some of those other young gods who had swept her off her feet and made her feel like a real women – vibrant, alive and beautiful.

Once again she relished that warm sensation in her body as she recalled some of the tricks of arousal and foreplay they had taught her and she was quick to learn and experiment for herself. Caius had not been able to match her raw, elemental sexuality and soaring abandon and she knew physically their marriage had staled years ago – well before the onset of her convulsions which, she felt, Caius had used as the final excuse to leave her and also because her very presence reminded him of his own inadequacy.

"That would be wonderful, mother," Drusilla welcomed this positive outlook. "You know how the men will love you. After you and father have agreed to go your separate ways they'll be fighting each other for your favours."

"And what of you, Drusilla...? How long before we find the right one for you? You could do a lot worse than marry one of Rome's consuls or perhaps a man who commands whole armies. They are extremely wealthy and only move in the most exclusive circles. The fame and the glory...."

"....And the absences from home," Drusilla cut in before the conversation led to her saying something she would regret. "Let's just get you on the road to full recovery before we start making plans for my own future."

But her future was already mapped out, clear and plain, walking down the years with a man of her choosing. Marriage or any other form of union recognised by the state was completely out of the question but, for now, all she wanted was to see him again and submit to his crushing embrace.

32

The atmosphere in the refectory at Ludus Gallicus was that of relief and camaraderie underscored with an element of self-satisfaction in work well-done – a state of preparedness for the days ahead, knowing those who remained had given their utmost and pushed their bodies to the limits of endurance. The large, airy room was lit only by candles and oil lamps whose dancing flames enhanced the mellow mood and sense of relaxation, and there was an overt sexual hungering in the air for this was the *Cena Libera* – the banquet held for the gladiators by the sponsor.

The guests were witness to a lavish meal that symbolised the boundary between life and death, the last supper for the condemned man as at least some of those present here tonight would no longer be alive this time tomorrow; and there were women too – beautiful women! Not solely the wives, girlfriends and lovers of those who had sold their freedom to train as fighters but wealthy, powerful and influential women seeking a night of illicit passion outside the marital bed with a man who may well die in front of her the following day. Many were the wives of senators, prefects, legates and tribunes and a host of other equally prominent civilian and military figures, either campaigning with the legions or engaging in questionable activities of their own.

The food was rich and plentiful and a welcome change to the regular dispensing of barley-gruel and beans. Wine flowed in seemingly limitless quantities while conversations became noticeably more animated and laughter finally relinquished its nervous edge. Crixus was seated with his fellow gladiators at the long wooden tables, taking full advantage of the sponsor's generosity but politely refusing the amorous attention of his many female admirers. He too was mentally preparing himself for tomorrow's action in the arena and unlike his comrades who would fight on a one-to-one basis he knew as the star attraction he would face at least three opponents simultaneously. The female presence here tonight was superfluous but he found himself highly amused by the antics of couples who made no secret of their erotic intentions. There was only one face he longed to see again and her absence tonight left him with a disturbing emptiness he had never known. She had promised to be there tomorrow, cheering for him, but whether she would be in the front rows with her father or relegated to the rearmost seats traditionally reserved for women he had no idea. Had he never met Drusilla and fallen into love's deep and bountiful pool he could easily have bedded as many of those women seeking his company tonight as he chose for they were all comely and clearly advertising their charms.

He had sworn a sacred oath pledging himself to Drusilla and as her face filled his world once more and he anticipated their next meeting in three days a small part of the loneliness he experienced seemed to melt away. And then a sobering thought occurred to him and he suddenly jerked out of his reverie. He had not even mentioned to the lanista if he might be granted leave of absence once more in order that he visit the apothecary a second time to replenish the elixir. In just two days it had restored an uninterrupted sleep pattern allowing him to waken fully refreshed and ready to face the trials of the day ahead. He was gazing into space mulling over this latest obstacle when he became aware of Lentulus Fulvius dropping down onto the bench next to him.

"The women are not to your liking?" he asked, a brimming cup of wine cradled in his huge hand.

"They are indeed tempting but alas I am sworn to another."

"Ah, I see. A love born out of enforced separation. Will it weather the test of time I wonder? You in here – her out there...? Tell me, Crixus, why is the young lady not here tonight for surely this is the one occasion when a man should not be without the company of a beautiful woman?"

"It is not possible for us to be seen together in public lest her father – especially her father, learns of our secret."

"She must be something special, young Crixus, if you are willing to pursue a fancy where your moments together are secret and stolen."

"She is the most precious thing in my life at this point in time and I cannot envisage a situation where Rome will ever consent to our union for I have the status of a slave and she is...."

"....Of the nobility," the lanista finished the sentence for him, nodding in understanding of their plight.

"Correct. Her father is a prominent citizen seeking election to praetor in the coming elections. You met him when he visited the school yesterday."

184

"Caius Attius Caecilius...?" he asked with incredulity. "You're fucking the daughter of Caius Attius Caecilius? She was with him, yes, I remember now. A great beauty with fire and spirit. Tread carefully, young Crixus, for Caius is not a man to be trifled with. He is spiteful and vindictive and would seek the ultimate punishment for you both if discovered together."

"We have only met once, purely by chance in the garden of the apothecary. Until then I was unaware of her existence and she of mine. I did not seek the encounter, nor did she. It was as if the fates had decreed our paths should cross and set us insurmountable hurdles. All I would respectfully ask is that I be permitted a return to the apothecary in three days, again at dawn, both to replenish the sleeping draught and also to spend a little time with Drusilla – the lady in question."

"The solution rests firmly in your own hands, Crixus. Win the contest tomorrow and let me hear eighty-thousand voices echoing across the sands like the trumpet of Poseidon as they acclaim the new champion. Do this and you may visit the woman as often as you wish. Fail and you will have no need of her for it will be a swift journey to the afterlife that awaits."

Crixus nodded in understanding for clearly his destiny now rested in his own hands.

"I will win and Rome will have its champion."

"Splendid!" Lentulus Fulvius boomed and delivered a great slap to Crixus' shoulder. He farted loudly and then strode off in the direction of a more rowdy gathering where two semi-naked women were having wine poured over their breasts to the accompaniment of raucous laughter and loud, suggestive comments. For Crixus another barrier had finally been negotiated and it was largely down to his own performance in the arena tomorrow to ensure crushing defeat on his opponents thereby securing his value as an indispensable asset at the school and buying valuable time to spend with Drusilla.

He would sleep well tonight for his mind was clear and his body rested. He had already assessed the likely tactics of those who would face him and considered the most effective response in order to make his mark with the blood-thirsty spectators.

He hoped she would be there to watch him and share the glory.

33

Amphitheatrum Flavium

The wild beast hunts that formed the morning's entertainment had been concluded for at least two hours and a team of arena workers had removed the portable scenery while others raked fresh sand over the pools of spilled blood. The midday execution of criminals had been something of an anti-climax and many in the standing-only terraces had left the arena in search of food and drink at local bars and taverns. As they now filed back through the maze of tunnels and corridors to the seating areas in eager anticipation of the afternoon's events, a written programme was distributed stating who would fight whom, how old each of them was, his country of origin and his fight history to date. A privileged few among the crowds would also have been present at the *Cena Libera* last night, held to honour the gladiators.

In accordance with tradition the entertainment commenced with the *pompa* – a grand parade through the streets and terminating inside the amphitheatre itself. The gladiators were dressed in their finest attire and marched alongside those with whom they were paired. The procession was impressive with a band up front followed by an array of attendants and circus performers adding a carnival air to the proceedings. The lead elements were already making their way around the arena in parade whilst the tail-end was still out on the streets enjoying the praise and adulation of those not fortunate enough to have gained access to the interior of the great building.

Most of the written programme was predictable and whilst much of the detail was kept vague for obvious reasons, one item caused much speculation and heated debate among those who would witness the spectacles. This was unheard of; a novice pitted against three adversaries on his debut appearance? There must be a mistake. It was indeed a mystery for none had ever heard of a gladiator by the name of

Crixus and as afternoon inevitably gave way to evening and the heat of the sun thankfully abated, anticipation increased to fever-pitch. Betting on the outcome of the contest was uncertain and odds fluctuated in a moment where outrageous fortunes could be won or lost. How could a neophyte hope to prevail against three proven fighters? Skilled combatants rarely pitted themselves against more than one opponent; the risks were too appalling. So what was going on here? If Crixus did indeed emerge victorious he would be hailed as champion and elevated to god-like status.

As the seconds ticked away, the herald clad in a gleaming white toga, strode to the centre of the arena and began to read from a prepared scroll while the general throb of conversation descended into nothing more than a whisper.

"Highness – citizens of Rome," and his voice carried to every part of the acoustically perfect enclosure, prolonging the drama and suspense with his deliberately measured tones. "We come to the climax of our entertainment today and an event not seen before in our great city. In an unusual contest a novice gladiator has elected to fight not one but three opponents lest his courage and quest for glory be doubted. From the Ludus Magnus, Brutus, Sextus and Lyden."

The three fighters made their entrance in single file to rapturous applause, turning in slow circles with weapons raised so they might acknowledge all in the huge circular auditorium. After several moments the crowds fell silent and the herald continued.

"From the Ludus Gallicus with training only recently completed, a former citizen now seeking fame and glory – Crixus!"

As one, the tens of thousands, seated and standing, burst into spontaneous applause and cheering when Crixus strode from the Porta Sanavivaria into the slowly gathering dusk punctuated by the soft luminescence of a myriad burning oil lamps and incense braziers, their combined haze drifting and spiralling up on the still, late-evening air. The noise was like a wave of concussion, assaulting his eardrums and shaking the teeth in his skull as it reverberated around the arena to collide with yet more pulses of sound reverberating off the high walls.

So this is what it's like!

In acceptance of their humbling accolades he too raised sword and shield and moved in a slow circle to the tumult of whistles and lustful invitations. The women screamed obscenities and bared their breasts as he stood before them, clad in leather armour with its bronze adornments, his massively-overdeveloped musculature seducing them in the manner of the most potent opiate. The initial long-legged stride of his entrance had now subtly evolved into a predatory stalk, even before the contest commenced and he approached his three opponents in the manner of an African cat, utterly confident in the kill and taking a degree of perverse pleasure in their discomfort as he drew closer.

Once again an uneasy silence descended and the herald made his final announcement.

"This contest is to the death. The vanquished will place their fate in the hands of the sponsor." He rolled up the scroll and began to walk away but paused momentarily as he drew level with Crixus. "May Nemesis guide your hand and grant you a glorious victory for your courage is an inspiration to one and all."

As one the group faced Domitian in the *pulvinar* – the royal box, and bowed respectfully. A distant raised hand signalled his acknowledgement and the referee's baton cut the air.

"Begin!"

Long before his three opponents could take up position in a calculated attempt to split his defences and divert crucial attention, Crixus seized the initiative in a blur of movement, delivering a savage reversal at the upper body of the man out to his right. Without checking to see if the strike had connected and done damage he continued his clockwise spin, letting inertia carry him in a full circle to deliver a heavy blow with the shield to head of the man on the opposite side. They had scarcely begun to move and already he was battering and harrying them with a rain of blows they could not match. A sword cut the air inches from his face but he brought the heavy shield to bear again, smashing through the man's guard and experiencing a sense of elation as his gladius ripped into his opponent's vitals, cutting upward with all the power he could muster. Blood and entrails exploded in a torrent of crimson, sending the jubilant crowds into paroxysms of lust and aggressive, wine-fuelled chanting as they urged and demanded even greater extremes of barbarity.

One down, two to go!

The remaining two adversaries seemed to rally and now gathered themselves so as not to fall victim in the manner of their comrade. Even so, none of their most determined attacks came close to finding their mark and they began to fall back, stunned, dazed and fearful of this spectre of death before them. What started out as a sure thing had rapidly developed into a fight for survival as the killing machine beat them down effortlessly, his gladius seemingly everywhere at the same time, hissing, cutting, slashing and opening flesh while the shield followed through like a battering ram. Already, one of their number was dead, his torso split from neck to abdomen while the bones of his ribcage pointed in every angle like accusing fingers. They were outclassed and the penalty for their folly and ill-judged grouping of tactics was death and they sensed it.

The crowds were on their feet again and the mood was ugly, bolstered by copious amounts of cheap wine as they hurled abuse and derision at the two unfortunates who were unable to do anything except go through the motions of attack, knowing Crixus would effectively counter and destroy all such attempts. It was time to end the debacle and he would take them both out at the same time for it was not worth pursuing such a contest any longer. At the outset he considered three opponents might have taxed his reserves and presented something in the way of a credible challenge but if they were all like this he might just as well have been blindfolded.

He rolled forward like an avalanche with gladius scything and hacking just inches from vulnerable flesh, causing his two adversaries to back up and give ground while the boos and heckling told their own story; and then, just as it seemed the end was only seconds away, Crixus paused and offered them their only chance but in the confusion of combat their reactions were slowed and the delay was fatal. In those few seconds Crixus ripped the helmet from his head and let it fall to the ground, reaching out and grasping the sword from his dead opponent. The wolf's-head shield was instantly discarded and within the blink of an eye Crixus had adopted the mantle of the dimachaerus – the one who fought with two knives!

He could see they had expended much of their reserves and were merely going through the motions of combat as fatigue and panic did their insidious work. They were finished and they knew it. Worse still, the crowds knew it too and were now howling for blood. They could expect no quarter and it might be a more dignified and glorious transition to the afterlife if they were to go out with heads high and swords in their hands. The two combatants exchanged imperceptible glances heralding what Crixus knew would be their final onslaught but they were to be denied their moment. In a blur of movement Crixus leapt into the attack with both swords held horizontally across his chest and the assault wavered as their nerve failed. For those who watched from the terraces the scene unfolded in shocking slow motion and time assumed a new dimension in the brutal climax to the contest. As Crixus drew level to his opponents with one man either side, his right and left arms lashed out in dual murderous retribution, ignoring the sting of pain as one of their swords found its mark and opened a deep laceration across his shoulder.

The impact jarred his arms and searing agony lanced through the injury site but his weapons had found their mark. Blood fountained and sprayed across his vision but it was not his own and he was aware of the forward impetus of his opponents faltering as they staggered and collapsed either side of him. As he halted and looked around him he could see each man twitching in the throes of death as his lifeblood ebbed away into the sand, a huge gaping slash wound in the side of the neck where the carotid artery had been severed. A new sound reverberated across the arena proclaiming Crixus' improbable victory and he now stood before his public with raised weapons. Blood from the vanquished mingled with his own, endowing him with a demonic appearance in the eerie twilight and flickering shadows.

It was over and the unthinkable had happened. One man had taken on three and defeated them with apparent ease and the engagement had taken less than ten minutes. As more solid blasts of sound echoed and bounced off the arena walls he became aware of the referee walking back to him from the edge of the seating area.

"Crixus, the sponsor has summoned you to appear before him. This is indeed an honour for a man who has fought as a novice and emerged a lion." Together they stepped smartly back to where the sponsor was waiting to greet Crixus and as he approached the man's position he leaned over the edge of the lavishly-decorated personal box with an item in each hand.

"Hail Crixus!" he intoned, "for you are indeed worthy of such felicitations. I have witnessed many contests in my illustrious career but never anything to equal this. An hour ago you were unknown but now the people have taken you into their hearts and worship you as a god of the arena. To the victor ludorum, the spoils," and he dropped the two items into Crixus' hands, a large purse of gold and his first laurel wreath. "Hail the conqueror," and as he raised his arms above his head the crowds responded with their own deafening acclaim while Crixus stood before them once more before marching back to the Gate of Life.

Drusilla and Caius had arrived only minutes before Crixus was due to fight and as the herald began the formal introductions she felt her stomach tighten with anticipation, knowing in this final contest she would see him dispense bloodshed and death on a scale she could scarcely believe. The very thought of his ruthlessness and immense power stood out in stark contrast to his touching kindness and sensitivity and made her weak with desire once more. When the three opponents entered she was truly frightened for him but as Crixus made his own appearance and they seemed to shrink back, her fears were allayed. They were totally outclassed, both in speed and tactical ability and could not hope to match his effortless, flowing grace that seemed alien in such a large man. She would relive the whole performance over and over until they met again a short time from now.

For Caius Attius there could be no doubt whatsoever he had found precisely the man he was looking for. The lanista had offered him generous terms and Crixus had delivered on his word. All that remained was to organise the games as a prelude to the elections and make himself known among the people. He would give them assurances of reforms and radical improvements to their daily lives, even if he could not deliver them; but what mattered most was that he appeared the kind and concerned benefactor championing the people's cause. If Crixus could win their hearts then it shouldn't be beyond the realms of possibility for Caius Attius Caecilius to do likewise. He wondered if he could lie so convincingly.

34

Darkness gradually receded and a new day dawned as the sun rose over the gentle hills of the eastern horizon. The early breeze was light and benevolent as a lover's caress but the cloudless sky offered no promise of rain to the scorched earth as flora and fauna alike baked in the seemingly never-ending heat of another Mediterranean summer. The sprawling vineyards either side of the dusty road stretched as far as the eye could see but even the fertile volcanic soil which had for centuries supported the rich red grape was unable to provide the key element upon which all life depended – water!

Even at this early hour an army of slaves was out in the fields sweating under the hot and demanding conditions as they carried thousands of clay amphorae and animal skins full of water from the nearby valley, up the slopes to artificially irrigate the vines so dependent on this basic requirement.

To Crixus the heat was of no concern in his present mood for he was nearing the place which had been uppermost in his thoughts these last few days. As he took in the smells of olive plantations, lemon and orange groves and clumps of wild sage interspersed by tall cypresses so his spirits lifted above the memory of the carnage and baseness of the arena and his pace quickened. As he rounded the final bend in the road and the welcoming sight of the apothecary's dwelling at last came into view, he felt his heart-rate begin to pound at the prospect of meeting Drusilla again. There had been no time to search for her in the vastness of the auditorium and the time before that her very presence had made it difficult to concentrate on the task at hand – especially with her father being present too. But he would not reflect upon that now for it was unproductive and detracted from his mission here today. As he stepped through the gap in the surrounding wall he again marvelled at the beauty of this natural setting with the lively spring tumbling over rocks into the deep pool and the indescribable attraction of the gardens.

He coughed politely to announce his arrival and rounded the corner of the house to find Quintina and Drusilla seated on a simple wooden bench chatting animatedly. Abruptly their conversation ceased and Quintina took the initiative, standing up to greet him with outstretched arms.

"Behold, great Mars has journeyed through the heavens in search of his consort! Welcome again to my humble home, you magnificent god of war."

"I am a speck of light in the vastness of the cosmos," he countered making an exaggerated deep and sweeping bow in acknowledgement of his host. "I have returned the amphora so you may refill it," and he held out the empty container.

"It may take considerable time to prepare so I will leave the two of you alone. I'm sure you have much to discuss," and with a flamboyant whirl of her stola she turned and made her way to the workroom. His gaze was fixed upon Drusilla and as she rose from her seat he knew if he lived to be a thousand he would never tire of her presence. She was tall and stately, possessing the grace of a swan and the majesty befitting a queen. She held out her hands and he took them in his own, kissing her fingers and feeling the world begin to tilt as he inhaled her fragrance and wondered how he had survived these last days.

"You are beautiful," and he felt his eyes misting over, "but my words are not adequate to describe that beauty for you are beyond words. I am only a mortal man but would gladly die in defence of those feelings I nurture for you. When I walked away from here four days ago I was only a shell for my inner spirit remained with you, where it truly belongs."

She made an unconvincing show of blinking away the tears and he could sense her upwelling emotions for the words she heard were an exquisite pain in her heart and confirmation of what she hoped he felt too. She leaned forward and he kissed her eyes, wondering at the soft, feathery touch of her lashes as she gave in to her feelings and allowed the tears to flood out. He was completely at odds with the turmoil that seethed violently within his own body, allowing him no respite from the conflicting, gut-wrenching extremes of his situation. He was a trained killer, a shining exponent of his trade and could butcher opponents as fast as they were sent to him; and yet, here like this with his woman in his arms, cradling her in this most tender and intimate of moments, he felt more vulnerable and unguarded than ever. He had fallen in love with her and there could be no turning back, as if he had plunged into the deepest precipice and his fate now rested in the lap of the gods. He ached to tell her how she had transformed his life where only the looming contest with Ferox was focusing his mind and preserving all rational thought; but he would wait until the time was perfect – for both of them.

After several minutes where they remained pressed together he became aware her crying had ceased and she stepped back a pace to gaze at him.

"Please forgive me," she whispered. "Your words took me by surprise and I had no response to such a beautiful declaration. I have wanted to hear it many times even though it is only our second meeting but I was unprepared when you spoke them." There was an undisguised invitation in her eyes and she moistened her parted lips with the tip of her tongue. "Quintina says there is a secret place at the bottom of the garden through an old gate where we can be alone for a short time. Let us go there now for my body craves your embrace and I need to hear the words you feel in your heart."

With hands linked they walked along winding paths inhaling the rich scents of exotic plants with their striking diversity of colour. Blossoms dangled pendulously from arbours and clung to the ancient stone walls while lichen-covered statues looked down from tall plinths with their unseeing eyes. Behind a dense leafy screen of figs and cicadas the narrow path came to an abrupt halt at another wall with a high wooden gate set into the rough blocks of travertine. The iron hinges had rusted over the years but when Crixus pushed gently, the gate opened without resistance and they stepped through the portal into a small circular area bordered by date palms and bougainvillaea with their pinkish-red blossoms and redolent scent. In the centre rested a small timber structure at the top of half a dozen steps. It was devoid of windows but a single opening led directly to the shaded interior and a modestly decorated room divided by a simple curtain. On one side, a large couch with sumptuous covers and tasselled cushions matching the blooms of the garden. It was the perfect hideaway from the outside world and its very location guaranteed a degree of privacy to be found nowhere else.

"I never even knew this place existed until a couple of hours ago," Drusilla declared with undisguised intrigue. "I wonder what other little surprises Quintina has up her sleeve."

"Is this why you brought me here this morning – so I might love you as I have wanted to love you since that first meeting?"

"Yes, I cannot deny the weakness of my body for where else can we be alone without the risk of discovery? How long do we have today, Crixus? How long before you have to leave me again and report back to the school?"

194

"As a special dispensation from the lanista I have until noon. That leaves us many hours to spend together unless, of course, your mother's ailment dictates you return to her before then."

"No," she replied with hooded, downcast eyes, coming to stand directly in front of him so he could feel the firmness of her breasts through the rough-woven tunic. "No, I do not have to leave so early today. She is much improved and the house slaves will be in attendance during my absence so you see there is no hurry at all."

Her words made his chest pound once more and the thought of caressing her flesh made his lower body ache unbearably. She moved back a pace within the shade of the small room and released the clasp on the solid gold fibula securing the shoulder fastenings of her stola but left the glossy, stylish black hair in place. As the garment dropped to the floor and she stood unashamedly before him inviting the attention of his eyes, he found it a little daunting to believe a woman could be so physically perfect and utterly desirable.

"Let me look at you for the first time," she demanded huskily, unbuckling the thick, heavy leather balteus at his waist and slipping the tunic over his head. At the sight of him her nipples firmed up to a new unbelievably sensitive consistency and her belly burned with the fires of her longing for he was indeed built like a god and not a single vestige of fat remained on his body. At the school she had only seen the great muscles of his arms and legs and in the arena much of his chest had been hidden by armour. Now she was able to study his form at her leisure and she lusted over his raw masculinity. His chest was huge and she could identify the individual pairs of abdominal muscles. The waist was relatively narrow but flared out again into great broad thighs. In his current state of arousal she wondered if she might accommodate him for even though she was well-versed in depictions of the male member as displayed in mosaics and frescoes, she had never seen anything quite like this.

But there was no hurry for time was on their side today and she could afford to let events unfold naturally. All the same, seeing him like this only served to reinforce her physical need and she felt her inner thighs quiver in delicious anticipation while the warm, slippery sensation spread a little further and began to slick her opening.

He gestured for her to lie on the ample couch with its soft, luxurious cover and she spread herself in a gesture of invitation while he gazed at the new shape adopted by her breasts. Much as he craved to bury himself within her and satisfy his own cruel need, he would not and began to explore her wondrous form, beginning at her toes and gradually moving higher. He had never seen the full extent of her legs before and was surprised by the sculpted muscle-tone and healthy appearance of her flesh where the sun had touched her with its golden rays. As he continued on his journey of sensual discovery he paused to kiss the little dimples at the back of her knees, teasing her body with the tip of a moist tongue and stroking with gentle fingers. Her fragrance was seemingly everywhere – even down here as he tasted her thighs and she began to move her pelvis in slow, sensuous circles. The first climax was already hovering on the fringes as he touched her slippery opening and she was aware of her own copious lubrication seeping out unchecked. Suddenly the world tilted and spun and her lower body contracted violently as the sensation of his fingers was replaced by a warm probing tongue lapping against the tiny bud of flesh that burned with its own fire. Her back arched and she shuddered with the intensity of it, biting down painfully on her lower lip so as not to call out.

It went on and on in a mind-numbing blur of spasms and contractions where his attention knew no limits and she thought she might die of her own lust and abandonment – and she had not touched him yet.

"Crixus, Crixus, what are you doing to me? My body is burning and every time the feeling grows stronger. Even in my wildest dreams it was never like this."

"In that moment of our first meeting I loved you more than life itself and the pain was like the thrust of a dagger for in my mind you were unattainable – as far from me as the moon is from the earth and I wanted you so. And now look at me for am I not the richest of all men?"

Once more he lowered his head and delved for her fleshy centre, losing himself in the wonders of her feminine scent and liberal secretions. It was warm and dark and safe and he experienced a degree of sanctuary impossible to describe, only that he could remain here like this for ever. Again and again she shuddered under his touch and rolled her head from side to side. He had made no attempt to enter her yet and seemed content to take pleasure from the sight of her voluptuous form and the knowledge he was taking her to heights she thought it impossible to reach. He was drawing out the pleasure for both of them as the stars continued to explode inside her head with unremitting brilliance and time assumed a new dimension in this sequestered little paradise. He seemed to have no regard for his own needs and she was aware she had not touched him yet, not gripped his length and teased him to the point of release with slim fingers and manicured nails. After the next trembling climax where her heart threatened to burst out of her swollen breast she at last managed to distract him with softly-spoken words.

"Crixus, enough, my love. Enough for now. Come and lay with me so I might worship your body also for I swear if you continue with your attentions I shall surely die with the intensity of it."

Almost reluctantly he lay down by her side, his head at a level with her breasts. As she reached out and closed a hand about his girth he moved his head and closed his mouth over the engorged nipple for it was the size of a ripe grape and succulent as the real fruit from the vine. Studying him as he feasted upon her she was filled with a surprising sense of protection and despite his towering strength and menacing qualifications as a star of the arena she detected an aura of vulnerability perfectly concealed by the tough, uncompromising exterior. She knew he had lost both parents many years ago and destiny had smiled upon him as he embarked upon his chosen journey to master the creation of structures that would endure for millennia. Just a few months ago that dream had been plucked from his hands by vengeful gods and he had now embarked upon a new, disturbing odyssey that saw him plunged into a world of blood, hideous cruelty and violent death as he sought to avenge the murder of a true friend and guiding light. This was not how it should have been and she pondered the predestination of life where their paths would have remained separate under different circumstances.

As she teased and stroked and ran her nails down the underside of his hard length she could surmise by his breathing he approached the moment of release and skilfully lessened the degree of contact so the wave might recede and gather itself once more. After a short while where neither of them spoke and satisfied the moment had passed for now, she resumed her deft touches and felt his size increase again. As she sensed the urgency of his movements and knew it was cruel to deny him a second longer, she slid her tongue deliciously into his mouth, searching, probing, demanding and in her hand she felt his reaction as the great wave finally rushed in and spent itself against the shore in a violent explosion of surf.

For long moments after, they lay unmoving, fearful to speak lest it shatter the fragile illusion of their situation. They were both aware their meetings were illicit and dangerous and their loving was born of the strict behavioural codes enforced by Rome's rigidly-stratified society. If their secrecy be compromised it would spell disaster with far-reaching implications for both of them. Even now, there could be no guaranteed tomorrows and promises made for the future. The best they could expect was simply to live for every stolen, forbidden moment where even the excitement of another chance encounter seemed as remote as the stars.

When he knew of Drusilla's true feelings and it looked as if they were destined to follow an uncertain path fraught with all manner of perils and insurmountable barriers, he had summoned one of the local goldsmiths whose reputation was deemed to be honourable. He could only guess the finger-size of the lady in question and made a simple drawing of his requirements with an urgent plea for haste as time was of the utmost importance. The man had been as good as his word and just before sunset last night delivered the goods to the school. After a careful inspection and nod of approval Crixus tossed the man a leather purse containing some of the coins presented to him on his first victory. It was perfect for their situation and he hoped she would approve of his bold gesture.

Grasping the nettle he reached out from the couch and retrieved a tiny package wrapped in a square of purple velvet from the pocket of his tunic. How thoroughly appropriate he should choose such a manner of presentation for that was the colour befitting her true status, the colour of royalty – the colour of a queen!

"Drusilla, I am painfully aware we can never be a couple in the true sense of the word and I am reminded of that every time I look at you. I know we can never be married for you are of the nobility whilst I am looked upon as a slave and the state would never recognise any union outside the law. In light of these things would you do me the greatest honour and accept that which I now offer as a token of love in the absence of marriage?"

As she took the small item and solemnly removed the outer covering with agonising slowness, he held his breath lest she be appalled and admonish his recklessness and stupidity. And then her eyes fell upon the ring and she wept with joy and the precarious nature of their situation. She had never known a happier moment in her life, nor would she give up a single moment of it in the months ahead.

"A betrothal ring!" she exclaimed through the floods of tears that threatened to overwhelm her. "A betrothal ring," she repeated with delight, slipping it over the third finger of her left hand, "and it fits perfectly. However did you manage this? It's simply lovely and I will keep it concealed about my person always. Thank you, and yes, I accept you as the husband Rome will deny me. May the gods witness I give myself to you completely and without reservation and hear me when I say I love you."

She half expected a clap of thunder accompanied by a bolt of lightning to strike her dead as the gods voiced their anger at her insolence and flagrant declaration but only silence prevailed and she visibly relaxed.

The expensive gold ring bore a relief carving of two young people clasping right hands and epitomised their own circumstances perfectly. Its beauty was in its simplicity and she loved it but Crixus was suddenly mortified by his own bravado.

"Drusilla, you cannot possibly wear this when you are at home or out in public for the significance is bound to be recognised and questions asked."

She was thoughtful for a few moments and then came back with a confident smile.

"There is a way I can wear it. I have a gold chain I can easily thread through the ring and hang around my neck so it rests just here," and she indicated the small gap in her prominent cleavage. It will remain perfectly concealed for no one but you and I will ever come so close...."

She touched him again and his arousal was swift and demanding. He kissed her and touched a gentle finger to the lips of her opening, sensing she too was ready and their moment was at hand. Their shared kiss became a lingering, passionate caress and bore an air of desperation at their imminent, frenzied coupling, reaffirming every word passed between them and containing a thousand other unspoken sentiments. It was a kiss symbolic of two people brought together by the suffering of others and circumstances beyond their scope of human understanding but because of the uncompromising laws of society and the whims of capricious gods, their future would be cut brutally short.

Her thighs were parted in the attitude of acceptance and as she reached out and found him hard and thrusting she knew, as if it had been carved in stone, this was the moment – the moment she had deferred for years in anticipation of he who would come to her in her hour of need and love her as no other.

As she felt him slide effortlessly into the core of her being she was again aware of that sense of protection toward him – an awareness of utter contentment where if she died right now there would be no regrets. She was touched by his gentleness and considerate comportment – placing her needs and feelings above his own and again she thought her heart might break. His movements became more urgent, assuming a note of abandonment she understood well as he passed the point of no-return. She closed her eyes and, squeezing her inner muscles so she might grip him even tighter, precipitated the onset of her own climax which had been lurking on the fringes of her soul.

In this attitude of peace and contentment where the ugliness and petty strivings of the outside world were consigned to a far-off place, the gentle mists of sleep enshrouded them with soft, protective wings.

Hours later they awoke as the sun cast its rays through the open doorway and Crixus judged by the angle of shadow it was still well before noon. A little guiltily he reflected Quintina would almost certainly have had their respective medications ready hours ago but then decided her hand had been instrumental in this unexpected interlude with Drusilla and their joint absences should not be entirely unexpected. As they dressed and prepared to make their return to the city once more Drusilla caught sight of a small written note attached to the polished-silver mirror and looked closer.

It read simply, '*May your love endure and the gods watch over you....*' No signature was required for only Quintina could have endorsed their love in such a manner. As Crixus adjusted his attire and Drusilla sat on the edge of the couch admiring the ring she would remove before she arrived home – just in case, she suddenly remembered her own gift tucked away in her stola. She had intended to give it to him earlier but the heated progression of events overruled any clear thinking and judgement, ensuring the opportunity passed by. She retrieved the object just as Crixus came to stand beside her once more and she patted the cushion next to her, inviting him to be seated.

"I intended to give you this when we arrived but I was filled with the magic of your own words and the chance was missed. I suppose now is as good a time as any...," and she pressed the small item into his palm, kissing his fingers as she closed them.

"A ring," he declared. "A silver ring. I have never owned a ring. This is too much. I did not expect...," and she silenced him with a delicate finger to his lips.

"Sshh.... There is no need of gratitude for this is my first love-gift to you."

As he read the inscription – Libera Vivas - May you live free, his resolve cracked and the tears spilled onto his cheeks. He wept with an unfamiliar happiness at his love for Drusilla who now cradled his head in her hands and he wept for Julius Quintus whom he loved like a father and was now gone for ever; but the monstrous cruelty of it all was that he would never be able to walk in public with this woman on his arm and see the envy in other men's eyes; that their love would be restricted to moments such as this, stolen, secret liaisons with the risk of exposure ever-present. He cursed his weakness for betraying such emotions but for Drusilla it was further confirmation he was a man – mortal, just like her and as such, vulnerable to human strengths and frailties and she loved him all the more because of it.

35

After witnessing Crixus' debut performance in the Amphitheatrum Flavium where he effortlessly defeated three opponents within the space of a few minutes and the crowds alternated between monumental cheering and stunned silence, Caius Attius Caecilius just had to show off this new sensation to his friends and colleagues in order he impress them still further.

Not being content to wait until his public games whereupon the ideal opportunity would have presented itself for Caius to demonstrate what a truly unique fighting phenomenon he had discovered, he decided in an impromptu display of decadence and one-upmanship to play his hand early and show off Crixus' skills at a private party held in one of his colleague's homes. Cassius Seneca shared virtually equal political status with Caius, enjoying the position of aedile along with its associated comforts and privileges, respect, influence and wealth. In an effort to assure Caius of his unstinting loyalty Cassius had offered the use of his own large domus with its immense banqueting room capable of holding up to a hundred guests, and there were heated, fragrant baths too. Caius had rewarded the man generously and given assurances of support in any future elections. The guests were duly invited and Caius was compelled to visit the Ludus Gallicus again to secure Crixus for one evening.

There had been no problems with the arrangement but Caius detected a note of secrecy and joviality in the air – a little hint of something he couldn't quite put his finger on, almost as if the lanista knew something he was not prepared to disclose. It irked him and he was on the point of voicing protest at this barely-concealed mockery when he thought better of it. He had gotten what he came for and the price had been reasonable too; one thousand denarii for what would in all likelihood be only a few minutes work for a man like Crixus but the increase in prestige and credibility for Caius would be enormous once they saw his ace card. The spectacles would need to be lavish indeed when the time came and on such a scale as to totally eclipse anything his opposition was planning.

But that was all in the future. Right now he needed to give them a foretaste of what they could expect in the days to come and he would do that as part of the entertainment at tonight's banquet.

Everything had gone according to plan and the main room was now humming with conversation as couples and groups mixed freely and socialised in the convivial atmosphere, feasting on the rich and plentiful food and limitless supplies of full-blooded wine. Couches were placed so as to facilitate the business of pouring and serving without house slaves becoming embarrassingly noticeable among the aristocracy.

The *Gustatio* or appetiser course had consisted of four choices which at first seemed inadequate in the face of such numbers but the caterers had done their arithmetic well and there had been no complaints about quality or quantity. Caius had chosen the menu personally and visually preened at the compliments. To tempt the palate there were jellyfish and eggs, sow's udders stuffed with milk and eggs, boiled tree fungi with peppered fish-fat sauce or sea-urchins with spices, oil and egg sauce. Predictably, those given to larger appetites had sampled all four.

After a short interlude during which the empty serving platters were cleared away and fresh supplies of wine brought in to be distributed among the guests, the main course of the evening – *Primae Mensa,* was carried at shoulder height by the serving slaves. The quantities were staggering, even for this number of diners and the rich, succulent aromas compounded by the tang of garum filled the air and blended with other, less-palatable odours of a hundred people in the same room on a hot and sultry night. There were scores of candles and oil lamps further adding to the heat and gradually the air thickened and fogged with smoke. But this did not in any way detract from the excellent cuisine on offer and many were demanding second portions before everyone had received their first.

Fallow deer roasted with onion sauce, Jericho dates, raisin oil and honey topped the menu tonight and to complement this there was boiled ostrich with sweet sauce, turtle dove boiled in its feathers, roast parrot, dormice stuffed with pork and pine kernels, ham boiled with figs and bay leaves rubbed with honey and baked in a pastry crust or flamingo boiled with dates.

Drusilla had placed herself at the far end of the banqueting hall in order to remain aloof from Caius' vulgarity and openly-disgusting behaviour where he was not only fondling the breasts of single women but some of the married ones too. As the wine flowed in ever-

203

increasing amounts and conversations became louder and slurred she felt completely out of place and regarded the whole episode with distaste. Initially the food had been to her liking but the obscene quantities spoiled her appetite and she pushed her plate away with a gesture of annoyance. She was bored out of her skull and longed to be anywhere but here. Unfortunately, her father insisted she accompany him for she might take a liking to one of the higher officials and make something of her life.

After heated protest her only reason for agreeing to be present at this indecorous soiree was because she knew Crixus would be making an appearance. Clearly he would not be partaking in the revelry and she hated her father with renewed venom for the way he intended to parade Crixus in front of his cronies, like a prized bull at one of the butchers in the forum. She also knew there would be a contest to the death once the tables had been moved aside and whilst she held no fear for Crixus in these matters she was aware of the miserable fate awaiting his opponent; robbed of a glorious death in the arena, his life seemingly snuffed out and ignominiously removed from the world before a handful of drunken, indifferent spectators who placed no value on his existence.

With the arrival of the sweet course – the *Secundae,* Drusilla experienced a mild sensation of relief, knowing the obscene gorging was almost at an end and the remains of the huge dishes with their sickly aromas would at last be removed from her presence. Mercifully, the smells of this last serving were not such an assault on her palate and she eyed critically the plates as they were laid out in front of her.

There was fricassee of roses with pastry, stoned dates stuffed with nuts and pine kernels fried in honey and hot African sweet-wine cakes with honey. She was relieved to see as appetites were finally becoming sated the guests did not pounce on the dishes like a pack of starving animals but approached them with an unfamiliar restraint and inspected what others brought back from the tables.

From the corner of her eye she became aware of someone approaching her; not her father for he was preoccupied fondling one of the pretty young things staring at him doe-eyed at the far end of the hall. No, this was one of a group of young males situated a short distance from her own table. Seeing how she sat alone apparently bored and clearly not spoken-for, the young man had decided to approach her having consumed sufficient quantities of wine to bolster his courage. In her current state of apathy she suddenly saw a way to liven up the occasion, both to the annoyance of her father and the embarrassment of the pathetic individual now almost upon her.

"May I join you?" he asked confidently, taking the seat next to her without waiting for a reply. "I have been watching you tonight and it seems you are listless and in need of male company. You do not partake in the feasting and celebrations with the rest of us and it is surely a crime for one so lovely to be alone."

His arrogance was unbelievable and she regarded him with undisguised hostility for he sickened her and she resisted the urge to walk away. He gave her the impression she had been waiting all evening for him to come across and sweep her off her feet but her reply was not the one he had been expecting and the sting in her tone caused the swagger to evaporate instantly.

"On the first count, I do not feast in the manner of those vile pigs surrounding me because, believe it or not, my appetite is spoiled and in any case I am particular with whom I choose to dine." With her downcast eyes she seemed a tempting proposition for his advances – a simpering virgin ripe for plucking and grateful of any male attention that might be shown her.

"Secondly!" she continued in a manner deliberately calculated to turn heads as her voice increased in volume and brought unwanted attention to the hapless suitor, "precisely what are we celebrating? Please, do enlighten me."

He was clearly uncomfortable with his mistaken interpretation of the scenario and she wickedly revelled as he squirmed uncomfortably and shrank away from her mounting anger.

"Well...," he continued hesitantly, "are we not celebrating Caius Attius Caecilius' imminent elevation to praetor in the forthcoming elections for it is virtually assured now he has arranged the games he will sponsor and his rivals will be swept aside?"

"An interesting observation," Drusilla replied confidently. "Tell me, is it not customary to hold celebrations *after* the successful even rather than before? To organise such activities in advance would not only seem a bad portent for the future but should the said occasion be marred by disaster and the predicted outcome not be realised then such revelry and jollification would appear a little foolish and premature, would it not?"

Heads were turning in her direction and conversations ended abruptly as the guests detected some other unplanned entertainment. Drusilla's unwelcome guest stood and made as if to take his leave for he was no match for this woman's acid tongue or monumental intellect. Instantly she was on her feet, throwing her chair back noisily and scattering plates from the table with an angry sweep of the hand. She derived a sadistic enjoyment from the cringing individual whose face was reddening under her verbal onslaught as he sensed his dreadful mistake for when his intention was to stroke the kitten he had unwittingly stepped on a viper.

"How dare you turn to walk away from me when I have not dismissed you? You think I am ignorant to your pathetic advances but I know what it is you seek from me. You care nothing for a lady's honour and respectability. All that concerns you is your own selfish need – your sexual gratification and you would gladly use me as the innocent receptacle for your vile and careless seed!"

The adrenalin was surging through her body now and she experienced a wonderful sensation of audacity bordering on recklessness. No one moved in the packed hall and a deathly hush descended upon the gathering. All she could hear was the blood thumping in her ears and a voice filled with outrage that bore little resemblance to the one she knew.

"Go and find yourself a whore worthy of your loathsome suggestions and pale, unmanly form for the only way you will enjoy female company tonight is to pay for it." She reached into the folds of her stola and retrieved a single silver denarius, hurling it into his face. "There! That should buy you a whore. This place is full of them!"

He was glowering with anger and the uncomfortable realisation he had just been bested by a woman – effortlessly and in front of his friends who, along with the remainder of the guests, were now dissolving into fits of mirth. He returned to his table and Drusilla found another chair, refusing to pick up the one she had sent skittering across the floor as she took to her feet. She poured a goblet of wine and sipped demurely, inspecting her manicured nails and admiring the many rings on her slim elegant fingers. The incident had not been lost to her father who remained silent throughout the heated exchange. He knew better than to become embroiled in another verbal confrontation with Drusilla, especially in a place like this where he could ill-afford any loss of face.

"A feisty one she is," someone called out above a scream of raucous laughter. "I like a woman with balls as well as spirit. Do you know her, Caius?"

"I know her," he grumbled like a simmering volcano and there was a mixture of anger at her outburst and a degree of reluctant admiration for he too had found himself on the business-end of her stinging tongue more than once and it had cut like a lash. All the same, he made a note to confront her about the incident but for now there were other more pressing issues to be dealt with for the tables were being cleared away to make room for the highlight of tonight's entertainment.

Chairs and couches had been arranged in a rough circle around the perimeter and satisfied everything was ready Caius took up position at the centre of the floor, red-faced from wine and visibly inflated by the prospect of the next few moments while the incident with Drusilla appeared forgotten.

"Distinguished guests – fellow Romans. I have arranged a little contest as the highlight of tonight's get-together so you might witness, as I did, the exceptional skills of a young gladiator I chanced upon only a few days ago. His competence and unmatched heroism were so great I have decided to include him as the main event in the games I will soon be hosting. I know many of you abstain from these spectacles through boredom or perhaps you are reluctant to be seen among the vulgar crowds who throng the auditorium. Rest assured, when you have seen him fight you will change your minds. The young man's name is Crixus and his opponent tonight – from the Ludus Magnus, Tysus."

As his name was called, Tysus emerged from the shadows into the semi-gloom and eerie flickering of candles and lamps. The room was bathed in unearthly yellow and orange light while smoke formed a dense layer in the high ceiling and obscured the delicate frescoes and artwork. He was bare-chested and wore no armour save for a heavy leather balteus studded with bronze rosettes over the waist of his simple loin cloth. There were no shields in this contest and each combatant would be armed with only a single gladius. Crixus too was waiting at the far end of the banqueting hall and the anger seethed within him for this parody, this mockery of a battle that bore no resemblance to a true contest of martial prowess. As part of his contract with the lanista he understood the necessity of being hired out for appearances as and when required, regardless of the location, but his place was in the arena and not some dismal, smoke-darkened function-room devoid of fresh air and adequate fighting space.

As he was summoned his two guards from the school were dispensed with but would remain on the fringes, alert and watchful – just in case. In the event of trouble it was unlikely they would be able to overpower their charge and relied largely on his good will and collaboration to keep the peace. Both fighters were of similar height and neither wore a helmet so it was immediately obvious from the whistles and ribald comments who appealed most to the women. Tysus was not an attractive man; his nose had been broken at some point and the line of his mouth was hard and fleshless. He carried a long scar from the outer corner of his left eye down to his chin – an ugly, vivid reminder of an earlier encounter in his career when the blood decorating the sand beneath his feet had been his own. He told himself there would be no repeat of that tonight. He exuded an air of cruelty, the countenance of the thug, the bully, the street-fighter and lacked any appeal for the female contingent.

When Crixus took the floor the air became deliciously charged with menace and sexual excitement, his body language calculated to instil confidence among the onlookers and the insidious worm of doubt in his opponent. Every muscle in his immense body was clearly defined as if forged by the Cyclopes in the foundry of the gods. Where Tysus had entered with a confident swagger, Crixus was disturbingly quiet and unsmiling and the latent menace in his near-naked form was apparent to all, even without the helmet and enclosing visor.

The referee was unknown to Crixus but he would watch the contest closely and ensure the strict rules were adhered to regardless of duration or outcome. He stood to one side and addressed both parties who now faced each other several feet apart.

"This contest is to the death, either directly by the hand of your opponent or at the wishes of the sponsor if he merits it worthy of a poor showing." He stepped back a pace and glanced at Caius who nodded for the bout to commence. "Begin!"

Without the protection afforded by shields they were both conscious to remain vigilant lest the gladius find its mark and end the contest prematurely. Tysus was quick and agile but lacked discipline and as he saw his most determined attacks countered with relative ease his anger mounted and his sword movements became increasingly wild and uncoordinated. It was impossible to launch feint attacks for Crixus anticipated his every move – and he had scarcely moved yet! Apart from the need to avoid some of Tysus' desperate lunges and great animated slashing assaults Crixus stood his ground and watched in amusement as the other man expended his reserves jinking and dancing to deny his man an easy target, but it showed on his face he was uneasy and his opponent was in a different league. There was no wild cheering and the atmosphere in the hall was strangely expectant, as if the outcome was foregone and being played out to its ultimate and predictable conclusion; but they were keen to see how both men acquitted themselves and how courage, valour and contempt for death assumed their places in the unfolding drama. The only sounds to be heard were the grunts of exertion and the metallic clash of blade on blade as battle continued.

They seemed almost mesmerised by the way Crixus was able to avoid being struck without flinching or backing away, in fact he remained on the same spot with both feet planted firmly on the marble floor while his huge torso swayed rhythmically, almost sensually in the manner of tall grass bending before a gentle breeze. Something had to happen soon. It simply could not go on like this indefinitely. In what could only have been a pre-arranged signal Tysus raised his left arm and clicked his fingers, the cue for one of his escorts to toss him a second gladius but in order to catch it he must momentarily avert his eyes from Crixus.

Whilst not actively searching for any particular opening in his opponent's defences for he was merely prolonging the end for the morbid curiosity of the spectators, Crixus was appalled by this glaring if only fleeting inattention to the other man's guard and without moving his feet simply thrust the gladius forward in a blur that deceived the eye and brought gasps of disbelief from those watching around the perimeter. As Tysus' arm was raised the point of Crixus' weapon found its mark, piercing the shoulder slightly below the collar bone and severing muscle and sinew. Tysus dropped the second weapon immediately but was unable to cover the wound or staunch the flow of blood. It was by no means a mortal blow but Tysus was maimed, unable to use his left arm and would be rendered weak from blood-loss and shock in a short time. His face was contorted in a mask of pain for he thought it impossible a man the size of Crixus could move with such speed. If he was going to stand any chance at all he would have to deliver a decisive attack of his own in the next few moments before his strength ebbed away completely.

Crixus sensed the end approaching rapidly and although it was not his intention to inflate Caius Attius' ego further and elevate the height of his already-lofty pedestal, he was mindful of his initial pledge to Lentulus Fulvius.

'I will give them something they have never seen before!'

At considerable personal risk where the virtual silence of the room was punctuated by barely-muffled screams from his female admirers, Crixus closed his eyes and turned his back on Tysus – the ultimate gesture of contempt for his opponent and a bold statement to his own fearlessness and self-belief.

In his all-consuming lust for victory and blind to the trap set for him, Tysus changed to an overhand grip on the sword, raising it up to penetrate Crixus' neck where it would sever the spinal chord and kill him instantly. Those who looked on with bated breath could only hope Crixus had not misjudged his opponent's intentions and left himself open to certain death. And then, as Tysus struck and it seemed there could only be but one outcome, the sword of Crixus was reversed and thrust backward and obliquely upward ripping into Tysus' ribs, cleaving flesh and bone and tearing into the heart, gutting him like a carcass on the butcher's block. The attack from behind immediately faltered as Tysus slumped to the ground and fell forward, face down into a pool of his own blood.

The heavy silence was broken by an uncertain smattering of applause and then the place erupted into a cacophony of sound as the guests stood and applauded, cheering wildly and banging clenched fists on the wooden tables. He stood unmoving and smiled, acknowledging their accolades and somewhere among the sea of faces he caught sight of Drusilla – aloof from the crowd but visually stunning in her jewellery and finest gown as she too smiled and applauded.

But Crixus' smile was a cover to conceal the resentment and hatred that burned like a flame as his roving eye picked out Caius Attius at the far end of the room, preening like a peacock and revelling in the blandishments being showered upon him. It was sickening and with a series of leaping strides Crixus took off in his direction, bringing the gladius up and launching it in a glistening, whirling arc. At the sound of screams Crixus came to an abrupt halt, just as the contingent of guards arrived and the gladius pinned Caius' robe to the wooden chair. They surrounded him with weapons drawn and he stood defiantly before Caius, hands on hips, feet apart and chin thrust out belligerently in a calculated display of insolence and overt contempt. Caius was spluttering with shock and indignation and his earlier euphoria evaporated leaving him mortified at the sight of the still-quivering gladius impaled deeply in the wood less than three inches from his throat.

"You bloody madman!" he bellowed. "I'll have you flogged and crucified for that. You almost killed me. Clearly, you are unaware that senatorial officials are inviolate."

"Almost!" Crixus' smile returned but his eyes remained cold as he shrugged off the guards' restraining hands. "Almost," he repeated, "and therein lays the truism for if I had wished it you would already be dead."

"Your insolence and treachery will be your death warrant. Mark my words, I will have you...."

"I have not harmed your most venerated person," Crixus interrupted the tirade, "and if it so pleases you I will replace the chair and pay for the repair of your garment but please, do not insult my integrity by inferring I *almost* killed you. At any time during the contest tonight I could have pierced your throat with a gladius and still continued the fight and defeated Tysus."

Embarrassingly, no one had yet approached Caius and attempted to remove the sword which kept him pinned firmly to the chair;

consequently, his position was further exacerbated by the fact he could not rise and must endure Crixus' censure whilst seated.

"And in reply to your threat," Crixus continued, "you will not have me flogged, crucified, banished to the farthest corner of the empire or anything else. Why? I will tell you why – because you need me! You need me to fight in your games and you need me to win every contest I am entered for. Even the great Crixus cannot do his master's bidding if his back is in tatters. If I lose, you lose also. Your credibility will vanish like a virgin's hymen and that vision of aspiring to provincial governor will remain just that – a vision!"

"You'll pay for this outrage with your life!" Caius threatened again but Crixus was by no means finished and, as yet, no one had intervened on his behalf.

"People such as your most noble self who float around on clouds of their own hot air should beware lest they fart and blow themselves out to sea," he continued and the tension was suddenly shattered as a burst of raucous laughter from some unseen location echoed around the hall. "Just remember, Caius Attius Caecilius, when I am treading the sands of the arena and you are watching from your box of privilege. Remember tonight. Remember how I pierced your robe and how easily I could do so again. Perhaps next time you will not enjoy the protection of the gods. If my aim is not so good or there should be a sudden vagary in the wind...," and the implied menace was unmistakeable.

"Leave us. Leave us this instant! Your lanista shall hear of your threats to me first thing tomorrow morning."

"I have no doubt it will be a most interesting conversation. However, before I take my leave there is one more thing you should know. By bringing Tysus and myself together to fight for your entertainment you robbed a fellow gladiator of a glorious death in the amphitheatre, before a crowd of eighty-thousand – a noble death and a warrior's death."

"He was paid well to fight, and to die if necessary. That is what gladiators do. They fight and they die – all of them!"

"There was no greatness about the manner of his demise and I would have defeated him regardless, but his passing will go largely unmarked and unnoticed. When I look at you I am reminded of the darker side of man and his failings, his greed, his lust for power and influence and the depths to which he will sink and the way he will permit his soul to be corrupted. You are many things, Caius Attius Caecilius, but honour does not rank among them."

Drusilla pushed her way through the gathering, edging closer to where her father struggled ineffectively in his seat while Crixus towered over him surrounded by his armed escort. As she remained partly concealed and unobtrusive within the crowd of fascinated onlookers she inwardly thrilled at the vision of Caius receiving his comeuppance.

"About time too!" she murmured and it was with an appreciable effort she prevented herself laughing out loud and incurring more of Caius' wrath when they left here.

"I will fight for you and I will vanquish those sent against me," Crixus continued, "but do not count on my cooperation in any other way. You will never command my respect and I hold no fear for your threats of retribution. I may kill in the arena but it is honest and open and I do not use people and lie and cheat to the furtherance of my own end. Underhandedness and deceit are not the tools of my trade and when a man looks into my eyes, what he sees is what he gets, unlike you, Caius Attius Caecilius, for you are a man of many faces and guises and as treacherous as a serpent."

"Get out of my sight – now!" and he was trembling with outrage once again. It left a bitter taste in his mouth to acknowledge his little party had degenerated into a farce with him being made to look like the fool while Crixus, who had essentially been an item on the entertainment agenda, walked away with all the glory. Had he played his hand too early? Should he have waited until the opening day of the games? It was too late now but, thank the gods, this had all happened in private and he still retained Crixus as the cutting edge of his campaign which he would commence in the next day or so. He would need to boost his popularity even more-so now and that would mean expenditure on a huge scale. He had the resources but he loathed to squander them when there was no guarantee on return and then he recalled something Crixus had said during their initial meeting at the school; something about giving them what they wanted, what they would remember you for. He had to think hard for time was of the essence and that magnificent, vote-winning public spectacle might not be the deciding factor after all.

For Crixus as he strolled back to the Ludus Gallicus in the company of his escort there were mixed feelings. There was, on the one hand, elation and a sense of championing Drusilla's cause at his scathing attack on Caius which had spelt out a few home truths and left him smarting from those angry words. He knew he had struck home and almost certainly there would be repercussions but he could not stand by and say nothing. There was joy at seeing Drusilla again, even if only fleetingly, and neither had shown recognition of the other although he yearned to hold her and kiss those soft inviting lips.

Finally, there was regret and an element of sadness to eclipse even the presence of his woman tonight. The outcome of his contest with Tysus was predictable from the first moment but it was the manner of his demise that troubled Crixus so. He had killed his fourth man tonight – not in the arena with a great crowd cheering them both on, but at a party for the rich and he felt no sense of victory at his own part.

36

Two weeks had passed since that unsubtle reminder of his own mortality – an assault on his person by the very man the feasting was intended to promote and whilst he had made threats to report Crixus' violent outburst and monumental insolence, he had thought better of it. Whilst the administration of a whipping might have placated Caius in the short term he was mindful of the implications if Crixus was unable to perform. Having witnessed his skill with the sword he knew it would serve no useful purpose to antagonise him further and put his own skin unnecessarily at risk.

The unfortunate incident had not been mentioned again although there were many references to the defeat of Tysus for no one could remember seeing a gladiator killed by an opponent facing in the opposite direction with eyes closed. The general consensus amounted to Crixus being a truly gifted fighter, possessing something other than sheer physical strength, skill and agility. If a lesser man had spoken to Caius that way he would have ordered his execution immediately without hesitation but despite his intimidating presence and a tongue as sharp as any blade, Caius reluctantly admitted he quite liked the man. Having seen many gladiators over the years and encountered villains and scum from all walks of life, he was further of the opinion there were no slave-like traits about Crixus despite the lowly status he had taken upon himself.

Crixus was scheduled to make his next appearance in the arena the day after tomorrow. After that, all would be decided one way or the other. So far the games had been a resounding success and well-worth the expense. First reports filtering back through his agents had been encouraging to say the least and whilst the name of Crixus was being heard all over the city and eulogised for his amazing exploits in the arena where he seldom repeated fighting styles in a bid to maintain the crowds' attention, people were openly praising Caius Attius Caecilius.

Whilst there was still no single worthy contender to pit against Crixus on equal terms he was, consequently, facing multiple adversaries whenever possible to thrill the vast numbers of spectators who not only dropped in to the performances out of curiosity but made the pilgrimage to Rome from further afield in order to witness the greatest spectacles held throughout the empire.

So far, all was proceeding as planned and for the grand finale he had laid on something they definitely would remember him for. Lentulus Fulvius had hesitated at first for such a suggestion was tantamount to stacking the odds against Crixus even further than they already were. Caius Attius Caecilius was indeed a hard man and drove an even harder bargain but then he remembered his firm pledge to Crixus and decided perhaps now was the moment to let destiny take its course.

"I will put the matter before him," the lanista replied thoughtfully. "If he is in agreement then perhaps both of us will witness history in the making. The final word must rest with Crixus for I will not knowingly send a man into a situation where he cannot prevail. Already he walks a thin line and what you are asking places a heavy burden upon my best fighter."

Caius had received his reply the following day and was ecstatic at the positive verdict. Crixus had trained long and hard for this – indeed his very presence at the school was pivotal to this moment and his most dynamic performance to date could be guaranteed. At great personal expense, Caius decided in order to reach the hearts *and stomachs* of the electorate, for a limited period of three weeks he would effectively double the corn ration and, in addition, dole out free bread and issue a daily amphora of wine to each household from his own vast reserves. The Caecilius estates produced huge quantities of wine annually and the weather this summer ensured another bumper crop, alleviating a small amount of pressure on his finances. He knew all citizens adored wine and food gifts were a welcome blessing too but the increased corn ration would be a vote-winner. As he contemplated the public's reaction to his big-heartedness he wondered how long it would take to recoup his expenses once the praetorship was safely in his hands and he could afford to live off the ill-gotten gains from his provincial governorship. After all, a prominent government position such as this had to have its fringe benefits, didn't it? Look at Gaius Julius Caesar. He had taken up governorship of Spain with enormous debts, only to return a short time later a wealthy man indeed. He had paid off his creditors and bought his way to the dictatorship. That was real power.

At the Ludus Gallicus news was good too for Crixus' ultimate goal was finally about to be realised. Ferox was en-route from Capua and the

215

two of them would face each other tomorrow as the closing battle in the games sponsored by Caius. In a historic event Crixus would be confronted by three opponents and after the bodies of the fallen had been removed he and Ferox would meet in what promised to be a truly unique and bloody engagement. Ferox was a big, powerful fighter in the league of heavyweight. His time of incarceration at Capua had done little to eradicate the ways of the brutal thug and he remained to all intents and purposes, a crude, undisciplined barbarian.

During a lull in the intense training and fitness programme Lentulus Fulvius approached Crixus as he sat alone on one of the seating terraces, his manner pensive.

"The meeting with Ferox is on your mind," the lanista assessed the situation flawlessly and Crixus nodded. "When you confront Ferox tomorrow do not rush, my friend, and govern yourself according to the dictates of your heart. To kill him will be simple but his immediate demise is not your ultimate goal. Whilst in essence it is an execution, for the crowds it must be a dance of death. This is your one and only chance to avenge the slaying of Julius Quintus and a quick kill will win you no acclaim for the public are aware of your skill in drawing out the inevitable and making a great drama out of any contest you are set."

"I understand your words for these things have been uppermost in my mind also and I have no desire for it to end quickly."

"Remember your mission when you are out there and keep the face of Julius clearly in your mind for it will help you focus and give added weight to your anger and hatred. The crowds will know why you and Ferox have been brought together and they will be under no illusion as to the outcome. Whilst the fires of vengeance burn inside you, keep a tight rein on them lest they weaken your resolve and you act impetuously. Kill with passion and the crowd will love you but give them blood. Give them more blood than they have ever seen and the women will bare their tits and beg you to fuck them. The blood seduces them in the manner of the most potent narcotic and they will scream and salivate and fuck unashamedly on the terraces in front of you. Do this and they will revere you as a god.

"Ferox is little better than a jackal, striking from the shadows at the weak and vulnerable but you are a sleek panther, a predator and your claws are lethal. Draw out the kill, Crixus, and let them see his fear. In the end he will beg for death and it is in this moment the crowds will remember you. At the end of it all, if you prevail the men will worship your sword and the women will be throwing themselves at your cock."

"I will kill him slowly but I will also keep him on his feet. There will be no missio for Ferox."

The lanista slapped him heartily on the shoulder with a huge paw and made to leave.

"Train until noon and then rest. If you are to defeat four opponents you will need your wits about you."

37

The small, single-storey domus Drusilla had found was ideally situated and hidden among the clutter of taller surrounding buildings close to the centre of the city. The Via Claudia ran approximately south-east from the Flavian Amphitheatre and the little house was placed virtually out of sight at the end of a blind alley and behind a high enclosing wall. It had been an impulse decision and she could not believe the idea had eluded her this long. She was out strolling, thinking about Crixus and when they might chance to meet again and then, realising she had strayed from her intended route, retraced her steps and seen the crudely-fashioned poster advertising the plot's availability. The vendor's office was only a short distance away and he had accompanied her back to the property which was accessed by either of two simple wooden gates set into the surrounding wall.

The house was small but would be perfect for her intended purpose and there was even a tiny garden and gurgling ornamental fountain in the centre of a mosaic-adorned terrace. The remainder of the area inside the wall was given over to twisting vines and shrubs with colourful rose, orange and bougainvillaea spreading their heavily-scented, flower laden branches to either side. The vendor seemed a little amused when Drusilla did not attempt to barter and haggle over the rental but as he studied her – the manner of her dress, her speech, body language and general deportment he judged she could probably have purchased the place outright with only the coins in her purse. However, he was pleasantly surprised when she paid him three years in advance and rewarded him with a beaming smile.

Inside, the rooms were modest after the huge open spaces of the family home on the Via Sacra but the air was refreshingly cool and there were shutters at the windows, both to afford privacy and keep out the worst effects of the fierce summer sun. There was no furniture but the place was clean and cared-for and it was with immense delight she envisaged the items she would purchase for their love nest now she finally had something to focus on. It would be their little secret – just the two of them and the very thought of inviting him here and being alone together made the goose-flesh come up on her bare arms while lower down the heat and melting sensation betrayed her more intimate thoughts. They would only be able to meet when Crixus could leave the school although she considered his chances of securing more short absences were markedly improved in light of his recent performances.

Even her mother, Agrippina, was making healthy gains after several weeks of taking Quintina's herbal preparation which Drusilla faithfully replenished every few days. Getting away during the daylight hours would pose no problem for Drusilla as she was now making regular trips to the forum and streets bordering the amphitheatre. However, spending whole nights away from the house on the Via Sacra would be a different matter altogether and she would have to come up with some credible and watertight excuses for being absent overnight if she was to avert suspicion and not come under the unwelcome scrutiny of either her mother or father.

'One thing at a time,' she told herself.

Already she had overcome one of the greatest hurdles that loomed seemingly insurmountable at the outset when they had declared for each other. At this relatively early stage in their relationship they had a secret meeting place and as long as she did not draw uninvited attention upon herself and they both utilised extreme caution entering and leaving the property, then she foresaw no problems. Care and vigilance would be the watchwords governing their meetings and she wickedly thrilled at the sinfulness of such wanton behaviour and flouting of social etiquette.

Tomorrow was the final day of her father's election campaign and would see the last of his public games in which Crixus would fight as the star attraction. Her bosom swelled with pride as she recalled how common folk and patricians alike were eulogizing him for the radical new phenomenon he had brought to the arena for every time he was billed to appear the amphitheatre was packed to capacity. The name, Caius Attius Caecilius was being heard too for they associated it with entertainment on a grand scale and, for a limited period only, improved food availability. They knew it was a game for all aspiring politicians played it in an attempt to woo the electorate and win as many hearts and votes as their empty promises and shallow pledges of reforms could muster. But, for a few days at least, life would be a little more bearable with the high-point of the games still to come.

On the darker side, Drusilla knew Caius left nothing to chance or interpretation and would have instructed his auditors to calculate every denarius and every sestertius his campaign had cost and worked out how to retrieve it with a huge profit over the coming months. He was barely able to contain himself after receiving confirmation of Crixus' agreement to take on a fourth opponent in this final match.

"Three more victims for the butcher's block," he gushed with childlike euphoria to Drusilla, his earlier threat of chastisement in the wake of her outburst at his social gathering apparently forgotten. "I have scoured Rome for the best and he will face them tomorrow. After a short interval they will send in Ferox. Ferox! The very reason Crixus chose to become a gladiator and, in a bizarre kind of way, my ticket to the praetorship for without Ferox there would be no Crixus and my dream might not be realised at all. It promises to be a great and glorious day."

Once again the urge to kill him was almost overpowering and she considered Caius fortunate she was not carrying a blade of her own.

Perhaps she should ask Crixus for lessons...!

He seemed incapable of grasping the scale of human tragedy here – treating people as if their only purpose in life was to serve him and safeguard his interests. To him they were not living souls but commodities to be bought and bargained with – minions to do his bidding, to be manipulated at leisure in the furtherance of his own high-born cause. Try as she might, she found it impossible to visualise what Crixus must be feeling tonight on the eve of his long-awaited meeting with Ferox. She was not overly-concerned for his safety in the first part of the match; rather, it was the opposition who should watch out. No, she was anxious for his emotional state as the rapidly-approaching climax to his months of training, barely-restrained anger and single-mindedness drew ever nearer. He would feel many things tomorrow – emotions she could not even begin to comprehend, but what would be left at the end of the day? Despite the greatness of the occasion, the pomp, the ceremony and the glory, despite the blood-lust and the screams and chants from the crowds as they urged and incited him to even greater extremes of barbarity, she knew he would abide by the rules of engagement, remaining ever-conscious of the fact he was there for the pleasure of the mob and not his own indulgence. Yes, he would give them what they wanted, at the same time exacting a terrible price from Ferox and they would love him for it.

There was a bitter irony here and she pondered the cruel gods who decided the fate of mortals. Without Ferox there would be no Crixus. Without Crixus and the changes he had wrought in her life there could be no future. He was the one she had waited for all these years. It was, in every sense of the word, an eternal circle of destiny.

She was also mindfully-aware she would need to comfort him when the violence and blood-letting were concluded and for this reason she had slipped away after dark last night and made her way to the Ludus Gallicus. Her name apparently carried more weight than she expected and the guards admitted her without delay, escorting her directly to the lanista's office. He bade her enter and poured wine for them both, unaccustomed to receiving visitors at this hour.

"You honour me with your presence, my lady, but you come here at great personal risk. Please – how may I be of service?"

"I will be blunt," she decided the direct approach would be infinitely more preferable with a man who was not renowned for mincing his words. "Crixus and I are lovers, a fact you may or may not be aware of. It doesn't really matter. Because of our class differences which I abhor, the state is not sympathetic to our cause and we can never be together. Even when you release him from his contract or he is awarded his freedom it will be no different."

"Yes," Lentulus Fulvius replied quietly, nodding his head in understanding. "I know these things for we have spoken of the matter. After his second visit to the apothecary he expressed his desire to spend more time in your company and when you visited the school with your father recently he admitted you were the object of his deep affections. I advised him to tread carefully for Caius Attius is not a man to forgive any wrong-doing against his person or reputation."

"He is spiteful and vindictive," Drusilla agreed, "and would go to extraordinary lengths to break anyone – man or woman, who threatened or openly challenged him."

"As a gesture of good will I let it be known if he defeated the three opponents sent to him in that first contest he could see his woman as often as he wished. For obvious reasons he would not be permitted to stay away from the school every night and apart from his obligation to continue training during the day I can well imagine your own difficulty arranging absences from home. If, however, your joint situation permits a little time together away from prying eyes then I see no harm in it. What is it you seek from me?"

"Tomorrow, on the final day of my father's election campaign, Crixus will fight three others and when he has defeated them he will confront Ferox. Only my father could have dreamed up such a spectacle but I know Crixus has entered into it of his own choice. After the contest he will be completely exhausted and I dread to ponder his mental state. Let him come to me, I beg you. Let me hold him and love him for one night before he returns to you. I have acquired a small house on the Via Claudia, not far from here, where we can be together.

Please, I know you are a good man at heart and Crixus speaks your name with pride. Let him come to me after the games. That is all I ask."

He was impressed by her candid, direct approach where the perils of their liaison could not be overstated.

"You are indeed correct for his proper care is of the greatest importance – to all of us. These training schools are generally regarded with disdain and loathing for we deal in slaves, barbarians and disreputable beings who have no rightful place in society. Even their status as human beings is denied them."

"Crixus could have gone to any of the other schools when he chose to train as a fighter. Why did he come here? What made him choose this one above the others?"

"Sometimes, destiny alone will guide a man's feet to his place of purpose while his eyes are focused on other matters. My vision, one day, is to purchase Gallicus from the emperor and then there will be no more slaves. I will choose who we accept and who we turn away and this school will be unequalled."

"I cannot overstress the importance of this arrangement remaining a secret between the three – sorry, the four of us. I had forgotten my friend, the apothecary. Should we ever be exposed I dread to think...."

"You have my word so please do not fear for your safety. Whilst my contract is with your father, the well-being of the men under my charge remains a priority. I know you have considered the pitfalls otherwise you would not have come here tonight. The very fact you would go to such lengths to be with a man you love, and at great risk to yourself, tells me many things."

"Despite that hard exterior I sense you are sympathetic to our cause, Lentulus Fulvius," she smiled for the first time.

"When your man is victorious tomorrow and the crowds have honoured him, then take him into your bed for he will surely have earned it. But mark my words," and he scowled like a friendly bulldog, "have him back here by noon the following day. I do not want him weakened and exhausted from lovemaking so he cannot hold a sword. I have amended the original terms of our contract and as long as Crixus continues to perform well and retain the hearts of the crowds then you and he may meet whenever you wish."

He refilled his wine goblet and raised it in salute.

"Hail Crixus, the new champion of Rome. I think now is a good time to reward some of his hard work and loyalty. May your love blossom and bring happiness to you both in these uncertain times. I salute you and the bond that joins you. You may come and speak with me any time but now you must go for the hour is late and it might be deemed improper if you were to be seen leaving here."

He opened the simple wooden door and she paused briefly, holding his gaze with her own and touching a gentle hand to his face.

"Goodnight, Lentulus Fulvius. I will never forget the kindness you have shown me," and then she was gone into the night, stepping briskly toward the gate where the guards let her through unchallenged.

'Even in the moonlight your shadow moves with grace,' Crixus pondered the image of his woman longingly as she passed close to his window, wondering why she had come to the school at this late hour. It must be something to do with the games tomorrow but whether she had attempted to intercede on his behalf he could not say. As she finally disappeared from view he lay back on the straw pillow and closed his eyes, any concerns for the coming hours banished to obscurity by the fleeting glimpse of his woman bathed in the luminescence of a full moon.

Lentulus Fulvius drained the remaining contents of the wine goblet and touched a hand to his cheek where the slightest hint of her perfume lingered and he smiled. He vividly recalled their last meeting where she had arrived late for no other reason than to anger an already-inflamed Caius still further, brushing past him without acknowledgement and positioning herself so as to remain aloof while they watched the activity in the small arena. She was the epitome of all the qualities he admired in a man, let alone a woman and he could well understand the attraction for she and Crixus were driven by similar ideals.

38

The breeze had veered into the west overnight, bringing with it cooler conditions and a welcome drop in humidity. As the early sun rose – flushing out the colours on the eastern horizon so the clouds began to build with the promise of rain later in the day. At the Flavian Amphitheatre preparations for the coming day's entertainments were already underway – removing huge quantities of litter and left-over food discarded by the mob as they vacated the terraces. A less-palatable task involved cleaning up the numerous pools of urine where spectators with aching bladders had relieved themselves on the spot, fearful of losing their place if they visited the latrines.

Fresh sand would be brought into the arena to replace the foul-smelling, contaminated material now being removed and beneath the floor in the *hypogeum* the beast-master and his attendants would be readying the many exotic animals brought in from across the empire for the first spectacles of the day. Wild-animal hunts generally began the day's activities and were seen as an effective and popular way of acclimatising the spectators to the more violent extremes of blood-letting that followed later.

On the maze of streets surrounding the amphitheatre the cries of hot-food sellers and wine vendors competed with the clamour of regular market traders bawling their wares. In addition to oil-lamps and trinkets on offer, the general public were now being treated to an array of action dolls and colourful glass figurines of their favourite gladiators along with the ubiquitous souvenir goblets infamously utilised as toilets by the less-discerning.

By mid-morning the amphitheatre was more than half-full and a seemingly-endless stream of bodies continued to pour through the seventy-six public entrances, making their way through the network of brightly-painted and fresco-adorned corridors to the numbered seats. In this rigidly-stratified society, social status and wealth dictated a person's seating position and many aristocratic families had their names carved into the stonework of the auditorium. Predictably, those seats closest to the action were occupied by the senatorial, equestrian and patrician classes along with provincial governors, heads of state, visiting dignitaries, prefects, consuls and magistrates. Prominent Roman citizens came next followed by the plebeian class with the rearmost seats and standing areas reserved for lower-class women and freed slaves.

As the wild-beast hunts drew to a close and the public execution of criminals commenced, large numbers of spectators vacated the auditorium, lured by the tempting aromas of hot, spicy food and the promise of cheap wine courtesy of the numerous vendors out on the streets. With the prospect of a long afternoon before them where the main events were not scheduled to take place until later in the day, the crowds would grow increasingly restless under a hot sun; tempers would become frayed, moods unpredictable with the potential for violent disorder ever-present as alcohol-fuelled aggression and blood-lust spilled over and an already-tense atmosphere became explosive.

As top billing Crixus would be last to fight and he was forced to endure a lengthy wait in the gladiators' holding area beneath the terraces. Now and then he would walk to the end of the tunnel and peer out through the iron gate leading to the arena. He appraised critically the individual pairs as they battled and nodded imperceptibly at the efficiency and tactical virtuosity of a quick kill or mentally applauded the missio duly awarded to a defeated but nonetheless valiant fighter. And then he would retire to the wooden benches, listening intently to the muted cadence of the mob as the waves of sound rose and fell from a gentle, barely-audible susurration, to a screaming crescendo of pulsating noise. It was as if the gods themselves had taken up a vengeful presence, affronted by this mortal intrusion on their celestial world; the trumpet of Poseidon blared across the open expanse of sand while the Cyclopes beat and hammered in their forge and an angry Vulcan hurled his thunderbolts across the sky.

Crixus had not yet found himself in the position where he must execute a defeated opponent, standing over the injured fighter awaiting the life or death decision from the sponsor. With the exception of practice sessions at the school, every opponent to date had been dispatched with ruthless efficiency and many had not even seen the blow that ended their lives. And so it would be again today except, of course, when he confronted Ferox for in his case special treatment was warranted. As the hours passed with agonising slowness and the sun at last dipped below the western horizon, Crixus made ready to face the greatest test of his life. The dancing flames from a myriad burning torches and oil lamps bathed the arena in a soft, flickering light and he felt a cool stirring of the air kiss his cheek as he gazed out through the portal of his destiny once more; a kiss as soft as the lips of his woman. Would she be there? He needed her at this moment more than ever, cheering for him, praying for him, willing him to survive the impossible odds he had shouldered. Under the mantle of Drusilla's love all things were possible. He would rise above the insidious and corrosive fear of death and assume the persona of a demigod. Fear was a trait of humans. It ate away at the spirit and turned the bowels to liquid.

'Please, let her be there. With Drusilla, all things are possible and I will transcend the bounds of mortality.'

His first three opponents were already defeated in Crixus' eyes and all that remained was the looming spectre of Ferox. He had been judged; there was no jury and the public gallery was full to capacity. The sentence was hideous, indescribably-violent death and Crixus was the executioner.

The breeze carried the words of the herald in the centre of the arena to him and he was able to judge the moment they made their respective entrances; three consecutive waves of sound as the seasoned veterans stood before their public with weapons raised up.

Enjoy your moments of triumph for they will be your last.

Once more an uneasy hush descended upon the vast gathering and as the herald at last began the final announcement Crixus stood poised behind the iron gate, waiting, waiting, waiting with barely-restrained impatience, waiting like a stallion at the starting gate in the Circus Maximus or a caged tiger about to be released into the hunting ground where vulnerable flesh awaited.

Please, let it come now!

Finally, the gate rose in front of him and he strode out of the Porta Sanavivaria into the lamplight and the cool of late evening while the air around him was rent asunder by the thunderous tumult of his audience. Every person was on their feet and the blur of faces suddenly became eighty-thousand individuals as his vision sharpened and assumed a new degree of clarity. He could smell the blood beneath his feet and the aromas of frankincense and sandalwood from the braziers on the periphery of the seating area. He could smell the remains of spiced food brought into the auditorium hours ago and the odours of garlic, olive oil and stale wine were unmistakeable; but, most of all, he could smell the fear of his opponents as they grouped together for mutual assurance and shuffled uneasily like gazelles at the watering hole when the lion approaches.

Lentulus Fulvius had indeed been correct when he briefed Crixus of what to expect from such a gathering for as he scanned the terraces he smiled at the sight of half a dozen women baring their breasts while others were rutting unashamedly in anticipation of the carnage.

"They are hungry for blood," Drusus, the head trainer observed in his seat next to the lanista

"They will not be disappointed," Lentulus Fulvius observed with a nod and a satisfied smile.

As the herald made his way back to the seating area and the referee took over, they turned and acknowledged the sponsor, Caius Attius Caecilius, in the front row of purple-and-white-adorned figures. He merely raised both hands in a gesture of approval while beside him Drusilla waited patiently, nails digging painfully into the palms of her hands. Otherwise, she remained radiantly beautiful, betraying none of the conflicting emotions surging within as she waited with a pounding heart.

"Begin the contest!" the referee's command barked out and Crixus' three opponents spread out in a rough semi-circle, wary lest they should come under attack before their own moment presented itself. From the outset they were handicapped by their superior numbers for they must spread out to afford one another adequate fighting space. Crixus had guessed the likely sequence of events well beforehand and he would make his opening gambit now with the Samnite out to his left, drawing the Thracian into the action and leaving the retiarius out of it for vital seconds. The Samnite was good, constantly probing with the gladius, ensuring Crixus maintain his guard but remaining ever-watchful of the other two out to his right. The man was fit and possessed good physique suggesting power, strength and endurance.

No good trying to wear this one down, dodging and weaving!

Always do the unexpected. The crowds will love you for that. One man against three – it should be a purely defensive contest with the odds stacked impossibly high against victory. Take the attack to the other man for three adversaries will not be expecting a violent and sustained onslaught from a single fighter. Crixus could imagine the eyes of the other man searching for his comrade beneath the restricted confines of the helmet, hoping the net-man did not move in prematurely and hamper their coordinated attack with the swinging net.

Let the Thracian come a little closer, just a few more steps. Come on, my friend, just a little closer and you won't know what hit you. Wait for it – wait for it – now!

As the Samnite predictably responded to Crixus' raised sword-arm, so the Thracian out to the right at last moved within range and as

Crixus struck, it was not a lunging stab but a right-handed vertical reversal with all the power he could muster; a vicious downward chopping stroke that cleaved the Thracian's bronze crested helmet just right of the centre-line, deeply creasing the metal and opening a large superficial wound. The attack immediately faltered for the man had been stunned by the impact and blood from the wound now ran unchecked into his eyes where the visor compounded his impaired vision. Crixus now brought the sword to bear again with the Samnite as his target for in that lightning-quick engagement he had not once averted his gaze from this most dangerous opponent. As the Samnite thrust into Crixus' deliberately-exposed right flank, he blocked with the wolf's-head shield and was impressed by the force of the attack – the impact travelling up Crixus' arm and jarring his teeth. But the blow had been delivered with unnecessary force for the gladius was now lodged firmly in Crixus' shield, rendering it useless.

Crixus merely relinquished his grip on the shield as his adversary now struggled with double the weight.

Watch out for the net!

He barely ducked in time to avoid the swinging menace as the retiarius sensed his opportunity and moved in.

Think quickly!

In seconds he had effectively blinded one opponent and temporarily disarmed another but the reprieve was only temporary.

Remember the training. Assess the risks and deal with the main threat first!

Directly in front, the retiarius was circling, fearful of becoming the third victim in less than a minute. As the raised, swinging net was furthest from him Crixus dug into the sand with his left foot, sending a shower of gritty material into the face of his unsuspecting adversary, blinding him for several crucial moments and arresting any further movement. He hated the tactic for it was akin to gutter-fighting but he had to reduce the odds against him if he was going to come out of this alive. Turning his attention back to the Samnite who had at last retrieved his gladius from the wolf's-head shield, Crixus began to methodically beat the man down in a withering barrage of strikes and beautiful flowing reversals. It had to end soon for he observed how the Thracian had now removed his helmet in order to wipe away the blood that still coursed into his eyes from the deep scalp wound. He would not need the helmet again and would almost certainly have been dazed by the impact. The retiarius too would be rallying again once his vision returned, spurred on by the anger of his humiliating ordeal. Crixus could easily have knocked the man to the ground, standing over him with the point of the gladius pressed into his throat as he waited for the decision, *'Mitte! Mitte!'* or *'Iugula!'*

However, such a tactic would have provided the other two with a valuable respite he could not afford and they would be ready for him. No, it had to be now while he retained the advantage. The Samnite was good – perhaps too good. In another situation where the odds were more favourable he may have been permitted a sporting chance but Crixus had another battle to fight when this one was ended and he needed to be strong. Speed and stealth were of the essence.

Let the crowds see it and wonder at this graceful ballet of death!

Amid the virtually uninterrupted flurry of blows he was landing on the Samnite, swamping his defences and effectively preventing all resistance, Crixus halted suddenly and flicked the gladius from right to left and then back to his right hand again. His opponent was slow to recover and Crixus repeated the manoeuvre, giving the man ample time to recover; a gesture of opportunity he would never have received at the hands of a lesser man.

Too late! You had your chance, my friend.

Crixus spun himself in a double circle and as he drew level with the Samnite once more he twisted the gladius so that it slammed into his opponent's neck flat-side on, knocking him off balance and theoretically rendering him out of the battle. But the man was still on his feet and showing no signs of capitulation and before he could kneel and raise a finger Crixus changed to a left-handed grip once more and plunged the gladius into his neck. He was finished and as blood sprayed in all directions he slumped to the ground while Crixus sought his next victim.

From the elevated terraces came a great roar followed by a wave of sound that caused the air around him to reverberate, sweeping across the sands with all the fury of Neptune's wrath. This was what they had come to see and it bore little resemblance to the traditional conflicts and struggles played out in the arena. The lone novice was selecting and dispatching his victims at leisure after incapacitating them and rendering all attempts to best him ineffective. His movements were completely unpredictable, baffling and confounding his opponents and performed with such speed and panache they tricked the eye.

Crixus considered retrieving the shield now adorned with a gaping rent, hesitated, then picked it up anyway, not that he genuinely needed it. The Thracian's battered helmet lay abandoned in the sand and blood continued to streak his face from the wicked gash in his scalp. The retiarius had begun to circle again too, eyes still streaming from the abrasive irritant. They would be walking a fine line between frustrating anger and the discipline of training for it was the equal of tactical suicide to attempt an attack on this behemoth who danced and pirouetted like a servant of Nemesis.

He had already given both fighters long enough to recover and he sensed the conclusion drawing closer; any further delay would see the crowds becoming restless and scathing, something neither he nor Caius Attius Caecilius could afford, especially today.

It was time to let them see more blood – and not necessarily that of his two opponents!

The retiarius, maddened by the futility of his actions and discomfort of his still-streaming eyes was swinging the net vigorously and jabbing aggressively with the trident while Crixus, seeing an idea, now appreciated his good judgement in retrieving the shield. Without taking his eyes off the swinging net he became aware of the Thracian moving in and, like his comrade, was seeking to exact retribution for the death of the Samnite. In order to bolster their courage and feign vulnerability he would let them draw next blood – and then he would end it!

As he deliberately turned his head in the direction of the approaching Thracian he knew the retiarius would be searching for just such an opening and within the blink of an eye the trident snaked out, catching him a hand's span above the knee with one of the viciously-pointed tines. It missed the femoral artery but the wound bled profusely, drenching his leg and spattering onto the sand beneath. From the terraces came screams and shouts of disbelief for Crixus had been injured, even if it was a calculated ploy as a means of securing a crushing victory.

Sensing his advantage the net-man exuded greater confidence, thrusting even more aggressively with the trident but fatally relaxing his attention to the movements of the net. On the next lunge Crixus stepped forward and met the assault with his shield, grunting with satisfaction as he saw how all three prongs perforated and became lodged in the metal. That left his opponent with net only – and maybe the dagger too if he remembered to use it. Now he could afford to discard the shield for the last time for it had served him well and bought precious moments in which to engage the Thracian on his own terms. Seeing Crixus injured, his leg awash with blood, he now moved in to finish it, confident of tipping the scales in his own favour.

But Crixus was by no means finished nor even remotely handicapped despite the wound in his leg and loss of the shield. The anger was upon him now and the stinging pain seemed nothing more than an annoying inconvenience as he confronted the Thracian for the final time. The man was being cautious, keeping his shield close to the body whilst hacking and slashing left and right with the gladius. Every move was predictable and there was no artistry in it despite the aggression and impressive energy employed in the seemingly futile movements. Crixus moved in relentlessly and the wild actions became less certain, more desperate as the Thracian detected his opponent's determination. They were almost touching now and there was hardly a space between them, no room to move, impossible to employ shield or bring the sword to bear. Blood from the scalp wound continued to run down the man's face but the eyes conveyed a new terror as he sensed death closing in from all around. He felt the gladius being torn from his grasp by a hand that could not possibly be human and then that same hand gripped the back of his head, pulling him down with such force he felt the sinews crack in his neck.

What, in the name of Jupiter...! The world erupted in an explosion of pain and bright stars as his blood-smeared face came into contact with the bone of Crixus' knee. He was finished; Crixus knew it and the crowds knew it too. There would be no *missio* – not in a contest like this. His face was smashed, his teeth broken and as he teetered and fell back he could see through half-closed eyes in the unearthly flickering twilight how it must be. The gladius pierced his heart with unimaginable force, being neither slowed nor diverted by the leather armour and the strange orange-yellow luminescence of the amphitheatre gradually faded into darkness along with the distant baying cadence of the mob.

The entire episode had taken less than two minutes while the retiarius continued vainly to dislodge the trident from Crixus' abandoned shield. Unable to retrieve his main attack weapon the retiarius now came at Crixus once more, net swinging with the dagger held at arm's length weaving and cutting the air inches from his opponent's bare chest. At last, the referee stepped in and separated the pair with his wooden baton for Crixus was now devoid of weapons and unable to defend himself. His gladius remained firmly embedded in the chest of the Thracian several yards away and the man's own armour was beyond reach.

"Crixus, you must place yourself at the mercy of the crowds for your life will surely be spared. Your courage is not being questioned but you cannot continue the contest without a weapon."

The retiarius was in a difficult position too for if he attacked and killed an unarmed man there would be no glory in it and the tens of thousands who packed the terraces tonight would demand his blood in retribution. Conversely, if he refused to continue a fight where his opponent had not technically given up the struggle, even though unarmed, he would be branded a coward and made to lose face.

There was seemingly no way out and Crixus' simple reply, "I will continue regardless," served only to elevate his own status and belittle the retiarius whose anger was now mounting visibly.

Seeing how his words apparently fell on deaf ears and he could not force the man to capitulate, the referee ordered the contest to continue, only too aware of how a living legend was being forged here tonight before this monumental crowd.

"Continue!" and the simple vine stick cut the air once more. Crixus took up the unarmed stance while the net-man continued his exertions with renewed vigour.

"A pox on your manly virtues," he hissed. "Your bravery will vanish like a virgin's hymen when the dagger pierces your guts."

An uneasy hush descended once more for this was quite unlike anything resembling the true definition of gladiatorial combat. Crixus should have given up the fight when his weapons were lost for an honourable discharge was guaranteed. And then, for no particular reason, he recalled that first trial combat at the school when he had confronted Septimus, another retiarius. Remembering also his anger at the time he knew exactly how to resolve this ridiculous situation. Abruptly, he ceased all defensive movements and folded his arms across his chest, smiling mockingly at his opponent, goading him. It was the ultimate gesture of contempt and, as predicted, incensed the other man to the point where he cast the net aside, his self-assurance telling him the dagger would be sufficient.

To the onlooker it appeared Crixus was dodging each of the stabbing lunges and wild slashing movements more by luck than any degree of skill or adeptness but unknown to the retiarius he was merely awaiting the moment. Three more times the knife came perilously close to inflicting mortal damage and then, without warning, Crixus' right arm shot out and grabbed the wrist of the knife-hand but not before the blade found its mark and inflicted a second wicked gash on his lower arm.

But Crixus was not about to relinquish his grip now and as the stinging pain of the injury was eclipsed by the age-old instinct to survive and fight again today he bent the wrist back until it snapped loudly and the blade fell harmlessly into the sand. As his opponent screamed in shock and horror at his own injury Crixus let the arm go and closed his grip around the man's neck, still utilising his right hand only. His thumb pressed into the larynx, crushing bone, tissue and cartilage while the retiarius merely clawed ineffectively and beat pathetically on Crixus' chest. The eyes bulged in their sockets and the mouth fell open slackly, releasing a stream of spittle that flowed onto his chest. With his face swollen and streaked with Crixus' blood he presented a visage of the utmost terror and as his executioner gripped and crushed one final time, his bowels voided involuntarily and he slumped lifelessly in Crixus' hand, his feet barely making contact with the ground.

Crixus threw the man aside, discarded like an item of soiled clothing amid the blood and shit surrounding him. It was over and he had defeated them all. Caius Attius Caecilius had scoured Rome for the best fighters to pit against him and he had beaten each and every one of them – not by employing tricks and ruses but by unmatched strength, brutality and sheer stubborn iron will. He became aware of another rising cacophony of sound sweeping toward him like a tempest on a wind-scoured lake. In this shrieking maelstrom that pummelled his ears and assaulted the air around him were other sounds that peaked in volume and ripped the tops from the green waves of the troubled waters – the foaming white spume carried away on the shrieking gale.

"Crixus! Crixus! Crixus!" they called on the balmy night air, demanding he stand before them and receive their accolades. "Hail Crixus!" they acclaimed him as a god of the arena. "Crixus Vitoria!" and as he at last faced his public, even devoid of armour and weapons he somehow conveyed the image of the supreme warrior, unassailable, magnificent, bloodied and battle-scarred. Yet there was an air of humility about him also as he stood quietly with arms raised, the madness of combat receding into the mists while he gathered himself once more. It was a wickedly-brief respite and a sudden flurry of activity told him they had come to claim the bodies of the vanquished, removing them through the Porta Libitina, the gate of death, as they commenced their journey to Elysium. Their would be no need of the usual grisly protocols where a figure dressed as Mercury touched each victim with a hot iron in search of remaining life. Two of the corpses were ghostly white where all vestiges of blood had drained away and the third was limp as a rag doll, his broken neck lolling from side to side as it bumped comically across the uneven ground.

A figure was approaching him from the shadows and he was somewhat gratified to see the welcome form of the physician carrying an amphora of cold water and a collection of medical supplies. He bade Crixus sit for a moment while he inspected the two injury sites and removed the stopper from a clay jar of lavender balm. While he drank copiously of the refreshing liquid the physician cleaned the wounds and applied a liberal amount of balm to each injury site, noting with a nod of his head and mumbled approval how the bleeding had ceased. Only a small amount of clear fluid was seeping from each puncture and laceration as the clotting process began but there would inevitably be much stiffness, swelling and discolouration in the days to come.

"Nothing to worry about," he commented. "You're still young. You'll be fighting fit in a day or two." He walked away without another word but the improvement was immediately noticeable. Binding the limbs would have reduced flexibility and he needed to muster every remaining degree of suppleness when they sent Ferox out. After that it mattered little in the bigger picture. Two more figures made their way across the sand to where he was seated, carrying a newly-sharpened gladius and shield to replace his own which had been damaged or destroyed. As he swallowed the icy water so his strength returned and he swore he had never tasted wine as good as this.

"Who is responsible for these hospitalities?" Crixus asked the referee hovering close by.

"Your lanista, Lentulus Fulvius, is here tonight along with your brothers from the school. When he observed your injuries he instructed the surgeon to attend for there are no rules forbidding such ministrations, as, indeed, there are no precedents for you agreeing to take on a fourth man when you have defeated three others."

"I am forever indebted to his concerns. My strength is almost fully returned and already the wounds do not pain me."

"Ferox will come to you soon and once again I will oversee the contest. May Nemesis guide your sword hand and Mars endow you with the wrath of the gods."

The bleeding had been staunched by the oil-based unguent and the fresh, icy water had revived him. His head was clear, his vision sharp, his mind perfectly focused. He was death incarnate and this time there would not be three opponents but one and he could afford to draw out the climax – not solely for the morbid pleasure of the hungry crowds, but his own indulgence as the rekindled fires of vengeance sent the blood coursing through his veins once more. The herald strode to the centre of the arena and began announcing the final bout of the night, deliberately drawing out the excitement as the seconds ticked by where tension was raised to fever-pitch. There were no great cheers, no outbursts of thunderous applause as Ferox made his appearance; rather, there prevailed a low murmur of disapproval, a muted, simmering undercurrent of hatred punctuated by an occasional deliberately-slowed hand-clap.

In stark contrast, as Crixus' name was called and he approached from the concealment of the shadows, the place resounded to the deafening blast of eighty-thousand straining voices.

Ferox had come to the greatest arena in the civilized world to meet his Nemesis and Crixus was to be the instrument of that retribution.

39

The towering thunderheads that had gradually built throughout the day now loomed tall and menacing over the city, obliterating the stars and raising humidity to intolerable levels. The earlier breeze had now dropped away and the heat lay trapped between the hills like a stifling blanket of oppressiveness. Still it did not rain and it seemed nature herself was holding her breath, waiting for this last great drama to be played out on the sands of the arena before she would finally relent and give up her precious, life-giving element.

The cheering, the applause, the whistling, stamping of feet and ribald catcalls now fell away into a distant, uneasy drone accentuated by an atmosphere heavy with tension, volatile and turbulent, waiting for a spark to ignite the world before Vulcan tore the night sky asunder.

Both fighters were similarly attired with minor variations in personalised armour. Both carried the gladius and a shield of preference but whereas Crixus' shield was relatively small, circular and easily utilised as a potent fist, Ferox carried a scutum – standard equipment of the Roman legionary. The scutum was a large, rectangular shield, slightly curved along its vertical axis with a heavy metal boss at the centre. It afforded an enhanced degree of refuge but was cumbersome. Ferox was indeed a big man and it wasn't all muscle. Clearly, the harsh regime at Capua had not honed him down to the extent where he exuded the fitness and grace of an athlete and he had not starved himself either. Whilst the traditional diet of barley gruel and beans promoted physical bulk and offered a degree of protection against superficial cuts and lacerations, it was prone to induce unwelcome fat around the body's mid-section if hard, regular exercise was not part of the daily routine.

Crixus tested the opposition by thrusting powerfully at the man's chest and was rewarded with a wild, swinging parry and a pathetic attempt to block with the large shield. Ferox initiated the next attack, an underhand thrust designed to gut Crixus which he sidestepped with contemptuous ease, noting how the other man used the scutum to protect his lower body leaving the head and much of the torso completely exposed – *and vulnerable!*

Crixus allowed him a little closer and Ferox advanced confidently, hurling a ferocious rain of blows only to have them struck away effortlessly or miss their target completely.

Had this man learned absolutely nothing during his incarceration at the Capua school? Crixus was disbelieving. The attacks were devoid of style and flowing motion. There was no strategy, no plan. There was neither grace nor beauty in it, just a succession of great unsightly swinging blows from right to left and back again with forward thrusts delivered as an afterthought. It was a grotesque, uninspiring performance from a barbarian possessing ugly, brutal traits. A more gifted adversary might have earned at the very least a small vestige of grudging admiration but at this rate the mood on the terraces would begin to flare up and spill over. It was all too predictable and, feeling the anger rise to the point where it scalded his guts and left him seething at Ferox' embarrassing show, Crixus struck the next blow away with a violent ring of metal on metal, immediately following through with two hits from the shield. Ferox was sent sprawling backward into the dust, dazed by the double impact to his head.

"On your feet!" Crixus demanded from several yards away, "or are you a coward too?" It would have been such a simple thing to stand over Ferox with the point of the gladius pressed to his throat, awaiting the sponsor's decision. But it was never fated to end in such a manner. "Before this hour has passed you will curse the bitch who spawned you and beg for death as a release from your torment."

"Fuck you!" he snarled, struggling to his feet. "It's not over yet."

"It is for you. Your fate was sealed months ago and tonight will see events come full circle."

"Continue!" the referee ended it.

Angered and humiliated, Ferox initiated the renewal of the contest with a determined barrage of thrusts and more great swinging blows from side to side. As another vicious forward lunge threatened to gut Crixus he deliberately collapsed his guard, angling the sword away to his left as it skimmed across the surface of the shield. The inertia of Ferox strike momentarily unbalanced him and Crixus simply reversed the action of the shield, slamming it into his opponent's face and although he was protected by helmet and visor the sudden force of the impact snapped his head back painfully. But there was to be no respite as before and Crixus stepped in mercilessly, drawing the edge of the gladius over one of Ferox' exposed shoulders and working it down to the bone. The sword dropped from nerveless fingers and as Ferox screamed in shock and pain Crixus reversed the action and opened the flesh of the second arm.

As the sand at their feet became splashed with gouts of blood and the terraces predictably erupted in cries for more carnage and butchery, it became apparent Ferox was not going to kneel and ask for the missio. In itself it was an act of defiance for they would not rob him of a warrior's death. He had never shown mercy in his life – to no one, and he would not beg for it now, snivelling like a wretch and shitting himself with fear. Crixus was aware of it too for as long as his opponent remained on his feet and did not raise a finger in capitulation, he could take his time and draw out the final moments.

He stepped forward and ripped the helmet from Ferox' head with such force the leather chin-strap cut more flesh before snapping. He had wanted to gaze into these eyes from the day he heard about Julius' slaying – wanted to search these fetid cesspools of hatred, knowing he would find nothing but darkness and brooding, simmering hostility. Crixus then unfastened his own helmet and laid it on the sand at his feet before turning to Ferox once more.

"Take a good look at me, you piece of shit, for I have trained long and hard in anticipation of our meeting and given up the life set out for me by the gods. Remember this face for it will be the last thing you ever see," and he thrust the gladius into Ferox' groin. The screams of agony would have woken the dead and echoed across the arena to reach those in the top, most far-removed seats.

"Please, put an end to this now, I implore you," the referee intervened but his hands were tied unless the sponsor called a halt. "The rules dictate I cannot step in and quell it while you remain standing."

"Fuck the rules!" Ferox blubbered through spittle and blood. "They were made for women!"

Crixus struck him again and the gladius went in deep, cleaving the right side of his chest.

"Do you remember a man by the name of Julius Quintus?" Crixus asked unemotionally as he twisted the sword and withdrew to the sound of more hideous, screaming protest that emanated from hell itself. There was no reply and he knew it could only be a matter of moments before Ferox collapsed to the ground. He walked slowly behind the swaying, teetering figure and thrust again, this time into one of Ferox' shoulders, twisting the blade on the return. "Julius Quintus was a kind man, an old man not given to antagonising others or inciting discord. He was like a father to me and you butchered him in a drunken, frenzied attack and left him for dead." He thrust again into the opposite shoulder and Ferox almost went down but Crixus wasn't done yet.

"Tell me, while you still draw breath for I am curious."

"I knew him," but the reply was only an agonised whisper and Crixus leant closer, cupping a hand to his ear.

"I'm sorry, I didn't hear. You'll have to speak up."

"I knew him but he was no fucking man!" and Crixus recoiled at the utter contempt and vileness as a gob of blood-stained spittle landed on his sandal. "Fucking upper-class elite! Fucking master race, looking down on people like me. Good as any of them, I was. Wrong place at the wrong time. Fuck him!"

He was raving and grinning evilly with eyes now rolled back into the skull while the blood and saliva mixed and flowed copiously onto the ground.

"Not much of a fucking man. Screamed like a woman and shit...." The gladius pierced his throat and emerged from the neck, abruptly cutting off the stream of filthy abuse and this time Crixus did not retrieve the weapon lest the tirade continue. It was an unlikely end to a bizarre contest and applause seemed the last thing on the minds of those who continued staring out across the vast enclosure. It certainly had not been a battle of martial prowess and tactical ability but rather an execution with the chance of a few combat highlights thrown in for good measure. Somehow, this was different because it was glaringly personal. Everyone knew the story of Crixus and Julius Quintus but to see a real-life drama of vendetta played out as the planned highlight to the games was simply breath-taking. The sponsor had certainly latched onto an idea and turned it to his advantage but the price in human suffering was beyond belief.

There had been no apologies and no begging for his own miserable life where Ferox remained unrepentant and poison-tongued right up to the end. Crixus sat down on the mired sand just a few feet from the corpse of his slain opponent and he wept, just as the first heavy drops of rain began to fall. The crowds at last began to disperse, filing along the rapidly-emptying terraces to the exits and regarding him with silent, macabre tribute. He wept for his remorseless victim who, in the face of prolonged, violent death had displayed nothing but contempt and blind hatred for a man who had never wronged him but who he saw as an enemy of the lower classes by virtue of their social differences.

He wept as his thoughts turned to Drusilla and how their continued existence as a couple hung by a thread. He wept for Julius and wondered if his spirit could now finally be at peace – that someone loved him enough to embark upon this terrible life-changing odyssey, but most of all his tears were those of release, a catharsis brought about by his public execution of Ferox and the months of denial, discipline and heartbreak that preceded it.

As the rain arrived in a deluge and the barrages of thunder rolled and echoed across the night sky he became aware of a presence and when he looked up through his streaming eyes Lentulus Fulvius knelt beside him and placed a friendly arm about his shoulder. A little further away the body of Ferox still lay in the sand, the gladius protruding from his throat where it had stemmed the torrent of filth. The rain was washing the blood away in rivulets as if trying to conceal the appalling violence by which the man had met his end; but even the force of this downpour could never heal nor disguise the wounds of the gladius and they averted their gaze.

"Come, old friend, for the deed is done and you are a true hero of the people. Three victims in one contest and now this. What a thing!"

"Will you see to it he receives a warrior's funeral?" Crixus gestured over his shoulder.

"You would wish that for the murderer of your friend?"

"He may have lived without honour but in death he was a man."

"He will be honoured with a stone marker in the gladiators' cemetery – you have my word. Enough of bloodshed and death for I have good news. Your woman came to the school last night under the cover of darkness to speak with me."

"I saw her leaving from the window of my cell. Does she fare well?"

"Let us get out of this rain and find some refreshment." They made their way out of the building which was now virtually empty and searched for a tavern. "Put your mind at ease, young Crixus. All is well - in fact all is better than you think. Your woman came to beg a favour – a favour I was only too pleased to grant. She was fearful of your health and well-being after the contest and wondered if she might spend a little time looking after you."

The handsome, chiselled features were split into a wide grin that told Crixus he knew exactly what *looking after* meant.

"But we have no where to be alone, unless she's planned another four-mile walk to the apothecary's dwelling and we sleep in the summer house."

"Relax, Crixus. Your woman has procured a house on the Via Claudia – just minutes from here. A place where you and she can spend the night, and many more nights I shouldn't wonder. It must be serious for her to take such pains."

"You have no idea how serious."

"Oh, I think I do. We had quite an informative little chat and she was most forthcoming about the two of you. You have my endorsement in all respects on the understanding she does not sap your strength and render you unable to defeat your opponents. As long as you return each morning and do not abuse the training regime then I foresee no problems. One other point. Don't get soft and out of condition! I have no desire to lose my most expensive asset until we have both made obscene amounts of money!"

"I am indebted to you yet again and I will vindicate your trust."

"You have brought great honour to my school, Crixus. Loyalty and commitment always have their just rewards. Perhaps it is a good time to repay those qualities."

"Where might I find this house on the Via Claudia?"

"Ah, I wondered when you might ask. Once you are on the road look for a narrow gap between two larger properties after you have gone half a mile or so. The house you seek is in a blind alley at the bottom of that gap. It is behind a stone wall with gates let in to the structure."

"How, in the name of Jupiter did she manage to find a secluded place like that?" Crixus was clearly impressed by the realisation Drusilla wasn't just sitting at home all day dreaming about the two of them.

"I gather your woman was out walking and strayed from her intended route. She discovered the vacant property after retracing her steps otherwise it would have remained hidden. Sometimes things are just meant to happen. Crixus, there is a more serious aspect to all this and I am loathe to bring it to your attention. Do not allow yourselves to be discovered. Your secret is safe with me but I cannot guarantee your immunity and protection if your liaison be compromised. These are dangerous times and a conspiracy such as yours could be worth much gold or used to bribe and corrupt others in prominent places. I will protect you but there are limits."

"We will exercise extreme caution and discretion in our movements and again I thank you for your generosity and understanding."

"Go, Crixus! Go to your woman for she awaits her man. Let her treat your wounds and comfort your body with the warmth of her flesh for you have surely earned it!"

40

For the first time in her life Drusilla had lied to one of her parents and whilst she viewed it as a mere distortion of the facts and no one was being made to suffer on her account, it troubled her deeply she must embark upon the road of deception in order she continue her new-found relationship with Crixus.

Immediately prior to leaving the family residence on the Via Sacra this morning she had bade farewell to her mother who continued to improve on a daily basis and, having rehearsed the words in her mind a dozen times announced her intentions almost as an afterthought.

"I shall not be returning home tonight, mother, so please do not wait up for me. I will be meeting friends after the games have concluded and attending a private party to honour Rome's new champion."

"Just as long as your father doesn't make an unexpected entrance and cast a shadow over the proceedings with his loud and disgusting behaviour."

"Father will, no doubt, be holding his own vulgar celebrations but I think it's reasonable to assume his elevation to praetor is secured. I don't think I could bear to be anywhere near him once victory is confirmed. It will be just another embarrassment."

"You go and enjoy yourself, my child, and do not worry about me. You have given so much of yourself these last months when you could have been indulging in other pleasures. The house slaves will be in attendance if I take a turn for the worse. When my strength is fully returned and we can leave the house together, perhaps then might be an appropriate moment to begin looking for your husband."

At the mere mention of such a possibility Drusilla's stomach quailed as she envisaged an arranged marriage to someone other than Crixus.

"Yes," she replied a little hesitantly, hoping the sensation of nauseating dread was not overtly mirrored in her voice. "Soon we will do all those things we spoke of for your resilience grows with every day the seizures do not return."

She had packed a few items in a small overnight bag and when the games were over she would make her way to the house on the Via Claudia, just a short walk from the amphitheatre. In the last few days she had purchased all the necessary furnishings including chairs, expensive woven rugs for the floors and a rather decadent cedar-framed bed. There were plush tasselled cushions for pillows and a beautifully-ornate silken overlay in rich purple with gold thread depicting the sun, moon and stars of the heavens. She pondered the spicier aspects of this last purchase for who could say to what new heights their loving would take them?

At the great amphitheatre she had, for once, been appreciative of her father's insistence she join him in the privileged boxes otherwise she would have been consigned to the rearmost seats. She desperately wanted to see Crixus again up close and this particular vantage point afforded a view of his most glorious moments yet, together with a chilling awareness of his emotions as he not only slaughtered his victims but basked in the adoration of the immense crowds. He had fought magnificently, keeping them on the edges of their seats with bated breath as the charged atmosphere alternated between death-like hushes and great thrilling outbursts of applause and roars of hero-worship.

This was *her* man they were eulogising and elevating to god-like status and as she saw how he moved like a panther confounding his opponents with his superior speed, strength and seamless flowing beauty of combat which made them appear clumsy and half-witted by comparison, she was physically aroused by his overpowering masculinity. When, in a flash of movement, he had been struck by the trident she knew it was a ploy to give them false hope and then he would finish it on his own terms. He had deliberately increased the odds against him, knowing how the massed ranks of spectators would venerate him. Then he had found himself without weapons and gone on to defeat the retiarius bare-handed. It was a spectacle even Caius Attius Caecilius could never have envisaged and Drusilla was barely able to conceal the tears of pride and the lump in her throat that almost constricted her breathing.

As he confronted the loathsome Ferox she knew from the outset how it must be and she watched, spellbound, as he exacted a terrible revenge while his adversary cursed and spat and his blood sprayed and drenched the sand.

It was frightful and horrific but she could not tear her eyes from the grisly drama and she knew Crixus must be exercising superhuman control in keeping Ferox on his feet and not submitting to the killing-rage of swift death. Each of his strikes was calmly measured, calculated to inflict maximum pain and trauma, drawing out the conclusion as he had promised. Then, as the heavens finally opened in a long-awaited downpour, she could see him huddled in the filthy sand, weeping - a giant of a man reduced to a small pathetic figure in the vastness of the surrounding enclosure. She could see it in the heaving of his shoulders and the set of his great body and she was filled with the need to go to him – to rush from her seat and kiss the tears from his face; but it was a situation in which she was powerless to intervene.

Her own tears had at last spilled over by her inability to render comfort. There was no applause, no cheering and even the footfalls of those vacating the amphitheatre were strangely muted. Crixus was alone on the field of battle and his own sounds of distress were carried away by the fury of the rain which descended with ever-increasing violence.

Caius Attius had already hurried away to his campaign headquarters, oblivious to the emotional extremes still being played out and when Drusilla looked up once more through her streaming eyes she saw Lentulus Fulvius with an arm draped about Crixus' shoulder. The amphitheatre was emptying fast and the majority were in for a soaking before they arrived home. She knew the storm would last well into the night for it was months since there had been rain of this magnitude and the earth was scorched and baked. In the blackness of the night she attracted little attention as she made her way along the Via Claudia and entered the garden terrace through one of the small gates. As she let herself in, so her spirits lifted and the sadness of the arena was briefly forgotten.

She lit candles and oil lamps and then, thankful to have left the window shutters closed throughout the heat of the day, stripped off her sodden clothes and hung them where they would dry sufficiently overnight. She towelled her hair and secured it in the style Crixus adored using the jewelled combs and clasps. As she found another body-sized towel and wrapped it about her nudity but deliberately left her breasts partially exposed, she became aware of her nipples firming up with the anticipation of being with her lover for a whole night. There was a meal of fish, olives, oil with herbs and vinegar and loaves of fresh crusty bread accompanied by two generous amphorae of wine. In a small curtained-off area to one side were bathing facilities, comprising a simple wooden table with more towels and two large bowls of water. She knew Crixus would be mired with blood and filth when he arrived and those injuries would need attention too. Hopefully, the deluge of rain would wash most of it away and once she had taken care of the immediate concerns they could perhaps relax a little and enjoy the lanista's generosity in this peaceful little haven.

All was ready and as she poured the fruity wine into two solid-silver goblets, she heard the outside gate open and close and seconds later, as he tapped at the door, she opened it and he fell into her arms – exhausted. Big as he was, she steered him into one of the chairs and closed the door behind him, bolting it securely. It was the darkest night she could remember in years for there was neither moon nor stars – just the relentless hammering of heavy rain and peals of thunder reverberating across a turbulent sky. Every few seconds the interior of the house would be illuminated by garish flashes of pinkish-blue lightning and she dreaded their flouting of social morals had incurred the wrath of the gods. She so wanted the night to be perfect.

He had come straight from the arena and was not only soaked to the skin and shivering from the icy rain, his wounds were beginning to stiffen. She unfastened the heavy balteus and lifted the rough-woven tunic over his head. He removed his own sandals and she covered him with a second bulky towel whilst rubbing him dry with another, watching with relief as colour bloomed on his cheeks and replaced the unhealthy pallor.

"I had almost forgotten what it is to be touched by you," he spoke softly as the thunder boomed and clattered across the rooftops. She gently touched the wounds and when he offered no protest removed the sealed top of a simple clay jar and applied a generous blob of the soothing lavender balm to the puncture on his left thigh. Mercifully it had ceased bleeding and although the rain had washed the wound almost clean it was swollen and discoloured a livid purple. Prompt attention by the physician would almost certainly have thwarted the onset of infection but he now required complete rest and more regular applications of the cold, fragrant unguent.

"I felt no trepidation whilst the contest was under way," she ventured at last. "But when it was over I became truly frightened. I knew your injuries would not be mortal for you would never deliberately allow another to come so close. My real concern began when I saw how you slumped onto the sand with head bent forward in the lashing rain, so clearly overcome by the moment and all that had gone before."

Throughout the heat of battle there was no time to ponder her whereabouts in the great auditorium but he was gladdened by her presence and the vow to watch over him like some benevolent and ever-vigilant custodian, completely at one with his actions and thoughts.

"I could see you were drained and tired unto death and needed me to take care of you, much as I too wished it could be so. But now you are here and we are together again until noon tomorrow. Quintina informs me lavender is a great healer and soon the stiffness will go out of your injuries."

She finished gently applying the ointment to his lacerated wrist where the dagger had opened his flesh and saw how close death had hovered in that instant. The blade had only narrowly missed the artery and inwardly she shuddered at the possibility of sustaining a more serious laceration. He was fit and would heal well but this particular injury only served to remind her like all other men he was not made of bronze or iron but flesh and blood.

He saw how the betrothal ring moved freely on its gold chain as it dangled invitingly between her large breasts and he yearned to press his face into the deep cleft of her cleavage. His body reacted with surprising abruptness and beneath the heavy towel draped over him Drusilla observed the change signalling in this department, at least, he remained fully functional.

"Actually," he seemed a little sheepish, "I am plagued by a terrible stiffness elsewhere and wonder if you possess a remedy for that also?"

She pulled the loose covering away and seeing the nature of his discomfort nodded in deep understanding.

"Jupiter!" she exclaimed. "That's a sizeable problem you have there. No matter, I have a solution. This will be only a short-term alleviation while I consider a more-effective method of keeping the unwanted swelling at bay. Later on, when we have eaten our fill and drunk well, I will endeavour to show you one or two other interesting procedures frequently employed in ridding the sufferer of this unwelcome stiffness."

She closed her slim fingers about him and began to tease and tug and manipulate for she could sense the urgency and knew release at this point would be a merciful relief and aid the healing process. After only a short time she felt his movements become more agitated, more demanding and as he reached forward and caressed her breasts tenderly she slid her tongue into his mouth. His reaction was instantaneous and as his pelvis gyrated under her skilled, teasing fingers she slowed and lessened the degree of contact so he might gather himself once more to please them both a little later.

"That's quite an effective method of nursing," he conceded, opening his eyes once more. "I never read about that one in any physician's journal. Have you practiced this branch of therapy before?"

"Actually, no. You are my first patient. Quintina taught me many things and this is my first hands-on experience. I have yet to develop my skills."

"You're clearly a most receptive pupil. I'd like to test it again when you've mastered your subject. Who knows – with regular practice and a willing subject...," and he let the statement hang tantalisingly.

As they sat at the table and Drusilla served the meal with pride, he became serious again and she studied him with wide eyes.

"I'm sorry," he ventured. "I did not bring you a gift as a token of gratitude for what you have provided here. It is rumoured a good portent to bring a gift into a new home I am told."

"You are the only gift I desire," and she reached across the table to touch his face with oil-smeared fingers.

"Tonight, in the arena, I witnessed an ugliness I could not believe – an unspeakable vileness and contempt for all things decent and good. I have never encountered such blind hatred nor heard words that belonged in the fires of the underworld. And now, being here like this with you, in the presence of great beauty, I can scarcely catch my breath."

She remained silent as she ate, watching him with those near-black eyes as he struggled to find adequate words to describe this bizarre paradox.

"I am at odds to explain my feelings, Drusilla, for your comeliness and grace makes me weak with impulse and yearning and our loving drains me in a way the most intensive combat and training can never equal. And then, on the other hand, when I am with you I assume the persona of a god – invincible, and I know all things are possible. Does this make any sense or is it fanciful nonsense I speak?"

She sipped wine from the silver goblet, inhaling the heady bouquet whilst never taking her eyes from him – eyes that reflected the flickering, dancing flames of candles and lamps.

"Your words would pierce the heart of any woman," she replied with an unimaginable promise etched on those slightly-parted lips as she popped an olive into her mouth and licked each of her slim, tapered fingers in a manner that left him in no doubt as to what she was thinking. "Who could have guessed only a few weeks ago we had nowhere to meet save for Quintina's gardens, and now look at us. Have our fortunes not changed for the better, Crixus? Have the gods not smiled on us at last and given us their blessing while the state remains defiantly opposed?"

"The lanista has been most generous and kindly disposed to our situation and if we are discreet and not seen in public together then I

247

foresee no problems meeting like this. For you the difficulties will be greater and you must not come under suspicion of your parents by reason of your absences at night."

"That is true," she nodded in understanding. "It may well be we can only spend the occasional afternoon and evening together before going our separate ways. I can't remember when father last spent a night at the house and I dread to think with whom he consorts after dark. It is only mother who needs me to be there and even she is not too demanding of my time in light of her health improving. It would attract the wrong kind of attention if all of a sudden I was to spend regular nights away and coming home the following morning." She was silent for a while and he could see she was deep in thought. An uncharacteristic frown creased her forehead and it was clear she was troubled. "Mother speaks of finding a husband for me when she is a little stronger and we are able to venture into the city and renew her social contacts. The very thought fills me with dread for I would rather die than be without you. If she insists then I will have to end her fanciful daydreaming forthright. I refuse to marry a man who is not of my own choosing for it is doomed to failure and only misery could ever come of it."

"Would your mother overrule your wishes at the risk of driving a wedge between the two of you?"

"I have stood up to my father often enough but mother and I have never exchanged angry words. If she persists then I will be left with no choice. It's my life and I will decide who I spend it with. I know she only wants me to be happy and financially secure but this wretched social status issue simply will not lie down and die. It makes my hackles rise when all I ever wanted in a man is right here in this room."

"You are beautiful," he replied simply. "Every time I see you I love you more than the last. I cannot influence the way your parents feel, nor will I attempt any course of action that places you in jeopardy. All I know is for another four and a half years I must live with the status of a slave, even though I am a freeborn citizen of Rome. The only release from my bond with the lanista is if I am awarded my freedom."

"Your status is immaterial to me. I would have waited a thousand years for you, let alone a few months."

"Until then we must live a secret life if we are to remain together and cherish stolen moments like this."

She reached across the table to recharge his wine goblet and then topped up her own. The topmost part of her towel had only been loosely secured and he stared in wonder as it fell away to reveal her large, perfectly-formed breasts. Never failing to be wonderstruck by the feminine form he gazed at her nipples which hardened and thrust out proudly.

"Let us drink a toast to our meeting tonight and ask the gods to allow us many such moments for if they are amenable then I can live with my own conscience and be damned with conventions and etiquette."

"To stolen times and nights of wicked passion," she echoed his audacious salute. She stood up and gestured for him to follow. "Come, for I wish to test the comfort of a certain acquisition situated in the next room." She led the way while he followed close behind, surprised at the new improved mobility in his leg. The bed was a joy to behold and raised higher off the floor than his own intolerable wooden-slatted abomination back at the school. This was a truly sumptuous affair with its plump cushions and tasselled pillows. Drusilla's opulent tastes were further in evidence when he observed the fine silk cover embroidered with real gold thread and saw how the outer edges depicted images of the heavens mimicking those on his fighting shield.

"This is indeed most lavish. I doubt the emperor himself boasts anything so grand."

"I have a little more time on my hands and besides, what else is money for if not spending? I have no children and I think there will be no call for it in the afterlife – now come here and kiss me before the night is gone and you must return."

He pulled her gently closer and ran a finger down her spine to where her buttocks flared out, teasing the cleft with delicious circular movements that brought the goose-flesh up on her arms. In turn she thrust her pelvis into his own and sought his tongue. It was a deliberate ploy for she relaxed the weight on her feet, becoming heavier in his arms and leaned back, upsetting the balance so they both tumbled onto the bed. She giggled at her own wantonness and he uttered an oath and then laughed too as he caught the leg injury on the way down. She spread herself invitingly and, taking him in a warm hand, guided him easily into her depths, feeling an overwhelming sense of contentment and well-being at this most wondrous union of man and woman.

Together they rode the waves of passion, rising to peaks of intense pleasure before subsiding into gentler, calmer troughs of quiescence. In this place so far-removed from the struggles of the outside world it was safe and secure and they took comfort from the darkness. Outside, the world dissolved in a maelstrom of confusion as great peals of thunder crashed and rolled across the sky while lightning briefly illuminated the small room with its garish, rapid flickering and the rain beat ever harder against the shuttered windows. It seemed as if nature too was in a state of wild abandon and competing against this mortal couple for dominance of the night and they were oblivious to her.

They came awake in the morning to bright sunshine streaming through the shutters and all was quiet save for the muted sounds of traders setting up their businesses for the day. Overnight, the storm had blown itself out while the remnants moved away leaving clear blue skies as its legacy and streets washed clean of filth and litter by the torrents of rain.

"It's beautiful out there," she greeted Crixus with an arm draped across his chest. "Do you think this a good omen and we have not incurred the gods' displeasure?"

"I'd say your screams frightened the storm away. Nature knew she was beaten and further competition was futile."

She nibbled his earlobe so that he shivered deliciously and reached down with a teasing hand.

"Young vixen!" he scolded with mock severity. "You need a lesson."

"What manner of lesson did you have in mind?" and her own pretended innocence rekindled the fires of wanting again.

"One you'll not forget in a hurry and a suitable punishment for such a misdemeanour. Stay exactly where you are for total compliance is required."

He moved out from under her embrace and as she spread her thighs for him again he placed his head against her slippery opening and probed with the tip of his tongue. She responded instantly, moaning softly while her movements became increasingly wild and abandoned and perspiration beaded her forehead. As her breathing was reduced to short, sharp pants and she rolled her head from side to side like a fever patient under the bouts of delirium she finally called out with the strength of her release. He had taken her over the top many times last night doing exactly as he was doing now and the vibrant streaks of incandescent lightning that forked and flared outside were rendered insignificant by the blinding white light that seared her closed eyes. Again and again she called out as the ripples and contractions gripped her and she thought her heart might falter.

"Enough, Crixus, enough. You must stop before the fire consumes me. Alas, I can take no more. Have I learned the lesson to your satisfaction or does the pupil require more tutoring?"

"On our next meeting I will test your memory but you show great promise." He moved again and went to lay by her side, tracing invisible circles with a fingertip on her belly. "We must not be seen leaving this place together. You had best leave first if you are to check on your mother and not arouse suspicion. When we have done this a few times it will be a little easier but we must be mindful not to create any kind of pattern in our meetings and departures."

He judged the sun's angle and decided it was not yet four hours until noon, nodding imperceptibly.

"If you are to bathe and dress you should be making ready."

"You are right," she sighed happily. "Last night was wonderful but I knew it would be. I could remain here for ever – just like this, but it cannot be so."

She rose from their bed and walked to the small curtained-off area where she found her clothes had dried sufficiently overnight. She bathed and dried herself then dressed and adjusted her hair. She gathered together the few simple items she had brought and placed them in the overnight bag, casting a critical inspection around her to ensure nothing had been omitted. While Crixus took his own turn she rinsed the food plates and stacked them tidily away after drying them carefully. There was still a small quantity of wine remaining and she shared it between the two silver goblets, offering one as he came to stand beside her.

"You are beautiful and it breaks my heart to watch you go."

"I love you, Crixus, and it breaks my heart to walk away."

They drank the wine in silence where eyes conveyed those final sentiments and as she turned to go, pressed a small object into his hand.

"There will be times when you must arrive first. No patterns – remember?" and he placed the key inside his tunic.

"I will guard this with my life – in fact I will wear it on a chain as you carry the betrothal ring."

"I will find a way to contact you but it may be only for an hour or two until I can spend longer. And now I must go. I love you more than life itself, Crixus, and I will count away the hours until we meet again."

She reached up on tiptoes and kissed him warmly before turning and walking out of the house where the air was redolent with the scent of bougainvillaea and orange blossom after the heavy rains. She did not look back as she bent slightly to negotiate the small gap in the perimeter wall so he missed the tragic expression and the single tear that spilled onto her cheek. He gave her an hour and spent the time tidying the room where they had slept – straightening the ornate cover and ensuring nothing was left behind. He was about to leave when he noticed the small pot of lavender unguent and decided to take it with him for although the injuries were unsightly they were without pain. One more check and then he too was gone, securing the door and exiting the garden through the opposite gate. Out on the street he took a different route back to the school and kept to the shadows lest he be recognised.

He walked slowly – his mind full of the vision of Drusilla, his heart heavy with melancholy because he had watched her go and the world was empty once more. Life was to continue along this path for the next eighteen months or so where Crixus enjoyed extended periods of freedom from the school as he continued to win resoundingly every contest he was entered for. There were no shortages of sponsors for the games and even the emperor, Titus Flavius Domitianus, requested his presence on major public holidays and feast days. He constantly faced groups of three and sometimes four opponents and consequently his prize-money was accumulating – as was the cost of his hire to the sponsors.

For Drusilla, there was still the frustration of lies and secrecy to cover up those illicit meetings and whilst her father had returned to the house only once it was, ultimately, Agrippina who remained the need for excess caution and constant vigilance. When the subject of marriage inevitably reared its ugly head once more Drusilla grasped the nettle and told her mother flatly she was enjoying herself too much at the moment to contemplate settling down on a permanent basis or even waste time searching for a potential candidate. Money was not an issue and the house was more than adequate for the two of them, so why the rush?

"Think of it this way," Drusilla tried to soften the blow. "If I marry a rich consul or fat senator and he whisks me off to the provinces hundreds of miles from here, how will we ever see each other again? However wealthy or generous he may be, I doubt he would appreciate the company of a permanent chaperone if you were to accompany us."

Agrippina seemed resigned to the logic of it and the subject was never raised again. Her daughter's mind was firmly made up and she would not be moved regardless of how forceful the argument to the contrary.

Caius Attius Caecilius had stormed to victory in the elections, sweeping all opposition away with his extravagant games, promises of reforms and generous food gifts to the populace. His elevated position within the senate had won him some powerful friends and he now conducted the majority of his affairs from the Curia itself located in the forum. He was, by definition, a magistrate in the law courts but he was also empowered to convene the senate and assemblies in addition to assuming the administrative duties of consuls when these were absent. Within a relatively short period the cycle would begin again as the vision of governorship materialised from the shimmering mirage of life's horizon. There would be untold wealth, power, influence, the command of an army – *and women!*

Life had been good these last years. His popularity had increased and he was accorded a new respect from his colleagues. He had finally managed to detach himself from the needy, cloying fingers of Agrippina and her incessant whining. He thought the fits might have finished her off by now but she seemed to have undergone a dramatic reversal to her condition attributed, he surmised, to the strange bond between Drusilla and her apothecary friend. He would not go down the slippery route of divorce, he decided after much soul-searching. Drusilla already knew too much about his extra-marital affairs and other incriminating business for the process to run smoothly and he could ill-afford any adverse publicity or scandal at this stage of his career. Keep them happy with money and a roof over their heads. It was a trivial matter and they could retain the house-slaves too. He wanted none of it. Just keep things running on an even keel for the next few months and all would be well.

He could never have foreseen it but Caius Attius Caecilius' dream of aspiring to a provincial governorship was to vanish before his eyes like the capricious early mists of a hot August morning.

41

Cyrenaica was a land of vast agricultural wealth and whilst not actually boasting the epithet, *Bread-basket of the empire,* contributed largely in other ways to the immense collective resources Rome laid claim to. With Numidia to the west and Aegyptus on its eastern border Cyrenaica was ideally placed to export its riches directly to the city of Rome itself. This was not only a region of great deserts and vast tracts of wilderness but also, by stark contrast, rich grazing pastures capable of supporting immense herds of sheep and cattle. There was an abundance of grain and other Mediterranean speciality crops and – in addition, there was Silphium.

Silphium proliferated on parts of the African coast but was especially abundant on the coastal plateaus near Cyrene where it flourished as a highly-prized commodity owing to its diversity. Perfumes were distilled from the yellow flowers and foodstuffs prepared from the stalks so nothing of the plant was wasted. Roots and juices were prized by apothecaries for their medicinal qualities where the plant was known to be an efficacious remedy for such ailments as sore throats, fevers, indigestion, seizures and general aches and pains. It provided an antidote for certain poisons, was used as a seasoning in foods and frequently employed as a cleansing agent in childbirth.

There had been Roman presence and influence in Cyrenaica for centuries and the province had come to be regarded as something of a backwater on the great imperial map. Consequently, the 3rd Cyrenaica Legion under General Maximus Titus Valerius was now based across the border in Aegyptus leaving only the garrison in Cyrene. Rumour had it Valerius would soon be returning to Rome where he would feature prominently in the consular elections. The present governor of Cyrenaica had recently succumbed to some mystery illness, leaving Valerius to administer the province until a suitable replacement could be found.

Within the great halls of the Curia in Rome the name of Caius Attius Caecilius was being submitted as the next likely candidate to rule this remote but prosperous and strategically vital outpost. With barely a week to go before he could assume the position was safely in his lap, Caius announced one more day of games and spectacle where Crixus would feature prominently as the star attraction.

"Twenty-thousand sesterces and a bargain at that," Lentulus Fulvius remained steadfast in the rate of hire for Crixus, knowing he could reasonably demand ten times that figure from anyone else. "To a lesser man it would have been two hundred-thousand but I can afford to be generous in my terms since it is largely down to you Crixus became an overnight sensation and the price of his talents rose to its current level."

"Twenty-thousand it is," Caius replied in agreement, placing a leather purse on the table in front of him. I brought extra but you may pocket the difference."

"I might have let you beat me down to fifteen."

"I would have paid thirty," and he offered his hand in order the deal be secured.

42

Drusilla locked the door of the little house on the Via Claudia and exited through one of the gates set into the surrounding wall – careful as always to check all around for familiar faces and any other signs of having been observed. But the narrow street remained completely deserted and she relaxed as her steps took her leisurely into the centre and back to the family home on the Via Sacra. As she approached the house she became uneasy, an increasing sense of foreboding that told her something was wrong.

Was it her mother? Had she taken another turn for the worse after all this time when Drusilla was convinced the darker days were in the past?

Please, let that not be the case!

As she walked through the house and into the living quarters she suddenly stopped in her tracks for there before her bearing expressions carved from stone, stood her mother and father. For Caius to be here alongside Agrippina it must have been an issue of considerable weight and she drew a deep breath, gathering herself for what was to come.

"Where have you been?" Caius demanded brutally and Drusilla could see the barely-restrained anger was simmering away just beneath the surface, ready to burst out at the slightest provocation. "I said where have you been?" and it seemed he was exercising monumental restraint in keeping his temper.

"I heard you the first time!" Drusilla snapped, "so don't you dare take that tone with me! I have been out with a friend – all night – not that it's any business of yours!"

"It becomes my business when I discover through a third party my daughter is fraternising with a slave," and the pieces finally tumbled into place. Their secret was out in the open. In a way she should have expected it for they had been fortunate to survive undetected this long.

"You know damned well he is no slave, nor anything of the kind!" she took the aggressive stance. "He is a freeborn citizen of Rome and would have remained so if his friend had not been so callously murdered. His motives are without question – unlike yours!"

"Do not provoke me, Drusilla. How long has this disgraceful affair been going on? How long have you been deceiving your mother and me?"

"Your mother and me?" she screamed back, the outrage coming to a head. "Your mother and me? You make it sound like you are an item. There is no 'your mother and me.' How dare you speak of yourselves as a couple! The dutiful parents concerned for their daughter's well-being. You should take a long, hard look at your own morals before you start questioning mine."

"You will tell me," he demanded with flecks of spittle flying from his lips. "You will tell me how long you have been engaged in this scandalous behaviour."

"Two years!" she screamed at him, her face just inches from his own. "Two wonderful years and I would not give up a single moment of it."

"On the contrary, young lady, you *will* be giving it up – *all* of it! I cannot believe this dreadful situation has remained undetected for two years and it was only by the merest chance you were spotted. You see, my dear, I have a loyal friend whose position within the senate takes him all over the city. An innocent survey of the Via Claudia revealed some interesting secrets. The plain clothes nearly fooled him but when your gladiator lover turned up as well there could be no mistake."

"Don't force me into making a decision. I will never give him up – not for you, not for anyone! Do you hear me? I will not give him up. I would rather die."

"It may just come to that. If you do not renounce your love of the slave I will have you publicly flogged as an example and Crixus will be transported in chains to the most desolate, far-flung corner of the empire where he will never enjoy free status again. Give him up now, Drusilla. It cannot remain a secret for ever. If this should become common knowledge the scandal will ruin us all. Give me your pledge this ridiculous infatuation is at an end and I will spare the ultimate punishment for you both. Do I have your word? Come, Drusilla, I am offering you a way out."

"You bastard!" she spat her reply. "The only thing you will ever have from me is my utmost loathing, contempt and hatred. I never thought it was possible to hate another person the way I hate you for it eats at me with a burning fire. Now I can understand how Crixus kept going all those months while he awaited the contest with Ferox. The lust for vengeance – to feel the agony of his victim and watch his lifeblood ebb away must have been overwhelming. Do not lecture me on my own private life when it is just that – private! We have always exercised the utmost care and discretion when meeting and have never been seen together.

"The way I see it, there are only two reasons for our relationship to become public. Either your friend sells his secret to the highest bidder or you spill your guts to the censuras when I inform them of your illegal practices. Yes – I can see now why you would not want that to happen for you would be finished. Even the great Caius Attius' influence would not help you weather the storm if this became common knowledge – that your own daughter was little better than a whore, bedding the champion of Rome under your noses all this time. You would be a laughing stock. The censors would conduct a full inquiry and once they were made aware of your own scandalous morals and disreputable behaviour your career would be finished.

"You would be forced into private life and forfeit any pension from the state so do not make your threats to me until your own house is in order. You would do well to remember I am a grown woman and not your simpering little girl any more and as such will make my own decisions whether you approve of them or not!"

"You dare speak to me that way!" he bellowed and it was clear all self-restraint had vanished. "Just who do you think you are, young lady?" and he slapped her across the face viciously leaving a huge angry welt on her cheek. She did not cry out nor cower in submission as he thought she might but came back at him with her own right hand, fuelled by more hatred and dug her nails into his cheek, dragging them downward in a manner calculated to open his face in four bloody furrows and it was Caius who called out with shock and pain.

"You bloody vicious little bitch!" he screamed like a girl. "Do you know the penalty for assaulting a prominent government official? You'll beg me to reduce the punishment to a simple flogging by the time I've finished with you. You bloody vicious bitch!"

"I can live with your insults and threats for I ceased to be afraid when you deserted mother. Your immediate concern is explaining those marks on your cheek. 'Has one of Caius' pussy cats scratched him?' they will ask. 'You really should exercise more discretion when choosing your liaisons, Caius,' and they will laugh secretively among their select little groups."

"You will give up your slave, Drusilla. Mark my words, you will give him up. Your illicit nights of passion and flouting of social morals are at an end. It is finished. You may see him briefly one more time where you will tell him it is over, for you both. The day after tomorrow

258

Crixus will fight in the games I will hold before leaving for Cyrenaica. I will leave strict instructions with my most trusted subordinates to ensure the two of you never meet again. Give him up, Drusilla, and let your mother find someone more suitable than a common slave."

"Someone like you?" she sneered. "Someone who might treat me the way you behaved when mother became ill? Someone who knows nothing of decency, honour and integrity? Someone who might beat me if I do not behave in the manner expected? Someone who cheats and lies and whores! I must say, you are without a doubt the perfect role model. Before you leave, for you have long overstayed your welcome, listen to me carefully lest there be any misunderstanding. I will not give up Crixus – not now, not ever. Not for mother and certainly not for you, now get out and never come back!"

"Make sure you're in the amphitheatre two days from now. I want to enjoy the tragic look on your face when your slave lover walks out, knowing the two of you will never meet again and it will be a just reward for your treachery and insolence."

"I'll be there, you can count on that. I wouldn't miss it for the world and I have a feeling the great Caius Attius Caecilius will be taking a monumental dive from his lofty podium into the gutter where he belongs."

"Are you threatening me – your father? I can see the sooner I make an example and whip some of that attitude out of your hide the sooner you might accept your place and show a little respect to those above you."

"My father is dead!" she interrupted with renewed hostility. "You bear no resemblance to the man I once knew!"

"You can do nothing to harm me," he continued, but her words had found their mark. "You could not even show just cause for the censors to convene a judicial inquiry into my affairs and have me removed from office or even remotely investigated so do not make your fine threats to me."

"I once swore I would see you finished and that threat still stands. I would not waste my time with disclosures to the senate regarding your abhorrent way of life for I am sure I would be confronted by an ominous closing of ranks. No. I think if I give you enough rope you will hang yourself and the most poetic aspect of it all – regardless of the price I must pay to see it happen, is your self-condemnation will be conducted in public. Now, for the last time, get out of my sight before I do you greater injury."

He stormed from the house still nursing his injured cheek. Blood streaked his face and ran through his fingers onto the folds of the toga and as he hurried along the street he made a curious spectacle where all dignity had vanished and he appeared the victim of an attempted assassination.

Let the bitch enjoy her small moment of triumph! She'll soon be paying a heavy price for such insolence, disobedience and that unprovoked show of temper.

Throughout the deeply disturbing and violent exchange Agrippina remained silent but shocked by the knowledge of Drusilla's indiscretion and the undisguised poison directed at her father. She was powerless to intervene – fearful lest Caius should strike her to the ground in his blind rage. She thought her daughter incapable of such venom and unbridled fury for Drusilla had always been her little girl. Circumstances now revealed Drusilla in a new, disconcerting light and secretly she dreaded the next two days where father and daughter would be instrumental in one another's destruction – a terrible real-life drama played out on the terraces of the amphitheatre.

Agrippina was fully conversant with the story of Crixus, despite the inflammatory and prejudiced stance of Caius. She also knew women and girls, from slaves to patricians, were sexually attracted to these stars of the arena but it was nothing more than lust-fuelled fancy and imaginary romance where only the stimulation of the flesh counted. Try as she might, she could not comprehend the reason why Drusilla should yield to this sordid temptation and give herself so unashamedly. Had it been merely infatuation or a serious crush similar to the ones she herself had experienced in her earlier years, she could have perhaps understood Drusilla's straying from the rules and practices governing a woman of her status – *but two years!* And she had even secured a house where they might spend their illicit hours together away from the public gaze.

Of course, she could never openly condone her daughter's choice of liaison but she could, perhaps, come close to understanding her motives; the thrill of seeing her lover fight for his life in the arena and the sound of the crowds as they venerated the new champion. What must that have felt like? How had they met? Was it by chance or had Drusilla's hand been instrumental in it? To have kept the magic alive for two years it must have been truly special – worth fighting for. Worth dying for....

As she recalled Drusilla's angry threats and declarations, '*I will never give him up – never! I would rather die...,*' she experienced an unfamiliar sadness and aching loneliness in the deep, empty place of her heart because she herself had never known such fire and passion and it cut like a knife.

43

For the first time in his life Crixus knew the meaning of fear – fear of living in a world where Drusilla was no longer a part of it. The killing of Julius Quintus had plunged him into a realm of carnage, butchery and monumentally-destructive anger but the prospect of losing Drusilla filled him with panic; his guts heaved in protest and the acid scalding in his chest felt like the blade of a gladius.

The crowds would remember today's spectacle, but not for the reasons Caius Attius Caecilius envisaged!

Today was the day it all came tumbling down – Crixus, Drusilla and Caius Attius along with an abrupt end to his dream of the governorship. Crixus would initiate the chain of events and Drusilla would effectively seal their fates even though she was unaware of it at the outset. For just a few short hours last night they had met in secret once more, knowing ultimately it was for the last time and even their loving had born an air of sadness and finality. As she explained the awful confrontation with Caius where each had lashed out with more than mere words, so he contented himself his decision was the right one and not a product of haste or heated emotions. Hopefully, when the final scenes were played out a short time from now she would understand his motives and feel their bond secured for all time – until their paths crossed once more. There had been no hugs – no goodbyes, and as they drew apart and went their separate ways it seemed there was an unspoken covenant between them, a tacit understanding this was not fated to be the end but rather a new beginning.

He thought about the little package wrapped in a square of purple velvet he had left for her at the house. In one respect it would break her and he tried not to think about the tears when she read the few lines on the accompanying parchment. Despite her grief, his promise would strengthen her resolve and give her the fortitude to see it through.

Next day in the arena, Crixus steadfastly refused to acknowledge the great crowds' applause and clamorous greetings as he made his entrance. He knew exactly where to find Caius Attius Caecilius and a quick glance confirmed his position – directly opposite the emperor's raised pulvinar in the front row of seats. Next to him – Drusilla, lovely as ever but she was unsmiling and there was a countenance of tragedy about her. Had she read his thoughts, his intentions and was now dreading the scenario about to unfold?

As the referee announced the beginning of the contest Crixus tore into the opposition with unbelievable speed and ferocity, giving them no chance to group or take up a defensive stance. It was utter carnage, unnecessarily bloody and brutal where his victims were killed over and over again as a mark of his all-consuming anger directed toward Caius. It lasted less than a minute and as he turned to face the object of his murderous hatred so the auditorium erupted in protest, a rising cacophony of discord, boos and jeers. They were not pleased and it reflected directly upon the games' organiser now scowling furiously at this shameful display of utter contempt and scorn. Incensed, he turned to Drusilla.

"This is your doing! You put him up to this – a conspiracy to discredit me yet again."

"Today's contest was not referred to and I did not taint our meeting by the mention of your name for it sickens me. Crixus is his own man and conducts himself accordingly. If he desired a quick kill then there was good reason for it. He owes you nothing – neither allegiance nor respect. As for my part in it, I wish it was you out there facing him now!"

Crixus observed the exchange and could see by Caius' florid face Drusilla was effectively holding her own in this latest battle of wills. He knew Caius would not allow it to end here like this. He must have formulated some contingency plan designed to swing the odds in his favour once more if it went wrong. As he stood defiantly in front of the sponsor, a sudden renewed bout of screaming and shouting rippled through the packed terraces when three more combatants emerged from the shadows and hurried toward him. It was a predictable reaction on Caius' part for he knew no bounds in his lust for power and unquestioning obedience. He turned away from Drusilla, confident of a greater spectacle in this second confrontation. No other man had ever faced-off six opponents in one single action. If he prevailed then Caius Attius' name would be up there with Crixus. If he was defeated, then it mattered little in the bigger picture. The problem of Drusilla and her gladiator lover would be finally resolved.

Crixus was daubed with the blood of his victims as he focused attention on this second group who were shuffling uncomfortably and eyeing the carnage around them. It was a scene of mayhem and butchery, severed limbs, spilled guts and faeces – enough to demoralize the most battle-hardened and committed opponents. In his short career as a fighter Crixus had gained a fearsome reputation and it was widely known the only time he ever faced odds of one-to-one was as a novice. Their fate was sealed and rather than face the wrath of the sponsor and retribution of vengeful spectators they would die with honour. Accordingly, they circled their prey who had now discarded the wolf's-head shield in favour of a second gladius, snatched from lifeless fingers. This man cared nothing for defence and immediately went onto the offensive with weapons hissing and cutting flesh in a tide of savagery and unprecedented force. More blood drenched the sand at his feet as two more victims fell before the steel in rapid succession leaving the third man completely alone.

Those who looked on saw how Crixus appeared to have steered the action to one side of the elliptical arena, beneath the six-foot-high marble wall and directly in front of the sponsor and his daughter. By contrast, Crixus' merciless onslaught had now given way to the expected moves and dispositions of combat that immediately aroused suspicion once more. Clearly, he could have ended the contest at any time so why was he prolonging the inevitable?

Drusilla felt the knots of fear cramping her stomach as she awaited some shocking, unforeseen outcome. Was Crixus simply toying with his opponent? He had not divulged any plan of action last night, nor had he said anything to frighten or unsettle her but as she watched his movements she knew something was wrong and became agitated. His opponent was giving a good account and the air resounded to the staccato clash of metal on metal. Crixus' superior speed and power inevitably began to wear his man down and it must end soon. Crixus was backing him up all the time and then – just as the brutal conclusion was only moments away, he froze, the dual weapons poised menacingly over their intended victim. Beneath the helmet with its enclosing visor his eyes bore into Drusilla's seated only a short distance away. Although facial details were completely obscured she felt the intensity of his piercing gaze as he uttered words too soft for her ears.

"Remember me, Drusilla, for I will always love you." In that instant where time had slowed and reality assumed a new shocking clarity, she saw with unbelievable horror what was going to happen. Before his opponent's strike had even landed in Crixus' unprotected chest, Drusilla's clenched fists covered her eyes and her anguished screams echoed around the great enclosure, now fallen silent with terrible expectation.

"No! No! Please, no!" It was a barely-human sound that emerged from her throat, the cry of a tortured soul in unbearable pain and despair as she heard the blow cut him down. When, after many moments, she dared look again, it was to the vision of Crixus kneeling on the sand in front of his opponent, mortally wounded. Blood was pouring from his chest but even as the crowds watched in morbid fascination they saw how he mustered sufficient strength to remove his helmet so they might gaze upon the handsome face one last time.

Drusilla was crying openly, her body wracked by great heaving sobs while Caius remained indifferent to the scene being played out, and now there was a glimmering of understanding among the crowds too. This was unbelievable – a woman of the nobility and her fallen gladiator lover. What a story! What an incredible end to such a contest. What an end to the champion's career and what a scandal would be born when this became more public than it already was!

The referee was standing close-by, ensuring no further moves by the aggressor until a decision was given by the sponsor. In the terraces, the crowds had already reached a unanimous verdict and once more the air thundered to the sound of one common accord.

"Mitte! Mitte! Mitte!" they demanded in deafening unison. "Let him live! Let him live!"

In the privileged seats Caius' face was lit up in exaltation at this unprecedented turn of events.

"See how the people love him," he turned to Drusilla and sneered. "Would you gladly see him executed as a measure of pride and defiance? I hold the power of life and death in my hand. A single gesture of the thumb will put an end to it one way or the other. I give you this last chance to renounce your love of the slave. Give him up now and I will accede to the wishes of the crowds."

In that instant it all became clear and Crixus' actions were completely understandable. There were no choices to be made and whilst it would bring about a merciful end to Crixus' pain and precipitate the means by which they might be reunited in a more-forgiving place, it would destroy her father also, as she had vowed.

"Tell me you renounce him, Drusilla, but hurry for his life hangs by a thread."

The fates had conspired to bring them together this way and by sacrificing his own life as a measure of his love, he had delivered into her hands the means by which to end Caius' political career. She saw how Crixus was beyond the assistance of any physician. If he was spared and carried out of here this very moment he would face a lonely death on the cold slab of the mortuary – hardly a fitting closure for such a man.

"Hurry, Drusilla, for he grows weak from the wound." His obscene voice galled her and she wished she had been carrying some kind of blade concealed about her person for she would have plunged into his traitorous heart.

Out on the sand the verdict was still being awaited as the feuding between sponsor and irate daughter continued; and then within the acoustically-perfect walls of the great amphitheatre Drusilla's trembling voice carried clearly to the tens of thousands now fallen silent as she took to her feet while Caius looked on with abject horror etched in his expression.

"Crixus, my love! Crixus! My father demands I give you up and renounce all there is between us on pain of death. I pledge you my solemn oath I will love you to eternity and beyond. I loved you the day we met, two years ago, and I have loved you from that moment. Your time on this earth is at an end, as mine too will be shortly. Go, Crixus – fly for me, spirit of Mars, for I will not live without you!"

Once more, the capricious fates had intervened and Caius now understood Drusilla's threat to finish him. In a bizarre way he had been instrumental in his own downfall. His daughter's affair with the gladiator was out in the open and he knew the subsequent investigation into it would highlight his own indiscretions and he would not survive it.

"Mitte! Mitte!" The crowds persisted in their aggressive demands but Caius was not listening. He was purple with rage and even as he gazed dispassionately at Crixus who was only moments from death, he remained devoid of any sentiment.

"Iugula!" the final command was issued. "Finish it!"

Crixus welcomed the executioner's blow for in a way it was a new beginning, no matter how long the wait. As he summoned those last rapidly-dwindling reserves and held himself erect with head tilted to one side, the sword pierced his neck and angled down to the heart – a noble death, a warrior's death secured by his woman and her public declaration of love.

44

'This impotent grief

Is taking my strength

And my life –

My beauty is in full bloom –

But I am a cut flower.

Let death come quickly – Carry me off

Where this pain

Can never follow.

The one I loved should be let live –

He should live on after me, blameless,

But when I go, both of us go.'

It was a sad, lonely walk to Quintina's home, made all-the-more poignant by the change in weather that brought a chill wind and rain squalls which dampened her spirits still further. She had not dwelt long on her next decision for delay would serve no purpose other than intensifying the desolation and merciless, relentless torture. There had been no more tears since the initial shock of seeing Crixus mortally injured and she vowed to contain them until she was alone again and could tell him she was coming to find him; but it had to be soon for the pain in her breast was without end and sapping her resolve. She needed deliverance and this final trip to her apothecary friend would bring about the relief she so desperately sought.

She pulled the woollen palla a little closer to her body and tucked her head into her chest as the rain came on again but as she rounded the last corner in the road and Quintina's walled gardens came into view, she knew it would be only a short time now and then the pain would be gone for ever.

It was a face of utter tragedy that confronted Quintina as she opened her door and some sixth sense warned her of a terrible misfortune that would alter the course of her own life within months. She could tell by Drusilla's slumped shoulders and deathly complexion that the very worst had befallen Crixus and she reached out to embrace the defeated body - the body of the woman she had come to love more than any man. Drusilla buried her face in Quintina's neck and as she began to speak the memories did their insidious work and her determination collapsed. Speech was impossible and Quintina let her cry, cradling the graceful form in comforting, encircling arms.

"My life has no purpose now," she managed after a lengthy pause, knowing a full minute-by-minute and blow-by-blow account was unnecessary. Quintina's eyes saw beyond the visionary limits of most humans and she was swift to gather a picture of events as they unfolded. "I implore you as one friend to another, help me end it now while my sanity is intact and I possess the fortitude to act decisively."

Quintina was horrified that a situation such as theirs could be so callously and irreversibly altered. The gods were known to be capricious and whimsical at the best of times but they had indeed dealt a cruel hand in this instance.

"Drusilla, think! Are you absolutely certain – without doubt or reservation, this is the path you wish to follow? I see your determination and will not seek to prolong the pain a moment longer but is there no other avenue of escape? I will do as you ask but you have to understand there is no going back, no antidote for the draught once it is taken and I am so unbearably saddened to let you go."

"My mind is made up. There is no going back now. Look at me, Quintina. Am I raving? Am I exhibiting symptoms of fever or delirium? Have I altered to the extent where my powers of reason and judgement have become impaired?"

"No," Quintina replied, studying Drusilla's eyes for indications of hesitation, "you are the same person I always knew and loved but your pain fills me with concern for your well-being. I simply could not bear to think of you writhing in agony after eating poison mushrooms or bleeding to death from an opened vein for such a manner of demise is beneath you. I will assist you on your final journey, even though my own life will be devoid of light and aspiration when you are gone. Come, we will do the work together and you will see the simplicity of such a lethal concoction."

They made their way to the workroom which contained shelves crammed with coloured-glass jars, pots and earthen containers labelled with every substance Drusilla could imagine. She watched with interest as Quintina selected a small amphora and removed the stopper, tipping the contents onto a wooden chopping board.

"Henbane," she remarked unemotionally and began to chop up the pile of leaves and roots with a sharp knife until they were nothing more than a mass of coarse fibres. Satisfied with the consistency she tipped the moist pulp into a large mortar and proceeded to reduce it still further with a heavy stone pestle. "By itself, an effective pain-killer and sedative but I'm going to radically increase its potency even though the dosage will remain unaltered. Instead of extracting the lethal elements by boiling in water I am going to macerate in alcohol and once the mush has been strained out you will have your ticket to oblivion. Drusilla, when you finally swallow this, drink it all with as much wine as you can accommodate. This will speed up the effects of the poison as it moves throughout your body."

She tried to appear nonchalant and unaffected but deep down she knew the next two hours would prove to be a turning point in her life. If she ever managed to survive the pain of Drusilla's passing it would be to the dawning of a completely new and perhaps unpleasant lifestyle. Certainly, the gods would test her many times and she would have to give good account lest they desert her. A single woman in a man's world – the prospect was daunting!

"What will happen?" Quintina nearly missed the question.

"I'm sorry...?"

"The henbane – what will happen when I take it with all the wine? Will there be pain and vomiting and other unpleasantries? I do so wish for this to be simple and uncomplicated. If Agrippina should ever find me I would spare her the less-palatable aspects of death by poisoning."

"You are such a strong, fearless young woman," Quintina placed a hand to the side of her face and then kissed her. "How I love you so...," and she wiped away the single tear. "As I said, the drug will act faster as your system becomes saturated by alcohol. Initially, you will begin to feel quite relaxed and untroubled, pretty much the way we all do after that first large cup of wine. Then, as the poison spreads throughout your body the brain and spine will become affected by the sedative element. You will undergo total loss of recollection, dimness of sight and insensibility. There will be no pain but your body will systematically begin to shut down as each function becomes swamped by the combined effect of drug and alcohol. You will lose the use of all limbs and within a short time breathing will be affected as the heart slows and eventually stops. It rarely takes more than half an hour and you will almost certainly be unconscious before breathing difficulties set in. It will be a peaceful death, Drusilla, and if you are still of a mind to go through with it then I applaud your strength and clear-headedness."

"You were always the wise owl. How I shall miss you."

"Drusilla, as you succumb to the effects of this drug you will hallucinate but do not be troubled. If you see Crixus call out to him for it will bring comfort in your final moments. That is all I can say to put your mind at rest. It breaks my heart to watch you do this but if the alternative is a lifetime of pain and emptiness, then who am I to stand in your way?"

"I must leave now for I shall go straight to the house on the Via Claudia to prepare myself. The pain is like a dagger thrust and I cannot end it soon enough."

They embraced for the last time and kissed each other's tears away.

"I hope you find your love again – that he is waiting for you," Quintina called out softly as Drusilla hurried from the small house and although she heard the words she did not look back, her face contorted in a mask of overwhelming grief and raw, lancing agony.

Daylight was fading rapidly when she unlocked the door of the small house and in the gathering gloom she went about her final preparations – lighting oil lamps and candles, ensuring doors and window shutters were securely fastened and a hundred other details she saw as vital. The neatly folded and sealed parchment for Agrippina was placed in the centre of the table and Drusilla reflected through tear-filled eyes how even the finality of this desperate heartfelt communication could not sway her mind. She would grieve but she would live and if the gods were willing might even chance upon a new husband.

Seeing there was little remaining but the final, merciful act, she carried the two small amphorae of wine into the cubiculum and drew the heavy curtain closed behind her. She set the wine down next to her and carefully broke the seal of the henbane; only then did her eyes fall upon the little package wrapped in purple velvet, laid on one of the tasselled cushions. Crixus had been the last one out yesterday and must have left it for her. She retrieved the item and saw it was attached to a fragment of parchment but the shadows obscured his words. As she slipped the simple fastening of the cloth a silver object rolled into her hand and as she recalled the circumstances under which it had been given so the gates finally opened and she gave vent to her raw, shredded emotions. It was the ring she had given him in Quintina's garden that summer day two years ago, simply inscribed, *Libera Vivas.*

She placed it to her lips and then, unfastening the delicate gold chain from around her neck, threaded the links through the silver ring. After re-fastening the chain she saw how the two rings sat perfectly, next to her heart. Then, with shoulders heaving she adjusted the light and read the few lines he had written just hours before his death.

'Where the setting sun surrenders to the moon, I will wait for you and one day we will have our time again. I used to think beauty such as yours was reserved for heavenly deities – not those of the earth, but in this I was mistaken.'

There could be no doubt. He had known it was the end – for them both. His actions were the final proof, if proof was ever needed. As she clutched this final declaration in trembling fingers and gazed upward with an echoed promise on her lips, her tears cascaded down her cheeks and dripped onto the parchment, diluting the lamp-black ink and streaking the words into rivulets.

Could there ever be more pain than this? Why had the gods not struck her down mercifully? Were they entertained by this spectacle, this bizarre ritual of torment and wretchedness? She would not cry out for Nemesis punished harshly and scorned those who bemoaned their fate.

She set Crixus' love-note aside and poured the first large cup of wine, downing it swiftly and refilling until it brimmed over. She had never drunk so copiously and the knowledge of her actions momentarily buoyed her spirits as blessed release loomed closer. As she emptied the first amphora and regarded the phial of poison with a critical eye, her resolve was unruffled and she picked up the slim glass container between two fingers, tipping her head back and swallowing the contents. After the wine it was horribly bitter and she drank thirstily to purge the brackish taste from her palate.

Then, she lay back on the ornate bed-cover and closed her eyes. She had not eaten all day and the wine was already surging through her body, making her head light and woozy. After the trials of the last two days she felt surprisingly relaxed and as her senses became more and more confused so the crying stopped. Eternal peace hovered seemingly at her fingertips but her arm would not respond when she reached out. The lightness in her head was incredible and all feeling had vanished in her lower body too. She could almost have been floating and in the mists of delirium she called out, smiling.

"Crixus – is that you? Is it really you? Oh, come to me for I fear the cold, the dark and the loneliness."

Her breathing had slowed and her heart-rate decreased, allowing her body temperature to drop and slowly, gradually, she slipped further and further into the mists of oblivion – into the peaceful darkness and into his waiting arms.

45

Caius Attius Caecilius was dead.

Within hours of storming from the amphitheatre amid open threats of murder and a barrage of thrown food, he had been forced to admit his ascent of the political ladder had come to an abrupt and decisive halt. With it had gone the coveted title of Provincial Governor and an end to his dreams of untold wealth, power and women. Again he wondered if, in his never-ending quest for popularity among the electorate of Rome, he had exceeded the realms of public expectancy by hosting this last day of games and should merely have accepted the senate's wishes and gone his way.

Drusilla's scandalous affair with the gladiator had been the ultimate cause of his disgrace, he reflected miserably, together with that openly-brazen and disgusting promise to follow in his footsteps as he knelt dying. He had not expected her to defy him so flagrantly and he realised his decision to go against the unanimous wishes of the crowds and order Crixus killed had not only played into Drusilla's hands it had done other, irreparable damage. He would ensure his daughter paid a heavy price for her behaviour and have her married off to someone not averse to using the whip.

However, that was the least of his problems for in the wake of her ruinous behaviour had come the inevitable probing questions into not just his private life but his public activities too and once suspicions had been aroused there followed a full senatorial inquiry highlighting certain aspects of his election campaigns. Caius, it would appear, had not been overly discreet when it came to offering bribes for votes and this embarrassing disclosure provoked even more in-depth examination which further suggested his resources were seemingly limitless.

When his disposable assets were taken into account – the properties he owned and the large expansive vineyards on the edge of the city, a tortuous web of deceit began to unfold because the figures did not add up and Caius suspected the hand of betrayal was at work. Looking still further the censors had discovered a disturbing imbalance in treasury funds to which Caius had enjoyed privileged access. The coincidences became too coincidental to ignore and Caius was subsequently charged with misappropriation and embezzlement of state property and hauled before a specially-convened senate hearing.

The knives were out and his persistent denial of the charges served only to ridicule him in the face of overwhelming evidence and give credence to his accusers and those witnesses receiving inducements. Caius was found guilty on all counts and he could only offer thanks they hadn't added bigotry to the list of charges. He was finished, in every respect. He had forfeited the Provincial Governorship, alienated the senate and lost most of his so-called friends. In addition, he would be seen as an outcast and a pariah. He had given up the splendid house on the Via Sacra, renounced the love of a beautiful woman when she became sick and pushed his daughter over the edge where she would kill him at the first opportunity. He was further sentenced to forego any pension rights bestowed by privilege and the vineyards which supplemented his income were confiscated to be auctioned off.

Drusilla's threats to destroy him had come to fruition. She had not lifted a hand nor reported him to any controlling body. In effect he was solely responsible for his own demise. She was the only winner here and compared to him, had come out of it virtually unscathed. Crixus was dead but she would soon find another. In a month or so this would all be forgotten.

As for now he had plans of his own and where he was going there would be no need of money, power or possessions. He was sick of it all and the sooner he was away from the back-stabbing, petty in-fighting and poisonous betrayal of allegedly-close relationships the better.

Paying one last visit to Cassius Seneca on the premise of his continued support and backing, Caius was informed of his friend's absence until later in the day but Juliana's cordial invitation to relax in the hot baths proved a fatal enticement for she had unwittingly provided the means by which he would take his leave from the world. As he soaked in the heated, fragrant waters of the luxurious baths and drank freely of Cassius' wine, he recognised there would never be a more opportune moment than this. The dagger was concealed in his toga praetexta, neatly folded at the edge of the pool and with a deft stroke he opened the large vein in his calf. There was no pain and he watched with amusement as his lifeblood ebbed freely into the hot water, rapidly discolouring it. After only a few moments his head became lighter and he felt the darkness closing in while all around him curly tendrils of

273

steam heavily scented with Egyptian aromatic incense rose eerily toward the high fresco-adorned ceiling.

Would they remember him for anything at all other than those magnificent spectacles and increased food rations? He regarded Agrippina as the ultimate millstone around any man's neck but Drusilla had ruined everything. The bitch! Her and that bastard slave gladiator.

Fuck them all! He was well out of it.

46

Drusilla was rushing headlong through a bottomless, swirling vortex of impenetrable darkness. It was totally without substance – no sensation of temperature, no feeling, no directional orientation. Nothing. How long had it been – a moment, a thousand years? Her last memory was of swallowing that foul-tasting potion and washing it down with a more-palatable beverage before her senses deserted her and the welcoming blackness beckoned seductively.

And then, just as she considered herself completely alone in this journey through the void of oblivion, a long-forgotten but achingly-beautiful and familiar voice echoed through the far reaches of space and time. Alas, hers was not the name being called but some other by the name of Tyra. What a strange title; it was neither suggestive of male nor female gender and certainly not a designation attributed to the Roman world she had left behind.

"Tyra," the evocative sound came again. "I sense you have gone as far as you are destined to go in your search and perhaps now would be an appropriate time to return to your own world where friends are ready to greet you."

My name is Drusilla. I am Drusilla Flavia Caecilius and my search is not yet ended. How can it be so? Where is Crixus? Where is my destiny?

"How can I return to such a place when my odyssey remains unfulfilled?"

"You will be entering a beautiful new world where your man lives and is waiting to embrace you," the sound filled her ears once more and she knew it was no fabrication, no trickery, no false hope for Quintina's words were pronouncements of the truth. It was indeed Quintina for the voice could belong to no other. Despite the pledge her man was ready to join her once more, the promise of Quintina's flesh proved decisive and she yielded to the soft, persuasive utterances.

What would it be like to kiss those soft, sweet lips again and delve for the honey at the centre of her flower?

"Tyra is unknown to me. I am Drusilla Flavia. Please, Quintina, what must I do to escape this infernal darkness?"

"You must place your continued existence in my hands. Do as I say and the darkness will be gone for ever. Your man is seated by my side, waiting for you to join him. All you have to do is heed my words and follow the light that now illuminates your world and gives direction to your journey."

"I am ready to do as you ask but please, act without further delay or impediment for the darkness is constricting and without end."

"Heed my words, Drusilla Flavia, and your journey will come to a swift end. You are seeking the light and Quintina's words will be the instrument of your escape. Concentrate every part of your being upon the distant brightness for soon it will fill your world and banish the shadows into your most distant memory. The light draws ever closer as your strange odyssey reaches its conclusion and when you are bathed in the luminescence of this new world you will know your man, Crixus, and the woman you have loved since your earliest memory are but a short distance away."

"The brightness increases with every heartbeat, surrounding me, searing my vision, paining my eyes with its intensity. Please tell me you are not far away now."

"You are close, Drusilla Flavia, and there is but a short distance to cover before it is done. Look straight ahead and you will see a tunnel, a corridor stretching into the distance. The light is kinder now and you can find your way without difficulty. On either side of you are doors bearing numbers. Those numbers are dates and I want you to read out loud the first date your eyes fall upon for this will assist me in returning you to your rightful place."

"The eyes of Quintina are indeed all-seeing for I am confronted by an ancient door. The timbers are gnarled, twisted and warped but there is a number fashioned from iron, now rusted but clear enough to read."

"Tell me the number, Drusilla Flavia," the familiar voice commanded.

"Eighty-four."

"You have done well and now we can begin the final part of your journey. I want you to walk at a leisurely pace along the tunnel before you, taking note of the dates on the doors as you pass them. With each door passed, you will narrow the distance between your old world and this new place. It may take some considerable time but your feet are light and the spirit is eager. You will leave many doors behind and the dates will blur into a succession of mystic and incomprehensible characters but your destiny is firmly rooted across the threshold of the final door when you can go no further."

"My progress is swift. Even though I have no awareness of movement the doors continue to pass me by."

"When you arrive at the last door, entering the portal will see your former world consigned to distant memory."

"The feeling is good and I sense our meeting is but a short time away. The light is brighter now and I am approaching a point where I cannot see beyond. Up to now the doors have been on either side but now I am confronted by a single entrance blocking my path."

"You may continue, Drusilla Flavia. When you have passed through door there will remain one last simple obstacle in your path and then it is done. A short flight of six steps will bring you to the arms of your man and the love of Quintina who has guided you all this time."

"I am standing at the bottom of the steps. Shall I ascend them?"

"Yes, begin and with each step you take I will call out a number. With that number your level of consciousness and awareness will return until you wake up with all faculties fully restored. One – take the first step, Drusilla Flavia. Two – take another step. Three – you're half way there and beginning to wake up. Four – another step and your eyes are feeling the need to open. Five – it's almost done and you're starting to come round now. One final step, six – and your long journey is at an end. Wake up, Tyra, and allow your eyes a moment of adjustment to this softer light."

The two stone replications at the foot of the couch were a sudden, startling reminder of her recent surroundings but she resisted the urge to call out.

"Can you sit up, darling?" Sophie asked, stuffing a couple of plump cushions behind Tyra as she shuffled into a semi-reclining posture. "You ought to drink something too. Your mouth must be absolutely parched by now," and she poured a glass of sparkling water. "How's your head? I can get you a couple of Panadol if you like."

"Thanks. I think I need them after that. Sophie, it's dark outside. How long have we been here?"

"Four hours, darling. A fraction over four hours. I simply cannot believe the amount of ground we covered. I've never presided over anything of that duration before. Do you feel up to talking?"

"In a moment. I need to get my head round all this first."

"We both got the whole story, Tyra. Now I can fully understand the reason for Adam's fragmented images over the years and why they were increasing at such an alarming rate. And then there's your own

277

part in this human drama. Who could ever have guessed the depth of your involvement and ultimate tragic outcome? Those verbal showdowns with your father were pretty scary and I have to say you acquitted yourself rather well in my books."

"I hated him, Sophie. I hated him for what he did to the man I loved. My own price was small by comparison."

"And now you are returned to the land of the living where your man has been waiting patiently these last four hours – or perhaps it was two millennia."

"I would have waited regardless," Adam leaned over and kissed Tyra's forehead. "I thought the love we shared now was something most people only dreamed of but to hear its very origins echoing through time gave me the shivers. I always knew you were there somewhere – a part of me I could never place with any degree of certainty, only that you were there."

"You are the image of Crixus, Adam. In every respect you are a carbon copy of the man I met that day in Quintina's gardens. How I loved you in that first instant but I knew it would endure regardless of our fates."

"I salute you, great Mars!" Sophie raised a bubbling glass of spring water. "Crixus is Adam, Adam is Crixus. What does it feel like to finally acknowledge half the known world witnessed your rise to power in the arena and elevated you to the status of a god? I suspected it for many months but now I know it to be fact. How uncanny!"

"Humbling might be a suitable expression."

"How did you know when to bring me back, Sophie?" Tyra was curious.

"Simple, darling. Once Crixus had been mortally injured and we both witnessed that utterly heart-rending declaration of yours to follow in his footsteps, I knew with absolute certainty it couldn't be long. When you made your wishes known to Quintina and then hurried away with the phial of poison, the writing was already on the wall, for want of a better expression. I could tell by your words and body language when you began to slip away and at that point it became critical you return here with the utmost speed. By the way, Drusilla Flavia, I simply adore that name. It was made for you."

"My mother, Agrippina," Tyra nodded in agreement. "She was blessed with good taste in all things except, perhaps, her choice of husband. It was good in the beginning but he turned out to be a total shit. She was well-rid of him, as was I."

"Tyra, can you now understand how love and destiny are so interweaved? It was your love of Crixus and his love for Drusilla that was to see your paths eventually cross once more in the distant future. But for that bond of unceasing love, faith and loyalty, Crixus would have merged with the dust of the earth and been forgotten and the same would have applied to you. Never doubt the power of love for you two are the living attestation to its wondrous potentials."

Tyra turned to Adam who seemed to be listening intently to these unearthly exchanges, barely able to comprehend the depth of his own contribution but resigned to Sophie's pronouncements and the undisputable facts which had emerged from Tyra's four-hour excursion into another time.

"Adam, we have spoken many times of our first meeting but can you now understand the fire and hunger between us that night at Russ and Julia's? The yearning passion of being united once more after the passage of two millennia? Neither of us could adequately describe the moment but we both knew with absolute certainty we were destined to be together – not just from that moment but an incredibly-distant time before. There was no denying it – we felt it but could not explain it. The sensations you felt every so often, Adam, and the fragmented images of a place you once knew well - reminders of your past, telling you it was time to seek confirmation of your destiny, not solely in this world but before you were born."

"Do you think we would ever have had the complete story of our lives if you had not done this tonight?"

"I cannot say for sure, but probably not. You were becoming increasingly-obsessed by the frequency and intensity of your experiences and I had been deeply affected by my own personal insights when we made love that afternoon. I found myself in the little house on the Via Claudia with him – you, it doesn't really matter, poised over me in the act of love, wicked, illicit, magnificent, soaring love. Eventually, more and more of the pieces would have been revealed but to what extent I cannot say. Many centuries ago our love was forbidden and the circumstances of that love ended our lives, but such was the intensity and tragedy of its end the fates dictated one day in the future we would meet again."

Tyra turned to Sophie and there was an unvoiced question in her eyes. The full details were too sensitive for discussion at this point in the proceedings – especially when Adam was present, but she needed to know.

"Sophie...?" and she seemed a little hesitant, "have you resigned yourself to the fact you and Quintina are the same person?"

"I have known for some time but I deemed it necessary for you to make the connection. Any premature move on my part would have been meaningless but I was certain once you embarked upon this odyssey of illumination the full facts would be revealed."

"All of them...?" Tyra blushed at the recollection.

"Yes, my darling," Sophie held her gaze with those piercing green eyes, "all of them. I am mindful of the love you and I shared and I know Crixus would not begrudge us a moment of it."

"What about Adam?" Tyra responded thoughtfully. "Would Adam begrudge us a moment of it?"

"Why don't you ask him, Tyra? We're all in this together. We have no secrets...."

She had been caught unawares by Sophie's candid admission but decided the direct approach would be infinitely more preferable on such a delicate issue. Certainly, his inquisitive nature would have been whetted by the disclosure but whether he approved or not was immaterial. More importantly, how did this latest revelation affect them as a group?

"Adam," she began a little tentatively, "long before Crixus came onto the scene, Drusilla and Quintina were sharing their own brand of love. Quintina had much to impart and Drusilla was ignorant in the physical aspects of male attentions. Drusilla was a willing pupil and Quintina proved a most competent and informed lover. You were my first man but Quintina ensured I was well-versed in giving pleasure as well as receiving it. I harbour no shame and freely admit my love has not changed. I love you, Adam. I love you with all my heart and would die for you if the need arose. But I also love the woman once known to me as Quintina and will not hide the fact. Without her I would be dead. I think we both know that. You are my strength and the reason for living but Sophie is the light of my life. She is the laughter on the telephone, the teller of wicked jokes, the reason for our dinner parties and the focal point around which all our lives revolve. Sorry if I've shocked you, Adam, but it needed to be said."

"Just as long as the two of you aren't planning to elope.... I think I can reconcile myself to a friendship like that. Anyone else and it would have been complicated."

He glanced at the luminous dial of his wristwatch, trying to focus on the hands in the muted, flickering light.

"Almost midnight. Is there any more we can do here, Sophie – anything else to be said?"

"I think we've covered everything," Sophie replied, barely stifling a yawn. "Other details are bound to crop up in the days ahead but I think we've addressed the major issues."

They were about to wrap it up when a thought struck Tyra and she turned to Adam.

"Unbutton your shirt!"

"Isn't it rather late in the evening for such...?"

"Just do it!" Tyra insisted. "There's something I want Sophie to see."

Obediently, he unbuttoned the garment and Tyra pulled the material from his shoulders exposing the horizontal scar about three inches long, high up to the side of his chest, just below the collar bone.

"Take a look at this!" Tyra invited. "I saw Crixus receive this in the final day of games held by that bastard father of mine. He was already injured but Caius Attius gave the Pollice Verso – the extended thumb and the victor's sword went in here, straight down and into the heart. The scar matches the width of the gladius and is in precisely the same place. Okay, Adam, you can get dressed now. Sorry about that."

They rose from their seats and made ready to leave. It was late and further discussion would serve little purpose tonight. Perhaps over dinner next time...?

"Goodnight, Sophie," Tyra resisted the urge to kiss her friend's soft, inviting lips and settled for a lingering embrace that set her heart pounding once more.

"Goodnight, my darling. We'll talk again soon."

"Thanks for everything, Sophie," Adam jumped in. "We both love you more than you'll ever know."

"Goodnight, great Mars," she replied. "You were the best."

47

"....And now we're going over to our live outside broadcast unit with Sarah Shaw, on site at the Roman Forum complex in Warchester. Sarah, this is something of a milestone in British construction projects according to critics and media coverage. What does it feel like to be standing there on this historic occasion?"

"Good morning, John. It certainly is a humbling experience to be here in the centre of this unbelievably-massive and beautiful complex. As you know, these buildings were raised on top of what used to be derelict ground and industrial landscape and it took a mere four years to produce what you see here today. It was originally hailed as the largest and most innovative construction project of the modern age and only began to take shape after several major companies agreed to backing and sponsorship. There's no government funding here at all."

There were TV cameras strategically placed around the vast sprawling site while roving reporters accompanied by sound technicians mingled with crowds and interviewed various dignitaries and prominent company men.

"The crowds have been building up since we arrived here earlier this morning and the roads into the complex are jammed with traffic. With the official opening less than an hour away there is an almost tangible air of expectancy among those present as they await the big moment. Police estimates of the numbers here remain conservative but a figure of around eighty-thousand was given and we know the immense car parks are virtually full. I've covered many official openings and state events over the years but they pale in significance compared to this."

"Sarah, we understand the man behind this project, indeed, the man who conceived the idea and oversaw construction, is going to make a speech just before the main ceremony. Can you tell us a little more about that?"

"Yes, John, I can. Adam Grant proposed the concept when the ground we're standing on was a virtual wasteland. He argued building such an edifice would be theoretically simpler than it was two millennia ago when the ancient Romans were erecting similar structures across the empire as a matter of course without modern mechanical aids as we know them today. This was a terribly run-down area and never recovered after coal-mining was axed in the eighties. Adam Grant saw this as a way to put Warchester back on the economic map of Britain and generate untold wealth for the whole area.

"During the four-year construction period, the many hundreds of workers billeted here brought more money into the town than it had seen since the pit closures – a fact which contributed immensely to the initial financial recovery. I can also tell you many of those workers never returned to their homes in other parts of the country. They struck up relationships with local girls, married and settled down here. It's a success story from beginning to end."

The vast array of heavy plant and earthmoving equipment had gone and the heaps of waste material removed along with the hundreds of portable accommodation cabins and site-offices. Finally, the surrounding bare, scarred earth had been landscaped and planted with a variety of imported ferns, palms, cypresses and umbrella pines further heightening the impression of a Mediterranean setting.

In and amongst the huge crowds that filled the open spaces, street entertainers attired in historic costumes provided thrills and laughter. Jugglers, acrobats and clowns showed off their skills for coins thrown while snake-charmers, illusionists and fire-eaters worked their magic in relative silence as the minutes ticked away in anticipation of the great opening when the hidden wonders of this recreation from the ancient world would be made known to the tens of thousands who had come to be a part of it.

In a large marquee separated from the crowds, a small group of well-dressed men and women readied themselves for the inaugural speeches while stewards replenished champagne flutes in a bid to quell those last-minute nerves. As head of Templeman Grant, Russ would speak first and give a brief insight as to the event, explaining the project in layman's terms from conception to completion. Then he would vacate the podium and allow Adam to hold the crowds' attention as he infected them with his own brand of passion – explaining how the ancient Romans had influenced architecture for thousands of years after their demise as a world power.

Adam was resplendent in a tailored dinner suit and black tie while Tyra added her own definitive touches of beauty and glamour - a statement of wealth, class, breeding and sensuous mature womanhood. In their many years together her appeal had never waned or faltered and it seemed in some ways today's events were to be underscored by celebratory issues of a personal nature.

Sophie was there too for no occasion of such magnitude could be complete without her presence. As she stepped into the sunlight to accompany Russ and Julia to the podium, she exuded an uncommon grace and elegance accentuated by the tilt of her head and stylish deportment.

"She's beautiful," Tyra observed thoughtfully. "I don't think I've ever seen her looking so wonderful. I can't believe she's still single. What a catch she'd make for the right man if ever he was to make an appearance."

In this great place full of the wonders and mysteries of the ancient world and listening as the crowds fell silent for Russ on the speaking platform, Tyra turned to face Adam, standing so close as to be almost touching and as he studied her intently while she gazed unblinking into his own eyes he knew this was the high-point of his life. The marquee was completely deserted and for just a few minutes they were alone together where nothing stirred and only a gently breeze ruffled the canvas structure soundlessly.

"I love you more than life itself," he whispered, and it seemed in this simple yet far-reaching statement was embodied the very essence of their existence again as a couple. "When I look at you I see so much more than the woman, the friend, the marital partner and the lover. There are depths and mysteries I may never come to know but perhaps that is all a part of the intrigue. Since that first night at Russ and Julia's I feel we have set out on a voyage of personal discovery and if we walk the same road for a thousand years you will forever retain all the attraction and magnetism I experienced on our first meeting."

He could see she was moved by his words and she pressed a little closer, moistening her soft, glossy lips with the tip of her tongue.

"I waited an eternity for you to come back and now, being here like this, just the two of us in this place we all know so well, I would do it all again but a day without you is too long."

She closed her eyes and leaned involuntarily toward him, closing the gap of those last few electrifying millimetres and pressing her warm and unbelievably sensuous lips to his own. She felt his arms encircling her, drawing her against the hard physique that had captured her from the first moment while he, in turn, could only wonder at the heat emanating from those large breasts. She hoped to God Russ was living up to expectations and holding the attention of everyone. To be disturbed at this most crucial of moments would be excruciating torture for, in a way, it was the wickedness of a stolen opportunity and the risk of discovery that heightened the occasion for them both.

He angled his head to one side and delicately kissed the flesh of her neck where the feminine scent of her arousal was now eclipsed by her chosen fragrance – subtle and evocative. Her nipples pushed out through the material of her dress – hard and demanding of attention and as she imagined his mouth closing about them, teasing, sucking, nibbling and fondling so her lubrication flowed in ever-more copious amounts. Her underwear was soaked and she felt the slippery, warm secretion beginning to encroach upon her upper thighs. Thank God it was a warm day and she had dispensed with tights. It would make the coming minutes so much easier even though Adam appeared to have a passion for them.

She sought his mouth again and inserted a moist tongue, reaching for the belt buckle and then the trouser clasp beneath. They were both beyond the concerns of discovery and her heart beat even faster as she felt Adam's hand beneath her dress, moving higher and higher with agonising slowness until he came to her opening, only modestly covered by the wisp of saturated lace. Before he had even inserted a finger she felt her body convulse under the first rippling sensations of orgasm and thrust her tongue into his mouth with even greater force. Again and again the world seemed to explode in dazzling, bursting pyrotechnics while the darkness behind her closed eyes was lit up by searing white light. The temptation to scream out loud was overwhelming as she imagined Adam standing naked and fully-erect before her while she flaunted herself, fully-clothed in the vibrant-red evening dress with its plunging neckline and those open-toed high heels.

"I want you inside me...," she gasped for breath as the next climax brought a renewed surge of the pleasant drenching sensation to her parted thighs, "right now. I can't wait another second. What's happening to us, Adam? I've never known it like this before."

He felt huge in her small hand but she guided him into her and the breath whooshed from her lungs in an attempt to muffle the cry.

"Promise me you will always love me," she called out in her abandon as the tears streaked her face.

"I will never give you up," he echoed Drusilla's pledge to Crixus. "I would rather die than be without you again," and as the great wave rose up and burst in a maelstrom of violent, booming surf it seemed for a brief instant in time they were back in the bedroom of the little house on the Via Claudia, entwined in body and mind on the purple silken bed cover with its embroidered depictions of sun, moon and stars for who could say to what new heights their loving would take them?

They became aware of a sudden barely-muted cheering and thunder of applause signalling the conclusion of Russ' speech and hastily they drew apart, adjusting their clothing.

"Thank God for waterproof mascara," Tyra exclaimed as she examined her face in the mirror of the powder compact she kept in her handbag. Apart from a little redness around the eyes she was okay but the feelings of a few moments ago seemed to be lurking on the fringes, waiting to burst out and deluge her crumbling defences at the slightest provocation.

Russ, Julia and Sophie strolled into the large tent just as the Master of Ceremonies announced Adam and Sophie's intuitive eye noticed the change in Tyra's body language.

"Darling! Whatever's the matter? Have you been crying?"

"I'm fine, Sophie – really. It's not what you think. We were alone for a few moments and something came over us both in the same instant."

"Ah – I see," Sophie replied, nodding in understanding at the cause of Tyra's ill-concealed distress. "Yes, I can see how that might have happened. The two of you dressed as you are in this enigmatic place which has connections and associations known only to the three of us.... Most harrowing! I hope Adam was able to offer comfort and relieve you of the worst effects...?"

"If only you knew....," but Sophie's expression said she remained perfectly abreast of her two friends' situation and a more in-depth appraisal of the spicier aspects could wait until they were alone together.

"Your time beneath the spotlight, buddy," Russ announced cheerfully to Adam as he sipped from the large cut-glass tumbler of Scotch and ice. "Give it to them straight and let them see why you're the best in the business. I've done the ground-work. It's your turn to break the hearts and make the tears flow," and he punched Adam's shoulder playfully.

"Time to go," and he took Tyra's hand. "Come and stand beside me and let the world see how a beautiful woman influences a successful man."

"I will always be at your side," she whispered huskily as she laid her hand on the lapel of his jacket and adjusted it with that proprietary feminine gesture.

48

The applause died away as Adam gestured for silence. Sophie and Tyra were ranged either side and he felt himself rising up to face the gods as an equal for what other man could possibly comprehend a moment such as this? The world and the media were here to witness the unveiling of this recreation from another world – an accomplishment no other civilization down the ages had managed to parallel. The ancient Roman architects may have conceived the original idea but he had brought it to life once more – resurrected it from the history books and tourist guides and turned into breathtaking reality, a magnificent statement of greatness and achievement dominating the skyline for miles around.

There was no typed oration – no prompts or notes to guide him as, indeed, there had been no initial blueprint of the edifice now towering above and obliterating the horizon in every direction. His words would come from the heart, following his creation.

"Honoured guests, ladies, gentlemen and friends. Look around you for what you see is not just the hopes of one man fulfilled but the aspiration of many men for contained within the structures you see before you today is the will of an empire embodied in stone."

He raised his hands up from the lectern and opened his arms in an embracing and all-encompassing gesture while his listeners huddled together in the silence lest they miss a word.

"When men raised monuments such as these, two thousand years ago and beyond, it was in the belief they would endure for ever despite the ravages of war, weather and time and they could only have dreamed one day in the far-distant future, one of their greatest achievements would be reborn – not for the purpose of national identity, but in honour of those who had gone before and set the benchmark for future generations to emulate.

"Look at the greatness of Rome! Look what she bequeathed to the world without modern building techniques and specialized heavy construction equipment and then look at what our world throws up today in the name of technology and advancement. Row upon row of grotesque red-brick terracing and huge concrete-and-glass monstrosities that reach up to the sky and not only cause offence to our eyes but despoil the very earth they are built upon. In every sense they are an affront to modern civilization, lacking beauty and form and are hardly representative of the abilities of an allegedly-intelligent society.

"Two thousand years ago there was – for want of a more-appropriate description, a piece of advice given to gladiators as they went out to face death in the arena. Give the public what they want – give them something they have never seen before and they will love you. Since I was a boy at school I have nurtured a dream that one day before I died I would recreate something of Rome's greatness here on English soil. After years of study and the attainment of the relevant credentials, the dream began to assume an air of reality.

"As you all know, the town of Warchester thrived on, indeed, owed its very existence to coal mining. It was as much a part of our heritage as the pits of Wales and Yorkshire. When the mines closed, this town's economy collapsed overnight. It was the death-knell for the people of Warchester and the small businesses which had sprung up to service the coal industry. Within a few short weeks this town had seen the life-blood sucked out of it and many inhabitants – dispirited and unemployed, moved out in search of a better life elsewhere. This was my town! This was my home! I had been born and raised here and it seemed Warchester had died a cruel, tragic death but was waiting – waiting to have the fire of life breathed back into her soul. And then she would rise – like a phoenix from the ashes to stand as proud as any city in the commonwealth."

Standing next to Adam and listening as he spoke with such passion, eloquence and mastery of his subject, Tyra felt her heart squeezed with love and pride. She edged a little closer and gripped his hand in a gesture she hoped would convey her deepest feelings.

"At last, the opportunity was here. Warchester didn't need factories and office buildings. It didn't need housing estates and blocks of flats which would spawn crime and anti-social behaviour among the masses of unemployed...," and his voice dropped to a barely-audible hush. "It needed investment – investment on a huge scale and the promise of something so controversial and theoretically impossible, many would doubt it could actually make it past the planning stage. The rest, as they say, is history. The proposal was accepted and once financial backing was assured it all happened. Warchester and its people received grossly unfair treatment by the government of the day and were completely neglected regarding future development. Once I qualified as an architect I saw the means by which to reinstate this town's prominence on the economic map and go a small way to redressing the balance of its forgotten status.

"I will take my leave of you now for we are rapidly approaching the opening ceremony and I'm sure you're all eager to find your way around. Before you go, there's just one thought I'd like to impart. As you journey through life, when something beautiful and utterly wonderful stops you in your tracks and takes your breath away," and he turned to face Tyra directly so there could be no mistaking his clear intentions, "then cherish that memory for ever. Hold it to you like a candle flame in the night and take comfort from the light she brings for when it is gone the darkness and despair are unbearable."

Sophie was applauding as enthusiastically as the surrounding crowds, tears streaming down her face for Adam's words had reached deeply and touched his listeners with a sense of pride. They had also witnessed the overt display of affection to his wife – that gorgeous raven-haired beauty in the red dress who had been pressed against him throughout the speech.

They stepped down from the rostrum and slowly made their way back to the marquee where Russ and Julia were waiting and he pressed a brimming wine glass into Adam's hand while Julia fussed over Tyra and Sophie.

"Thanks. I need this. Any other day I suppose we'd all sit down and enjoy the great British cuppa – but, what the hell! When in Rome...!"

"My sentiments entirely," Russ replied as his gaze lingered on Julia's curvaceous buttocks and shapely legs in the tight skirt and high heels. "Just the drunken orgy now and it's been a perfect day."

Julia smiled sweetly having overheard the none-too-subtle remark.

"I can hardly wait. So – tell me, Russell. How will you be wanting me tonight? Would you like me naked on the kitchen table while you do your little trick with the grapes or should I screw one of your friends after dinner and you can discuss my sexual performance over pudding?"

49

A gentle breeze wafted through the open window, redolent with the scent of aromatic herbs and colourful blossom on this fine, late-summer evening. There were no sounds to be heard from outside – no traffic or city-bustle and even the cattle in the adjacent field had sensed the imminent sunset and adopted their sleeping positions in the shelter of the low, dry-stone wall.

The small room remained unlit and in this peaceful setting away from the telephone and life's thousand and one distractions, Tyra and Adam were alone together. For two weeks the workplace would be a distant memory and after the frantic days leading up to the official opening of the Roman Forum along with the constant intrusions of the media, they could at last take time out for themselves in this untroubled little backwater.

He had wanted Tyra to choose their ultimate destination but in the end she had told him simply, "Surprise me," and left him to make the arrangements. "Rome!" she had almost squealed with delight as she opened the envelope containing their tickets and Adam's relief was transparent. "Rome for two weeks. Just you and me, no work and no disturbances. How absolutely delightful. I've never been to...," and she regarded his innocent smile curiously.

"I thought we might see what's changed over the years, and you'll not have to endure any crowded city-centre hotel either. I've arranged a private charter flight and we'll be staying in a modest villa in the hills just outside town. The hire-car will be waiting at the airport and we can please ourselves. Two weeks, Tyra. It'll be wonderful."

The villa was a joy to behold and the tiny bedroom was strangely-reminiscent of another location which held deep associations from way back. Outside, there was little in the way of borders and flowers but an olive plantation sat close by and the house was effectively screened by tall stone pines with their broad canopies and mature, slender cypresses.

"What would you like to do tomorrow?" he asked as she lay next to him with an arm draped over his chest.

"I've been thinking," she came back after a pause. "We can do the tourist thing any time, can't we?"

"We're on holiday. There's no pressure to do anything."

"Well...," she seemed to be experiencing difficulty coming to the point, "you'll probably think I'm totally off my head but I'd like to go for a little walk along the first part of the Via Claudia – you know, just to see if – if there's anything, oh hell, you know what I'm trying to say. I'm curious, that's all, especially since that night at Sophie's."

"I think it's a splendid idea," he replied quietly. "We can set off straight after breakfast if you like and I think we should also pay a visit to the archives office to see how much of the original area has survived over the years."

"There's probably a supermarket there now or maybe a hotel or even a car park," and she became fretful and pressed closer to him. "Adam, what if there never was such a place and it was all a trick of the mind – a cruel deception and the product of a fanciful imagination?"

"Don't expect too much from this, Tyra. I believe it as much as you but it was a long time ago. Places change, buildings come and go. We'll search and if there's anything at all we'll find it but I do so want for you not to be disappointed."

The office of archives and records was situated in a narrow, unglamorous side street off the Piazza Venezia. It was a dismal, unimposing structure and gave no hint as to the priceless treasures contained within. The reception area was equally uninspiring but despite the aura of gloom about the place they felt their spirits lift as they considered how their journey of illumination could begin right here. The archives would undoubtedly contain much more than a political history of the city and the works of celebrated orators, statesmen, poets and satirists. Locked away in the repository would be detailed street plans – the Forma Urbis. The blueprint of Rome!

Twenty minutes later after making their request known to the archivist on duty, Adam and Tyra found themselves alone once more in a sealed reading-room where the temperature and humidity were maintained at a constant level.

They both studied the box file on the table and after a moment's indecision Adam invited, "You do it. You're used to this kind of thing," but as she released the fastening and opened the hinged top she saw the contents were not the originals but photo-copies which, in a way, were more conducive to the nature of their inquiry. There was never a chance of reefing through page after page of the actual two-thousand-year-old

291

documents if, indeed, they still existed. This way, at least, they would be able to handle the drawings without fear of damaging them. After slipping on disposable gloves Tyra reached for the first handful of papers and lifted them carefully out of their protective box.

"I should have brushed-up on my Latin before we left home. I'm not sure I can understand all this."

Despite the unfamiliar wording, abbreviations and overall presentation, they were soon able to recognise the drawings had been classified into two distinctive sections – one for the buildings on the left of the Via Claudia and one for the right and they appeared to be in chronological order as the development expanded, radiating out from the centre.

"Cast your mind back to that night in Sophie's room when Drusilla was walking from the Colosseum to the place we're looking for now. Can you remember on which side of the road it was? It would save us an awful lot of time and needless searching."

She left the papers for a moment and seemed to stare into space as she concentrated her mind on that period of her life that could start her crying again without warning. He held her hand and saw how her eyes had now taken on that almost hypnotic gaze and he remained silent as she searched her mind for the single detail that might unlock this bewitching mystery.

"It was late afternoon," she began. "I had left the amphitheatre and was walking slowly along the Via Claudia toward the house. The sun was on my right but still above the level of the tallest buildings. It was midsummer and the shadows were few. I was walking on the right where there was always a small amount of shade. Yes, I can see it now. If I had been walking on the left I would have been in full sunlight. I liked to enjoy the shade but never crossed the road. I only ever walked on the right."

Her eyes suddenly focused again as she returned to the present.

"It was on the right, Adam. Of that I am certain."

"You're a clever girl and you've just reduced our workload by fifty percent."

"Oh goody!" she exclaimed and felt the aura of excitement begin to wash over her in the hope of unravelling more facts and clues. They immediately discarded those drawings relating to the opposite side of the street and their next task was to ascertain how far Drusilla travelled before turning off into the cul-de-sac between the two tall buildings.

"Tyra, can you recall how far it was to the place where you turned off into the blind alley? I've an idea it was about three quarters of a mile from what you were saying at Sophie's and considering the density of the housing along that stretch we could be looking at a fair few drawings before we find it."

"Adam, I can't describe any particular details of the route but I know the journey used to take about fifteen minutes at slow-to-normal walking pace. I never hurried in case I drew attention to myself."

"Okay then," and he made a quick mental calculation. "Let's say in the space of fifteen minutes without stopping you passed by fifty individual plots. That would bring you to roughly....here!" and he jabbed his finger at an apparently random spot on one of the drawings. "This is an optimistic estimate because you'd never have progressed further in the time."

The survey documents were meaningless to Tyra and she could not begin to fathom the intricate mass of lines and figures where only the clearly-demarcated border of the Via Claudia stood out in the clutter; but to Adam's trained eye it all made perfect sense and despite the ancient Latin text and Roman numerals he was able to decipher the relevant information and skip the rest.

"Actually, when you look at modern plans and surveys, very little has changed and considering their age these are spot-on. You have to think of it as an aerial perspective, Tyra – a view from an elevated position and then it's just like looking down on the foundations. We don't need any of this technical detail. What we're searching for is a likely gap between two large structures – possibly tenements or something similar, that leads us to a dead-end and I don't mean that literally. Something similar to a blind alley or no-through-road with a surrounding wall."

As Adam used his finger to trace a path along the line of buildings, studying every detail of the individual structures, Tyra called to him and there was such urgency in her voice he looked up suddenly and lost his place.

"What is it?" he asked, seeing how the colour had drained from her face. She had been studying one of the related drawings spread out on the large table, merely inspecting the details in the bottom right hand corner when the name seemed to jump out and startle her.

"Adam, look at this! This is the index number of the worksheet and this figure below corresponds to the area we are looking at now, a map reference if you like. This is the date of the survey – August 84 in the reign of Titus Flavius Domitianus and the signature right at the bottom belongs to the name immediately above. Does it ring a bell, Adam? Think! Where have you heard the name before? Shall I tell you? You heard it when I was undergoing my little session at Sophie's a few weeks ago. He was one of several officials who supervised public

293

buildings and would have commissioned surveys exactly like this as a matter of routine.

"Cassius Lucius Seneca! My heart nearly stopped when I saw it. Do you understand the significance of this, Adam? Seneca shared equal political rank with Caius Attius Caecilius and it was he who discovered Drusilla's and Crixus' secret. He must have been in the vicinity that very day to have seen the two of them, even though they arrived separately. What are the chances of that happening? It was in Seneca's baths Caius Attius ended his life. It all fits, Adam. This cannot be just another coincidence. I knew nothing of these people before my regression and now the evidence is here right under our noses."

Adam resumed his original scrutiny of the road, clearly impressed by Tyra's discovery so early in the proceedings. He felt they were drawing ever-closer to the little clue he sought so avidly and if it was there at all he was certain to find it.

"You're a star and I have a feeling this innocent-looking document is about to yield another secret."

He moved further and further along the outline of buildings with agonising slowness and then stopped abruptly, not daring to breathe lest the sound shatter his concentration. His finger was poised above what could only be described as a narrow gap between two large structures, a constricted alley barely wide enough for two people to negotiate side-by-side. After a few dozen yards the narrow passage seemed to turn back on itself before coming to an abrupt halt at a much smaller plot of land behind a surrounding wall. It was here. She had not imagined it and they had found it.

"This is it," he stated flatly but with absolute certainty. "It fits the description perfectly. The shape is right and the location's spot on. Shall we take a closer look? It's only a short distance from here and we could drive or walk. How do you feel about it?"

"Let's walk, Adam. I want to savour every moment of this, even if there's nothing left when we get there. We've come so far and we now have proof the house, or something like it, really did exist. Do you need any more from this?" she asked, indicating the drawing which had given them the all-important detail.

"No, I know exactly where to begin searching," and he became serious for a moment as another thought occurred to him. "Tyra, we've just confirmed the previous existence of this place but there's no guarantee of it being there now. Our information has come from a two-thousand-year-old street plan and there's every chance the whole area has been redeveloped many times since then. We may not even recognise it."

"I don't care, Adam. I really don't. If you'd told me yesterday we'd find documented proof of the location I'd have been happy with that. But we have nothing to lose, have we, Adam? Nothing at all?"

"I suppose not," he agreed. "Okay, we're done here. Let's go and see what secrets the Via Claudia has to offer."

50

They walked hand-in-hand, just another couple of tourists enjoying the warm sunshine and architectural splendours of the route that would take them past the Colosseum and onto the Via Claudia. As they finally came to stand in the shadow of the great amphitheatre Adam experienced a momentary cold shudder and the goose-flesh that flared up on his arms was not due to the absence of direct sunlight. She sensed it too and drew a little closer while they both halted and stared at the immense structure where the slaughter of men and beasts had entertained the Roman public for over four hundred years.

"You can't deny the beauty and symmetry," Adam commented as he studied the edifice with a critical eye, "but it's also sinister. The sheer size and the way those arches are configured one above the other. I can see why slaves brought here to fight and die must have been terrified when they first saw it and wondered what manner of man could possibly conceive such an idea. It's strange how photographs never quite prepare you for the impact of the real thing – how standing beneath its walls can be so intimidating...."

She was quick to hone in on his apparent discomfort, placing an arm about his shoulder while they continued to gaze up at the towering monument.

"Do not be cowed, Adam, for in a way it is a part of you and will always be so. It was the stage upon which the final act of a great love story was played out. Had you not followed your heart and placed your destiny in the hands of the gods then I fear we may never have found one another again. Think only of what this place was for us, Adam, and not the theatre of death and misery portrayed in the history books."

"It's strange, Tyra," he continued. "I was never directly affected by the appearance of this building and in most respects remained completely indifferent to its design. For me it was just a place of work where I came to entertain the crowds because I had entered into a contract and swore to honour it – but when I look at it now and remember...."

"Come on, let's go," she ended it before the dwelling on past memories threatened to cast a shadow over the remainder of the day. She linked her arm through his once more and smiled, just as the sun emerged from a puff of fine-weather cumulus and chased away the cold feeling of a few moments ago.

As they skirted the circumference of the imposing and enigmatic structure and negotiated the busy roads around the Piazza del Colosseo they picked up the first signboard announcing their arrival at the start of the Via Claudia. The street was nowhere near as wide as Adam first surmised but then he remembered his attention had been focused on the buildings themselves. His heart sank when the imposing facades of hotels and guest houses loomed all around – their garish pink and blue neon signs advertising vacancies and star-ratings. As they progressed further – past souvenir shops, insignificant fashion outlets and electrical retailers he grew more uneasy and it began to dawn on them both the entire area might, as he had speculated, have been redeveloped leaving nothing of its past above ground.

He tried to exude a spirit of optimism although he was reasonably sure Tyra must be experiencing the same aura of gloom and disappointment, even if she was not voicing her thoughts; and then for no explicable reason, after they had gone about half a mile the street narrowed again and they came into an area of much older buildings whose style of construction was ancient in comparison; slums by any other word. It was like stepping into a forgotten world, a place discarded by civilization and he could find no reason for it. It was nothing more than a ruin. Whole walls had collapsed and those still standing were riddled with cracks from which strands of ivy dangled or clung to the rough masonry. There was filth and litter everywhere but no other obvious signs of recent habitation or human presence. All around was shabbiness, decay, sadness and neglect and a vivid contrast to the bustling activity and vibrant colour of the centre only a relatively short distance away.

"This looks encouraging," Adam spoke at last as he pondered the chaos and shambles of a disintegrated world. Had it not been for the fact they were walking amidst piles of cream and buff-coloured stone as opposed to red brick, his mind told him they could be in 1940s London during the height of the Blitz. Those few walls that remained intact supported rotten, timber-framed windows devoid of glass whose flaking paint was bleached and faded by the sun. "It's like a ghost-town,"

Adam continued. "I wonder why no one's bothered with it all these years."

Tyra was clearly of the same opinion for her expression was one of perplexity as she struggled to find some feasible theory supporting this degradation all around them. They ambled further along the dismal street and the sensation of gloom intensified as the increasing height of the derelict buildings gradually reduced the amount of sunlight until they were in permanent shadow. Adam now began to actively search for the features memorised from the drawing in the archives office and as they drew ever closer to where the narrow gap must surely be, Tyra lapsed into a fit of the giggles and couldn't stop.

Adam regarded her suspiciously for although their sense of expectancy had mounted noticeably and they both experienced the sensation of butterflies in their stomachs, he could find no reason to account for her strangely-out-of-place merriment.

"Careful you don't wet yourself," he teased. "It's a long way back to the car."

"Sorry," she replied with a smile and rosettes of embarrassment blooming on her cheeks. "It must be nerves getting the better of me. I just needed the release."

"I can think of a more suitable way to release you from all that nervous tension," he remarked salaciously, running a hand over her curvaceous buttock and casting a lingering gaze over her breasts beneath the thin cotton jacket.

"Later, tiger," she admonished him fondly. "When I can give you my complete and undivided attention."

"We've got to be close, Tyra," and he had become serious again. "I reckon we've come a good three quarters of a mile already and I know we haven't missed it," and then, quite suddenly – after just a few more steps, it was there, exactly as the blueprint had described. The gap was indeed narrow and as Adam looked upward he could see the high walls were completely devoid of windows and nothing stirred in the dismal, funereal shadow that partially obscured the cramped walkway.

Adam led the way, mentally cursing his inattention to detail where a flashlight would have been a blessing at this particular moment. Tyra followed close behind with barely a gap between them and after a hundred yards the path turned abruptly into what, Adam knew, must be the dead-end she had described and there – directly in front of them, was a wall!

"This is the place," and the words were spoken with a certainty he could not question. The darkness of the long, narrow alley had given way to a more natural watery daylight revealing details of the solid

298

obstacle confronting them. The wall was about ten feet high and although it had fallen into disrepair over the centuries and was crumbling and riven with cracks, they could not see what lay on the other side. There was no visible way over the top and the exposed surface had been weathered to the point where climbing might be regarded as suicidal; but they had come too far to be cheated of their goal at the eleventh hour. As he continued to scan the large masonry blocks of the rampart there was further evidence supporting the accuracy of Tyra's words under the shroud of hypnosis. Two gates had once formed portals into the world beyond but at some point had been removed and replaced by more dressed stone blocks.

"Someone went to a lot of trouble maintaining this – if not recently. It's in a damned sight better condition than all the other stuff around here. Have you noticed?" And then something else caught his attention. "Hello, what have we got here?" he remarked thoughtfully as he returned to the right-hand corner of the wall where it was joined and buttressed to the neighbouring property. He had barely glanced at the feature when they arrived but first impressions suggested a dead tree or extremely dense bush of incredible age that had once grown against the stonework. Clearly, the soil was of poor quality for the massively-deformed serpentine roots had broken out of the ground at some point in search of moisture and nutrients. The enormous but dangerously-rotten trunk had split and divided while the gnarled branches resembled grossly-distorted, arthritic limbs accentuated by the covering of grey, reptilian bark.

As Adam inspected the tortuous mass of tangled roots and branches more closely in the poor light, he could now see how several of them had lodged in the tiny gaps between the stone blocks. Over the centuries they had increased in width, enlarging the joints and opening up yet more cracks and fissures to the point where it might just be possible to dislodge one or two stones and gain access to the far side.

But how?

Looking around him Adam could see nothing that might be utilised as a lever or probe with which he might loosen part of the masonry to the point where others would collapse under their own weight.

"So close," he whispered. "There just has to be a way through," and then a thought occurred to him and he removed the khaki safari jacket and began to unbutton his shirt. Tyra's curiosity was immediately aroused and she moistened her lips with the tip of her tongue at the sight of Adam's semi-naked body.

"You only had to say if you couldn't wait, although the ground looks a little unforgiving. I suppose we could always try it standing up...."

"You sexy little vixen," he replied fondly. "There's nothing I'd like more but it wouldn't help us get through this wall. If the offer still stands later on I may be interested...."

He scrambled into the confusion of branches and after more close scrutiny finally selected a likely place about four feet from the ground where, he thought, a little gentle persuasion might just force a gap. As he positioned his back against the rough stonework and planted the rubber soles of his desert boots firmly into a suitable junction of branch and trunk, Tyra saw what he was about to attempt and her concern was immediate.

"Adam, please be careful. That wall looks awfully strong and I don't want you injuring yourself if it collapses," but she knew he had weighed-up the odds and not rushed into this haphazardly for as she glanced around her she could see no other way. All the same, she didn't want him crippled. She had plans for both of them later.

"I'll be okay," he joked and tried to sound convincing. "It's just a matter of opposing factors – the immovable object against the irresistible force. Let's see which one of us caves in first," and he began to push. Nothing! He adjusted his feet and lowered his position against the wall by a couple of inches, then pushed again – harder this time. As he strained and heaved the sweat broke out and slicked his upper torso while his face became suffused an angry red and the sinews creaked and popped in his spine. His vision starred and he felt the blood rushing in his ears but, at last, he sensed movement and heard the first satisfying grating sounds of stone upon stone. He pushed again, even harder than before, summoning every last ounce of strength and felt the wall yield another inch to this monumental force.

As the great muscles of his chest flexed and bulged he wanted to call out, to scream with the pain of it and give vent to his frustration and mounting anger as the wall stubbornly refused to breach. He paused for breath and Tyra remained silent but watching him with fear etched across her face. This was something completely new to her – an uncharacteristic display of brute force that threatened to break him. He was pushing himself beyond anything she had ever seen – beyond the limits of human endurance and it was as if he had become a different person, transcended into something more than flesh and blood by the all-consuming urge to smash through this final barrier between present and past.

His face was twisted into a mask of pain as she watched him take the strain again and she knew it must come now or not at all for he would surely kill himself if he continued in this manner. Her hand was pressed to her mouth – a precaution against calling out and destroying his concentration but still she heard the tremor in her voice as she whispered in a barely-audible prayer.

"Please stop, Adam. Please stop now before you do irreparable damage to yourself," and as he at last bellowed like a wounded animal she suspected the worst and closed her eyes tightly – afraid to look lest she see him spent and broken upon the ground. And then, incredibly, the sound of his agonised, breathless laughter as he leaned forward, bent double in an attitude of total exhaustion – but he was alive and apparently unharmed. She opened her eyes and the relief was transparent as she saw him thus. She threw her arms around his neck and kissed him with a passion that invigorated him and left her weak at the knees.

"Christ, Adam! Don't you ever bloody dare do that again! You scared the hell out of me."

"Sorry," he replied lamely, "but I wasn't going to be beaten by a humble garden wall." He straightened up and reached behind him to massage the aching muscles in his lower back but grimaced with pain and when he inspected his hands they were streaked with blood.

"Let me take a look at that," she demanded firmly and when he turned around she was horrified to see how the skin was torn and bleeding and there were areas of livid swelling and discolouration where the abrasive contact of stone had taken its toll. "This is awful, Adam! Your back's in tatters and I've nothing to patch it up. I'm beginning to have my doubts as to whether this trip was worth it now. You weren't supposed to require hospital treatment as part of the itinerary."

"You should see the other guy!"

She reached into her bag and found an opened cellophane pack of Kleenex which she used to dab away the worst of the blood that had dribbled down and soaked into the waistband of his trousers.

"This will need proper attention," she remarked with a frown. "If you're not too uncomfortable we'll sort it out as soon as we get back to the villa."

"I'll live," he added. "Right now there are other more-important issues," and he slipped his shirt back on and handed Tyra the jacket. As they turned their attention to the wall once more they found there was no great collapse feature for them to walk through or even a single hole where part of the masonry had tumbled. Rather, the wall had bulged noticeably outwards under Adam's relentless exertions. The enlarged cracks attributed to the tree's growth over countless decades had proved its weak-point. Adam simply braced himself against two of the branches – one to either side, and kicked upward and outward with both feet and it was done. The centre of the wall collapsed, leaving a large opening about three feet wide through which they both scrambled excitedly.

As they gazed around the small rectangular plot with its totally-enclosing high walls they both experienced a sense of anti-climax after Adam's impassioned exertions for all traces of the little house that once stood here had now vanished. It was hardly surprising for although the surrounding area had clearly fallen into decay and surrendered to the forces of nature over the years, this place had been effectively removed from memory. Not a single stone remained. A small sand-coloured lizard scampered across the ground in front of them and disappeared beneath a fragment of roof tile. Adam crouched down to investigate and as he carefully lifted the shard of baked red clay they could both see the tiny reptile had vanished into the darkness of a round opening no more than two inches across.

"The water supply for the fountain," Adam commented flatly. "At least we have evidence this place was not a flight of fancy on your part."

"There's nothing left!" Tyra exclaimed and she made no attempt to conceal her disappointment. "I can't honestly say if I expected to find anything at all but it's just so empty. I suppose I should be happy really – finding out it was real and we were part of it."

"Don't be too dispirited," he consoled her with an arm draped about her shoulder. "We knew at the outset there might be nothing here. At least it's not lying under twenty feet of concrete. There's something not quite right with all this. Why would someone clear away a structure – not just demolish it but effectively remove every last stone and tile from living memory? Why the high-quality workmanship employed on the surrounding wall when a simple repair-job would have sufficed? It's almost as if...?"

"Adam, please don't. You're giving me the creeps again," and she felt the superstitious chill run up her spine despite the warmth of late afternoon. The colourful wisteria, orange and bougainvillaea had long-since vanished but she could still savour their heady fragrances as they wafted through the open window on the evening breeze.

'In their anger and hatred they have torn down the place of your meeting but such a love does require stone as its epitaph!'

302

Adam had wandered across to the far side of the small enclosure and appeared to be gazing up and studying intently something on, or set into the wall.

"Tyra, quick!" his voice alerted her. "Come over here and take a look at this. It could be important."

"What is it?" she inquired, coming to stand beside him.

"What do you make of this?" he asked, indicating the inscribed stone with an outstretched finger. "You're better-versed in Latin than I am. There doesn't appear to be a date so I think that has to rule out any commemorative plaque or celebratory event."

As she struggled with her limited working knowledge of the ancient Latin which was further exacerbated by the badly-eroded surface, it suddenly dawned on her that what they were seeing was indeed no homage or memorial but something infinitely more sinister. Immediately, the goose-flesh came up on her bare arms and he heard the unmistakeable tremor of unease in her voice.

"Adam, this is a warning – a statement relating to a great wrongdoing." As she lowered her eyes to the base of the inscribed slab and saw the name, the pieces fell into place at last and she became visually agitated. She returned to the top and began to translate haltingly. "This site has been razed to the ground lest its continued existence taints the memory of future generations. Henceforth, let no man build upon this ground which is now cursed and despoiled. By decree of the praetor, Caius Attius Caecilius, the will of the senate and the people of Rome."

"Bloody hell, Tyra!" Adam tried to keep his own trepidation and sense of wonderment under wraps. "This is all starting to come together in a way I never expected. We made this little pilgrimage purely on a hunch and look what we've discovered already. We could so easily have missed everything and it would all have been lost."

"He must have ordered this place be demolished just before he killed himself in Seneca's baths."

"I'm afraid you're right. There can be no other explanation. His very character tells me this is typical of the man – spiteful and vindictive to the last. It's a wonder he lived long enough to end his life with the blade. The hatred alone would have been enough to kill him. Look at the way he's distorted the facts to inflame public opinion – 'The will of the people.' The average Roman would have loved the scandal generated by Drusilla's outburst in the amphitheatre and Crixus was their hero. I think this inflammatory and not representative of the true feelings predominant at the time."

"I'm still trying to work out why no one's attempted to build here – after all this time. Do you think they really believed all that stuff about the ground being cursed and they were fearful of some kind of retribution? Also, why was the stone placed inside the wall rather than outside where everyone could see it?"

"That's how Caius would have wanted it," he replied grimly. "Don't forget, Tyra, this whole area lost its charm and appeal God-knows how long ago. It's hardly a magnet for regeneration."

Sobered and somewhat elated to see themselves carved in stone with only the actual names ominously missing they wandered around the empty plot but saw nothing to justify remaining longer. Perhaps their flagrant breaching of the wall had broken any sense of doom and ill-fate, perceived or otherwise and Caius was now reeling in anger once more that his bitch of a daughter and that bastard slave lover of hers had defied him from beyond the grave.

"Shall we go, Adam?" Tyra's weary tones brought him back to reality. "I don't think there's any more to see here. We've already found more than I could have expected, and anyway, I think we ought to get your back cleaned up. It's a mess and you're going to be sore tomorrow."

"I agree," he echoed her own thoughts. "Do you think we should come back in the morning and fix the wall?"

"Don't even think about it, mister," and she reached up to kiss him warmly. "I'm quite accustomed to seeing you in the role of Adam, the builder, Adam, the designer – Adam, the constructor of great monuments. Witnessing Adam, the destroyer has left me slightly flustered. Such brute strength and raw power...."

They made their way to the partly-collapsed wall, stepping carefully over the tumbled blocks and Adam stood to one side, allowing Tyra to exit first. She may have viewed this as just another display of manners but Adam's motives were infinitely more down-to-earth and unpretentious.

"My God, woman," he studied the erotic shape of her backside as she clambered through the gap. "Why the hell didn't you wear a skirt and high heels today? We could have indulged in a little poontang for old-time's sake." She wiggled her bottom and replied in a manner that would ordinarily have set his heart racing with anticipation but the words went unheard for his attention had been diverted as he stepped over the loose stones. In the earlier excitement of their dramatic entrance and possibly because his gaze had been focused directly ahead, the small package – seemingly nothing more than a wrapped and secured parcel that would have sat in the palm of one hand, remained unnoticed and he could now see why he had missed it. For some inexplicable reason this unremarkable, insignificant item had been sealed away – locked up for all time within the structure of the wall. By whom, he would not know for several years and he could only guess as to its contents.

As the blocks of stone had tumbled under Adam's frantic efforts the package had spilled out and come to rest in a gap between two of them. The sky had brightened considerably throughout the afternoon and the shadows cast by the surrounding high buildings had moved, rendering the mysterious bundle immediately conspicuous. He pocketed it and continued on his way through the wall to join Tyra in the narrow alley beyond. He would inspect the contents later but, for now, his back was stiffening and there was still the best part of a mile and a half to walk before they picked up the car. After an hour's drive through the busy streets and out to their villa in the hills, they could relax, indulge in the luxury of a hot bath and discuss the day's startling revelations over several bottles of Chianti. Tyra would treat the abrasions on his back with her skilful, deft touches and then she would prepare one of their favourite meals with her usual flair.

Again, his pulse quickened and the blood sang in his ears as he envisaged making love to his woman while the candles flickered eerily and the smells of the open country wafted through the open window.

With this enticing prospect not too far away the small item in his pocket was forgotten – for now!

51

She wrinkled her nose at the evocative smell of carnations in their spray on the crisp white linen cloth and thrilled at the way the silver cutlery sparkled in the flames of the two slim and tapered dinner candles in their pewter setting.

She was the epitome of elegance, refinement and raw, sensual beauty in the stunning, figure-hugging strapless evening-dress, its vibrant red contrasting vividly with the black, twisted braids purposely-styled for the occasion and the large pink orchid at the back of her head. Around that long, slender neck she wore the Anubis pendant which had enthralled him so on their first meeting and added that subtle aura of mystery to an already-intriguing situation. In every sense she was the one he had waited for – a stranger in many respects but someone he knew more intimately than his own body. She was indeed a delicious conundrum, a riddle, a mystery and a puzzle with her most deep-seated and enigmatic secrets hidden away behind a screen of long-forgotten memories and the passage of countless centuries.

"Adam, this is simply delightful," she reached across and laid a carefully-manicured hand upon his own. "You certainly know how to show a girl a good time," and he inwardly breathed a sigh of relief. It had been the devil of a job to find something like this, even in Italy, the food, wine and romance capital of the world and he had searched diligently for exactly the right place. It was tucked away in a remote side-street, far-removed from the bustle of traffic and flocks of tourists and for a Friday evening it was virtually deserted. Only one other couple shared the intimate ambience of the subdued lighting and soft music, oblivious to all other presences in this sequestered little haven.

He had found it quite by chance this morning when they drove into the city for Tyra's appointment with the stylist so she might look her best for tonight's celebratory dinner. Also, there had been the other matter requiring his attention – the issue of the little package hidden away among the tumbled stone blocks. He had barely two hours to locate an up-market restaurant and have the contents of the package cleaned and polished. Time was of the essence and he had offered the jeweller a handsome cash incentive.

When, at last, he collected Tyra from the hair-stylist, he was feeling somewhat self-congratulatory. He had found the perfect place for dinner tonight and his other little surprise nestled comfortably against his chest, tucked away inside his jacket.

They were enjoying one of their favourite dishes – spaghetti vongole with fresh clams and it was an echo from the past when she had cooked for him in the early days before their marriage. As always they drank a fine Chianti for what other wine embodied the story of their lives to date? She would forever be the flame that burned in his heart and as their raised crystal glasses came together and rang with the toast he knew he was indeed a god among men and blessed by the influences of providence.

"Happy anniversary!" they chimed in unison and laughed at their synchronised salutation; and then she was apologetic.

"I'm so sorry, Adam. I didn't buy you anything. Surely, twenty-seven years together deserves a gift of some kind," and she was crestfallen by her own inattention.

"Why would I need a gift to remind me of my life with you when I have the object of my desires right here before me? Anyway, don't fret. I have something for both of us," and he reached into his jacket and retrieved a small but luxuriously-presented gift-box covered in purple velvet for that was the colour befitting of such a woman and the one he would always remember her by.

"Accept this now with all the love I have to offer, as you accepted it once before a long, long time ago," and he pressed the purple-covered box into her hand, kissing her fingers.

"Adam...," and the voice had assumed a note of uncertainty at the sound of his words, the sparkle and smile in her eyes vanishing in an instant. "Adam..., what is this?" and as she raised the lid and gazed upon the contents, the room suddenly tilted and swayed about her and she thought she might faint. His pleasure rapidly turned to consternation as he observed her reaction and considered he might just have made a dreadful mistake. But she was swift to regain her composure and simply stared at the gift, unable to speak lest the words choke in her throat.

Inside the box were two rings nestling in a bed of purple silk. One, made of the finest gold, depicted a young couple with joined right hands – a betrothal ring which might have been seen on the finger of a young aristocratic female two millennia previously, or, perhaps, worn around her neck on a slim gold chain if their love was a secret.

She could see they were the originals for there was just the slightest trace of pitting but so faint as to be almost negligible. What was their story and how had Adam found them? It must have been tied up with their excursion along the Via Claudia yesterday for there had been no other opportunity and Adam would have said something before now, surely. Had they been placed secretly in the wall at some point and Adam's frantic efforts had dislodged them? But why and who had deposited them there and what if Adam had forced an entry in a different place? Questions, questions. So many questions but all paths seemed to have converged at one indisputable point. Proof of their life before. Unequivocal proof. What would Sophie have to say about it?

"Many years ago you wore this ring on a gold chain around your neck, such were the circumstances of our love it could never be seen in public lest we be punished by the state."

Reverently, he lifted the ring and as she offered him her exquisitely-manicured slim hand, he took it in his own and slid the gold band over her third finger, sitting it snugly next to her wedding ring.

"In this public place – as indeed when we were married, I pledge my love to you and swear there will never be another. I would rather die than live without you again."

She wanted to cry but fought back the urge with considerable difficulty. She was amazed by the appearance of the ring and how it fitted with such perfection – almost as if it had been made for her. The second ring was fashioned in silver and bore the inscription, libera vivas, may you live free. Solemnly, she took it between two fingers and placed it upon his own hand, just as a big tear finally escaped and rolled down her cheek.

"When I first gave you this, you were a world away from achieving the wish inscribed upon it and you passed from that world never again knowing the freedom you had been born into. You forfeited your liberty to avenge the death of a friend and in doing so embarked upon an odyssey that would see your own life cut brutally short before too long. But somewhere along that journey our paths crossed and we were never to be the same people again. As I return this ring to its rightful owner it is with as much of my heart now as then and I too give you my word that whatever life brings our way there will never be another. I let you slip away once before – you won't get away so easily next time!"

52

The following morning it was in a mood of considerable enlightenment they vacated the small villa and made their way along the minor roads to Leonardo da Vinci airport for their return charter flight to England. This close to the city it was impossible to avoid human presence and influence but as they at last emerged from the clutter of housing and light-industry they came into an unfamiliar and untypical area of parched, uncultivated wasteland.

Adam pulled over and consulted the ordnance survey map but it yielded no clues as to their precise whereabouts. The city lay to their west behind a small rise and to the east the land sloped away into the foothills of the much higher ground. It was just after midday and the sun was behind them so they were definitely heading north. The road they were on appeared as little more than a thin line on the map – pencilled in as an afterthought and there was a disturbing lack of signs. There were no rich pastures upon which cattle might graze nor were there manicured terraces supporting those regimented columns of vines reaching to the horizon and it was almost as if the hand of man had not moved here for an eternity.

In the absence of lush vegetation, only scrub, rye-grass, stunted trees and wild sage interspersed with gangly thorns managed to scratch an existence for the soil was dry and of such poor quality the land had been discarded over the millennia by those seeking a living from it.

But man *had* been here – albeit only briefly, a long, long time ago and in his own inimitable style had left his mark so others might one day see what great deeds he had accomplished. Just a few hundred metres from the dusty road where Adam and Tyra now passed by and virtually obscured by the accumulated scrub and pale grass which had encroached as it lay toppled and flat on the barren earth, a single stone hewn from a slab of white travertine marble. The edges had been eroded over the years and were now rugged and spoiled but the otherwise unmistakeable uniformity of the rectangular monolith gave hint as to its purpose.

As it lay here for two millennia the carved inscription had weathered to the extent where it was now virtually unreadable but a historian on his travels or, perhaps, an archaeologist with a gift for deciphering the past and an understanding of the ancient Latin, might just chance upon this uninspiring tablet and kneel before it while he gazed at the mysterious, half-completed eulogy.

CRIXUS – CHAMPION OF 137 CONTESTS IN THE GREAT ARENA
THE WOLF WHO STOLE THE HEART OF A QUEEN

As he stared at the headstone and pondered the type of man who might have inspired such an epitaph, he would become aware of an eerie silence now descended upon him; a silence punctuated by the breeze as it came over the hills, rustling the tall grass and sighing through the thorn bushes. It would indeed be a sigh, a hushed and distant whisper, soft as a lover's declaration with the promise of their first kiss.

'Where the setting sun surrenders to the moon, I will wait for you and we will have our time again.'

'Oh, Crixus, my love. I followed my heart to the ends of the earth for I knew you would be waiting.'

53

Warchester, England

One Week Later

Summer was drawing to a close, yielding inevitably to the processes of seasonal change where the days were shorter, the nights cooler and the air buzzed with a strange expectancy unlike the anticipation of spring.

Barely three weeks had elapsed since embarking on what would ultimately turn out to be a journey of illumination and once again Tyra pondered the list of chance happenings that had made it so, deciding it was down to far more than coincidence. Sophie had been most explicit in her pronouncements over the years and held the view life was preordained whether we chose to accept it or not; accidents and misfortune were all part of the bigger picture and freedom of choice was simply there to make life interesting.

Tyra could have picked the holiday destination herself but left Adam to do the work and surprise her. Would she have chosen Italy? How could she know? What was the thought process behind Adam deciding on Rome? They could have gone to any of the Mediterranean resorts – Capri, Sorrento, the Amalfi Coast and Ravello or perhaps somewhere more secluded like the isle of Ischia.

Then there had been the compelling urge to seek out physical evidence of a location that may never have existed at all, only in her mind. The street-plans stored in the archives office had certainly revealed the distinct possibility of something resembling the area Tyra spoke of under hypnosis and their subsequent visit to the Via Claudia confirmed this. There were names too, not solely her ancestral father but the senatorial official who had chanced upon Drusilla's affair with Crixus. There was the ominous threat of retribution from Caius Attius Caecilius himself, etched in stone within the perimeter of the plot and

311

finally – confirmation beyond all doubt as to her and Adam's true identities. The rings; walled up for two millennia. By whom, remained another mystery to be unlocked at some future point.

It could all have been so easily overlooked and she inwardly shuddered at the prospect of never making the discoveries where only the tenuous threads of far-distant memories remained. If anything, Sophie's presupposition relating to matters of destiny, kismet and serendipity had been validated yet again and she would be suitably impressed to learn of her two friends' recent enlightenment into the mystical workings of fate and providence.

As one door in their lives closed, another was soon to open and lead to the most startling revelations yet where nothing was as it seemed and they would welcome an unlikely fourth member into their coveted circle.

There was also the matter of that strange, age-old, unearthly sexual magnetism between Tyra and Sophie, smouldering away just beneath the surface and held in check only by a combination of circumstances and their own rapidly-crumbling willpower. How would it pan out in the greater picture and, more importantly, how would it affect her relationship with Adam?

The next year would tell.